SALTED EARTH

A SEAHOUSES MYSTERY

KATHERINE GRAHAM

QUARTZ BOOKS

To my fabulous mum,
and my wonderful dad.

CONTENTS

PROLOGUE

THE SHRIEK OF THE TELEPHONE PIERCED HER SLEEP, WAKING her with a start. Sue slid upright as she grabbed the handset, her head meeting the headboard with a thud.

The familiar voice at the other end of the line was breathless. 'There's been another one. Another murder.'

Her legs were tangled in a knot of duvet and she tried to straighten them, orienting herself in the darkness. 'What time is it?' Sue whispered. Her sister was a light sleeper and the wall between their bedrooms was thin.

'What's that got to do with anything? Didn't you hear what I just said?'

Sue rubbed her eyes. It was dark – either very late, or very early. Inky shadows pooled in the corners of the room. The haze of an unidentifiable dream draped over her mind like a dawn fog before it faded to forgotten, retreating into the murkiness of the night.

It took a moment for the words to sink in. *Another murder.* 'Who?' Her fingers, now icy cold, gripped the phone.

'I'll give you a clue...'

'For goodness' sake, Diana. This isn't a game!' she hissed, unable to hide her frustration.

'Well, don't worry, dear. It won't take you long to guess. We ran into him yesterday, and you told him he "would get what's coming to" him.'

Sue emitted an involuntary gasp. *Him*. How could *he* be dead? She pressed the heel of her hand to her mouth, not trusting herself to speak.

She winced as she recalled their encounter. He wasn't a particularly pleasant chap by any stretch of the imagination – in fact, he was perfectly vile. At the time, she'd been proud of herself for standing up to a bully. She had walked home with her head held high, her shoulders set back, feeling three inches taller.

Now she groaned inwardly. Why had she said those things?

Too late to take it back.

'How was he killed?'

'Ah ha!' There was a tremor in Diana's voice. An audible frisson of excitement, rather than the result of her advancing years. 'You asked "how was he killed", not "how did he die". Does that mean you can see what's going on now? With another murder on the cards, we can no longer deny that there's foul play afoot.'

Sue sat up properly now, tugging the duvet high on her chest. A single fragment of her almost-forgotten dream nibbled at the edge of her consciousness.

The girls.

For as long as she could remember, she had kept a phone on her bedside table. If there was some emergency, if either of her nieces were in any kind of trouble, she wanted to be the first to know. When it rang just now, a metallic clang that had shocked her awake, her immediate worry was that something had happened to Izzy in Hong Kong. Her heart was still galloping from that thought.

She took a steadying breath. 'Stop saying that. Stop saying *another murder*. We don't know—'

'You asked how he was killed. Don't you want to know?'

Was that a note of glee in her elderly friend's voice? Everyone in the village knew of Diana's penchant for melodrama. Not to mention her fondness for murder, mystery, and intrigue. Seeing shadows where there were none. Only this time...

The bed creaked as Sue shifted her weight. Her eyes were growing accustomed to the dark now, the pattern on her curtains slowly emerging. Beyond the window, the night was still.

When she spoke again, her voice was small. 'How did he die?'

'Now here's where it gets interesting,' said Diana. 'A heart attack!'

A shiver rolled down Sue's spine, a tingle that reached her fingertips, which were now icy cold. This was precisely the last thing she wanted to get caught up in: idle gossip, busy-bodying, wicked whispers. Although this felt... different. She'd had a peculiar feeling in her stomach else ever since—

'A heart attack at that age isn't even plausible.' Diana pressed on. 'At least there'll be an inquest with an autopsy and a thorough investigation. No one will be able to fob the police off this time.'

Sue sighed. 'Nobody fobbed them off last time.'

But was Diana right? Not everything was an Agatha Christie mystery, after all. The Nile and the Orient Express were far away – things like that didn't happen around here, not to people like them. She had to focus on the facts, and not let the over-active imaginations – or paranoia – of others cloud her judgement. And yet... doubt needled at her.

Diana continued. 'So, you can see where that leaves us. We've got two men dead, less than three weeks apart, and an identical cause of death.'

Sue didn't like the sound of this. A heart attack in someone so young was suspicious. She shivered, trying to shake off a sudden chill, and stared out into the gloom.

Diana, firmly in her element, was persistent. 'You know what all of this means, don't you?'

Sue wasn't sure if she expected an answer or not.

'My dear girl. We've got ourselves a serial killer.'

1

SIX WEEKS EARLIER

LUCIA WOUND DOWN THE WINDOW OF HER CAR. AT LAST, THE SEA WAS coming into view. Just a glimpse at first, here and there, snatches of navy infinity that grew longer and wider the closer she got. She inhaled deeply, savouring a lungful of salty air.

As soon as she'd seen Seahouses, she'd known it was the one. The way some people feel about a man, she guessed – not that Lucia ever had. Guys were nice enough, but she didn't need a boy to make her happy. She didn't need anyone at all. With her, it was all about places. Some places had it, some didn't. And what was *it*, exactly? A vibe? An energy? She struggled to give *it* a word, even to herself. But when you knew, you knew.

She had never been to Northumberland until last year – never even really thought about this corner of the country. Of all the far-flung places she passed through, very few still had the power to take her breath away. The further she travelled, the worse it became.

Just three weeks ago she had watched the sunset from the beach in Cabo San Lucas, surrounded by misty-eyed honeymooners who ooh'ed and aah'ed at the dusk display of whales playing in the surf. Lucia had felt nothing.

The week before that, she'd been the only passenger on a seaplane to Vancouver Island, the pilot taking a diversion from the scheduled route to give her a private tour of the skies. She pretended to be impressed, just to be polite.

And yet during that long weekend in Seahouses back in December, she'd had to pinch herself every time she looked out her hotel window. The golden sandy beach was impossibly wide and stretched on for miles, punctuated by ancient castles. The blue of the sea was a different colour and mood every hour, broken only by foamy waves rolling out to the horizon.

Such mesmerising beauty, and it had been right here, all along. A small part of Lucia almost felt cheated that she hadn't discovered it sooner.

She'd come for a friend's wedding, one of the few girls from college that Lucia still kept in touch with. Or at least Emma – the friend – kept in touch with her. She seemed to think Lucia would be interested in the mundane details of her life in Durham, with her new build semi, twice-yearly package holidays and a very vanilla fiancé.

Lucia wasn't the keeping-in-touch type, but she never begrudged emailing Emma a polite response from time to time. She'd been surprised to receive an invitation to the wedding, though.

As it happened, she had been due to travel to Scotland the week before. Close enough. She bought a dress, hired a car, and drove down.

And there, when she least expected it, she fell head over heels in love.

After weeks of consideration, once she'd made her decision, it had taken just a fortnight to uproot and head back here. Her apartment in Barcelona was now being rented to a man named Hector, and her room in Berlin was empty, with just an envelope of cash and the keys left for her flatmate. Everything she owned – everything she needed – was in two rucksacks.

She was smitten with Seahouses. And it was time for a fresh start.

'Another one?' Mum said when she told her the news. Lucia rolled her eyes.

She had hoped her parents might be pleased – Seahouses would be the closest to home she'd lived in years. But she understood. They weren't getting any younger, and they wanted to see her *settle down*, whatever that meant. Or at least for her to stay in one spot for more than a few months. She was already older than Mum had been when they'd got married and had her. Manchester was only four hours' drive away, she reminded them. She'd be able to visit more often.

Mum hadn't said anything to that, years of distance hanging in the silence.

The breeze was picking up now, blowing coils of hair into her eyes. She used her sunglasses as a hairband, pushing the errant strands back from her face, allowing her to focus on the road and the view beyond it.

Before long, Seahouses appeared on the horizon, postcard-perfect. Even at this distance, it was just as lovely as she remembered.

She would be happy here, Lucia decided. It wouldn't be like all those other times.

Because in a place as wonderful as Seahouses, what could possibly go wrong?

2

LUCIA CHECKED THE ADDRESS IN HER NOTES, EVEN THOUGH she had studied the map long enough to know exactly where she was going.

She'd found the most gorgeous place on Airbnb: a rose-pink cottage in a terrace perched on the crest of a hill, overlooking the harbour and offering unobstructed views of the sea. She slowed to a crawl, squeezing her hire car along the narrow back lane.

Each house on Sea Street was a different colour: candy shades of seaside rock. She spotted Puffin Cottage immediately, its blush standing out among the pastel hues. Her stomach knotted with anticipation as she pulled up outside.

A wrought-iron gate creaked open, leading onto a pebbled yard that was sheltered from the breeze. Already, Lucia could picture herself sipping a morning coffee out here, enjoying the feel of the sun on her face. A welcome committee of seagulls paraded overhead, caterwauling to the skies.

She peered inside the cottage, curving her hands around

her eyes as she pressed her face up to the window. The interior was dark, a tiny kitchen and dining table just beyond the entrance. Through an open door she made out an armchair in the next room, silhouetted against a sea view. She couldn't wait to get inside. This, she had a good feeling, was everything she had been looking for.

The owner had emailed instructions to collect the keys from the local pub, a five-minute walk away. Lucia left her bags in the car and headed back down the lane in the direction she had come from. The air carried the note of something sweet, and despite the unseasonable warmth of the late afternoon, there was the unmistakable scent of a log fire. Her arms were bare, and after being stuck in the car for so long, the salty breeze tickled her skin like a kiss. She grinned, unable to help herself.

As she turned the corner, the harbour came into view. It was almost empty of fishing boats, but several smaller vessels were tacking across the open water towards the point where the harbour wall ended. Day trippers milled along the waterfront, clustering around a blue and white ice-cream van.

Finding the pub was straightforward. Lucia was good with maps, and it usually took her little time of studying a place on paper before she was able to navigate it in person. Few things riled her more than asking for directions and having to listen to some random person – inevitably a man – explain the simplest route in the most excruciatingly patronising detail. That didn't mean that she didn't get lost from time to time, especially in big cities. Some places just had a way of swallowing you whole, no matter how hard you tried to fight it.

The Ship was like nothing she had seen before. Every

inch of the walls and ceiling was covered in souvenirs of the village's maritime legacy: brass dials, gauges, diving gear, ropes, knots, and buoys. Antiques, by the look of them.

Lucia was a confident sailor thanks to a summer crewing a vessel up and down the coast of Croatia, but she couldn't figure out what half of these things did. Her eyes grew wide as she tried to take it all in.

She barely registered the conversations that stopped mid-sentence, nor the faces that turned in her direction, eyes assessing the new arrival. Lucia had become adept at not noticing. The hush that descended as people gawped at the beautiful stranger did not bother her in the slightest.

In the porch that separated the main bar from the back rooms, there was a noticeboard. A younger, slim woman – the only person not staring at Lucia – was studying something pinned to it. A poster of some sort. Pink. Lucia edged towards her for a closer look.

'Book club... Awesome. I love reading,' she murmured, as much to herself as to anyone else.

The woman turned to face Lucia and tucked a strand of sun-kissed hair behind her ear, her face creasing into a smile.

'You must come! We're only just starting. First get-together is next week.'

Lucia nodded, a slow nod. This she could do. Make friends. Socialise. Live a normal life. Stay in one place.

Her heart fluttered. *Deep breaths.*

Yes. She would *settle down* here, and making friends was an important first step.

'Great,' she said, trying to sound as enthusiastic as possible and before she lost her nerve.

'Super. I'll look forward to seeing you there.' The

woman's smile put Lucia at ease. She had kind eyes, flecked generously with gold that sparkled in the late-afternoon light.

'I'm sorry,' the woman said, offering her hand. 'But I don't think we've met. I'm Amy.'

3

'THAT'S EIGHT SIGNED UP ALREADY,' AMY CALLED OUT TO HER aunt as she tugged her boots off, kicking them to the side of the crowded shoe rack.

Sue emerged from the kitchen, drying her hands on a tea towel. 'You what? For the book club?'

'Yes.' Amy laughed. 'What else?'

Her aunt's eyes widened, her chin dimpling in worry. From upstairs came the thundering rumble of three small pairs of feet.

'Don't look so alarmed,' Amy said, just as the children hurtled down the stairs and threw themselves onto their mother, immobilising her in the hallway. 'It was your idea. You wanted to do this, remember?'

Sue bit her lip. 'Perhaps we needn't have bothered with the posters...'

Amy had to resist rolling her eyes. This was so typical of her aunt, especially of late. When Amy and her sister were growing up, Auntie Sue had been so sure of herself, so certain of the world. The old Sue wouldn't have given a second thought to something as banal as a book club. It crushed Amy to see her declining confidence and she couldn't understand what had brought it on.

Life, she supposed. The passing of years and the fading of time.

She scooped up her youngest daughter and carried her towards the kitchen. At seven, Betsy was already becoming too heavy to do this. Amy reckoned she had another year before she wouldn't be able to carry her further than a few feet without needing physio afterwards.

Her babies were growing up so fast, and the moments when they needed a cuddle from their mum were becoming fewer and further between. Amy willed the seasons to slow, pleading with the universe to give them more time. Betsy buried her face into Amy's neck, the tip of Betsy's nose a cool pebble against Amy's collar bone.

The kitchen was misty with steam, despite the open window. Lucas, Amy's only son and the Sanders's mild-tempered middle child, had been helping his great-aunt with dinner. At ten years old, he was more than a head taller than his little sister, although Amy didn't fancy his chances if the two of them ever got into a fight. Betsy, she was quite certain, could more than hold her own. Thankfully, Hannah kept the peace between them.

Amy gazed at her eldest daughter. Already twelve. The disappearance of childhood was so unfair. Amy was torn between wanting Hannah to forever remain a child, and curiosity to know the brilliant young woman who emerged little by little, day by day.

Hannah had also picked up on Sue's agitation. Unselfconsciously, she flicked her light brown hair over one shoulder and gave her great-aunt a peck on the cheek.

'Is Mike not back yet?' Amy asked.

Sue shook her head, still biting her lip. Her mind was elsewhere.

Amy poured wine and handed a glass to Sue. 'I almost forgot to tell you, I met Diana Wheeler's new tenant. Ever so pretty.' She was about to tell Sue that the woman, Lucia, was among those who had signed up for the book club, but decided to drop that topic of conversation for now. 'Remember? Diana mentioned someone booked up for six months paying mid-season rates.'

'Who?' Sue frowned, glancing up from the stove. 'What was that?'

Dear god. Auntie Sue really was twisted up. Amy knew this was about more than some silly book club.

She took a deep breath. She didn't know what was going on with her aunt right now, but she thought back – as she often did – to a dark day many years ago when she and Izzy were desperately in need of someone, anyone. Sue turned up to answer their prayers. Now it was her turn to be there for her aunt.

4

THE MERE MENTION OF DIANA'S NAME HAD BROUGHT SUE OUT in a feverish sweat that even the walk home failed to break. She had no doubt her formidable old English teacher would join the book club. In fact, knowing Diana Wheeler, she wouldn't be satisfied unless she was front and centre of the entire bloody thing.

Probably best to just let her take it over, Sue thought idly. After all, what did she, Sue, know about fiction?

The idea of starting a club had come to her a few weeks ago. Nothing big or fancy. Just a casual reading circle for like-minded ladies. A chance for Sue to get out and mix with people other than her sister for a change.

She loved to read, and she was... what was it? Listless? Lonely?

Sue spent her days gardening, reading, and looking after Amy and the children – she still thought of it as *looking after* Amy. She might as well turn one of them into a social activity.

One day, she picked up a book and noticed a sticker on

the front: a stamp of approval by a book club. Well, if that couple from the telly could do it, she could, too.

Only now she was having her doubts. It was suddenly impossibly hot, there in the kitchen of the home she shared with her sister. The heat prickled at her neck as she imagined Diana, who would no doubt have lots of insightful opinions and a head full of intelligent questions that Sue wouldn't have a clue how to answer. The flush rose higher, lapping at her cheeks. This was worse than the menopause.

It wasn't as if this was her first book club. Back in Aberdeen – those short years when she had flown free, tethered only by the lightest of threads – she'd joined a feminist book club. They'd debated their reading material into the wee small hours, fuelled by cigarettes and whisky and the heady rush of being young and liberated. It was glorious. And yet, when Sue thought back to that woman – the woman she had been, back then – she barely recognised herself.

Of course, it wasn't her fault that she'd had to return to Seahouses. And it wasn't her sister's fault that she had stayed all these years. It simply was what it was.

Only, lately, Sue hadn't been feeling quite herself.

There was a French phrase for feeling out of sorts. *I'm not on my plate*, or something like that. That summed up Sue's feelings to a tee. Some days, she couldn't even see her plate.

She took two pieces of vegan lasagne from the freezer. Anne was back to her vegan phase, and it was easiest for everyone if Sue simply toed the party line. With a bit of luck, it wouldn't last too long this time.

It was already starting to get dark, the sky melting into a rich velvety blue. Her sister hadn't eaten since breakfast – quite typical of Anne once she got into a project. Anne was one of those people who claimed that they simply forgot to eat, whereas Sue structured her entire day around mealtimes and had the hips to show for it.

The light was on in Anne's workshop at the end of the garden. The workshop that used to be the shed, until Anne had repurposed it, and Sue had to move all the gardening gear into the garage. Far better to have the craft things in there, though, out of harm's way.

Anne's latest obsession – because Sue's sister only ever had obsessions, and nothing less – was mirrors, set into handmade frames adorned with shells and sea glass. *Upcycling*, Anne called it, even though they had been perfectly good mirrors to begin with. Several finished 'pieces' already hung in their home, and goodness knew how many more she was working on.

Sue gazed into one of them, contemplating her reflection.

The pixie cut that had seemed daring and edgy during her Aberdeen years was still the same, except these days, she kept her hair short because it was practical. Where once a fierce young woman smiled out at her, Sue now only saw a slightly overweight, slightly lost middle-aged lady. Even Anne, who was six years her senior, had none of the worry lines that crisscrossed Sue's forehead. When had those appeared? Where had that bright young woman gone?

She inched closer to the mirror, the sea glass catching the light, until her reflection was no more than a kiss away.

'Are you still in there?' she asked herself.

5

THE NEXT MORNING, SUE FOUND ANNE SITTING AT THE TABLE, nursing an unidentifiable herbal tea in place of breakfast.

It was her usual Ayurvedic, yoga-tastic, tantric whatever-have-you, but to Sue it looked like pond water. She watched as her sister took a sip, feeling positively queasy at the mere sight of it.

Anne kept her eyes on the newspaper. 'Where are you off to, looking so smart?'

'I'm not smart,' Sue said, immediately regretting her defensive tone. She smoothed a hand over her hair. Amy had given her a beauty set for Christmas, which contained something called *sculpting wax*, and she had tried it out for the first time that morning. She prayed it wasn't too obvious.

Anne shrugged. 'Nice blouse.'

Sue didn't tell her it was a charity shop find. 'I'm heading over to the pub. Fancy it?'

'No thanks, love.' Anne sighed, slowly turning a page. 'I've got so much work to do.'

Sue's jaw tightened. By 'work', Anne was referring, in the

loosest sense of the word, to her *collection.* 'Any idea what you're going to do with them all?'

Anne glanced up at her, a blank expression on her face as if this were a silly question. 'I'm going to sell them, of course.'

'Right. Yes, of course.' Sue hesitated. A beat. 'Where?'

'Good question.' Anne closed the paper and turned her full attention to their conversation. 'Do you think Helen would put them in the gift shop?'

Somehow, on some level, Sue had known this was coming. Anne was doing her best to make it look like the idea had just occurred to her, but Sue could see now that this had been her intention all along. Asking Sue's best friend to sell her 'works of art' was too easy.

Or perhaps it had only just occurred to Anne now. Occasionally, Sue worried she knew what her sister was thinking before the idea had even entered Anne's head.

'Do you want me to speak to her?' Already, Sue's mind was racing ahead to how, exactly, she would manage Anne's disappointment when Helen said no.

'That would be marvellous,' Anne said, turning back to the newspaper.

Sue left her sister to a day in her workshop and headed out into the pale light of spring sunshine.

Unlike everyone else in Seahouses, Sue preferred the winter months. Almost all the businesses in the village depended on good weather to draw in tourists, and most locals pictured day trippers with pound signs in their eyes. But Sue saw only litter, queues, full carparks, and crowds.

The rational part of her knew that many of their neighbours earned most of their income during high season, and yet she still yearned for the days to get shorter again, for the nights when she could light a fire before tea, and those cold mornings when she wouldn't be able to feel her nose after five minutes on the beach.

Pinned to the noticeboard in the Ship's porch, a pink poster invited passers-by to join Sue's book club. The posters were Amy's idea and she'd printed them off at work. What on earth had possessed her to use pink? Didn't they have normal paper at the hospital? At the bottom there was a sign-up section, where several names were already scrawled.

Amy had written her name first in an effort to encourage others. Her niece was good like that. Below that, she'd signed up her friend Rachel in identical handwriting. And there, of course, was Diana Wheeler, her name scrawled in a flourish with the 'D' taking up at least three lines. Sue read the list out loud, mumbling to herself.

'Helen, Gina, Carrie, Fiona, Lucia... Tom?' Sue's face knotted into a puzzled frown.

Who on earth was Tom?

In more than ten years as The Ship's landlady, Sue had never seen Gina looking anything less than bombshell. Low-cut tops, big dangly earrings, and even bigger hair. Gina, it seemed, had no off days. She greeted Sue with a friendly smile.

'Y'all right, Sue? What can I get you?'

'Diet Coke please. I see you've put your name down for the book club.'

'Yeah,' said Gina, looking proud of herself. 'And my friend Carrie.'

Sue pictured the skinny woman who sometimes hung around the pub, her short bob dyed dark red, and her pale face caked with make-up.

'Any idea who the others are?'

'One of them's a bloke.' Gina raised an eyebrow suggestively.

'Yes. I did wonder about him. But a man... He probably won't show up?' Sue said it like a question, but Gina didn't have an answer.

Whenever Sue had pictured the book club, she hadn't imagined any men joining. There certainly hadn't been any back in Aberdeen. Not that she had anything against men in principle, it was just... she struggled to put her finger on it.

'Who knows, Sue? He might be fit. This mysterious Tom could end up being the man of your dreams.'

Sue couldn't describe to Gina just how unfathomable of a suggestion that was.

Gina leaned conspiratorially towards her. 'I don't know about him, but I can tell you everything you want to know about Fiona Gallivan.'

Sue's eyes grew wide, her mouth rounding into a small 'o'. *That* Fiona.

Everyone had heard of the Gallivans – after all, they were practically celebrities. The husband was a high-flying businessman who'd made his fortune from a chain of shoe shops. He had been stung in some sort of offshore tax scandal, but the shops were still going. They even had a branch at Berwick. Years ago, they'd had an annoying advert that showed during Coronation Street.

The wife – Fiona – was something of a minor socialite. She'd had interviews in celebrity magazines and was often in those *Who's Who* pages; not that Sue wasted her time with that sort of thing.

There had been huge excitement when the Gavillans bought a house in Seahouses – nobody could talk of anything else for weeks. There had even been a rumour that

Hello! magazine was coming to do a feature on their move to the countryside. But that was six months ago, at least. So far, no one had even met them.

'I know, right?' said Gina, mistaking Sue's silence for excitement. 'Seems her ladyship is finally ready to grace us with her presence.'

Sue swallowed against the knot of anxiety that rose in her throat. Why had she ever thought this was a good idea?

It was one thing meeting up with your niece and a couple of old friends to talk about a good book, but quite another to have complete strangers there. People you didn't know, picking over your taste in fiction and your opinions. What if they all hated it? Suddenly, Sue couldn't think of anything worse.

Get a grip, she told herself. *It will all be fine.*

The reading list was the result of hours spent on the internet, researching best-seller lists, cross-referencing reviews and blurbs from different websites and magazines. Sue's idea was to have a carefully curated selection of feminist fiction – nothing too revolutionary, but enlightening all the same. She had taken books off, added more, and then taken those off too. It had been through several drafts before she had anxiously shown it to Amy three weeks ago.

'Very *woke*, Auntie Sue,' she'd said.

Sue hadn't wanted to admit she wasn't sure what 'woke' meant, but by the way her niece said it, she had a hunch it was a good thing. She looked it up that night, back at the computer, and felt quite proud of herself. Perhaps the unapologetically radical Sue of her youth would have given her a pat on the back.

'Great.' She forced a smile for Gina, pretending she wasn't feeling completely overwhelmed.

.   .   .

Sue pulled her coat tight against the sea breeze and made the short walk to the gift shop, mulling over the list of names on Amy's poster.

Gina had agreed to let them use the back room of the pub for their get-together. It was little more than a snug, dating from the days when women sat separately from men. These days it provided space for overspill on busy nights and extra seating for lunch on weekends. And from now on, on the second Wednesday of every month, it would be the meeting place of Seahouses book club.

Neither Gina nor her friend struck Sue as being big readers, and she hoped they would actually discuss the book rather than simply sip wine and gossip... then she instantly felt appalled that such a snobbish thought had even crossed her mind.

It was interesting that Fiona Gallivan was coming, though. Was this a sign that the mysterious newcomers were finally taking an interest in village life?

The Gallivans had bought their house from the Millers, who'd run it as a bed-and-breakfast for years. It was an enormous property, standing proudly at the top of Seafield Road that ran along the coast to Bamburgh. The Gallivans had slapped solar panels on the roof, extended the side and back of the house, and replaced the windows with a strange reflective glass so that nobody could see in.

If rumour was to be believed – and in Seahouses, it often was – they had even installed a hot tub in the back garden.

According to Gina, who heard from one of the builders that worked on the place, the Gallivans would be dividing their time between Northumberland and their house in Spain. But they kept themselves to themselves, and after the initial novelty of the high-profile newcomers had died down, Sue had more or less forgotten about them.

The gift shop was empty apart from a young couple browsing the display of wooden bird feeders. Helen's face lit up when she saw Sue, and she dipped into the back of the shop. Seconds later came the click and purr of the kettle, and the chink of a spoon against ceramic. The couple had left by the time she re-emerged clutching two steaming mugs of tea, and the knots in Sue's shoulders began to ease.

There were only weeks between them, but Helen's hair – which she had worn in the same jaw-length style since she was a girl – had far fewer grey streaks than Sue's. She had what Sue affectionately thought of as an outdoorsy complexion: perpetually rosy cheeks and a year-round golden tan.

They took their usual seats behind the counter and Helen extracted a packet of biscuits from the pocket of her gilet – no doubt one of the many causes of the soft thighs and rotund hips that dogged them both.

'How's Anne?'

Sue sighed. Anne was... just Anne, she supposed. 'Still working on her "art".' Sue wiggled her fingers, miming inverted commas. 'And still talking to herself. Well, talking to Edward.'

Anne's husband Edward had been dead for more than twenty years, but having cosy chats with him was not the strangest thing her sister did. Not by a long shot.

Helen shrugged. 'Whatever makes her feel better, I suppose.'

'And the meditation, of course,' said Sue. 'And the chanting, the energy cleanses, the rituals. To be honest, I think she's getting worse. She's been quite withdrawn lately.'

The words came tumbling out before Sue had a chance to think them through. In truth, she worried about her sister. And it was easy to talk to Helen about all of this.

There was a comfortable familiarity between them, like a trusty pair of good walking boots that have seen you through more seasons that you can remember. Sue knew only too well what the local gossips said about her sister, but she could rely on her oldest friend not to break her confidence. Helen wouldn't tell anyone, not even her husband, Roy.

Sue knew from experience that Helen could be trusted to keep a secret with never a word whispered, even between the two of them.

6

———

THE SHOP WAS QUIET AFTER SUE LEFT. HELEN REACHED FOR another biscuit, then hesitated, remembering her struggle with the zip on her jeans that morning. She guiltily shoved the half-eaten packet in the drawer, out of temptation's way.

Since Matthew left home, she had gained more than a stone, her sadness for her son manifesting itself as a craving for anything sweet, buttery, or creamy. Roy didn't seem to notice how quiet the farmhouse was, nor the expanding roll of soft white flesh around his wife's midriff.

To distract herself, she picked up the book that Sue had chosen for their first read. There were only a few chapters left, and Helen was enjoying it more than she had expected.

The back cover mentioned the word *dystopian,* and that had been enough to make her think it was probably not worth the £7.99 that Tesco charged. Thankfully, Alnwick Library had a copy. It was all about equality and liberation – stuff that usually made Helen's eyes glaze over, but wrapped up in a plot she found easy to follow. She was even optimistic for a happy ending.

How typical of Sue to choose a feminist book. *Although they probably don't even call it feminism anymore,* Helen thought, and made a mental note to ask Matthew when he called. She wanted to sound intelligent when they discussed the book. Or at the very least, avoid sounding like an ignorant country girl.

She remembered the first time Sue came home for a visit, the Christmas after she went off to university up in Aberdeen. She was still Susan when she left, six months earlier. Now her hair had been lobbed off into a crop, and she was telling everyone to call her Sue. She had already grown a world away from Helen, who was working on her dad's farm by then and engaged to marry Roy Tattershall.

If anyone had asked her – not that they ever would – Helen would insist that her life was perfect, and she wouldn't change a thing. But secretly, deep down, she had always wished she was just a little more like Sue. And although she knew Sue wanted to be anywhere but back in Seahouses, Helen was glad to have her around.

She wondered what the mysterious Fiona Gallivan would make of Sue's reading choices. Or perhaps the book was the reason she was coming? Who knew? Perhaps Sue would have her own army of feminists marching through Seahouses before the end of the week.

Apparently, a man was coming, too. So far, they only had a first name: Tom. Helen didn't know any Toms, and she had to agree with Sue that, in hindsight, it would have been sensible to ask for surnames on the sign-up sheet. In a village where everyone knew everyone, nobody liked to be surprised.

Not long after Sue left, a young woman came into the shop. A striking creature – one of those people who are so perfect, you can't help but stare. And natural, too. It was awful, what you saw on some of the young ones these days: the fake eyebrows and hair extensions, and all that rubbish they injected into their lips. But not this girl. She picked up a scarf, examining the delicate silk between long, slim fingers.

Helen cleared her throat. 'That's hand-painted by a local artisan.'

She always referred to them as *artisans*, although most of them were merely hobby-artists who made and sold crafts to get them through the low season. Women like Anne, who had apparently got it into her head that Helen would stock her ghastly mirrors.

The beautiful stranger smiled at Helen, pale green eyes the colour of summer rock pools. She didn't look like she was from anywhere near here. Cinnamon skin, and those honey-coloured curls piled haphazardly on her head. She looked good enough to eat.

'Are you here for the day?' Helen didn't know what had got into her. She wasn't usually this nosey.

'I just moved here, actually.' The lady selected a silver bracelet from the jewellery display and held it up for closer inspection.

'You live here?' Helen couldn't hide her surprise.

The woman flashed a perfect pearly smile.

'Yes. As of today, I guess. I'm Lucia.'

The way she pronounced it, *lu-chi-ya,* made Helen think of expensive perfume.

Lucia spotted the book on the counter, face down on the page Helen had been reading before she walked in. 'Are you enjoying that?'

'Yes... very much so.' Helen scrambled, trying desperately to think of something else to say – some witty insight or opinion. Nothing came. 'I, er, really sympathise with the main character.' *You idiot,* she cursed herself.

She saw a way to recover. 'I'm reading it for our book club. You can join us if you like.'

The young woman beamed. 'Funnily enough, I've just signed up.'

7

SUE PICKED UP LUCAS AND BETSY FROM SCHOOL AND HEADED back to Amy's.

This was possibly her favourite time of day. The little ones were always so pleased to see her, and without toys or television to distract them, their great-aunt could bask in their undivided attention during the short walk home.

Sue had never had children of her own, and that was quite all right with her. She'd never particularly wanted them. It wasn't a conscious decision. There was never an epiphany, a moment when she had decided, definitively, that motherhood wasn't for her. But some days, particularly when she was younger, she had wondered whether she had missed out on something.

By the time she had returned to Seahouses and moved in with the girls, they were already teenagers and were largely self-sufficient. It wasn't until Amy had her children that Sue got to experience being around babies and toddlers. Watching as their little personalities emerged, observing as they discovered and experienced the world with such wonderment – and the endless and unconditional love. The best part was that she could give them back after a couple of hours.

The arrangement she had with Amy suited her perfectly. And as much as she wished Anne was more helpful, Sue loved the role she played in the family. She was the surrogate mother, the step-in grandma-slash-cool-great-aunt. Those kids – and her niece – they meant everything to her.

But was that all her life had come down to? A few hobbies, her family, and this village? Weren't her dreams bigger than this, once upon a time?

That's what she missed the most. Excitement. The thrill of not knowing what the future held.

Amy was sitting in her favourite chair when they crashed in, shattering her peace.

'I'm more than halfway,' she said to Sue, waving the book in the air to show her progress.

The kids barrelled straight to the kitchen in search of snacks as Sue sank into the sofa opposite her niece.

'You'll never believe who signed up for book club – Fiona Gallivan.'

Amy's forehead creased in surprise. 'At last, we get to meet the mysterious Gallivans. Or one of them, at least.'

'I do hope she likes the book.'

'Please stop fretting.' Amy patted her aunt's hand. 'I don't know what you're so nervous about. It's just a book club.'

They followed the children into the kitchen, consistently the warmest spot in Amy's house thanks to the oil-fired Aga, one of the original features that Amy and Mike had kept. The old stone house was in quite a state when they bought it, and the early years of their marriage had been devoted to lovingly renovating it.

'There's another thing,' Sue said. 'Some *man* has signed up.'

'What's wrong with that?'

'Nothing, nothing. Except...' Sue searched for the right words.

A smirk danced on Amy's lips. 'Are you going to tell me that men can't read?'

'Of course not,' Sue scoffed. 'It's just that... well. I didn't choose the books with men in mind.'

At this, Amy laughed. 'Auntie Sue. You were one of only two women to graduate from your master's programme. You spent four years working on an oil rig – the only female in a sixty-mile radius. It's kind of ironic that you wouldn't want a bloke in your book club.'

Sue sighed. She didn't want to tell Amy about Aberdeen, the delights of an all-women reading circle, those unique friendships that she had cherished. Those years – her life – that was something sacred, secret. Something she wasn't willing to share, not even with her beloved niece.

And then it struck her – perhaps that's what this was all about? Trying to recapture something of her life back then. Recreating some of that joy, the excitement, that, until now, she thought was lost forever. But could she be that woman again? Or was the old Sue, like so many things, beyond her grasp?

8

From her favourite chair, Fiona could see for miles.

The view from upstairs was one of the most attractive things about this property. While Peter got agitated about converting the pantry into a temperature-controlled wine cellar and bringing in an audio-visual expert to wire up his new media room, Fiona had fantasised about putting an armchair right here in this corner, angled just so.

It had been one of her few requests to the designer, who presented the idea back to her weeks later as *the library*. They installed made-to-measure bookcases and painted the walls in shades of stone and sand that echoed the hues of the beach below. All that, when all she'd asked for was a reading chair.

It was ironic that she had barely read a page since they moved in.

Fiona had anticipated Peter's retirement with equal measures of longing and dread. Dread because, after all these years together, she wasn't confident that they had much in common. And longing because Peter's work, frankly, had become the source of her worst nightmares.

Seahouses – like the boat, the villa in Marbella, the Arctic Circle cruise last year – had been his idea. Apparently, it was Peter's lifelong dream to have a home on the coast, looking out across the beach. Fiona had wanted to ask him how this lifelong dream had never come up in conversation during forty years of marriage, but didn't ask, in the end.

Life in Durham had suited her – she loved the city with its winding medieval lanes, the Gothic cathedral perched on its hilltop, the wide river that flowed through its core. And she had friends there. Good friends, women she could trust.

Or at least, she thought she could.

Once or twice a month she would get together with *the girls*, as they called themselves – despite all being in their fifties and sixties – and go to a wine bar where they would sip Chablis and laugh like teenagers. Now she was stuck up here with only Peter for company.

They weren't supposed to live here full time, not at first. Their initial plan had been to split their time between Durham and the coast, escaping to their weekend bolthole whenever they felt the urge to take some sea air. And of course, they had the house in Spain for whenever the sunshine and cava called. But after everything that happened, that plan was revised.

Seahouses was so much colder than she remembered. In the six months since they got back from Marbella, she had only ventured out on to the beach a handful of times. It had been bitter, squally gusts whipping and biting at anything they touched. It was already April, but even now she had a throw over her lap like an old lady. Sitting in her reading chair, she shivered at the memory of the wind.

When Peter first showed her the property listing – two days after he put in an offer to buy it – Fiona had a vaguely romantic vision of them taking daily walks together on the beach. Goodness knows Peter needed the exercise. He had promised to take better care of himself after that last scare, but Fiona knew better than to push him. At least he was playing plenty of golf.

She listened now, trying to decipher where in the house, exactly, he was. It was unnerving to spend so much time in a confined space with her husband. From somewhere downstairs – probably that media room that he had made such a fuss over – she heard the distant drone of his snores.

Three days. That was how long it took Fiona to pack up and move out of the home they'd lived in for twenty years.

A young family lived there now, in that beautiful red brick house with its sweeping driveway and white-columned porch. Sometimes she liked to picture the new owners. The woman tending to the vegetable garden that Fiona had cultivated, the man washing his car in their driveway. The kids running around on that vast lawn or playing in the nursery that she had painted herself when her own children were still small. The four of them sitting by the fireplace in the family room, just as the Gallivans had once done.

She missed it. And she missed the girls, even if they had turned out to be not quite such good friends after all.

The bay window of the reading room had become Fiona's lookout post. Without even moving from her seat, she could see the imposing stature of Bamburgh Castle on the horizon. She spent the days waiting for a familiar car to approach their drive, expecting visitors that never came.

Most days, she took a walk through the village. Seahouses was the type of place where people greeted one another in the street, even strangers. For an hour each morning, Fiona could pretend that she wasn't completely alone.

She had been passing the pub last week when something caught her eye. There was a community noticeboard of sorts in the entrance, and sometimes Fiona crossed the street and popped her head in the door, just to get a glimpse of what was happening.

Waiting for the day when she might work up enough nerve to join in with any of it.

The pink poster stood out among the Lifeboat Institute fundraisers, bake sales and Farne Islands tours, calling to her. And despite not having been able to pick up a book in over six months, Fiona signed up to join a book club.

Reading had been a great distraction over the years, one of her go-to escapes from Peter. On those many occasions when he drove her to despair, she'd been able to find comfort and calm between the pages. Until that last time, when he tipped her over the edge, and she couldn't concentrate long enough to follow even the simplest plot.

Now, finally, with the pressure of a deadline, Fiona was finding her focus. The book club was meeting this week, and she was determined to not only finish reading but have something to say about it, too. You only had one chance to make a good first impression.

She half-thought about getting up to make another cup of tea, but the kitchen was so far away. Just one more chapter, she promised herself.

Caitlyn would enjoy this book. All that girl power and what-not. Fiona smiled to herself, then wiped away a tear that came out of nowhere.

She wouldn't cry. She would not cry.

During their worst row, Caitlyn had accused her mother

of not standing up for herself. Of being a victim. *It's not like that*, Fiona had pleaded with her in desperation. And anyway, what did Caitlyn understand? She barely knew the half of it.

At least Ben was still speaking to her. Such a good boy. She wouldn't have got through it if it wasn't for him.

She was really crying now. Big, silly tears. Some days, it all got too much. Especially when she thought about Caitlyn.

Fiona padded along the plush carpet of the upstairs hallway to her bathroom and dabbed at her eyes with a tissue. People always remarked on how much Caitlyn resembled her. For Fiona, it was like looking at a younger version of herself, a mirror of youth that reminded her how she used to be. So sweet and naïve, with so much hope for the life that lay ahead.

Her cheeks dry, she brought out the jar of La Mer face cream and patted it into her skin.

'I don't know why you're still with him,' Caitlyn had said. 'You don't even like each other.'

It was true, she and Peter didn't like each other terribly much. And they certainly no longer enjoyed one another's company. But their marriage was beyond such trivialities as shared hobbies.

The glue that kept them together was the secrets they shared.

9

Gina was not enjoying the book. There were too many characters to keep up with, they had some stupid superpower that she couldn't understand, and there was no sex. Even after skipping ahead to the last chapter, she still couldn't work out what was happening. Worst of all was that she'd paid eight quid for the privilege.

Last night she had stayed up late just to try and get the damn thing finished and hadn't switched her light off until gone 3 a.m. She'd had to use extra concealer to cover up the dark circles under her eyes this morning. Gina's days of late nights were well and truly behind her.

This whole book club thing was starting to feel like a stupid mistake. Not only was she taking a night off the bar, but she had agreed that they could use the back room for their meetings. She would have to pay one of the lads to cover for her. It was madness.

But it would all be worth it for Carrie. She had come over yesterday and looked worse than ever. The poor wee thing.

Gina had known girls like Carrie growing up. Rudderless ships lost at sea. That lass had been bounced around between family members and foster carers and god knew what else. And after all of that, she'd had the misfortune to fall in with a man like Chris. Gina shuddered.

Gina had been able to see Chris for exactly who he was from the very first time she met him.

Carrie had been smitten, basking in the attention of her affectionate new boyfriend. *Very* affectionate. And very attentive. There were flowers, gifts, and even talk of a tattoo of Carrie's name, at one point.

To Gina, it was an alarm bell, sounding in her skull.

Chris would text Carrie constantly, her phone pinging all day. Even when Carrie was upstairs cleaning the bedrooms above the pub, Gina could hear it. *Ping, ping, ping.*

The problems started if Carrie took too long to reply.

One day they'd been up against the clock – after a full occupancy the night before and the other girl calling in sick, Carrie was left to clean all ten rooms herself. Even Gina had pitched in to help, the pair of them sweating with exertion as they hoovered, polished, mopped and dusted.

They were almost done when Chris showed up. He was red-faced after running to the pub in a panic that something had happened to her.

Carrie thought it was sweet that he cared so much.

A sense of recognition prickled at Gina's skin, the hairs on the back of her neck standing on end, even after Chris feigned embarrassment at causing a fuss over nothing.

Run, Carrie, she wanted to yell. *Get as far away from him as you can.*

Less than a month later, Gina caught him looking through Carrie's phone. She had left it on the table while she nipped to the loo, and he simply picked it up and started scrolling. How did he even have her passcode?

It left Gina speechless, and it wasn't until the following day that she calmed down enough to raise it with her friend.

But Carrie shrugged off her concerns. 'It's not like I've got anything to hide.'

'That's beside the point, Carrie. Doesn't he trust you?'

'Of course he trusts me. He goes through my phone. He can see for himself that I'm not up to anything.'

'And do you go through his?'

Carrie said nothing in response, her face reddening.

As the months went on, Gina saw less and less of her friend. Thanks to the reliable sources that propped up her bar on a weekly basis, she was vaguely aware of arguments between the couple, money troubles and problems with Chris's job. But Carrie had clammed up.

Now, Gina could see Carrie was fading into a shadow of her former self. She gave a startled jump whenever her phone made a sound, her face permanently etched with a frown of worry.

In the stillness of her flat above the pub, Gina heaved a heavy sigh. It was no use telling Carrie to break up with Chris. Her friend was already in too deep, and Gina couldn't risk driving a wedge between them. The best thing she could do was to hold her tongue, bide her time, and be there to dry Carrie's tears when they finally fell. She would eventually crack. They always did.

Gina shuddered. It was all too horribly familiar.

10

SUE TRIED ON THREE BLOUSES AND ENDED UP GOING BACK TO the first. She smoothed her hair down to one side with the sculpting wax and looped a long string of glass beads around her neck. The eyeliner pencil in her make-up bag was so old that she couldn't remember buying it, but it did the job.

'Make-up too?' Anne said from the doorway.

'Why not? I feel like making a night of it.'

Anne made herself comfortable on Sue's bed. 'What time do you think you'll be back?'

Sue watched her sister in the mirror while she carefully applied lipstick. Anne was impossibly supple and folded herself into a cross-legged pose that made Sue's knees ache just watching. 'Why don't you come with me?' she asked, for what felt like the dozenth time.

Anne's shoulders sank. 'No, thanks,' she said in a quiet voice.

Sue could sense her patience ebbing away. Anne had been sulking all day and Amy would be here any minute. If her sister didn't want to come, that was her choice – but Sue wasn't going to feel guilty about it.

Her thoughts were interrupted by the sound of Amy letting herself in.

'We're up here,' Sue called out.

Amy appeared in the bedroom doorway. 'You look great.' She smiled at Sue.

Anne was making an effort now, hiding her huff behind a broad smile for her daughter's benefit. She followed them down to the door.

'Have fun,' she called, waving them off as they stepped out into the street.

––––––

Amy threaded her arm through her aunt's, pulling her close. It was a mild evening, the warmth of the day lingering even as the sun began to drop.

'It was a really good idea this, Auntie Sue.'

She didn't want to tell her aunt that Mike hadn't been quite so enthusiastic. Amy couldn't put her finger on when, exactly, it had started. Mike's mother had been a stay-at-home housewife, always there to look after her husband and only son. He'd said this to her once. *Always there to look after us.*

As if Amy wasn't.

She pictured Mike's mother waiting by the door for the men to get home, her husband's slippers in one hand and his pipe in the other.

Of course, Mike didn't begrudge his wife having a career. At least he saw that in that respect, his parents were of a different generation – and that was putting it politely. The possibility that Amy stay at home had never been up for discussion. Mike had cracked open a bottle of champagne when she was finally appointed district nurse team leader two years ago, after Rosie Baker took a well-earned and long-overdue retirement.

No, work wasn't the problem. It was all the other things he wasn't so keen on: the extra hours she put in with the school governing body, the Lifeboat Institute committee, the harbour festival group. When she'd told Mike that Auntie Sue was starting a book club and she was going to join, he had the nerve to roll his eyes at her.

She wouldn't say any of this to her aunt, though. Sue was still a bundle of nerves and Amy wondered again what had got into her aunt, and most importantly, if Sue would ever snap out of it.

11

TOM WAS THE ONLY MAN. HE FELT THE BLUSH BLOOMING ON his cheeks as soon as he realised this and forced himself to take a deep, steadying breath. For a second, he considered making a run for it – it would be easy to spin on his heels and leg it back out of the pub.

But one of them spotted him, and before Tom had even finished processing the thought, she pounced. His window of escape closed as the petite white-haired lady steered him by the elbow into a lounge opposite the main bar.

'I'm Diana,' she said, shaking his hand. 'Diana Wheeler. I assume you're Tom?'

His hands were sweaty, but Diana didn't seem to notice. He nodded, somewhat dumbstruck.

'We're so very glad you could join us.' Her sapphire eyes sparkled in the warm light.

Tom hadn't had the faintest idea of what to expect. He only hoped he wouldn't stand out and on that, he'd failed before he started.

But what an interesting group.

Diana was the oldest, by quite a bit – not, Tom

suspected, that anyone would have the audacity to enquire as to her age.

She gestured for him to take a seat, and he squeezed into the banquet beside a pear-shaped middle-aged lady.

'I'm Helen.' She smiled, shuffling along to make room for him.

'Now that we're all here,' Diana raised her voice and the chatter instantly diminished. 'Might I propose a round of introductions?'

The lady with the grey cropped hair cleared her throat. 'Yes, Diana. I was just about to suggest that.'

Tom might have imagined it, but she sounded annoyed.

'I'll go first. I'm Sue Palmer.' She hesitated, a beat. 'I'm from Seahouses and I've lived here for my entire life. Well, almost all of it.'

The introductions continued, and Tom did his best to commit names to memory while fighting against a wave of anxiety that made his lunch curdle in his stomach as his turn drew closer.

One of the younger women – she must have been a model or something – told everyone that she was new to the village, having fallen for the scenery and fancying a change of pace from city life.

That was the line that Tom had planned to use.

He froze in panic as the group turned to him.

'I'm Tom.' He heard the inflection in his voice and took a steadying breath. 'I've just moved here too, funnily enough.' He attempted a casual laugh, imagining it would move the discussion on. It sounded forced, and he stopped abruptly, the heat rising in his neck.

Sue fixed him with a look that seemed to go beyond curiosity. 'From where?'

'Oh, er, London.' Tom shifted his weight in his seat. The blush lapped at his cheeks, and he willed it to subside.

'And how long have you been here?'

Tom spoke again, his voice reduced to little more than a croak. 'A couple of months.'

Sue continued to stare at him, even after Diana invited everyone to give their first impressions of the book.

The discussion itself lasted a solid forty-five minutes. It started out as a polite exchange of opinions but rapidly escalated into a good-natured and wine-fuelled debate, chiefly between Diana and Sue, until one of the others – Sue's niece, he was sure that was her – called for a truce.

Despite having prepared notes – which he had sensibly left at home – Tom was barely able to get a word in. And yet, it was exhilarating. He didn't mind not saying much. Just being around other people was more than enough for him. He hadn't appreciated just how isolated he would feel up here, or how lonely he would get. His face began to hurt, and he realised, with a pang of sadness, that it was from smiling so much.

It was getting late. He stifled a yawn and decided to give himself another twenty minutes before calling it a night. It was warm in the back room and several of the women were rosy-cheeked, although he suspected that was more from the wine than the central heating. He tried to decide who was his favourite.

The others seemed quite taken with Fiona, who'd come dressed in white jeans and cream cashmere despite the forecast suggesting showers later that night, and who hadn't been subjected to anything remotely close to the grilling Tom received.

Gina – now she was quite a character. Those fake nails looked like piano keys, and you didn't see many forty-something-year-olds in leopard print – not around here, anyway. At least the next time he came to this pub, he would have someone to say hello to. Wouldn't that be something?

As he watched Gina, a shadow fell over her face. Something like anger flared behind her eyes, just for a second, before she recovered herself.

She had spotted something – or someone – over Tom's shoulder.

He resisted the urge to turn around and kept his focus on Gina. Her eyes tracked the new arrival.

'Fancy seeing you here,' she said to whoever was now right behind Tom. The skin on the back of his neck prickled.

'Just came to walk Carrie home.' The voice was deep, the accent heavy.

At the mention of her name, the skinny redhead looked up and Tom swore her shoulders sank an inch. She smiled at the newcomer, but her eyes were cold, pale. Tom recognised that look when he saw it.

Gina's mouth drew into a pinch.

'Actually, Chris, we're not finished yet. Why don't you go and have a drink in the bar while you wait?'

'It's fine,' said Carrie, standing to leave. 'I'll just—'

'Stay.' Gina kept her eyes on the man, then turned to Carrie, her tone softening. 'You're having a good time, aren't you? Chris can have a pint while he's waiting.' She glanced back at the man. 'Can't you, love?'

By now the well-groomed lady with the expensive dye-job – *Fiona,* he remembered – and the supermodel had stopped talking and were observing the stand-off. Tom still had not dared to turn around and was doing his best to pretend he hadn't noticed anything was amiss. The heat rose in his neck.

'You all right there, mate?' The man put the emphasis on

mate, and Tom realised with icy dread that the remark was directed at him.

'Yes, perfectly fine, thank you.' Tom stuttered, feeling the burn in his face as he turned to smile at the stranger. His heart pounded in his chest.

One by one, the ladies stopped talking, the chatter giving way to silence.

Carrie stood, snatching up her bag. 'See you tomorrow,' she muttered to Gina as she shrugged on her jacket.

She flashed the group a trying-too-hard smile as she grabbed the man's arm. He hesitated, glowering at Tom, before following her out.

Oh dear, thought Tom. *Not again.*

12

THE LIGHT WAS DIVINE IN THE BATHROOM AT THIS TIME OF day. Filtered by a veil of cloud, the last dregs of golden sunlight reflected in the sea as the sun slunk towards the horizon. Lying there in the bathtub, Lucia had watched the sky turn from blue to golden, casting a hypnotic light show of purple, pink, and amber across the ceiling.

Tonight, she was celebrating her one-week anniversary in Seahouses. As the days ticked by, her customary disquiet was dissipating. The inner voice that was usually so quick to point out flaws and imperfections, the one that pushed her to keep moving on to the next place, was growing quieter as time passed. Whenever that little voice stirred, she promptly shut it down.

Some people called it itchy feet – for Lucia, it was more of a whole-body ache. Wanderlust that bordered on obsession. It was a compulsion. She recognised that, but she just couldn't get comfortable. There seemed to be nowhere on earth where she belonged. She had spent years scouring the planet for perfection, and although she'd come close once or twice, she hadn't found it.

Until now.

She hoped.

A week after arriving, it still felt right. That was a good sign.

She filled her days with beach walks, reading, and simply gazing out the window. That last job in Prague had paid generously, sufficient to keep her going for another couple of months at least. Earlier today, one of her regular clients in New York had emailed a brief. She would get back to them next week and decline. Right now, she just wanted to relax.

The book club had been exhausting. Fun, but exhausting. Social events like that – especially with a group of strangers – just took it out of her. All that small talk and requisite niceties. It felt, to Lucia, like learning lines for a play and performing on stage. She said all the right words and went through the motions, but she was playing a part.

She patted herself down with a towel and threw on the silk bathrobe that she'd picked up last year in Ho Chi Minh City. Downstairs in the tiny kitchen, she brewed a chamomile tea. Earlier in the day, she had prepared a fire, carefully stacking the logs and coal, filling in the gaps with scrunched-up newspaper, just like Nana used to. She struck a match and watched as the flames licked to life, the light dancing on the tiled fire surround.

Puffin Cottage had been a great find. Each time she walked through the honeysuckle-framed door, it felt like she was stepping back in time. The worn Persian rugs, capiz shell lampshades and cut-glass crystal goblets spoke of timeless glamour. Lucia loved spaces like this – real, lived-in homes, with traces of real people. She sought them out on all her trips, choosing back-street bed-and-breakfasts over contemporary hotels whenever the agent hadn't already organised the accommodation.

Her landlady had been there last night. An older woman, a tiny little thing, who kept touching Lucia's arm as if they had known each other for years. When Lucia told her how much she was enjoying her stay in Puffin Cottage, Diana jovially announced that she would call in for tea one day next week.

The book had been pretty good – not her usual thing, perhaps, but wasn't that the entire point? To try new things?

It was an interesting group of women – and that one guy, of course. A real mixed bag, several of whom were excited to talk about anything other than the book.

One of the women had wanted to set Lucia up with her son. She shyly suggested he was about Lucia's age, and she apparently thought – despite having known Lucia for less than an hour – that they would have lots in common.

This happened to Lucia with surprising frequency. In airports, supermarkets, on the street. Women asking if she was single, saying they knew someone. What on earth did they see in her? What was it about her that convinced complete strangers she would be a great match for their son, or brother, or friend? She unfailingly declined, always politely.

But this was a fresh start. And this time, she was doing things differently. Besides, it was just one harmless date.

There was something about the lady, Fiona, that made Lucia eager to please her. She'd offered no personal details apart from her first name, but Lucia could see in the glances traded between the others that this woman was *someone*. They deferred to her in the way that wealth and status tend to command respect – although such things did not impress Lucia. No, it was more than that. It was a sadness, a certain sorrow, that Lucia could see just below the surface of the beautiful blow-dried hair and expensive clothes. Lucia had put the son's name in her phone and promised Fiona she would call him.

It was already late. She would text him tomorrow once she had fully recharged her batteries.

She hoped Carrie was all right. The atmosphere in the pub had changed after her boyfriend showed up 'to walk her home'. Yeah, right. Despite the warmth from the fire, she shivered just thinking of the way he snarled at poor Tom with the undeniable threat in his voice. None of them felt quite so convivial after that.

From the battered leather armchair, Lucia gazed out the window. It was properly dark now, the blackness rich and satiny. The stars were so bright here that the sea caught their reflection. Far down below, at the bottom of the steep drop, boats bobbed silently in the harbour.

Lucia closed her eyes, quieting her thoughts, listening to see if the little voice was awake.

All she heard was the distant rhythm of the sea.

13

ONCE UPON A TIME, FIONA HAD IMAGINED THAT THEIR retirement would be an endless carousel of holidays abroad, long walks, and nights out with friends. Even when they first moved here, while it was all still sinking in, she had pictured them making new friends and spending evenings in quaint country pubs. At least now, finally, she had some friends to call on.

Their retirement. Because Fiona did think of it as her retirement, too, despite not having worked in thirty years. Life with Peter had become a full-time job in itself.

Her gaze drifted over to him, sitting opposite her across the dining table. Had he always chewed with his mouth open like that? Peter ate too fast – he blamed growing up with five brothers, but Fiona couldn't imagine what his excuse would be now.

'Ben might come and visit this weekend,' she said, testing the water. She hadn't even asked Ben yet but wanted to start laying the groundwork, give Peter time to get used to the idea.

He grunted a non-committal response. A crust of blood

had dried on his neck where he cut himself shaving that morning.

'His new job is going well,' she started, before remembering that Ben's career as an estate agent was one of the many things his father, apparently, could not abide about him. 'And he booked up to go to Ibiza this summer with some friends, which sounds super...' she trailed off.

The grandfather clock in the hallway sounded out the empty seconds, echoing in the dining room.

'Anyway, so he might come up for a couple of days, which would be nice. Maybe you boys could go for a round of golf?'

Peter didn't take his eyes off his food. 'We'll see.'

Fiona poured herself another glass of wine and nudged a square of ravioli around her plate with a fork. Even after everything Peter had done, it still fell on her to make all the effort.

She thought again about Lucia, that ethereal creature with those magnificent jade eyes. Fiona didn't know what had come over her, suggesting that she'd like to introduce her to Ben. *A date.* The words came out before she had thought it through, hoping that young people still called it 'a date'. Even now, she blushed at the memory. Thankfully, Lucia had said yes.

It was selfish, really, but if Ben had a girlfriend in Seahouses, he might be inclined to visit more often. It would certainly be something to counter how much he detested his father's company.

Besides, seeing Ben and Caitlyn settle down was at the top of Fiona's wishlist. She longed for weddings and grandchildren, some light at the end of the tunnel.

Ben was too fussy, that was his problem. And fickle. She'd never known him to maintain a relationship for more than three months, breaking up with them for the most ridiculous reasons. Somewhere in the back of her mind, Fiona was vaguely aware that Ben's perspective on what went wrong possibly didn't tally with the girls' accounts. But it was her prerogative as a mother to take his side.

Still, she wished the boy had more staying power.

Perhaps she was to blame. It wasn't easy for either of them, growing up with that kind of wealth. Or that kind of father. But it was a common problem these days, from what Fiona could see. Too much Instagram and airbrushing and reality television had given the younger generation unrealistic standards. You only had to watch an episode of *Love Island* – and Fiona had only watched it that once – to see how nit-picky everyone had become. The relationships they were looking for simply didn't exist in the real world.

When Fiona had married, she understood it was for life – no question about that. Only twenty-one years old and so certain. But she had been right. She and Peter had done their best to set the children a good example of what marriage meant. It hadn't always been easy – in fact, it had been bloody hard work, at times.

Quite a lot of the time, actually.

Peter finished his supper and stood up from the table, the abrupt movement snapping Fiona back to the moment. His napkin dropped onto his plate, where it landed in a pool of tomato sauce. Fiona watched the red stain seep through the linen as Peter headed wordlessly towards his media room.

The half-eaten meal on her plate had gone cold.

14

AN ENTIRE WEEK AFTER THAT STUPID BOOK CLUB, GINA WAS still fuming at the way Chris had dragged Carrie off. A dog that he called to heel. And, if Gina was being honest, she was angry with herself for not doing more to stop him.

She spent the mornings thunderously clattering behind the bar, smashing her favourite coffee mug and breaking a nail in the process. But as the days wore on, her fury turned into agitation, then a growing unease. Most worryingly, she hadn't spoken to Carrie since that night.

The girls had been booked to clean every day that week, which should have given Gina ample opportunity to get Carrie on her own. She planned to steal her away for a coffee once the housekeeping was done. But Chris had been hanging around like a bad smell, turning up early and waiting to walk Carrie home. Gina's heart sank lower each time she saw him. His eyes, as vacant as a shark's, avoided her accusing glares.

And Carrie was dodging her.

At first, Gina thought she was imagining it. They had been at full occupancy on Saturday, so there was plenty to do the following morning, and the last check-outs didn't finish their breakfast until the housekeeping girls were almost done. It gave Gina no time at all on Sunday to pull Carrie to one side. But by Monday, she started to get the sense that Carrie was avoiding her.

By Wednesday, caving into her frustrations, Gina cornered her.

This feat was made more difficult by the constant presence of the other cleaner, Margaret, who would not stop yapping on and on, oblivious to the awkwardness. Carrie's texting was becoming more frantic, forcing Margaret – who, Gina always thought, looked like she was half a Mars bar away from diabetes – to make the last two beds on her own, leaving her breathless with the effort.

'Time for a chat?' Gina struggled to disguise the eagerness in her voice.

'About what?' Carrie frowned.

'You know... the other night. Chris. You running off like that. I just wanted to check everything was OK.'

Carrie sighed. 'It's fine. Honestly, I don't know what your problem is.'

Her problem.

Recalling it now, Gina dug out the pack of cigarettes that she had hidden from herself at the bottom of the freezer and sneaked out to the back yard. Her first tab in seven weeks, but desperate times and all that. She exhaled and uncurled her fists, pins of pain where her nails had pressed into her palms.

It was because another man was there. That's what set him off. That poor bloke. Tom. He didn't have much to say for himself, not even when he popped back into The Ship over the weekend. Seemed content to sip a glass of wine at the bar on his own. Of course, Gina had been friendly with him. It was good for business. Now it was Thursday again, and she was ready to put money on him coming in tonight.

The nicotine went straight to her head, and she leaned back against the yard wall, feeling the tension in her muscles diffuse. At last, her brain was calm enough to focus.

Once upon a time, Gina had known a man just like Chris.

A dangerous man.

She'd had boyfriends before him. *Going out.* That's what they used to call it, even though they never went anywhere except down by the river. In that rain-soaked place-between-places, that town which had teetered for centuries between two countries, there wasn't much else for bored teenagers to do. They occupied themselves with juvenile relationships that were all-consuming for all of three weeks before they fizzled out and each party moved on merrily to the next. But none of that had prepared her for Tony.

In the stillness of The Ship's back yard, Gina said his name out loud, exorcising an old ghost, his name bitter on her tongue as she forced herself to confront the memory.

More than twenty years later, and he still haunted her dreams. Not always his face, or his name, but undeniably his presence. Even the thought of him brought on a cold dread, the memory of a sensation that someone had once *controlled* her, and she had been powerless to stop him. Of seeing her friends and family slowly drift away, and not realising until too late that her hand had pushed them. The feeling of being a puppet, dragged along by a string around her neck.

Every time he appeared in her dream, it morphed into a nightmare and she would wake, panting to catch her breath, her hands fisting in the duvet and ribbons of tears on her face.

She eventually escaped his iron grip, the chokehold he

had her in, but it took two years. She would wear the scars for the rest of her life.

Gina dropped her cigarette, watching it land in a splatter of orange sparks. A gust of wind chased itself around the tiny yard, the sudden chill making her shiver. She was powerless again. All she could do was bide her time, observe, and be there when it all came crashing down. This was a waiting game, and there was no shortcut to the final conclusion.

Or was there?

15

For an entire week after the book club, Sue was buzzing. The evening had gone swimmingly.

There had been a good discussion, in the end. Sue hadn't even minded when Diana took charge, unable to resist the temptation. By then, Sue barely cared about how clever she might have sounded. She was mellow, two glasses of Sauvignon Blanc fizzing through her veins, the collective enthusiasm of the group rendering her the most at ease she had felt in a long time.

Tom wasn't what she had expected. The clothes. That's what gave him away as an outsider. Dressed like the tourists in their 'weekend-in-the-country' gear.

She'd pegged him at a few years younger than her and Helen – a few, but not many, although he had none of the deep lines that scored Roy's face, nor the callouses on his hands. A real city boy.

It took quite some cajoling on Diana's part to get him to join in with the discussion. Amy scoffed afterwards, when Sue pointed this out, and said he was probably just shy. But a reluctance to share opinions was not, in Sue's experience, an affliction shared by most men.

He hadn't wanted to tell them anything about himself. And it wasn't like Fiona Gallivan, who they could just google. No. Tom was something else.

And there had been that business at the end when Carrie's boyfriend showed up and dragged the poor girl home. *Chavs*, that's what Amy and Izzy used to call people like that, although Amy seemed to have forgotten this fact as she got older and now chastised Sue whenever she used that word.

Whatever you wanted to call him, the man had 'low-life' written all over him. Sue could see past the tattoos, shaved head, and skin-tight t-shirt. It was, from what she understood, considered quite the look these days. They probably had David Beckham to thank for that. But with Chris, it was more than just the outside.

There was something dark about him, something that was rotten to the core. It was that jaw set permanently forward in a jut, that grimace of a smile and those cold, hard eyes. It was the way the atmosphere turned gloomy when he entered the bar that night, like a cloud blowing over the sun.

Sue had been quietly indignant and now, a week later, still found herself riled over the whole affair.

The bell tinkled as she entered the gift shop. Helen had generously agreed to display three of Anne's mirrors right at the entrance – prime retail real estate – as a favour to Sue. As much as she knew it would buoy her sister's mood, Sue secretly hoped there hadn't been any buyers. She was already looking forward to a new obsession – hopefully one that would take up less wall space.

At this time of year, the shop was quiet on weekdays, the

tourists still limited to weekenders and only the most committed day trippers, giving Helen plenty of space to host and time to chat.

Mug of tea in hand, Sue helped herself to a Garibaldi from the packet Helen had just opened.

'Matthew couldn't believe we met Fiona Gallivan.' Helen blew steam from her tea. 'I was telling him how she's lovely and not at all what you'd expect.'

Sue frowned. 'What on earth did you think she'd be like?'

'Oh, I don't know.' Helen dismissed Sue's question with the wave of a hand. 'It's just... all that money. They say it corrupts.'

'And how do you know she's not corrupt?'

Before Helen could answer, something beyond the window caught her attention. 'Speak of the devil...' she said, her eyes on the entrance.

Sue glanced over her shoulder as the bell chimed and a briny draught blew Fiona Gallivan into the shop.

'Fancy that, we were just—' Helen started to say, but caught herself. 'We were just saying how much fun it was last week.'

Fiona was much more appropriately dressed today, thought Sue. It was warm for April, but a cool easterly breeze blew in off the sea. She had swapped last week's all-white outfit for jeans, hiking books and a Barbour, and looked like an authentic country lady – although perhaps not with that blow dry. Sue hadn't used the sculpting wax this morning and now regretted it.

'I don't know why I've never stopped by here, when we're practically neighbours,' Fiona said, her eyes roving around the shop. 'You really have some lovely things.'

Helen shrugged and offered a bashful smile.

Fiona's gaze landed on Anne's sea glass and shell mirrors, where it briefly lingered, her expression quizzical. She paused, hesitating. 'I don't get out much at all, these days,' she said, quietly.

Sue and Helen exchanged a glance, a wordless agreement not to interrupt the woman so clearly in need of unburdening herself.

'When we lived in Durham...' Fiona's voice trailed off. She quickly caught herself and shook off whatever had just come over her.

'Anyway.' The brightness was back. 'I was just passing when I spotted you in here, and I thought you might fancy tea. This evening, I mean. At my house. Or coffee. Or wine.' She was bumbling now.

Sue ignored Helen, whose eyebrows had jumped to the mid-way point of her forehead, and focused squarely on Fiona. 'That would be lovely.'

———

Fiona stuffed her hands deep into her pockets as she walked, her fingers searching for warmth. She didn't know what had compelled her to call by the gift shop just now. And it certainly hadn't been her intention to invite those two women over.

Ben was driving up tomorrow after work, his first visit in nine weeks. Not that she'd been counting. After the last row, she desperately wanted to convince him that she was happy. She pictured her son in her kitchen. She would casually hand him a bottle of that craft beer he was into, and say, 'Why yes, dear, of course I've made new friends. As a matter of fact, they were over here last night.'

She muttered it to herself as she walked along, rehearsing her line. Would he be convinced?

It was supposed to be parents who worried about the kids, not the other way around. That alone made her feel like a failure. At least Ben's concern was preferable to Caitlyn's silent treatment.

Fiona had dressed for a walk along the beach, but now, as the wind blew, she wondered if she should call back at home to put on an extra layer.

There had been an article in *Good Housekeeping* about how walking was beneficial to your mental health. Fiona could have sworn she'd never even heard of *mental health* until a couple of years ago. Now people went on and on about it, bandying it around as casually as they talked about a common cold. But, as the days grew warmer, the appeal of walking along the beach was growing. And when Ben asked her if she was getting out, at least she could give him an honest answer. Fiona was a terrible liar.

The gift shop was only along the road from their house. It really was astounding, now she thought about it, that she'd never even ventured inside. What exactly, she wondered now, had she been hiding from?

Forget the extra layer. This would have to do.

She walked past her own house, glancing up at those big reflective windows that stared out at the sea, empty and soulless. Looking down on her. Judging her.

It would be nice to have visitors, she mused. There were already two bottles of white in the fridge – maybe she should add some rosé, too. All that Cotes de Provence that Caitlyn and her friends liked to drink. No point in it just sitting there. Perhaps she would make some hors d'oeuvres, too.

Few things excited her more than entertaining, the

house buzzing with people while caterers glided through the throngs, holding trays of champagne and canapes at shoulder height. The finer details. That's where Fiona excelled. Printed menus. A dedicated cloakroom attendant. Musicians, but never the same ones twice.

The house in Durham had been perfect for parties, with its long salon that opened up onto the orangery and the terrace at the back. She'd had solar-powered lights installed all over the garden, hidden in the borders and along the paths, and as soon as it got dark enough, they lit up the night like stars.

After that last party, that fateful night when it all came crashing down, she had gone out there alone. She plonked herself in the deckchair and drank champagne straight from the bottle, wondering where it all went wrong.

She sniffed, the cold now beginning to bite at the tip of her nose. As she reached the bottom of the dune path, the beach unfurled in front of her and Fiona made long, determined strides, her calf muscles straining from the exertion. The sand glistened with salt, and closer to the shoreline, gleamed from the receding tide.

Fiona had known that there were other women. At least Peter always had the decency to be discreet. Well, he tried, at least. The problem was that Peter didn't always do discretion terribly well. He was still, and always would be, the working-class lad who made a million before his thirtieth birthday and wanted the world to know.

In the right frame of mind, she thought his infidelity was rather continental. The French were always up to it, weren't they?

And on her bad days, she wanted to strangle him.

She had hoped that last heart attack had finally put an end to his shenanigans. How wrong she had been.

At least it was all over now. There were some humiliations that there was no coming back from.

Her sister called her spineless for staying with him.

No, thought Fiona. *You're wrong.*

To hold her head high after everything Peter had done proved that she was made of steel.

16

———————

'I'm not wearing that,' said Sue. 'It's just drinks over at her place. A casual night in.'

'Fine. Have it your way.' Amy hung the garment on the front of Sue's wardrobe, giving it the same careful consideration she would offer a piece of art hanging in a gallery.

Sue bit her lip. 'Do you honestly think...?' She trailed off.

It was a gorgeous top. Silver sequins that shimmered in the light like a mermaid's tail. Amy had worn it last Christmas and was now trying to convince her that it would look great with jeans for a casual night round at their new friend's place.

'It's not some big girls' night out, you know.' But Sue knew she didn't sound convinced. And the longer she stared at the top, the less crazy the idea seemed.

Amy shrugged. 'Don't bother if you're not going to be comfortable...' She paused. 'You know what I think?'

Sue shook her head.

'Life is short,' said Amy. 'Wear the damned sequins.'

· · ·

Helen was waiting for her on the corner. They linked arms, huddling close for warmth as they walked down Main Street, steps that they had taken together a thousand times. The village was quiet, their footsteps echoing in the dusk. They passed the gift shop and Coxton's ice-cream parlour, now in darkness save for the blue pallor of the freezers. The sun was beginning its slow descent towards the Cheviots, casting glints of gold across a tarry sea now void of boats.

Sue took a deep breath as the Gallivans' gate swung closed behind them, the latch clunking into place. The house had been extended, but only part of it was visible from the main road. The new annex was constructed in stone that almost matched the original Victorian masonry, and even the windows had been framed sympathetically in stained wood to complement the original woodwork. Only the solar panels on the roof hinted at the scale of the renovation.

The old door had been replaced with a wider one in oak, flanked on either side by two bay trees in tall stone planters. They'd kept the original doorbell, an enamel button set into a circular brass surround. Someone had recently polished it, so she had to assume it still worked. Sue's heart fluttered as the chime echoed inside the house.

A man answered.

'Come on in,' he said, his red face creasing into a smile. She detected the faintest twang of a Brummie accent and the smell of cigars and hair oil.

It took Sue a second to recognise Peter Gallivan. He looked different, somehow, from the pictures she'd seen. Less glossy.

She recovered quickly, offering a smile.

'Lovely to meet you.' Helen held out a hand only for

Peter to pull her towards him, his meaty hands swallowing her shoulders.

Sue registered the shock on Helen's face as Peter kissed her, European style, with a peck on each cheek.

They were saved by footsteps thudding the length of the tiled hallway at a pace that almost matched Sue's pulse.

'Ladies,' said Fiona, eyeballing Peter. 'I see you've met my husband.' Something in her tone made Peter back off instantly.

Fiona smiled at Helen and Sue, her jaw tight.

'These are for you.' Helen offered a bunch of daffodils wrapped in brown paper that suddenly, to Sue, seemed ridiculously modest for this grand house.

'How beautiful.' Fiona cooed, as if she really meant it. 'We'll be through here this evening.' She gestured down the hall towards the kitchen, light spilling from the open door.

Sue kicked off her ankle boots and followed Fiona. The hallway had been transformed since she was last here only a year ago, for a coffee morning when it was still the Millers' B&B. Where there was once an umbrella stand overflowing with beach toys, and a bookcase jammed with paperbacks and board games, there was now an elegant half-moon console table and a large oriental vase, glazed in an intricate design flecked with gold, no doubt an antique.

The kitchen was equally unrecognisable. Even old Lucile Miller would struggle to navigate the new layout. Gone were the old pine units, the terracotta floor and tiled walls. In their place was a combination of marble, granite, and gloss white surfaces, all framing a stainless steel island in the middle. It looked more like a chemistry lab than a kitchen, apart from the velvet bar stools clustered around the island.

Velvet, thought Sue. *Who puts velvet in a kitchen?*

A decadent floral display stood proudly in the centre, and next to it, a sweating ice bucket of champagne.

'Please, make yourselves comfortable.' Fiona waved in the general direction of the island as she put the daffodils in a vase and went to retrieve something from the oven.

'Is that your son?' Helen gestured to a photograph in a chrome frame. It was a candid shot, a young man with his face screwed up in mock protest as Fiona pressed a kiss to his cheek.

'That's Ben. My baby boy.'

Sue wasn't sure if she imagined it, but there was a flash of hurt in Fiona's eyes. Whatever it was, she quickly shook it off.

'Voilà,' Fiona said, setting down a tray of party food.

Sue held up a doll-sized ceramic dish of gooey cheese, unable to hide the question forming on her face.

'Miniature *tartiflette*,' Fiona laughed with forced joviality. 'I was feeling quite creative this afternoon!'

Sue surveyed the buffet, wondering what half of it was and where to even start, as Fiona poured three glasses of champagne. Not even prosecco, Sue noted. She couldn't wait to tell Amy.

Fiona's silk blouse was sheer, something that most women half their age would struggle to pull off, and Sue was glad that her niece had pushed her to dress up. How often did she get a chance to drink champagne these days, anyway? That alone had to be worth the sequins. She exchanged a wide-eyed glance with Helen, who was already working on a smoked salmon blini.

'Cheers.' Fiona held her glass high. 'To new friendships.'

'To new friendships,' they echoed.

17

FIONA RINSED THE CHAMPAGNE GLASSES AND PROPPED THEM upside down on the rack to dry. With the dishwasher purring, she could relax.

She emptied the last of the rosé into her glass and climbed onto a bar stool. The house was still. Apart from the clock in the hall and the ever-present distant murmur of the sea, it was silent.

Peter had taken himself off to bed hours ago, with only a curt wave goodnight to her guests. *Her* guests. At least he had got the message to leave them well alone.

They'd got through three bottles in the end – one champagne and two of the Cotes de Provence. There was still a third bottle in the wine fridge, just in case Caitlyn ever did show up. Drinking that final bottle would be too close to acknowledging that it would take a minor miracle to get her daughter back.

She had got quite carried away with the food this afternoon, but it had been worth it to see the look Helen and Sue exchanged. It wasn't all made from scratch, and the vol-au-vents were in fact from the M&S freezer section, but her guests either didn't notice or were too polite to ask.

Caitlyn would like these women. The thought crossed Fiona's mind before she had a chance to fight it and she let it sit there, imagining what Caitlyn would say if she was here. Helen had the most wicked sense of humour and was already offering Fiona tips for the garden. Sue, it turned out, had not only gone to university, but studied something very scientific and rather impressive, although she had modestly shrugged it off.

Fiona had been surprised to find herself enjoying the evening immensely.

Of course, it wasn't a patch on the old days, when she used to hire a chef for their dinner parties and bring in wait-staff. Students from Durham University that Fiona booked through an events agency. There was something deliciously thrilling about having toffee-nosed public school kids serve her at her own table.

Male students, of course.

After that one occasion, when she interrupted Peter in a compromising situation with a young waitress in the utility room, she'd made a point of requesting male staff.

Fiona had almost forgotten about that. It was funny, the things that were coming back to her now that she had so much time on her hands.

At least Ben would be here tomorrow. She checked his message again, her reading glasses balanced on the tip of her nose.

He planned to set off at lunch time, which meant he would be here by early afternoon. That little car of his went at quite a lick. She would buy fresh bread in the morning and have a doorstop cheddar and Branston sandwich ready and waiting for him. Perhaps with a garnish of that micro-green salad that he liked the last time he was over. Fiona made a note to drive up to Berwick in the morning to see if Sainsbury's stocked it.

The cleaning lady had made up a bedroom for him, and after Fiona's initial indecision, she was confident it would suit him best. It lacked a sea view, but the ensuite had a rain shower and, most importantly, it was well out of the way of Peter's study.

Fiona had planned the whole weekend for them. Only in her head, of course. Ben hated it when she confronted him with a written itinerary, and he was a big fan of *chillaxing*. As far as Fiona could see, that meant doing next to nothing, preferably while mindlessly scrolling on his iPhone. But she wouldn't mind, if it came to that, so long as he was doing next to nothing in her house.

The most exciting part was that he was taking Lucia out on Saturday night. He hadn't been too enthusiastic when Fiona first texted to inform him she'd arranged a blind date. But sure enough, he eventually warmed to the idea. He'd probably looked her up on Tinder or Instagram, or wherever young people seemed to find each other online.

Fiona hadn't wanted to push him too hard on where, exactly, he was planning to take her. Much better to wait until he arrived to do that. She had taken the liberty of jotting down some ideas in her notebook, just in case. Ben didn't know this area very well, so she was simply saving him a bit of time by researching the best restaurants and pubs.

Nursing her wineglass, she idly wondered what Ben and Lucia's children might look like. A crazy thought, and she had to laugh at herself – they hadn't even met yet. But there was no harm in letting her mind wander, surely? She pictured babies with Ben's eyes, skin the palest shade of biscuit and sunshine-blond curls, lighter and looser than Lucia's.

Simply thinking of Ben caused a warmth to spread through her, thawing her loneliness. Parents weren't supposed to have favourites. Fiona understood that – and of course, she didn't. But there was something special about a mother-son bond.

With girls it was different – too many hormones, perhaps. Caitlyn had morphed overnight from a kind and softly spoken little girl to an opinionated and unappeasable teenager. The rows they'd had... Fiona gave an involuntary shudder.

But it had always been different with her little Benny. He would never abandon his mum.

18

Amy zipped her fleece and adjusted her headband to cover the tops of her ears. She conducted a final check of her gear and stepped outside to stretch.

The wind had been blowing off the sea all week, an easterly gust that could be bitterly cold. She quickly recalibrated her pace, thinking about the parts of her route where she'd be up against the headwind and on which sections she might be able to gain a bit of ground. She set off down Sycamore Street, listening to her breath as her heartbeat fell into sync with the rhythm of her footsteps.

Amy used to hate running. At school, they were forced to do cross country no matter how bad the weather. Her abiding memory was running along the banks of the Aln, the ground frozen solid, her chest aching so badly that she thought she might throw up.

Her cadence increased as she turned onto the coast road. *Inhale through the nose and exhale out the mouth. Back straight, touch down on the balls of your feet.* The burn in her lungs felt good, now. She was resilient and determined. It had taken the feat of growing three humans in her body for

Amy to understand the extent of her power – not just her physical strength, but her willpower. Her *superpower*. All that time, and she had been stronger than she realised.

Amy's children were the greatest thing that had ever happened to her, but being their mother – was that what defined her now?

Some women even wrote it in their profiles. *Wife, mother.* Women who measured their worth in relation to the people who they loved. And Amy got that, she did. She just didn't *get it*. She'd had a first-hand close-up at what happens when the centre of your world crashes out of the universe and she was determined to never let it happen to her.

Her trainers were like a second skin, moulded by the miles, snug around her feet. She was already passing the carpark, her childhood home coming up on the left. Amy kept her head down, as per habit, pushing away the memories of that tragic year when they lost Dad, only to lose Mum so soon afterwards.

As usual, her thoughts drifted to Izzy. She saw her sister's latest post on Instagram that morning, Izzy posing alongside two impossibly good-looking men aboard a boat, the skyline of Hong Kong harbour in the backdrop.

It never failed to amaze her. That adolescent fantasy of running away to the other side of the world, all that silly talk about wanting to live somewhere hot. Amy always thought it was just something they fantasised about, a coping mechanism for dealing with everything they had been through.

It transpired that not only had Izzy meant every word, she'd actually gone and done it.

Good for you, thought Amy, whenever she scrolled through her sister's pictures on social media. Evidence that dreams could come true, even for people like them.

Perhaps this year Amy would finally get out to visit her.

If Mike didn't like it, he'd just have to lump it. Besides, between Auntie Sue and Rachel, he'd have plenty of help.

Poor Rachel. Amy had watched her friend's hope of ever having her own children slowly diminish, a light dimming month by month, year by year, until it vanished entirely. You can grieve for those you never knew just as deeply as those that you had lost, Amy realised. Amy was more than happy to share the affection of her brood. Love was infinite, and there was more than enough to go around.

As she passed the first houses on the coast road, a green sports car pulled up outside the Gallivans' place. A Porsche, maybe? Mike would know.

Curiosity getting the better of her, Amy reduced her pace, observing.

A young man climbed out of the car and stood there for a moment, a hand to his eyes as he took in the view. Aviator sunglasses, grey suede bomber jacket, boy band hair. *Too cool for school,* thought Amy. Fiona appeared at the front door, trotting down the garden path, beaming at the new arrival.

The son. That had to be him.

Amy had forgotten his name but could recall with vivid precision the look in Fiona's eyes when she had talked about him last week.

He dropped his bag on the path and ran towards his mother, his arms outstretched.

Amy suddenly felt like an intruder, a spy, an uninvited spectator to a private moment. She put her head down, fixed her eyes on Bamburgh Castle, and picked up speed.

———

A familiar figure was jogging along the coast road. Diana pipped her horn and waved to Amy Sanders, all the while never taking her eyes off the road. It must be Amy's day off. She would call over later, on the off chance that her friend wasn't too busy for a coffee.

As she turned onto the roundabout, a lone coach with curtained windows was belching day trippers into the carpark. Diana kept her eyes forward, doing her best to avoid becoming distracted by the knot of tourists.

The council was forever changing this section of road, and for someone who had been driving for as long as Diana, un-learning old habits could be quite troublesome. That's what she told herself, at least. After the last redesign, when they moved the pedestrian crossing twelve yards further down the street to make space for new flower beds, Diana had to admit to two near misses. Possibly a third, if she was being honest with herself.

One of them had been a child. That left her quite shaken up, even though everyone had been perfectly fine. It took her a couple of weeks to get back behind the wheel.

Of course, she'd hidden it from Sandra, who seemed to take a perverse delight in watching her mother age, glee-fully watching the balance of power and control teeter slowly towards her favour. She made no attempt to hide her desperation to get her paws on her mother's old cottage and had even consulted an interior designer who drew up the most ridiculous renovation plans.

Whoever wanted to stay in a seaside holiday home that owed its inspiration to a cocktail lounge? It was downright vulgar. Which Sandra would see for herself if she had a modicum of good taste.

Diana heaved a sigh of sadness. She wouldn't be cold in

the ground before her daughter swooped in, brandishing her ensuite bathrooms and breakfast bars.

The fragrance of honeysuckle hit her as soon as she opened the gate to the sheltered yard at the back of Puffin Cottage. Suddenly she was a newlywed again, her dear Lionel about to pick her up and carry her over the threshold. She closed her eyes, inhaling the scent and letting the memories wash over her.

She was pulled back to the present when the door opened.

'Dear girl.' Diana smiled at... Lucia.

That was it. *Lucia.* She blamed forty years in an all-girls school for her loosening grip on first names.

Lucia held the door open wide. 'Welcome home,' she said, flashing Diana a broad grin.

Under Diana's instructions, Lucia prepared a pot of tea. The girl had already set the table with the gold-rimmed bone china cups and fashioned a bunch of wildflowers into a modest display in the green glass vase. Very tastefully done, Diana thought. Lucia poured the tea with a steady hand.

'Thank you for inviting me over,' said Diana, before remembering that, actually, she had invited herself.

'This place... your cottage. It's gorgeous.'

Diana smiled. 'Yes, it is rather lovely. Even if I do say so myself!' She chuckled. 'It was my home for a while. A long time ago.' It was hard to keep the sadness from her voice. Diana gazed wistfully around the kitchen, her eyes lingering on the ghost of herself as a young woman cooking at the stove. She took a sip of tea. 'Do you believe, dear, that places have memories?'

Lucia nursed her cup in two hands. 'Yes, I do, I suppose.'

'Whenever I'm here, I remember...' Diana trailed off,

searching for the words. 'This cottage. I think part of my soul will forever remain here.'

Lucia said nothing, but let the words hang there as a comfortable silence filled the space between the two women.

Diana's eyes pricked with the threat of tears. 'Anyway,' she said brightly, shaking it off. 'I didn't come here to talk about myself. You never told me where you are from?'

The younger woman hesitated, just a beat. 'My mum's Sicilian and Dad's from Ghana. They met at university in Manchester and decided to stay when I appeared. That's where I grew up.'

She took a sip of tea, clearly hoping this information was sufficient.

But Diana found her curiosity piqued. 'And were you living there before you came here?'

Lucia squirmed, but quickly composed herself. 'I was travelling a lot. For work. My base was in Barcelona, but I was hardly ever there.' She laughed uneasily.

'How wonderful,' Diana exclaimed. 'I did so love to travel. And what is it that you do for work?'

'I'm in marketing. It's all online, remote. Digital nomads, that's what they call us.'

'And what, exactly, does being a '"digital nomad" entail?'

Lucia drained the rest of her cup. 'I'm a content creator – digital content.'

'Forgive me, my dear.' Diana offered an apologetic shrug. 'But I am something of a Luddite. You might as well be speaking a foreign language.'

'I'm sorry, excuse me.' Lucia smiled and held a finger to her lip, resetting herself. 'It's hard to get out of the jargon. I write copy for social media posts, edit photos, design graphics for online content – websites and internet adverts. That sort of thing.'

'Why, that sounds absolutely wonderful.'

'It is. I really enjoy it. And the best part is that I can do it from anywhere in the world.'

'How splendid.' Diana dropped a sugar cube into her cup and gently stirred. 'Good for you.' She beamed at Lucia.

It did sound wonderful, she thought. A job that you loved, that you could do from anywhere, something that allowed you to decamp to a place as splendid as Puffin Cottage and still call it work.

The only problem, Diana realised, was that none of it was true.

At the beginning of her career, when Diana Wheeler was still Diana Foster, she spent two torturous years teaching at an inner-city comprehensive in Newcastle. Fresh from her postgrad, nothing in her genteel rural existence could have prepared her for it. But the experience toughened her up and helped her to understand one key fact of life: girls and boys are radically different species.

She knew some would consider her viewpoint to be old-fashioned, and she recognised that popular opinion – not to mention teaching methods – had moved on. But no one could argue with basic human nature.

When boys fought, it was ferocious, oftentimes bloody. Yet they could be friends again within days. They were transparent in their dealings with one another, and with their teachers – to a fault, sometimes. The male of the species, in Diana's opinion, was a simple sort.

Girls, on the other hand, were not.

Their fights were vicious campaigns of mental torture

and emotional abuse, vindictive and malicious. They could be cruelly two-faced and the majority of them had a somewhat casual relationship with the truth. Yet they were also generous and caring, and when they were supportive of one another, they could achieve incredible things in a world where the odds were stacked against them.

At some point, Diana arrived at the realisation that anyone can teach boys. She wanted more. She decided to dedicate her life to educating girls, nurturing and shaping them into the fine, upstanding women the world needed them to be, the women they had the right to become.

And thanks to many years in a classroom full of girls, Diana had developed a keen nose for a liar.

She could tell by the way this young lady regarded her as she spoke, watching for Diana's reaction, checking to see that the story had landed. The way her shoulders sank with relief when she mistakenly believed it had.

It wasn't an issue, she supposed – people routinely misplaced the truth on all manner of topics, and Lucia could have any number of plausible reasons why she didn't want her landlady to know how she earned her living.

The interesting aspect, as far as Diana was concerned, was what else she might be hiding.

———

'Can I pour you another tea?' Lucia asked.

Her palms were sweaty, and she discreetly wiped them on her jeans before reaching for the tea pot. Diana's questions echoed in the tiny kitchen.

Where are you from? A question that, for Lucia, was difficult to answer. Multi-layered, like an onion – you peeled back one layer only for another to appear. A human Russian doll.

What did Diana really want to know? Where she grew up? Where her ancestors came from?

Lucia understood that her appearance prompted curiosity and had long ago reconciled herself with others' desire to understand what ethnic cocktail made her turn out the way she had. Or did her guest want to know where 'home' really was?

Even Lucia didn't know the answer to that one.

She hadn't been prepared for the questions about her job. Lying usually came easily, but Diana unsettled her. Few people ever challenged her cover story beyond the 'digital nomad' line, and those that did were usually satisfied with 'content creator.' At one point she thought Diana was going to ask to see actual examples of her work.

Lucia didn't like people knowing what she did for a living. After that first job, she'd made the error of telling a couple of friends about it. Back in those early days, when she couldn't believe how much money she had earned for doing something so simple.

But neither could her friends, and that became a problem. She had a hard time convincing them that there was nothing illicit or morally wrong with it, nor was she putting herself at any risk. They still didn't believe her.

Lucia moved on soon afterwards. A fresh start somewhere else, another city. Another apartment, new friends.

Lucia disliked the grubbiness of people prying into her life, the weight of their doubt bearing down on her. Crushing her. She understood that her work would always lead to questions, and Lucia was no longer prepared to explain herself. So, she started to work on a cover story.

One evening at a party in Beirut, she met a French guy. A

digital nomad, he called himself. She imagined herself alone in a Bedouin tent, the glow of her laptop the only light in the blackness of the desert. Something clicked. Yes, that could be her. Mobile, forever roaming. A nomad – that's what she was.

She stuck with that story ever since, and it had worked perfectly.

Until now.

Somewhere, in the furthest corner of her mind, that little voice stirred. The teacup in front of her was still full, untouched.

'Drink up, dear,' said Diana. 'Don't let it get cold.'

'Gosh, sorry. I was miles away.' Lucia realised she needed to change the subject. 'I have a date tomorrow night with Fiona's son.' She blurted out the words before thinking them through.

'How splendid, dear! But I'm sure there's nothing to be nervous about...'

'I didn't say I was... I mean, I'm not—'

'Of course not, and how foolish of me. I'm quite sure you're rather looking forward to it.'

'I am,' Lucia replied, her voice smaller now. 'Can't wait.'

Diana had struck a nerve, though. In truth, Lucia was anxious about her date. She didn't know anything about the man, apart from his WhatsApp profile picture and the fact that his mum lived in the village. She hadn't even asked for his surname, knowing that she wouldn't be able to resist the temptation of looking him up online.

Ben, she had decided, deserved a fair shot.

As they sat in companionable silence, Lucia listened carefully. The voice – that little voice in her head that pushed her to run – was now wide awake.

19

GINA WANTED TO SCREAM. ANOTHER DAY HAD GONE BY AND she still hadn't had a chance to get Carrie alone. How exactly had Chris managed to convince her that Gina was in the wrong?

The pub was busy, and she was grateful for the distraction of a full bar. She'd brought in Gavin, one of her weekenders. His wages would make a significant dent in her takings for the night, but it was a long-shot bet on Carrie and Chris calling in. If there was any opportunity for a chat with her mate – even if it meant following her into the ladies – Gina wanted to be able to take full advantage.

The odds of Chris bringing Carrie to the pub may have seemed miniscule, but Gina weighed that up against the likelihood that he wouldn't be able to resist sending a message.

He knew now that Gina was on to him. She had seen it in his body language, the way he was stalking Carrie, never allowing her alone time with Gina. Never risking the chance that she might whisper in Carrie's ear.

But Gina knew Chris better than he realised. A depraved

bastard like him would be thrilled at the thought of cutting off his girlfriend from her one real friend, and would be unable to resist the spectacle of Gina floundering awkwardly for Carrie's attention. If there was one thing Gina knew for sure about guys like Chris, it was that they got a kick from this shit.

———

Tom was back at The Ship – third time that week, and second night in a row. Talk about getting out and about. Mixing and mingling. It was almost as if he was *someone*.

Gina greeted him with her usual polite banter, pouring him a Sauvignon Blanc before he ordered. Flashing him a matey smile, as if they were real friends.

How he wished they were.

He'd spent that afternoon listing topics they could talk about. He approached it as if studying for an exam. After reading up on local and national news issues, he'd looked at the bigger picture and decided that Gina was probably, on reflection, more of a pop culture girl. Woman. Whatever.

He pored over blogs about the latest Netflix movies and TV series, skimming over other people's opinions of bands and reviews of reality shows, hoping that some of this – any of this – might intersect with Gina's interests.

And yet, as Friday night arrived and he took his seat at the bar, Tom was tongue-tied. He couldn't see his way in.

Underneath her convivial exterior, Gina was visibly agitated. Her jaw was set, her lipsticked mouth fixed into a harsh line. In between serving, she tapped the bar with the long nail of her index finger with the pulse of a metronome, while throwing intermittent glances towards the door.

Tom willed her to notice him, to come and talk to him,

to say anything – he had the next line ready and set, he just needed that push to get him started, some chink in the facade, a crack of light to show him the way in.

Nothing.

Until someone even more riled than Gina walked in.

A man – a very good looking man, despite looking so shaken, who marched right up to the bar.

'Scotch, please.' He brought his head down to meet his hand, a fingertip and a thumb massaging his eyelids without so much as a glance at Gina.

'I've got a Glenmorangie twelve-year single malt, a twelve-year Speyburn, a Macallan eighteen—'

'I'll take the Macallan.' He looked up for the first time. 'Please'.

Now, thought Tom, *there's something you don't see every day.*

So handsome that he had almost – almost, but not quite – made Gina do a double-take. Expensive clothes – you could tell just by looking. A hint of designer stubble and thick glossy hair in the same cut as Harry Styles. And he had just ordered the most expensive whisky without even asking the price.

The man slid a fifty-pound note across the bar but kept his finger on it. He necked the whisky, then tapped the glass on the bar.

'Same again, please.'

By the time the second arrived, the newcomer had calmed sufficiently to glance at the people seated around him. His eyes met Tom's, fleetingly, before he continued to scan the crowded bar, assessing, appraising.

As the stranger's gaze turned back to his drink, Tom felt a familiar sensation. *Invisible.* That's what he was.

Because in a world where beauty and money and power are everything, who would ever notice a man like Tom?

————

'I'm off to change the barrel,' Gina called out to Gavin.

She descended the steep stone staircase to the cellar and went directly to the makeshift vanity station she'd constructed for precisely this kind of emergency. After readjusting her bra, she pulled the V of her top as low as she dared it to go. A fresh smear of lipstick and a spritz of perfume later, she was set.

'Ready for another?' She leaned forward across the bar, giving the handsome stranger the perfect view of her cleavage. Now she had his attention.

'Not just yet.' He smiled back at her, a flash of perfect teeth.

'Just visiting? Here for the weekend?'

She could see the second whisky was kicking in now, replacing his agitation with a mellow haze.

'Yeah.' He took a smaller sip. 'Visiting the folks.'

Only the slightest hint of a local accent, almost too delicate for Gina to have noticed, were it not for her intense fascination with this man sitting at her bar. And the way he spat out the word *folks.*

'And how's that visit working out for you?'

He took another sip, his perfect lips meeting the glass in a delicate kiss. He must be a good ten years younger than her, maybe more. A challenge, perhaps, but not an impossibility. She glanced at the clock on the wall, calculating the hours and minutes until closing time and the odds of this man hanging around until then.

His eyes shone in the warm light of the pub. Brown, she

noticed. And his face was vaguely familiar, as if they had met before.

'My dad's a bastard.' His delivery was deadpan. But then he laughed, then laughed again, finding his own joke funnier the longer he thought about it.

Gina smiled, but something stirred inside her. She wanted to hug him – to hold him in her arms and make everything all right. From behind the bar, she caught a whiff of his aftershave and inhaled deeply.

The man was on a roll now. 'He's a bastard to me, he's a bastard to my mother, and he's been a bastard his whole life.'

The edges of his words were softening. He leaned in towards her, closing the gap between them. 'Can you imagine – sorry sweetheart, I didn't catch your name?'

Sweetheart.

'It's Gina,' she said, softly.

'Right, yes. Gina. Gina – can you imagine being such a bastard that your wife, kids, your best friend and your business partner – they all hate you? And still—' He took a deep breath. 'And still... you just don't give a shit?' His voice cracked, his beautiful eyes glossing. 'That you would just be OK with that?' He drew a deep breath, shaking his head. Composing himself.

'What kind of man does that?' he asked quietly. A question that didn't invite an answer.

Gavin threw her a raised eyebrow, and she gave a subtle shake of her head in return. Telling him *it's OK. I've got this.* She lowered her voice to a hush.

'And while we're making introductions...'

'Ben.'

'Ben...'

She was going to ask him where his folks lived, who his

dad was, anything to help her understand just who in god's name he was on about. But then she worked out why he looked so familiar. It wasn't him that she had met, but his mother.

All at once, several things fell into place.

20

LAST NIGHT HAD BEEN AN ABJECT FAILURE, BY ALL ACCOUNTS.
Tom felt utterly wretched.

Still, he'd been out for two nights in a row. That was
worth a pat on the back, he reminded himself. It was all
about chalking up the small victories. He tried to focus on
the quantity – the fact that he had socialised (of sorts) with
actual people (kind of) for two consecutive evenings – rather
than the quality of his engagements.

That was important. Focus on what went right, not what
went wrong.

Gina had not only acknowledged him, but actually
exchanged pleasantries. *Banter.* Only a little, but still. And
he had certainly been ready for a conversation. Goodness
knows he had done enough preparation.

Then that man, the whisky-drinking rock star, walked in
and stole the show. Who on earth did he think he was,
paying with a fifty-pound note? Mr Flash indeed. But it
worked. Within minutes, Gina had been fawning over him
and had quite forgotten about Tom. She left it up to that

other chap to serve everyone else so that she could give Mr Flash her undivided attention, making several shameless plays to get his in return.

Tom despaired.

He wasn't even sure what it was about Gina that had captured his attention. Proximity? Availability? That he always knew where she would be, or that she had shown the slightest inclination to friendliness – surely, he wasn't *that* pathetic? Or was it that she reminded him of someone? Someone from before?

Fran would advise him to diversify his interests. Look elsewhere for a new friend. Don't put all your eggs in a Gina-shaped basket.

Joining the book club had been Fran's suggestion. Well, not specifically the book club, but the idea of signing up to take part in social activities. Getting out and meeting new people – these were things that Tom needed to work at. Apparently, these were the things that would help him recover.

He ignored that little Fran-voice in his head. It was Saturday night, a chance to try again. The pub would be busy, because that's what normal people did on a Saturday night. And he was a normal, ordinary man. This was not about Gina.

Tom now had a regular seat at the bar of The Ship. He liked that. It was like that show from the eighties. A place where everyone knows your name. Well, Gina, at least.

From here, he had the best view of who came and went. His stool – a high, studded leather thing – sat directly under an antique oil lamp, suspended from the ceiling. Preferable to the next seat, which had a large brass artefact hanging above it. You could never be too careful.

He had thought about wearing a bowtie, or something just sufficiently out of the ordinary to spark a conversation. But he'd felt silly and shoved it in his pocket before he left the house.

Gina was still tense, the poor thing, and Tom had the vague notion that her unease might be connected to something serious. Hopefully nothing to do with that ghastly bloke who turned up to their book club.

Her eyes were joyless, and when she wasn't remembering to smile at punters, her mouth tightened into a pale, flat line.

But she brightened up when *he* walked in.

Mr Flash.

Oh, here we go again, thought Tom, his heart sinking to his shoes. Perhaps he should have stayed in with Agnes after all. He could have been watching *Come Dine with Me* by now.

But Mr Flash didn't sit at the bar this time. After greeting Gina and sheepishly ordering a Diet Coke, he took one of the small round tables at the side of the room.

When Lucia turned up moments later, things became clearer. Everyone turned to look – Tom now understood that the expression 'turning heads' was not just figurative.

On sight of her, Mr Flash's face lit up. Lucia – in Tom's head, he still thought of her as the supermodel – scanned the room and their eyes met. It was like a scene from a movie – Tom couldn't believe it. Did things like this actually happen in real life?

Mr Flash was already on his feet and as the supermodel made her way towards him, and the bar collectively exhaled.

Of course, that makes sense, they were thinking. *The supermodel and the rock star.*

Everyone except Gina.

Tom chanced a glimpse at her over the top of his glass. Her expression was stormy, a tempest brewing behind those blue eyes, her hands balled so tightly that her knuckles paled.

A jealousy that was so reflexive, he was quite sure that she wasn't yet aware of it herself.

21

THEY STARTED AT THE PUB. IT SEEMED AS GOOD A MEETING
point as any, and it was part of Lucia's escape plan: if he was
awful, she could end the evening there.

Ben surprised her by ordering a Diet Coke, and after one
drink, he invited her to go for a drive. It was almost too
corny, and she almost said no, until she remembered the
promise she had made herself to give this place – these
people – a chance.

A fresh start.

At Bamburgh, he took a right turn after the castle green,
zipping down a lane that curved and ran parallel to the
beach. The sun hung low, dipping towards the hills in the
west.

Where is he taking me?

Lucia kept one hand on the door handle and one eye on
the lock as she scanned the road for familiar landmarks.
She had explored this stretch of beach by foot, getting as far
as the headland that gave way to a steep bank of dunes and
eventually, a small cliff. The only thing out here was a golf
club, as far as she knew. She watched the sun setting, calcu-

lating how much time remained before darkness swallowed them.

Halfway down the lane, Ben slowed the car to a crawl, crunching over gravel. Not exactly the middle of nowhere, but at that hour of the day, there was no one about.

She began to wonder if she had made a foolish mistake.

'We're here,' he said with a grin.

Lucia was about to ask where 'here' was when something caught her eye on the opposite side of the road: a makeshift campsite, consisting of a white tipi on a rug, the entrance surrounded by candles.

'Oh my,' she murmured.

Ben grinned but said nothing as they climbed out of the car. The candles, on closer inspection, were battery-operated. He crouched down and peeled back the cover of the tipi. Inside were several large cushions, a wicker hamper, and a perspiring ice bucket brandishing a bottle of champagne.

Despite her efforts to retain her composure, Lucia let out an involuntary giggle.

'Before you say anything, it wasn't all me.' Ben held up his hands in mock surrender. 'I have to confess – I might have had some help from my mother.'

She laughed as Ben plumped up the cushions.

'And I'm sincerely hoping you don't think it's too much?'

It was, but there was something heart-warming about such a grand gesture for a first date and how readily he admitted that his mother was involved. Lucia's pulse quickened. She shook her head.

'In that case, mademoiselle, would you like to take a seat?' Ben gestured to the stack of cushions.

Lucia sat on the rug, folding her legs to one side as she eyed the spread. Ham and cheddar sandwiches, Scotch eggs, hummus and crudites. Ordinary picnic food, a desperate attempt to reduce some of the *extra-ness*.

Ben popped the cork. 'Care for some champagne?' He registered her hesitancy. 'I will only have one glass, so you needn't worry about getting home in one piece.'

The tent was small, forcing them to sit so intimately close that she could feel the heat of his body. With blankets draped over their laps, it was easy to forget the chill of the evening outside.

The conversation flowed easily. Ben was funny, and despite his good looks, his humour consisted mainly of self-deprecating jokes and stories. Lucia was reduced to tears of laughter at his story of a boys' weekend trip to Dublin, which saw Ben call an ambulance for a mate who turned out to have nothing more than heartburn. And the time he'd been stung by a wasp on his backside on his first day in a new job and had to find excuses to avoid sitting down.

It turned out that Ben liked to talk. *A lot.* And that was fine with Lucia. It was infinitely preferable to talking about herself. Whenever he asked something too personal, too close for comfort, she subtly steered the conversation back to him with short, deflective answers. Within an hour she learned all about his job (estate agent), his home (apartment in Newcastle), and his hobbies (football, tennis, skiing).

'What if I'd said no?' she asked at one point, gesturing to the setup. 'What would you have done with this lot?'

Ben held up his glass, inspecting the champagne by electric candlelight. 'Invited my mother instead?'

She batted him with a cushion and he caught it just as it landed squarely on his chest. In a heartbeat, they were holding it between them, their eyes locked, faces just inches apart.

Lucia backed away first. 'Are you close to her?' she asked.

Without hesitating, he nodded, but Lucia noticed the sadness in his eyes. A sadness she knew, too. 'And your dad?'

Ben sighed. 'That's a tough question.' He avoided her eyes, seemingly searching for the right words.

She left him the silence to continue.

'My father... he's not a good man. The way he treats my mother, it's... well. Frankly, it's appalling.' Ben pressed the heels of his hands to his eyes, and Lucia's heart broke, just a little.

'There have been other women,' he went on. '*Lots* of them. He just doesn't care, I guess? Not about Mum. Not about any of us. I mean, he's successful. If you can call it that. Started on a market stall in Birmingham and turned it into a multi-million-pound business.' Ben shrugged. Swallowed. His voice shrank, catching in his throat. 'It all went to his head, I suppose. And for my whole life, I've just had this certainty that no matter what I do, no matter what I achieve, I want to be the exact opposite of whatever he is.'

Lucia doubted Ben had set out that evening with the intention of unburdening himself on a complete stranger, and he was too troubled by the telling of his story to notice the impact he had on her. He did not register, in that moment, that something clicked inside her, satisfying an urge she had scarcely been aware of.

They picked over the food, after that – appetite evaded them both. At one point, Ben's eyes started to glisten so Lucia lay back on the stack of cushions, gazing up towards the top of the tipi, giving him as much privacy as she could.

Eventually, Ben exhausted himself.

'I am so sorry – I have no idea what came over me.' He sat up, shaking his head, blinking back to the moment. Disbelieving himself.

'It's OK. You needed someone to talk to. I'm glad I was here.'

His eyes were chestnut in the low light. 'Thank you,' he said. He held out a hand and when she reached out, her fingertips meeting his, she could have sworn she felt a spark.

22

LUCIA STRETCHED OUT ON THE COUCH IN HER SILK ROBE, A
languorous evening spent solely in her own company. The
flames lapped in the hearth, the gentle cackle of the fire
providing the only sound.

After three weeks, she had grown quite used to this little
cottage. The creaks and cracks of the timber frame, the
groans of the ancient stone, and the rattle of the windows as
the sea gusts tested them. Within its walls was a constant
cacophony, an undulating hymn that sang in chorus with
the weather outside come rain, wind, or shine. Noises that
helped to quiet the voices in Lucia's mind.

She set her book down, slicing the corner of a page over
in a fold to mark her position. An inspired choice, Lucia
thought, grinning to herself. It would be interesting to see
what Diana made of it. Lucia had a feeling her landlady was
a traditionalist, someone who had been perfectly at ease
with the classic version of the story and wouldn't care much
for a contemporary retelling. But then again, her new
friends seemed to be constantly full of surprises.

She should phone her parents, tell them that she was settled. Perhaps invite them up to visit.

The idea troubled her more than would have liked, more than she was prepared for. It was hard to picture her mum and dad in here, in this place that had become her sanctuary. There simply wasn't enough room for her parents and all their baggage – metaphorical and literal – and the thought caused her head to throb, a dull pain at the base of her skull.

It was her fault, Lucia supposed, for allowing the gulf to grow. For allowing silence to take root in the space that lay between her and her parents, in the fissure that appeared when she was only just a woman and yet still a girl, unable and incapable of bridging it. A chasm filled with all that had gone unsaid.

She closed her eyes, listening out for the voices. But only the sea called to her, a reassuring whisper from down below.

Lucia's mind, once again, turned to Ben. He hadn't been far from her thoughts all week. She had felt something that night; a sensation that she had not experienced in many years. A pull, a push that sent a tingle down her spine.

Her fingertips prickled, the memory of the spark she felt as his hand brushed against hers. As if the universe was telling her something, urging her on.

To do things differently.

They were seeing each other again this weekend, and Lucia was annoyed to find herself counting down the days. She tried to keep herself occupied with long walks along the beach, venturing even further beyond the headland she had previously explored.

Her phone buzzed, and she glanced down, then tossed it to one side when she realised it was just a delivery notification for an online purchase.

How daft, she thought, as her heart rate steadied. Her excitement felt in that split second, and her disappointment when she realised the message wasn't from Ben.

They conversed exclusively by text, and even though she ached to hear his voice again, a frisson of excitement fizzed through her limbs each time her phone vibrated, his words appearing on the screen.

Lucia traced the memory of that evening, exploring the details. His brown eyes, glinting in the candlelight, the dimples that puckered his cheeks when he smiled. The crook of his cupid's bow, the curve of his laugh. The moment when something clicked inside her, and she realised that she had stumbled across something special, something unique. Something she hadn't even known she was looking for until it stared her in the face.

She had the distinct feeling Ben planned to keep it low-key this time, and that was fine with her. Besides, it would be hard to improve on a clifftop campsite with a candle-lit picnic. And Lucia just wasn't into fuss or frills, no more than she was into champagne and fast cars.

She just wanted *him.*

23

'WHAT DOES THAT MEAN, "IT WAS GREAT?"'

'Exactly that, Mum. *It was great.*' Ben shrugged and bit into a slice of toast, spraying crumbs onto the floor.

His mum stared at the crumbs, clearly struggling against her temptation to wipe up straight away. 'Did Lucia enjoy herself?' she asked, failing to conceal her excitement that he'd taken Lucia on a second date last night.

'I think so.'

'So, do you plan to see her again?'

Ben rolled his eyes, acutely aware that his mum wanted a salacious blow-by-blow account and not feeling quite prepared to let her in. The first date had been – he cringed at the thought – emotional. Raw.

At least last night he had redeemed himself.

His mum did a solid job last weekend – god knows where she got that tent from. But he wanted – needed – to do things his way. More... chill. More *him*. He wanted Lucia to see who he really was.

Despite a busy week at work, he'd found himself counting down the days until he would see her again. Last night, he had taken her to a gastropub in Bamburgh. They sat side by side in a booth, barely touching their food, unable to take their eyes off one another. They had connected pretty deeply, and he sensed Lucia felt it as strongly as he did.

He hoped.

But he couldn't share all of that with his mother. Some things were sacred.

Lucia was so easy to talk to. Almost *too* easy. On their first date, he told her stuff he'd been too embarrassed to tell even his closest mates – about how Dad fired him for under-performance, based on nothing but spite and a misdirected desire to teach him self-reliance. About how Dad had promised to help him buy the flat and then backed out at the last minute, saying it would be a more valuable life experience if Ben was forced to stand on his own two feet – leaving his son saddled with a mortgage he could barely afford, and a debt too embarrassing to admit.

Even now, Ben felt vaguely mortified as he recalled telling her about the time his dad walked out on lunch.

It had been Peter's invitation, a cosy father-son chat that was supposed to reconcile the previous falling-out. His dad ordered crab, steak, and dessert wine, and then upped and left, disappearing from the restaurant and not answering his phone. Ben spent the afternoon there, squirming under the curious stares of the waitresses, until he finally got a message through to his mother to come down and pay the bill.

He tried to laugh it off as relayed the story to Lucia, making light of it.

'I don't think that's very funny,' she said.

'No. Me neither.'

The one thing he hadn't shared was just how badly his

dad had betrayed his mother. That was the most painful thing of all.

Ben ate the last bite of toast now. 'We might have kissed.'

His mum's eyes grew wide. 'You did not...'

He grinned at her, one eyebrow raised, a wouldn't-you-like-to-know look. 'A gentleman never tells, mother.'

The kitchen door opened, startling them. Peter eyeballed his wife and son and shuffled over to the fridge. 'What's this about a gentleman?'

Neither of them answered.

'I'm talking to you, boy.'

'Yeah, well, you know what, Dad? I wasn't talking to you.'

Fiona caught Ben's eye, silently pleading with him.

Peter stood with his back to them, the glow of the fridge illuminating his profile. 'What's for lunch?'

'Actually, dear, Ben and I might drive down to Craster. You're welcome to join us, if you'd like?'

They both knew he would never come. Accepting the invitation was about as likely as him apologising.

Peter closed the fridge door. 'Please yourselves,' he grunted. 'I'm staying put.'

His father was almost at the kitchen door again, and Ben sensed that the dark cloud he had brought with him was about to break, that the sunlight would burst through any second.

When Ben spoke, he took even himself by surprise. 'It's not enough, is it, Dad? It'll never be enough.'

The old man stopped and looked over his shoulder. 'What's that, lad?'

'It's not enough for you to fuck up your life. You've got to take everyone else down with you. Why can't you just let her be happy?'

'Ben,' his mother hissed, her eyes wide. Pleading. 'Stop that.'

'Don't push me, lad.' His father turned now, slowly, towards him. 'Don't push me—'

'Or what, eh?' Ben jumped to his feet, his fists instinctively balling at his sides. 'Or what?' he snarled.

'Please.' His mum's voice was a croak. 'Please stop this. Not again.'

Father and son stared each other down, but they both knew who had won. His father always won.

'Get out of my house.'

'Peter, no—'

'Quiet, you!' He held a meaty palm towards Fiona.

If he hits her, thought Ben. *If he touches her, god help him.*

'Don't talk to her like that.' His voice was smaller.

Peter laughed. 'Or what, son? What will you do? What will *she* do?' His face was red, and he leaned closer to Ben, his breath hot and smelling of onions. 'If the ship is sinking, why don't you all jump on a lifeboat?'

Ben's heart thundered in his chest, and he felt his resolve melting. Once again, he was the seven-year-old whose father locked him outside in the rain for not taking care of his trainers. The thirteen-year-old who was driven to the woods at night and left there 'to toughen him up'. The man who was sacked by his own father in front of the entire regional sales team.

'Yeah,' snarled his dad. 'I thought so.'

'I hate you,' Ben murmured as Peter walked away. 'I hate you!' he shouted louder, the words bouncing off his father's back. He couldn't stop the tears, then – hot, angry sobs – and he hated himself for crying on his mother like this.

'Ben, please...' His mum was crying too, and he knew

that yet again, he had let her down. He grabbed his overnight bag and car keys.

'Come on, darling. Not like this,' she started, but he was already striding out into the hall.

Peter was back in the media room, the door ajar, light spilling into the far end of the hallway from the giant screen. It was an old comedy. Peter guffawed along with the canned laughter, a deliberate, over-dramatised, hateful laugh. Salt and spite in Ben's wounds.

Lava-hot rage smouldered in the pit of his stomach. He had to get out of there.

He ran to the door, his mother chasing after him. Pleading with him to stay, to slow down. Shouting at the top of her voice.

Still, Ben didn't stop.

He jerked the door wide with an explosive clatter.

His mother ran after him down the garden path. 'Please, Ben, don't—'

But he was too angry to reply. If he tried to speak, he would properly cry.

He threw the bag onto the passenger seat and revved the engine. As he pulled away, he watched his mother shrinking in the rear-view mirror, leaning over the garden gate.

She doubled over, the pain of hurt, of grief, of loss, crippling her. He watched her through a blur of tears, watching him – the last of her hope zooming off into the afternoon.

———

Apart from her usual spot next to the Aga in Amy's kitchen, the beach was Sue's happy place. One of the mildest days of the year so far, and it had luckily fallen on a Sunday. Jeans and a jumper weather. Still, Sue huddled next to her niece on the sand, for the comfort of proximity as much as sharing body heat.

The tide was low, the sea a mirror. A perfect day for splashing in the water. Mike played with the kids in the surf, wet-suited and life-jacketed, as they jumped on and off their boogie boards. Amy's eyes trained on them, her body tense and ready to jump in at the slightest sign of trouble.

'Relax,' said Sue, giving her arm a gentle squeeze. 'They're only in the shallows. You and Izzy did far worse at that age.'

Sue remembered the girls as they had been back then, when she would come down for the weekend to visit. Climbing trees, making dens, rock pooling. Forever trudging home with scraped knees and nettle stings.

'I know.' Amy's eyes didn't move from the children.

'Have you spoken to her?'

'Izzy? Yes. I mean… no. Just texting.'

'How is she?'

Sue couldn't hide the hunger in her voice, the constant itch for news of her other niece. It was one thing to go and live on the other side of the world, but she wished Izzy would call home more than twice a month. True, there was the time difference, and her travel schedule, and the job that purportedly consumed every waking hour of the day.

'She's good, Auntie Sue. Honestly. She's just… living her life for her.'

And who did Amy live her life for? Her kids? Mike? Who would she be if not for them? What, Sue wondered, about the day they no longer need her?

She watched Mike now, playing in the baby waves with Betsy and cheering Lucas on as he rode a small crest of salty foam, tummy-down on his board.

Mike and Amy had met when they were young, and

everything fell into place so quickly. With her inheritance from Edward, they'd been able to buy one of the largest houses in the village and do it up.

Was Amy happy with how *her* life had worked out?

Now Betsy tired of the fun and ran towards them, her little heels kicking up pinches of sand with every footfall. Sue was ready with the towel by the time her great-niece reached them. She folded Betsy into a tight embrace and kissed the top of her head, slick with sea water and salty on Sue's lips.

'Let's go and get you changed.' The little girl's teeth were already chattering.

'You don't mind?' Amy still kept her eyes fixed on Lucas and Hannah. The wind carried their laughter over the purr of the waves.

'Of course not,' said Sue, leading Betsy away by the hand.

They had parked the car at the top of the dune path, the boot ready to double up as a makeshift changing room. She was dressing Betsy in dry clothes when she heard a clatter, followed by shouting so loud that it startled the little girl.

It came from the Gallivan place over the road.

A young man – Fiona's son, that had to be him – marched down the garden path, a brown leather holdall slung over one shoulder. His mother trotted after him, yelling, but it was impossible to hear what they were saying with the wind blowing the opposite direction.

The window of the open car boot gave Sue cover to watch without being seen. Was the lad crying? It certainly looked like it from here. His mother wailed, a pained howl that originated from somewhere deep within her. Sue winced at the sound.

The man jumped into a fancy little car and slammed the

door, never once looking back at his mother. Sunlight glinted off the roof as the car shot off, definitely too fast for this section of road.

Sue couldn't take her eyes off Fiona. She fell to a crouch, one hand on the gate, her body folded in half as if she'd been kicked in the stomach.

Dear me, thought Sue. Now there was a family with problems.

24

IT WAS DAYS LIKE THIS THAT MADE SUE APPRECIATE HER LITTLE family. They had been fractured and fragmented, but they had healed and reformed into something different. Something beautiful.

She once saw a programme on the Discovery Channel about a Japanese tradition of repairing broken pottery by bonding the pieces back together with molten gold, making it whole again. *Kintsugi.* Not ignoring the break or trying to conceal the damage, but celebrating it.

The late-afternoon sunshine streamed through the windows of her kitchen, dappled by the ancient maple tree in the garden and casting streaks across the table which, just an hour earlier, had groaned under the remnants of a Sunday lunch. Veins and mottles of gold, filling the spaces between them and making a whole.

Their post-war brick semi felt unnaturally still after the raucousness of a full house. After cleaning up, the sisters sat in companionable silence, appreciating the peace while simultaneously missing the noise.

The phone in the hallway rang, a bright clatter so loud

that the side table jumped under the force of the sound. Sue jolted to her feet, barely registering that she had been nodding off.

'Sue? It's me. Fiona.' Her voice was little more than a croak, and Sue pictured the scene from earlier that afternoon, her heart breaking for this woman who was still practically a stranger.

She clutched the phone. 'Is everything all right?'

'Yes.' Fiona sniffed. 'Yes, it's fine. I could just... really appreciate some company, that's all. I was wondering if you had any plans?'

'What, now?' The few plans Sue made these days were typically fixed at least a week in advance.

Fiona hesitated for a beat. 'Not now, of course. How silly of me. Another time, perhaps.'

Sue could tell she was trying to sound breezy, cheery. As if some harmless detail had been lost in misunderstanding.

'I don't have any plans right now.' Sue glanced through the open living room door. Anne was scrolling through Sky, searching for something to watch on TV. They would have a cup of tea and be in bed by ten. She made the invitation before she had thought it through. 'Would you like to come over?'

A short time later, she and Anne stood in their kitchen. A thorough scavenge of the larder had turned up a few old Quality Streets, some honey-roasted almonds past their sell-by date, and a tube of Pringles.

Sue pursed her lips, worry entrenched in a crevice between her eyebrows. 'Not much of a spread, is it?'

Anne dismissed her concern with a wave of her hand. 'If she's hungry, we'll order a pizza.'

There goes the vegan phase, thought Sue.

White light swept over the hallway, the beam of head-lights tracing an arc across the ceiling as a car pulled into their driveway. The clop of heels on the paving stones and then the doorbell.

'Please, Anne.' Sue placed a hand over her sister's. 'No... funny stuff, all right?'

Anne frowned, dejected. She was about to protest when Sue stopped her.

'You know what I mean. It's... she sounded upset on the phone. She might just want to talk. About *herself.*'

Anne's lip jutted in the pout of a sulk, but she followed Sue to the door.

Apart from her perfect hair, Fiona had the appearance of a woman barely holding it together. Her eyes were puffy and red-rimmed, although her make-up was freshly applied, and her tailored blazer and white jeans made Sue wish she'd spent less time rummaging through the kitchen cupboards and more time riffling through her wardrobe. She was still in her sweater from the beach.

'Your home is lovely.' Fiona's compliment was no doubt rehearsed, a social skill honed over years of practice, but it felt sincere. 'And you must be Anne?'

'How wonderful to meet you.' Anne accepted Fiona's handshake in a two-handed hold that lasted just a few seconds longer than it needed to. Fiona was gracious, but Sue shot Anne a warning look and steered their guest towards the living room.

'Tea?'

'Not unless there's anything stronger on offer?'

'Oh dear,' said Sue. 'One of those days, is it?'

From the cabinet at the back of the living room, she retrieved a bottle of sherry and three of the good glasses.

'Tell me all about it.' She handed one to Fiona.

'Well, I...' Fiona trailed off. 'I feel ever so silly. It's just that...' She took a breath, waiting for the threat of tears to pass. Composing herself. 'I suppose I just miss female company from time to time.'

Sue nodded. 'I saw you today, when we were leaving the beach. You were with your son?'

She felt bad now, admitting that she had been watching, but thought it would help Fiona to divest. The other lady said nothing, her tears glinting in the glow of the side lamp.

'Children, eh?' Sue continued. 'They always know how to press our buttons, no matter how old they get.'

Still, Fiona said nothing. Sue refilled her glass, already drained.

———

Fiona mustered her bravest smile, but inside she was on the brink of eruption. She dared not speak. Her patience had been worn down from a solid sheet of silk to a single gossamer thread, and she feared the lightest tug would break it.

She wanted to tell Sue that it wasn't Ben who had upset her, that it wasn't about one afternoon but an entire life-time, not one argument but a thousand cuts. That she had made a mistake, many mistakes, and didn't know how to fix them.

The prospect of unburdening herself to this woman – a kindly but relative stranger – was as tantalising as it was terrifying.

She swallowed, pushing away the temptation.

And did what she had always done.

Sitting up a little straighter, she brushed an invisible

thread from her blazer. 'You know what? I'm already feeling so much better.'

―――――

Anne insisted on an energy cleanse as soon as Fiona left.

She wafted burning sage into the corners of the living room with a feather fan, chanting softly to herself.

Sue retired to the kitchen for tea and toast while she waited for her to finish. Somehow, she didn't quite trust her sister not to burn the house down.

'So much negativity.' Anne reappeared, her smudging ceremony concluded. 'You could feel her pain, couldn't you?'

'She wanted to tell me something, but something made her hold back.'

Anne tutted. 'Well, the energy reading is betrayal. One of the worst cases I've ever seen.'

Sue looked up from her book. 'You're telling me you can see what she's going through by the energy she left behind?'

'Oh, yes.' Anne looked pleased with herself, glad to have Sue's attention. 'It was all over the place. She left such a mess.'

'In our living room?'

'Yes.' Her tone was insistent, as if all of this should be obvious. 'Negative traces of energy. If you look hard enough, you can see the cause – she's been hurt by someone close to her. It's appalling prana. I'll have to reset the Vastu Shastra.'

Their discussion was interrupted by the shrill clang of the telephone in the hall, making both sisters jump. *I must get a quieter phone,* thought Sue. That strange visit had set her on edge.

'Auntie Sue?' Amy was breathless, rushing.

The skin on Sue's neck prickled. 'Yes? What's happened? Who is it?' Her mind traced over the children, their tiny bodies that she expertly knew the weight and density of, and imagined all the terrible injuries and illness that might befall them.

'We're all fine. It's Fiona.'

Sue listened to the sounds between Amy's words – the clatter of her car keys in her hand, her footsteps on the hallway floor.

'Fiona Gallivan?' Sue glanced at the clock. She'd left less than forty-five minutes ago.

'Yes. Listen, I'm on duty tonight, and I just got a call out to their place. Fiona rang 999. They've dispatched an ambulance from Alnwick, but I'll be quicker.'

'Dear god, what's happened to her?' Sue's mind raced with the possibilities as she grabbed her car keys. Fiona had drunk two glasses of sherry – it couldn't be that, surely. They were thimble sized. But still... 'She's at home? What do you need?'

Amy was outside now; Sue could hear her footsteps on the path, her car door shutting.

'It's the husband, suspected heart attack.' Amy's voice was level, controlled. Methodical and calm, the district nurse in charge. 'It sounds as if she's gone into shock. I could use an extra pair of hands.'

'I'll meet you there.' Sue didn't say goodbye before hanging up.

25

The door was ajar when Sue arrived at the Gallivans'. She let herself in.

'Hello?' she called out. Something gritty crunched under her feet. She quickly squeezed out of her boots and kicked them to one side.

From a room across the hall, she heard Amy's voice. Calm, low, clear. She followed it into the living room, dimly lit by a side lamp, the television glaring.

Horizontal, Peter Gallivan looked even larger than he did while standing upright. That ruddy face was now a pavement-grey, his lips tinged blue. Amy was performing chest compressions, an earpiece connected to her mobile phone, trading updates and instructions with a colleague on the other end. Discarded packaging and medical paraphernalia littered the floor.

She glanced up at Sue, her eyes heavy with worry, and nodded towards Fiona.

As still as a millpond. That was the expression that came to Sue, in that moment. How their father used to describe the sea on calm days. Untroubled, at peace.

Someone had muted the TV, but the show – a police drama – played on silently. Fiona looked pallid in the fluorescent glow from the screen, but other than that, only her hands clenched in her lap offered the slightest indication that anything was bothering her.

'What do you need me to do?' Sue asked Amy, trying to disguise the panic that swelled her in chest.

'Take over for a second. My arms need a break. Here,' Amy gestured to Peter's chest. 'Like this.'

Sue's hands trembled as she folded them and pressed down on Peter's chest, avoiding his eyes.

'Harder,' muttered Amy.

Before long, Sue was out of breath.

'That's great, thanks.' Amy said, returning to the task. 'Maybe you could take Fiona to the kitchen?'

Fiona still had not moved from her spot on the sofa. Sue threaded an arm around her shoulder. 'Come on.' She tried to sound cheerful, bright. 'A nice cup of sugary tea is just what the doctor ordered. Amy's got everything under control in here, I'm sure.'

Her niece continued the compressions, more urgently now; her brow sheened with exertion. Sue tried to stop the thought forming, but it didn't look good for Peter.

Amy spoke without looking up, her face knotted in a frown of concentration but her voice level.

'Keep her talking. That's very important, OK? Just keep her talking as much as possible.'

'Got it.' Sue steered Fiona towards the kitchen, passing once again through the hallway. Something about the space looked different, but she didn't have time to work out what it could be.

She brewed tea while firing questions at Fiona. Silly questions – the first things that came into her head. *What did you eat for breakfast today? What's your favourite soap opera? Where did you go on holiday last year?* Anything that forced her to speak without thinking too hard about her husband lying on the living room floor or the son Sue saw her clash with that afternoon.

Perhaps it was all related, she wondered. Fiona was clearly upset after the row. Presumably Peter was too. Maybe it wound him up so much that it gave him a heart attack. How would that poor lad feel when he found out that he tipped his father over the edge?

She wanted to ask Fiona if there was someone they should call, but it was best to leave that stuff up to Amy. She'd know what to do. *What's your favourite sandwich filling?*

'Honestly.' Fiona held up a hand, signalling that she'd had enough of this game. 'I'm quite all right.'

Sue took a seat on the velvet bar stool, the same place she sat just last week, and wondered how Amy was getting on. It already felt like they had been waiting forever for an ambulance. As if she willed it into existence, the first note of a siren's wail pierced the night.

Fiona's gaze was fixed on some unseen point in the dark of the garden, but there was no tremble in her hand, no tears in her eyes. The screams of the ambulance grew as it drew closer, eventually exploding into a crescendo of flashing blue light, voices, and boots. Fiona sipped at her tea.

After an eternity, Amy came into the kitchen, her shoulders low. She looked tired, older in the harsh light of the chandelier above, and Sue knew instantly that Peter was gone. She could read her niece like a book.

Fiona had been sitting with her back to the door and she turned, a slow twist from her waist, eyebrows raised, as if Amy was some unexpected visitor.

'Fiona. I'm so sorry, but Mr Gallivan – Peter. I'm sorry, he didn't make it. We did everything we could.'

Amy shifted her weight from foot to foot, looking down at the floor the way she did as a frightened adolescent. 'I could drive you to the hospital, if that's what you want to do. You might prefer to come and say goodbye before they take him away...' she trailed off, registering Fiona's indifference.

Sue placed a hand over Fiona's. It was cold to the touch. Maybe she was in shock after all. 'Do you want me to call someone? Ben, perhaps?'

Fiona shook her head. She coughed, choking back a sob, spluttering into her hand.

Sue tore off a sheet of kitchen roll, ready to catch the tears. 'We could also—' But then she stopped. She shot a puzzled glance at Amy, a frown forming. Doubting what she was hearing.

Because Fiona wasn't crying. She was laughing.

26

Amy sat on the doorstep, the orange tip of her cigarette glowing in the darkness.

Her aunt eased herself down beside her. 'Do you know that's bad for you, or did you miss that day of your nursing degree?'

Amy exhaled long and languidly, enjoying the release. She had never smoked, not properly, but something about the shock of losing a patient punctured a craving that didn't exist the rest of the time. 'Just this one, I promise.'

What she didn't say: *until the next one dies.* She pointed a thumb back towards the house. 'How's she doing?'

Sue squirmed. 'At least she stopped laughing. It was some hysterical counter-reaction, I reckon.'

'I gave her something to help her sleep. She should feel better in the morning.'

Sue shuddered. 'It must have been a dreadful shock.'

'Not that much of a shock. It wasn't his first heart attack.'

Amy felt better to acknowledge this out loud. The paramedics had shared his patient history, as if that would offer some small consolation. No doubt Peter Gallivan had been a ticking cardiac time bomb.

Just like Dad.

It wasn't my fault. There was nothing more I could have done.

She chanted the words silently to herself.

Amy remembered the exact moment she decided to become a nurse. She thought back to that awful day. Hearing the ambulance and watching from the upstairs window. Spectating as the paramedics lifted the man onto the stretcher, her shock when she realised it was her father strapped down under that oxygen mask. That sensation of helplessness.

Maybe I could have saved him.

She should have gone on that walk with her parents that day, but she had been sulking after a daft teenage row with Izzy.

If only I'd been there.

At least she could have said goodbye.

The thought continued to fester, keeping her awake many a night, and eventually pulled her towards nursing. She hadn't saved her dad, but maybe she could save others.

After they loaded Dad into the ambulance, Izzy bummed a cigarette from one of the paramedics. Failing, perhaps, to appreciate how young the girls were, he offered one to Amy, too. Amy followed Izzy's lead, not knowing how to smoke but not knowing how to decline. Safer to copy her big sister. The smell of tobacco, the rush of nicotine to her brain and limbs, always took her back to that day.

'The son is going to feel terrible.' Sue heaved a sigh. 'He was here this weekend. He had a row with Fiona this afternoon, and he stormed off. Packed his stuff and left. I saw them from the car when I was dressing Betsy after the beach. There was shouting, she was crying.'

Amy stubbed out her cigarette under her shoe and tucked the butt into a giant stone planter next to the door. Sue went to protest, and Amy stopped her.

'Don't worry. I'll take it with me when we leave, I promise.'

But it was the plant pot, not the cigarette butt, that now held her aunt's attention. Sue stroked the stone, then held her finger up, trying to get a better view in the weak light from the front door.

'What are you doing?'

'Nothing.' Sue's eyes were on the plant pot, her head tilted to the side, momentarily lost in thought.

'Well, if she's in bed, we might as well get going. I'll just grab my bag.'

————

They tiptoed back into the house, mindful of being as quiet as possible in that cavernous hallway. Sue slipped her boots on and again noticed a crunching grittiness underfoot. She crouched down for a closer look.

Against the while tiles of the hallway, she spotted something. She picked it up, squinting in the half-light to get a better look. It was sharp, but not glass. Ceramic, perhaps? It was hard to tell. She glanced around her feet, noticing several fragments.

Tiredness hit her then, a needle point between the eyes. She would have gladly taken Fiona's sofa if Amy hadn't cajoled her out the door.

'Come on,' she said. 'I'll drop you home. You can call over to pick up your car tomorrow.'

Sue nodded, her eyelids heavy, and climbed into Amy's passenger seat. Everything would look much better in the daylight.

27

AMY FELT RAW, THE MEMORY OF LAST NIGHT COMING BACK TO her within seconds of waking. Those final seconds as Peter's light extinguished.

She should have called his wife back into the room to say goodbye. She should have done another round of chest compressions, she should have got there sooner. *Should have, should have.* Those twenty minutes replayed like a film on a loop in her mind.

It shouldn't have happened.

The meds he was taking were supposed to protect him. It wasn't an exact science, but Peter should not have had such a massive heart attack.

Amy had felt powerless as his blood oxygen levels tumbled and he failed to respond to the CPR. She went over it again and again, examining her memory frame-by-frame, wondering if she could have done something differently. Trying not to think of her father going through the same thing.

Poor Fiona. She had been in quite a state. The ones who broke down crying – that normal, instinctive reaction – they were easier to deal with. Sadness. Anger, even. Far worse were the ones who showed no emotion at all. It was easy to fall into shock and hard to climb out of it. Too many times, she had seen shock become the foundation stone for a grief that stretched on and on.

It was the first time she'd had someone laugh, though. Her skin prickled at the memory.

Mondays were her day off, but she would call in on Fiona this morning. For a district nurse, the boundary between work and neighbourliness was occasionally blurred, and Amy didn't give it a second thought. Hopefully, the son would be home, no doubt full of remorse and regret and ready to help his mother pick up the pieces.

She sent a message to her aunt, suggesting they meet over at the Gallivans' place. Amy wasn't sure what, exactly, but something was unsettling her to the point that she didn't want to go alone.

———

Sue had been awake since 5 a.m.; as soon as the thinnest trace of dawn light touched her eyelids. Despite her exhaustion, she had spent the night tossing and turning, sleep just beyond her reach.

The harbour was quiet, the fishing boats already out for the day. Toy-sized vessels dotted across the cobalt expanse. Sue took deep breaths of the cool salty air, which reinvigorated her and steadied her nerves.

When Amy's car pulled up just as she approached the Gallivan house, she exhaled with relief. Although she could barely admit it to herself, she wasn't sure what they would find when they got there.

Amy waited for her at the garden gate. 'Ready?'

The doorbell chimed brightly, echoing in the hallway. Sue's attention turned again to the planter she noticed last night.

In the daylight, she could see it even more clearly. An old stone urn as tall as her mid-thigh that must weigh a ton. It had been planted with a small bay tree, from which several leaves lay scattered on the soil. On its side, a filigree patina, peppered with mustard-yellow starbursts of lichen.

Ordinarily Sue would be struck by the beauty of the lichen, the exquisite hardiness of an organism that could survive on nothing but air. She could see the smear where she drew her finger through it just last night. She'd been right – something was amiss.

'Auntie Sue?' Amy muttered. 'Are you OK?'

'Yes. It's just...'

The sound of footsteps snapped her back to the moment, and Fiona appeared at the door.

'Sue. Amy.' She beamed at them. 'Come on in.'

She had washed her hair. That was the first thing Sue noticed. She had also got dressed, which was significantly more than most people managed to achieve the day after losing a loved one. With a barely perceptible glance at her niece, Sue followed Fiona inside, trailing in the fragrant wake of her perfume.

'Tea?' Fiona was barefoot, her toenails a freshly painted fuchsia.

The radio was playing in the kitchen. *Good vibrations.* A half-eaten bowl of granola sat on the counter.

Fiona took Amy's hands in hers. 'I just want to thank you for what you did. It can't be easy for you when... well, you know.'

Amy nodded and offered a weak smile.

As Fiona turned to retrieve two mugs from the

cupboard, Sue stole a sideways glance at her niece. This was all starting to feel quite peculiar.

The chime of the doorbell startled her.

'Ladies – please excuse me,' said Fiona.

Sue waited until she had left the room. 'What's going on?' she mouthed to Amy.

'No idea', came Amy's reply, just before they heard a familiar voice.

28

'HONESTLY, IF I'D KNOWN I'D HAVE COMPANY, I'D HAVE BAKED a cake!' Fiona's laugh was shrill. She reappeared at the kitchen door, holding it wide for the latest arrival.

Amy couldn't hide her confusion. 'Diana. Fancy seeing you here.'

The old lady's face was sombre. She clasped her hands in a prayer at her chest. 'I came to offer my condolences as soon as I heard the terrible news.'

Amy might have imagined it, but her old schoolteacher's tone was almost defensive. Diana gave Fiona's arm a squeeze. 'It's incredibly sad, dear.'

'Yes, well…' Fiona trailed off, distracted by something outside. Her eyes followed a magpie as it hopped along the wall of the old kitchen garden. She blinked, coming back to herself. 'Oh yes. Tea.'

Diana cleared her throat. 'A heart attack, I heard?'

Amy groaned. It was remarkable just how quickly unfortunate news travelled in a place like Seahouses. And trust Diana to be first on the scene – the woman couldn't help herself. After a couple of sherries at last year's Lifeboat Institute Christmas party, she'd told Amy that she considered herself the 'eyes and ears of the village'.

Fiona nodded. 'He had been ill for quite some time, as Amy will tell you.'

Amy cradled her mug in two hands. That wasn't quite how she would have put it. Peter's previous heart attacks weren't severe, and he was on blood thinners and beta blockers.

'I suppose I'll have to think about clearing out his things.' Fiona mused.

Sue's eyes widened, pools of surprise.

Amy gave her aunt a swift kick to the shin. 'I think you can wait a while before you see to that sort of thing.' Amy heard herself – she didn't sound certain at all.

Fiona shrugged and stared off again into the garden. A new song was playing now. The women sat in awkward silence.

Diana was unfazed. 'When my Lionel passed away, I couldn't bear to get rid of his things. In fact, I still have one of his dress shirts hanging in my wardrobe. Just to hold on to one last piece of him.'

'You're right.' Fiona nodded. 'I'll focus on the funeral first. They said his body could be released by the end of the week.'

'That sounds about right,' said Amy. 'I wouldn't expect there'll be a post-mortem, given his medical history. He saw a doctor recently.' *Although a doctor might question why his medication failed to prevent a massive heart attack.*

Diana went to stand. 'Nature calls, I'm afraid. Fiona, would you be so kind as to show me the way to the loo?'

'Of course.' Fiona helped her down from the high seat.

'And while I'm on my feet, I'll take the full tour.' Diana

chuckled. 'Only if you're feeling up to it, of course,' she quickly added.

Sue waited until she and Amy were alone again. 'Don't tell me that's a healthy response,' Sue whispered, jabbing a finger towards the door through which they had disappeared.

Amy rolled her eyes. 'Relax. Everyone deals with these things in different ways. It'll hit her in a day or two.'

Except she wasn't sure she believed that.

The days after Dad died floated to the surface of her memory. It was strange, the details she could recall. How the wind whipped off the sea, so loud that apparently people didn't hear her mother scream for help. The red blanket they covered him with. The sand in his hair. She couldn't remember what he was wearing, but she remembered the sand in his hair.

Maybe I could have saved him.

'We'll see,' Sue whispered.

Tea, tours, and loo visits exhausted, Amy suggested they left Fiona in peace. The woman was distraught, she was sure. People had different ways of showing it, that was all. They shuffled into the hallway.

'Darn it!' Diana slapped a palm to her forehead. 'You know, I do blame old age. I'm so sorry, dear, but I seem to have dropped my scarf during the tour. Perhaps it was in the master bathroom while you were showing me the steam room.'

'No problem.' Fiona glanced at the two other ladies, something like confusion behind her eyes. 'Let me just run and get it for you.'

'You're an angel,' Diana purred. Her smile fell as soon as Fiona reached the upstairs landing.

'Quickly, dears.' Diana whispered, an urgent look in her eyes. 'I need to show you something.'

————

Sue didn't have time to object. Moving with much more agility than she had before, Diana dropped to a crouch.

'Look!' she whispered, pointing to the floor. 'Evidence of a disturbance. Something broke here.' She gestured to the tiled floor by the console table. 'And someone trailed sand from the front door into there.' She nodded towards the living room.

Sue was about to protest, but stopped herself. She had noticed something on the floor last night. Now, she crouched to take a better look in daylight. She picked up a single piece, turning over the fragment of ceramic between her fingers. One side was adorned in a delicate pattern, flecked with gold.

And then she remembered – the vase. On her first visit, she had admired an antique vase, right there on the side table. Now, the table was bare.

And with the sun streaming in through the window at an angle, bright and unfiltered by cloud, she could also see sand. Illuminated and glistening in the light, as if someone had walked from the front door and straight into the living room. Whoever trailed it in must have had wet shoes to carry so much sand all that way.

So what? She thought. It was probably the paramedics. Presumably, they were more preoccupied with saving a life than making a mess.

But it wasn't raining last night. And presumably, the ambulance crew had not been hanging about on the beach waiting for someone to call the emergency services.

Against the pristine tiles, the trail of sand shimmered, glinting white in the sunlight. Pale sand, thought Sue. *Very pale.*

She licked her thumb and pressed it against the tiles, holding it up for a closer inspection.

Fiona was on her way back, her footsteps already audible on the first floor landing. Reaching for Amy's hand to support her, Sue straightened up. She shoved her hand into her jacket pocket and wiped her thumb against the inside of her handkerchief, folding it over with her finger.

'Here it is.' Fiona waved a silk scarf. 'It was in one of the guest rooms.'

Diana took the scarf from her, moving slowly again now. 'Heavens, dear, I am awfully sorry.' She heaved a sigh of regret. 'Old age comes for all of us, eventually.'

When they reached the garden gate, Diana turned to face them. 'Excuse me for saying so, but that was highly irregular.' Her voice lowered to a whisper. 'I suggest we *rendezvous* back at Amy's house and compare notes.'

Sue wasn't sure quite how much more of Diana Wheeler she could take today, but she wouldn't leave Amy to deal with her on her own. Besides, the prospect of sitting by Amy's Aga with a plate of biscuits was always a tantalising option, no matter who joined them.

'What do you say, Ames? Amy?'

But her niece wasn't listening. She was looking back up at the Gallivan house, lost in thought.

Sue followed her gaze, to those windows made of sea and sky. What *was* going on in there?

29

The kitchen windows beaded with crystals of condensation. The Sanders would need to strip and repaint the sill again soon – Sue could see where the blue gloss was beginning to peel back at the corners.

Diana lowered herself into a chair at the head of the long wooden table. It was already in this room when Amy and Mike bought the cottage, a slab of solid oak worn smooth over goodness knows how many years. Sue took the seat at the end closest to the Aga, and Amy placed the biscuit tin between them.

Diana helped herself to a chocolate digestive. 'I'll just come out and say what everyone is thinking – it's all frightfully suspicious.'

'Diana—' Sue cut across.

'Indulge me a moment, Sue. I'll state my case concisely: a wealthy man with a problematic family suddenly drops down dead.'

Amy winced.

'Now come on,' said Sue. 'You can't label them a "problematic family"' – she hooked her fingers into inverted commas – 'just because of one little row.'

'What row?' Diana's eyes glistened, fiery sapphires of curiosity.

A knot tightened in Sue's stomach. She was no better than the busybodies she had vowed not to become. She sighed. 'We— I saw the son leaving yesterday. They were arguing, and Fiona seemed upset. That's all...' She waved her hand dismissively, as if the incident she witnessed yesterday was nothing out of the ordinary.

Diana clasped her hands. 'The plot thickens! I didn't even know about that.'

'I'm sorry, but when you said, "problematic family", what exactly were you talking about?'

'My dear.' Diana leaned in closer. 'They have lived here for six months and have barely left their house. Certainly not to venture into the village.'

'Fiona joined the book club. Perhaps they were just settling in, taking time to get their bearings?'

Diana ignored her. 'And in all that time, how many visitors have they had?'

'How would we know that?'

'Richard.' Amy pinched the bridge of her nose. 'Richard Pringle lives next door.'

Of course, thought Sue. The headteacher at North Sunderland Primary. A friend of Amy's and Diana's. Definitely no stranger to gossip.

Diana neither confirmed nor denied her source.

'In six months, their son has visited three times despite only living an hour away. And,' she waved a finger in the air for dramatic effect. 'Not one single friend.'

Sue huffed. 'Maybe they don't have any friends?'

'Well, there's one way to find out...' Diana eyed them

over the rim of her cup, glancing from Sue to Amy, neither of whom responded. 'Facebook, anyone?'

Amy shrugged and sloped off to fetch her laptop, her shoulders slumped.

Sue knew that her niece already felt rotten, and combing through Peter Gallivan's social media presence would not help. But somewhere in the back of her mind, a small voice urged her on.

It was true that the Gallivans had kept themselves to themselves. And there had been that trouble with their son. Who really knew what was going on with that family?

Sue had never seen the appeal of Facebook. She was familiar with the concept, of course – it was hard not to be. Amy had tried several times to convince her to join. Apparently, the thing was so smart that it could connect you to people you had lost touch with. An algorithm so powerful that it knew what you were thinking, according to Amy, who seemed impressed by this. But for Sue, the prospect of reconnecting with old acquaintances held no appeal. The past belonged firmly in the past.

'Here we go,' said Amy. She angled the computer so that Diana and Sue could see the screen. 'Peter Gallivan.'

In his profile picture he smiled broadly at the camera, a creased-eye toothy grin. It was taken outdoors – blue sky and the bright green of a well-kept lawn. The picture was a few years old – the man Sue met just a few days ago had more silver in his hair, but she was reminded of how young he was. At fifty-nine, he was only a few years older than her.

'Founder and CEO of Sparkbrook.' Amy read from the screen. 'There's not much else to go on – it looks like he wasn't a big social media fan.'

Diana frowned. 'Let's try her.'

Fiona's profile was wide open. Amy scrolled through a

carousel of profile photos – Fiona with Peter, Fiona with some other ladies. Consistently with a smile on her face and typically somewhere exotic. Posing by a boat in a marina, wearing a hat to the races, sitting under a palm tree. This was a woman who lived the high life – until recently. In the past six months, Fiona had only posted once – an image that Sue recognised as the sea view from their house. Amy clicked back to the last images Fiona had shared before the social media blackout.

'Oh my,' Diana said. 'Is that...'

Sue squinted for a closer look. The resemblance was remarkable.

'She never mentioned a daughter...' Amy hovered the mouse over the image, prompting a tag to pop up. 'Caitlyn Gallivan. It's got to be.'

Diana steepled her hands under her chin and sighed. 'As I said. A *problematic* family.'

30

GINA WAS DOING THE CROSSWORD. SHE HAD A MILLION THINGS to do – clean the optics, do the cellar inventory, file the caterer's invoices – and couldn't muster the energy to tackle any of them. Even the crossword was making her cross-eyed.

She heard footsteps on the stairs, the sparrow-light tread of Carrie followed by Margaret's laboured dawdle. Gina glanced at the clock. They were finished early, and there was no sign yet of Chris.

She seized her opportunity, grabbing her bag and intercepting Carrie in the porch. 'Want to go for a walk? Just the two of us?' She tried not to sound too eager.

Carrie glanced about. The pub was empty, but a straggle of lunchtime punters would arrive soon.

'Don't worry, I'll lock up.' Gina was already shrugging on her jacket. Missing one Monday lunchtime's worth of takings wouldn't sink her.

Carrie hesitated, biting her lip.

'Once around the harbour and back, get some chips.' Gina struggled to hide the desperation in her voice.

Carrie broke into a smile. 'Sure. Sounds good.'

'Well, don't mind me, will you now?' Margaret tutted as Gina ushered her out the door.

Gina looped her arm through Carrie's as they walked. This felt clandestine, illicit. On some level, she knew how ridiculous that was, but she was acutely aware that if Chris had been hanging around, Carrie wouldn't have come.

The breeze lessened as they descended the bank.

'Chips or ice cream? My treat.'

Carrie shook her head. 'You don't have to do that. Especially when I've been…'

'It's all right, pet.' Gina pulled her closer. 'I've missed you, that's all.'

Gina ordered two portions of chips from the takeaway window at Neptune's, and the women sat on a bench at the top of the bank. It was easier to talk sitting side-by-side. Gina was worried about the quality of her poker face and whether she was capable of masking her resentment of Chris. She held a steaming chip on a small wooden fork, letting it cool.

'So, how've you been?'

Carrie thought about it. 'I'm fine, now,' she said. 'Me and Chris were fighting, and I just wanted to keep my head down, you know?'

'Want to talk about it?'

Carrie hunched forward, bringing a bony knee to her chest and wrapping her arm around it, giving herself a hug. 'It's just him—' She caught herself. 'It's me. I wind him up.'

Gina wanted to scream. She took a deep, calming breath, biting her tongue as Carrie continued.

'I mean, that's what he says. And he knows he's got nothing to be jealous about. But he's had his heart broken in the past and he's just…'

'Paranoid?' Gina offered.

Carrie winced. She saw a thing on Facebook last week about the long-term effects of smoking weed, and that was the exact word they used. *Paranoia.* And Chris had smoked that stuff for years.

In fact, a lot of what they described in the post fitted him down to a tee: irritable, paranoid, low self-esteem. His mood swings were getting worse.

Carrie was suddenly struck by the feeling of being watched. Was someone listening to their conversation?

She instinctively looked around, goosebumps rising on the back of her neck. But their only companion was a large seagull with its eye on her chips, and Gina remained oblivious. *Now, who was being paranoid?*

She often got this weird feeling, sensing Chris's presence when he wasn't there. It was probably a sign of how much time they spent together.

Last summer, she went to Berwick to see Auntie Pat – the only foster mam that actually gave a shit about her. All weekend, she felt like Chris was there, somewhere, watching them. She kept catching herself glancing over her shoulder, only to see that the street behind her was empty.

'Does he pay the bill for that thing?' Auntie Pat had asked, nodding at her phone as Carrie checked it for the hundredth time that afternoon. 'You've only been away for a day. He'll not miss you if you carry on at this rate.'

Carrie had texted Chris:

Auntie Pat is telling me to get off the phone, LOL.

As an afterthought, she'd added a smiley face sticking its tongue out.

She hadn't had a weekend at Auntie Pat's since then.

Gina pinched a chip from her carton.

'Gerroff, man! You've got your own!' Carrie giggled.

'Serves you right for not paying attention.'

They fell into an easy silence, their eyes tracing a fishing boat as it backed into its pitch, its engine spluttering like an old man coughing.

'You know what would be nice?' Gina turned to face her. 'A girls' night in. Nothing crazy—' She held up her hand, stopping Carrie's protest before she had a chance to fully form her objection. 'What about this Friday? I'm thinking a Brad Pitt film, a bottle of wine. Maybe a Chinese takeaway. Just me and you, you know?'

That did sound good. Carrie knew what Chris would probably say, but it couldn't hurt to ask. The more she thought about it, the more reasonable it seemed. How could he say no to that?

And then another thought occurred to her: that she was second-guessing his mood, his rules, his permissions. What he would *allow* her to do.

How had it come to this?

31

HELEN WAS LATE OPENING THE SHOP. THE MORNINGS WERE getting lighter now, and she relished the occasional extra ten minutes beneath the duvet, thin sunlight pooling at the foot of her bed. This morning, ten minutes became twenty.

Of course, it was still dark when Roy got up, creeping from their bedroom and slipping out to get to the cows before they woke. If she pulled back the curtains, she would see him, sometimes, striding across the dew-soaked fields, guiding a heifer back to the pasture or bringing a calf in to the barn. No wonder he was always so tired. Farming was hard work for a man of any age.

Some of the other landowners had diversified. *Glamping*, that's what they called it. Daft little tents called yurts that people paid a canny penny to sleep in.

Helen had looked up the costs, calculated the return on investment, shown him a spreadsheet. Right there in black and white, numbers that actually made sense. But Roy had laughed until the heat crept up her neck, the flames lapping at her cheeks.

Too stubborn. That was his problem. And too stupid to

see that unless they did something, this was all they would ever have. All they would ever be. The same as their parents before them, and theirs before. Nothing ever changing.

At least she had the shop to keep her busy, and the money did come in handy – although Roy would never admit as much. It was her pocket money, as far as he was concerned. But her pocket money paid for the broadband they'd had installed at the farmhouse, the repayments on the new sofa after the old one finally bit the dust, and two years of Matthew's tuition fees. *Some deep pockets those must be*, she mused.

Now, she stood on something in the shop entrance and heard a crunch beneath her boot. She bent down to inspect the culprit and rolled her eyes – another shell had fallen from one of Anne Morton's bloody mirrors. Helen swore under her breath.

There had been a couple of middle-aged walkers in the shop over the weekend, down from Carlisle for two nights. They'd admired the mirrors – the first people to do so, as far as Helen was aware – and had even swallowed her local artisan line. Then a piece of sea glass fell off mid-sales pitch, landing squarely on the woman's toe. She wasn't hurt, but it had cost Helen the sale and ten minutes of faffing about with superglue.

Not that she expected to make a profit on the mirrors – she just wanted them gone. Anne had thanked her for displaying them in such a great spot, right beside the door, so that people would see them as soon as they came in. The truth was that Helen had put them there so that she didn't have to look at them all day. Two feet further to the right and they'd be in the sodding carpark.

She chided herself for thinking like that. It wasn't Anne's fault that she was so... fragile. That breakdown after Edward died had been a terrible business, and Helen still felt guilty that she hadn't worked out what was going on back then. Those poor girls had a terrible time of things and she wished she'd done more. Still, it had got Sue back.

There wasn't much in the post, so she brewed a tea and sat down to read the paper.

When she saw the front page, her jaw dropped.

Sue answered on the third ring.

'Have you seen the news?' Helen was breathless. 'It's Peter Gallivan. He's dead!' She didn't intend to sound quite so excited and regretted not waiting until she had calmed down before picking up the phone.

She heard Sue sigh, heavy and resigned, and remembered how much her friend resented gossip. But this was hardly idle chit-chat – it was front page national headlines, for heaven's sake. Seahouses hadn't featured this high on the news agenda since Grace Darling rescued a boatload of sailors back in 1838.

'It says here that he died of a heart attack on Sunday night. The poor man.' She scanned the next line and gasped. 'And he's worth four hundred and twenty-three million quid.' Helen couldn't quite compute how much money that was. She repeated the figure again, whispering it to herself. How could one person have so much?

And then the thought struck her – if her worth was measured, what would the grand total be?

'Stay there,' Sue said, as if Helen might have somewhere else to be. 'I'm on my way.'

. . .

Helen was still reading the front page when Sue walked in fifteen minutes later, the tinkle of the bell finally prompting her to look up.

'Can you believe it?' She waved the paper towards Sue.

'Which part – that the man was incredibly wealthy, or that he has died?'

Helen didn't have an answer.

'Sorry,' said Sue, 'that was uncalled for. But this media attention can't be very pleasant for Fiona. I'm worried about her.'

'You've seen her? Since that evening we were over there?' Helen tried and failed to hide the hurt from her voice. She should have known that Fiona and Sue would become friends and wouldn't need her tagging along. After all, what did a farm girl like her have to offer someone like Fiona Gallivan?

Sue nodded glumly. 'I was there on Sunday night. Amy got called out for the resuscitation, or whatever it is they do. I sat with Fiona while we waited for the ambulance.'

Helen winced. So they hadn't exactly been gallivanting around the village together.

She jabbed at the paper. 'It says here that they have a son *and* a daughter.' She squinted at the text, double-checking. 'Fiona never mentioned a *daughter*. Did she?'

She thought back to the evening of the book club. Fiona had banged on and on about her son while she tried to pair him off with Lucia, and hadn't so much as whispered about having a girl, too. Or that time Fiona hosted them over at her place. In fact, the more Helen thought about it, the more it seemed like Fiona had *deliberately* avoided mentioning a daughter.

The colour drained from Sue's face. 'To be honest, I'm not sure that's the only thing Fiona is hiding.'

32

THE WIND WHIPPED AT THE SEA, ANGRY AND BITTER, SPITTING starbursts of white foam high in the air as the waves pummelled the harbour wall. The fishing boats looked tiny now, precariously fragile next to the vast strength of the sea.

Lucia had watched some of them leave early that morning, only to beat a hasty retreat when the weather turned, their engines groaning under the strain of outrunning the elements. The dark clouds rolled out as far as the horizon, with no end in sight.

She hadn't heard from Ben for over a week now. Several times, she'd gone back over their conversations, reading between the lines. Seeing if there was something she could have missed.

If she closed her eyes, she could still feel the warm brush of his finger against her face as he tucked a curl behind her ear. At night, she dreamed of him, the sparks of copper in his eyes and the way the corners of his mouth dipped down at his own jokes. A dimple in his left cheek, a perfect flaw. The spark when their hands had touched. That had been real, hadn't it?

There were rules, apparently, about who was supposed to call who and what was an acceptable timeframe for replying to messages. Lucia had never paid much attention to all of that and was beginning to wish she had.

And how, exactly, did the rules change after a death in the family? Perhaps she was naïve, but Lucia had assumed that Ben would turn to her for comfort – especially after that night. It was true that they hadn't known each other long, but she had never felt such a profound connection with anyone. It was more than simply wanting to be there for him. There was an ache in her gut to comfort him, a sense that the universe had thrown them together. An instinct that told her she – and she alone – was what he needed right now.

But she would not push, nor force her way in.

Peter Gallivan's demise had slipped from the front pages but was still in the news.

She realised with a pang of sadness that she might never hear from Ben again. In the messy grief of his father's death, he might completely forget her.

If that's what fate had in store for her, she couldn't fight it. *What will be, will be.*

Poor Ben. He was so full of anger, but Lucia recognised it as resentment that masked something else. He hadn't always hated his dad. Maybe *hate* was too strong a word, anyway. Those feelings had been honed over time, sharpened into something that no longer resembled what they had originally been.

She went over their last date again in her mind, scene-by-scene. Touch by touch. It was all such a crying shame.

The funeral was this morning.

The newspaper quoted a spokesperson saying that it would be a private event. That seemed strange, thought

Lucia, for such a high-profile man. Peter Gallivan must have had thousands of acquaintances. Surely some of them would want to come and say goodbye?

When Nonna died, there had been a three-day festival in the village and some of Lucia's aunties wore black for an entire year, all for a humble *commessa* from Catania. Perhaps 'private' was simply aimed at keeping the press away. Besides, Ben might need her.

Her mind was made up, but Lucia chewed on a nail, fighting a small knot of worry in her stomach. She would wait until the service started, slip into the church, and sit at the back.

She got up before she changed her mind again and set off for the walk to St Cuthbert's.

———

'We can't *not* go. It wouldn't be proper.'

'Auntie Sue – they've said it's private. *Private* means we're not invited.' Amy squared her jaw and went back to her book.

'But she's our friend.' Even Sue could hear that her protest was half-hearted, and her stamina for arguing with Amy was waning. She couldn't work out what had come over her niece, but clearly, Peter's death had left a deeper imprint than Sue first realised.

Besides, was Fiona actually a friend? They only met a few weeks ago, and Sue hadn't heard from Fiona at all in more than a week. Perhaps the grief had finally hit her. Sue had sent a couple of texts and called around once at the house with a shepherd's pie. There was no answer, so she left it on the doorstep. The urn had caught her eye again as she turned to leave.

It was Diana who suggested they go to the funeral. She was firmly of the view that 'private' was simply aimed at minimising media intrusion and that, as neighbours, they should be there.

But Sue decided to defer to Amy's judgement. There was no way she was risking any more upset to her niece. She would call Diana and declare herself out.

She had found Amy the other day curled up asleep on Betsy's bed after putting the littlest ones down, her face pressed against the top of her daughter's head, Amy's cheeks tear-stained. It confirmed what the dark shadows under her eyes already told her. Sue left her to nap for a while before rousing her.

Of course, Diana's desire to attend the funeral had nothing to do with paying respects or offering condolences. Sue knew she was just being downright nosey. Diana was still convinced there was something off with the whole affair.

Sue shivered, a sudden chill catching her from nowhere.

Diana had a working theory that someone had broken into the house. She didn't have an answer to the question of 'and then what happened?', but she was adamant the mess of sand trailing across that gleaming white hallway and the remnants of a shattered vase were proof that the Gallivans had received an unexpected and uninvited guest. Telling her that Fiona's son had argued with his parents had poured petrol over the flames.

Ordinarily, Sue would have dismissed her, but there was something else. The tall urn by the door. Sue had a feeling it had been moved, and on that, she had a theory of her own. And then there were the shards of porcelain that had crunched under her shoes. But what about the rest of the vase? Would an intruder have cleaned up after themselves?

She exhaled slowly, stacking up the pieces in her mind and seeing how they might fit together. Perhaps Diana did have an overactive imagination. Or, just maybe, her friend's wild theory wasn't so crazy after all.

————

From this side of the street, Diana had a reasonable view of St Cuthbert's.

It was a pity she couldn't convince Sue to come with her. With such excursions, safety in numbers was infinitely preferable to flying solo. Still, at least she had her age to fall back on. The one saving grace to getting older was just how much one could get away with.

Satisfied that everyone had arrived and would be installed inside, she slipped her theatre binoculars back into the glove compartment and made her way across the church yard, remembering at the entrance to slow to her old lady shuffle.

In the cool of St Cuthbert's the musty air hit her, the smell of centuries. Diana paused, just a beat, inhaling the memories.

Only the first couple of pews were occupied. Diana slipped into the last pew, only to notice another solitary figure had already taken a seat back here.

Lucia seemed surprised to see her, but composed herself quickly and jumped to her feet, offering Diana an arm.

She didn't take it. It was one thing to affect an old woman's hobble and quite another to accept help that was entirely unnecessary.

The girl wasn't dressed for a funeral, although she had at least managed to wear black. Her tight-fitting jeans – the poured-into variety that Diana couldn't fathom how girls took off at night – and black silk shirt were smart enough, but only just.

'That date went well, I assume?' Diana whispered.

Lucia gave a shy nod.

Although not well enough to sit among the family.

Diana made a quick headcount. 'Not the turnout I'd imagined,' she mused.

A private funeral – Diana had never heard of such a thing. Whoever asked mourners to stay away? It was obscene.

But the knot of people gathered in the front pews was miniscule. From here she could make out Fiona and the son, and one had to assume that the other head of lustrous blond hair belonged to the mysterious daughter. Caitlyn, according to the internet.

Diana watched her now. As if sensing eyes on her back, Caitlyn threw a glance over her shoulder, her steely gaze lingering on Diana and Lucia. She whispered something to her brother, who bristled in response. Ben hesitated before turning and did a double take when he saw Lucia.

How interesting, thought Diana.

———

Lucia had been busted. First by Diana, and now by Ben's sister. So much for getting in and out without anyone spotting her. But when Ben turned and his eyes met hers, Lucia felt that little elastic band snap in her stomach. He offered a feeble smile before turning his concentration back to his mother.

It was remarkably dry-eyed for a funeral. Perhaps that was a rich people thing, Lucia mused. Stiff upper lip and all that. Although Ben didn't strike her as that type, and nor did his mum.

Of course, they all knew the Gallivans were wealthy, but her jaw had dropped when she read how much he was worth. Lucia couldn't imagine why anyone would want to accumulate that much money. As Peter proved, it couldn't buy happiness. Nor could you take it with you. It certainly didn't look like they'd blown much of it on his funeral.

There were so few people. Lucia counted twenty-four, not including her and Diana. Impossible to go unnoticed. The thought made her mouth dry, her stomach twisting in knots.

The sister threw another scowl over her shoulder, sending Lucia's heart hammering in her chest. At least Diana gave her some cover. They could leave quietly, as soon as it was polite, and slip away before the family left the church.

If Ben wanted to see her again, he would call her. She would give him space and be patient.

She flattened her palms together in her lap and raised her eyes to the eaves, praying that it wasn't the end.

33

THE LAUNDRY FINISHED, SUE CAME BACK IN THE LIVING ROOM to find Amy asleep on the sofa. She dragged a crochet blanket over her, tucking it around Amy's feet. She'd wake her in an hour, just in time for them to walk down together to fetch the children from school.

Sue took a seat next to the Aga and picked up the newspaper. There was more coverage of Peter's untimely end. Photos of him and Fiona with a TV chef at a black-tie charity gala, Peter cutting the ribbon on a new Sparkbrook shop. The journalist was generous in his praise for the working-class lad who grafted his way to millionaire status and made only the briefest mention of the tax scandal that thrust Peter into the headlines a couple of years ago. According to the paper, Sparkbrook had also been caught up in the row over zero hours contracts and employment rights. She would research that on the internet later. A perverse curiosity was creeping in, a desire to find out all she could about Peter Gallivan.

Another question bothered her, too. She padded along

the hallway in her socks. In the living room, Amy was still fast asleep.

Sue's coat was hanging on the rack by the door. Slipping her hand into the pocket, she carefully fished out the folded handkerchief that had lain there for more than a week. The word 'sample' came to mind, and she pushed it away, tutting to herself. But something about that sandy trail in the hallway didn't feel right.

It was years since Sue had used a microscope. She'd bought one for Hannah two Christmases ago, hoping to nudge at least one of the children towards science. Sue had set it up for her great-niece on Boxing Day, showing her how to prepare the slide with a drop of water from the pipette. She remembered the awe in Hannah's eyes the first time she saw a piece of onion skin magnified to a thousand times its size. Sadly, the novelty had quickly worn off.

Sue found the box tucked away on a high shelf in the girl's bedroom, now dulled by a film of dust. She cleared a space on Hannah's desk and gingerly unfolded the handkerchief.

There was more sand than she remembered hastily gathering that day at the Gallivans'. The grains glinted like stars against the stark white of the handkerchief. Even to her naked eye, it was obvious. She prepped a glass slide for a closer look.

Back in the lab, they used to run through a sequence of questions when identifying samples of rock. There was a process to follow, a system for classification. For a young woman confused about her place in the world, losing herself in the rigour and discipline had been a balm to Sue's troubled soul. She might not have fit into a box, but with science, she could find order amidst the chaos. It came to her now, the echo of a memory from a lifetime ago.

'What are you doing?'

She jumped, startled by Amy's voice behind her. She held her hand to her chest, feeling the percussion of her heart beneath her fingertips. 'Remember that day we went to Fiona's place?'

Amy yawned, leaning against the door frame. 'What about it?'

'I took a sam— I picked up some sand from the hall. There was a trail of it, leading through to the living room, and Diana thought it was suspicious, given how Fiona had everyone take their shoes off at the door.'

Amy cocked her head to one side. 'I remember. But it was probably from one of the paramedics. Or even me.'

'That's what I thought, at first.' Sue hesitated. If she was going to leave this here, now was her chance.

Amy sat on Hannah's bed. 'The house is two hundred yards from the beach. It'll get sandy sometimes, no matter how immaculate Fiona wants to keep her floors.'

'I don't think this came from your shoes. Come and look, you'll see what I mean.'

With a frown knotting her brows, Amy squinted into the eyepiece. 'Tell me what I'm looking for.'

'The beaches here, the sand – it's a mix of all sorts. Different types of rock, some of them thousands of centuries old, minute fragments of carbon, fossils, tiny pieces of shell. Each grain is a unique colour, size, composition.'

'That's not what I'm seeing here.'

'Exactly.'

Under the LED light of Hannah's microscope, the grains looked even more pale, spherical crystalline orbs. They were uniform, too, almost identical in size. You wouldn't need a master's in geology to spot that.

Amy looked up from the microscope. 'Maybe it came from another beach?'

Sue shook her head. 'This didn't come from *any* beach. It's silica sand. Mined and chemically processed. The kind they use in construction.'

Amy shrugged. 'So what? Maybe one of the paramedics was called out to a building site beforehand?'

'It's a possibility. But there's something else you should see.'

It would be easier to show Amy, rather than try to explain it to her. In daylight, it would be obvious, even to an inexpert eye.

Sue had pulled a blackberry crumble out of the freezer. That was their cover story.

Defrost – six hours. Heat for twenty minutes at one-eighty. She scribbled on a card, adding her condolences after the cooking instructions.

At least they knew the house would be empty. Nevertheless, they took the precaution of parking Amy's car on the side street beside the gift shop. Close enough for the short walk over to the Gallivans', and far enough that folk wouldn't think they were intruding on the family's grief.

Amy put the frozen crumble on the doorstep, carefully placing it to one side to avoid potential accidents.

'Right. What am I looking at?'

The urn hadn't been moved. Sue crouched down beside it.

'See this?' She stroked the delicate yellow crust that decorated the surface of the stone. 'This is lichen. It's a living thing – it implants itself onto stone and wood and feeds off moisture and oxygen in the air. Normally, it doesn't like direct sunlight, so it grows in shady places. On a tree, for example, you'll see more lichen on one side of the trunk, or in the crevices. But look here – this is concentrated on the side facing south.'

'The side that gets the most sun...'

'Exactly. Just the place it doesn't belong. That means the pot was moved. Quite recently, I'd guess.'

Amy pursed her lips. 'I'm still not sure what this has to do with the sand in the hallway?'

'What if someone broke in? Or, perhaps, let themselves in with a key?' Sue could hardly believe she was giving this theory oxygen, but she'd been mulling it over for the past few days. A smashed vase and sandy hallway might not mean much, but if there was a spare key, perhaps there *was* more to it?

The pot was solid stone and must weigh a ton – far too heavy for most people to pick up. But it hadn't been lifted – it had been rotated. She could picture how it was done. Someone would have tilted it, twisted it on its base before carefully setting it back down in a new position.

Amy studied the urn. 'Only one way to find out,' she said, as she rocked it towards her.

'Careful! It's heavy—' Sue stopped short. In the damp shadow beneath the urn, a silver key winked at her.

'So?' Amy asked.

Sue nodded, resigned. 'It's there.'

Together, they set the urn down, sliding it back into position.

'I don't see what this means, though,' said Amy. 'Diana will always have a theory about these things – she reads too many murder mystery books. Everyone has a spare key hidden somewhere, Fiona could have got locked out or—' She stopped short, her eyes growing wide.

'What's up—'

Amy grabbed Sue's hand, tugging her away from the doorstep. From the road at the bottom of the garden came the sound of car doors closing.

'They're back!' she hissed, pulling Sue away from the porch just as the garden gate opened.

They crouched down at the side of the house, behind the corner of the original cottage where it joined the annex, just out of sight of the path.

'What are you doing?' Sue hissed.

Amy held a finger to her mouth.

Sue leaned back against the stone wall, her heart hammering. What on earth was Amy playing at? Wasn't the whole point of the crumble to have a cover story, an excuse to be here? This was the height of stupidity. How would they explain themselves if someone saw them hiding?

She stole a glance at her niece, who had flattened herself to the wall in a crouch closest to the corner of the building.

The voices grew louder as the trio approached the door. Sue could make out Fiona and two others. She guessed one of them must be Ben, the son.

'I just think you should lie low for a while,' he was saying. 'Just until this is all done and dusted, you know?'

'I'm fine, honestly.' Fiona's words were strained. 'And he's gone now. That means we can go back home.'

The third voice was a woman. 'Ben's right. We need to keep our heads down until the dust has settled. Then I never want to hear the name Peter Gallivan again.'

The daughter, thought Sue.

Fiona sighed. 'You can't say things like that.'

'Don't worry. I'll be slightly more circumspect in public. But I'll say whatever I like about him behind closed doors.

Anyway, it's not like he's here to take offence. It's time to do what's best for us. For *all* of us.'

'Exactly.' Ben was now so close that Sue could hear him sigh. 'And there's no rush to— hey, what's this?'

They paused.

Had they noticed the urn had moved?

'There's a note. Give it here.' Caitlyn's tone was brusque. 'It says, "Reheat... blah blah. To Fiona. Our thoughts are with you. I'm here if you need anything. Sue." Who's Sue?'

Sue felt the burn rising in her face as the pounding in her chest grew to hammer blows.

'She's a friend.' Fiona sounded defensive. 'From the village.'

'Right.' Caitlyn's voice sneered. 'I bet they're swarming like flies around the proverbial. I told you, Mum, you need to be careful—'

'Come on, Caitlyn. It's not like that.' Sue could hear the exasperation in Fiona's voice. 'No one around here knows a thing. It's been nice, getting out and about again. Not stuck at home with your father all the time.'

There was the jingle of a key, the clunk of the door being unlocked. A burglar alarm beeped urgently. 'Besides.' Fiona's tone was cooler now. 'It's not like I've had either of you to keep me company.'

There was a shuffle of feet into the hallway, and finally their argument receded behind the closed door. The hammering in Sue's chest continued long after their voices faded.

34

AMY'S HANDS TREMBLED ON THE WHEEL. SHE COULDN'T believe she had done that. Spying on a grieving family. Poor Peter wasn't yet cold in the ground.

They had been caught off-guard when the Gallivans came home from the funeral so early. In her panic, Amy forgot all about the blackberry crumble, as well as the line she was supposed to use if anyone saw them. Perhaps it was because she already felt like they were snooping.

The funeral must have been short and sweet. *Very short.* No wake, no hosting everyone back at home. It pained her to admit it, but perhaps Diana was right. There was something fishy about that family.

She and Auntie Sue had waited until the three of them were inside, then legged it, like schoolgirls playing knocky-nine-doors. The stress of it had given her aunt heartburn. She would have to do the school run herself and leave Auntie Sue to chill at home for a bit.

They pulled up behind Diana's car, which was parked on the street outside Amy's house.

'Now what?' Amy groaned. She didn't have time for any more conspiracy theories today.

Diana was waiting on the doorstep with her new lodger, that pretty mixed-race girl. Lucia. *Such a beautiful name,* thought Amy. And those exquisite eyes the colour of sea glass. They were both dressed in black, Diana sporting a pillbox hat pitched at a jaunty angle.

Amy hadn't even closed the gate before Diana launched at her. 'Ladies, I think an intelligence gathering is in order.'

'Looks like I'm hosting, then...' Amy muttered under her breath. She caught Lucia's eye, and they exchanged a knowing glance, just short of an eye roll. Diana seemed determined to cajole them all into joining her mystery tour.

Sue busied herself with the tea while Diana got started. Amy kept one eye on the clock – she only had thirty minutes before she needed to leave to fetch Lucas and Betsy. As much as she adored her former teacher, her indulgence had a time limit today.

'Now, Lucia,' Diana said, very solemnly. 'You have been getting acquainted with Ben. What can you tell us about him?'

'I... er—' The colour rose in Lucia's cheeks. 'He's a nice guy...?'

Amy tutted. 'Steady on, Diana. Some things are not meant for public consumption.'

'We don't have time for privacy policies today, my dear girl. I get the feeling that something is going on with those Gallivans and Lucia here might be able to give us a clue as to what that may be.'

'And so what?' The words came out harsher than Amy intended. She softened. 'What's it got to do with us? Peter wasn't getting along with his kids. Wealthy families fight all the time. Inheritance, control of the company... they could have fallen out for any number of reasons. It doesn't make it any of our business. Some things belong behind closed doors.'

She couldn't help it – her memories of the year Dad died came back, when Mum went missing and their misery became nothing but fodder for the village gossips. Two grieving teenage girls left to fend for themselves and all anyone did was whisper about them behind their backs. No wonder Izzy couldn't wait to get away from this place.

Of course, Diana had shown them kindness. She was one of the few to offer genuine sympathy and practical support – one of the reasons Amy was still good friends with her today, even if she did find her exasperating at times. Amy wasn't sure if it was a suspicious mind or an overactive imagination, but one thing was certain – her former teacher was getting worse with old age.

Diana brought her hands together in a prayer, pressing her index fingers to pursed lips and frowning in concentration. 'A high-profile and successful man lives like a hermit, cut off from the world – including his children. Who or what was he hiding from? That's our first line of inquiry. And secondly, did whatever – or whoever – he was hiding from catch up with him in the end?'

Sue bit her lip as she set the tea down on the table. 'Fiona said something earlier. She said that "no one around here knows a thing".'

'Ha!' Diana clapped her hands. 'That confirms it. They are hiding something.' She seemed to consider this. 'Something that other people elsewhere are aware of, but they have managed to keep hidden from us here in Seahouses. Something – or someone – that resulted in a trail of sand and a smashed vase in their hallway. I wonder if it has something to do with the daughter? Strange, that Fiona omitted to mention her.' She drummed her fingers on the table absentmindedly.

'I'm sorry, but I have to get going.' Lucia blurted out. 'I have a deadline this afternoon for work.' She stood and pushed her chair back under the table.

Amy saw her opportunity to escape and grabbed her car keys. 'I need to collect the kids from school; I'll drop you off.'

'Thanks.' Lucia flashed her a weak smile of relief.

————

It wasn't entirely a fib – Lucia really did have work to do.

She had been sitting on a brief from her London agency since Monday and she owed them a response. Despite the savings in her account and her planned hiatus, she was thinking of accepting this one. It was Kuala Lumpur, a relatively simple commission. Most crucially, it would get her away from Seahouses for four or five days. That had to be better than sitting around and moping about Ben.

Amy grabbed a bag from the passenger seat and tossed it into the back, clearing space for Lucia to slide in. At Lucia's feet was another bag, this one full of books.

'It's library day tomorrow,' said Amy, as Lucia arranged her legs around it. 'I'll forget otherwise.'

Lucia stole a glance at the back of the car. A child's car seat was fixed in one of the passenger seats and the footwell was littered with toys, odd socks, a welly, and several empty water bottles.

'Kids,' said Amy, shaking her head as she reversed out of her spot. 'There aren't enough hours in the day to clean up after them.'

Lucia squirmed with guilt that Amy felt the need to excuse her standards of cleanliness to a complete stranger.

Why did people constantly find the need to justify themselves to others? It was one of those things Lucia just didn't get, no matter how hard she tried. She gazed out of the window as the cottages passed by, snatches of sea view peeking through the gaps between them.

'Ben told me his dad was a bully.'

She said it without thinking. She didn't know why she felt the need to explain Ben to Amy – to anyone, for that matter. After all, they had only been on a couple of dates, officially.

But Amy simply shrugged. 'No family's perfect. Mine certainly isn't.'

They pulled up outside Puffin Cottage. Lucia climbed out, then hesitated. 'But he doesn't hate his dad. *Didn't*, I mean. They might have fallen out, but Ben's a good person. I can tell.'

'Like I said,' Amy muttered. 'No family's perfect.'

As Amy drove off, Lucia wondered whether she should have said anything at all. Maybe it was a good idea to get away, just for a while. She would leave next Friday and be home by mid-week. Because she would come back.

She would definitely come back.

The voice was stirring.

This was how it always began. An offer, an invitation, a job – something that caught her attention. The opportunity to explore somewhere new, or a ticket to somewhere she had been before, the chance to see how it had changed. To Lucia, it felt like catching up with an old friend.

Karissa Chang. She'd got her that first job. Karissa was in her sociology class at college. They'd studied together from time to time, sometimes grabbing lunch in the cafeteria between lectures. Karissa had been one of the few to notice when Lucia dropped out, her texts growing more frantic by the day until she eventually turned up at the door of Lucia's flat.

Lucia didn't tell her what had happened, and Karissa didn't pry. They drank tea. Lucia hadn't had any milk in the fridge, so they both took it black.

A week later, Karissa called. She had this side-line, she said, the odd job she occasionally did for her uncle. He wasn't actually an uncle, more like a family friend from Hong Kong. Struck down with a cold, she couldn't go, and wondered if Lucia wanted the gig.

Lucia balked when she heard how much money it was. It seemed too good to be true. 'Completely legit', Karissa promised her. 'I swear'.

She remembered that first job so clearly, the texture of her emotions suspended forever in her memory. How she sat awake for the whole flight, too nervous to sleep. She had never flown so far, never even travelled abroad on her own. The tremor in her hands – she had been convinced she would get caught, or someone would stop her in the airport or at the hotel and tell her that it was a scam, a set-up. Surely, it could not be as straightforward as this?

The fact of travelling itself, of covering all those miles, was exhilarating. The lights of Hong Kong were seductive, the silhouettes of skyscrapers stretching taller than the shadows of the mountains behind them. Once the deed was done, the uncle – Tony Chen – asked if she was open to another job. This one paid even more.

She went on to Taipei, where everyone spoke a slightly different version of Chinese and touched her hair. Strangers in the street stopping Lucia to tell her that she was a beautiful girl. A taxi driver gave her a kiwi fruit. 'For good luck', he said. She spent a day by the pool in a luxury hotel before her flight home. For a college drop-out from Manchester, it was thrilling.

All of a sudden, her problems were left trailing far behind her. She was reminded of when astronauts talk about seeing the earth from space. A blue marble, they call it, a wistful sheen glazing their eyes. How peaceful it looks from so far away. Distance puts all difficulty into perspective.

Lucia learned a valuable lesson back then. When things get tough, the easiest way to make them better is to run.

35

Sue envied the way Amy bolted out of there at the first opportunity. That was Sue's problem: she wasn't fast enough.

'Now that they're gone,' Diana said, 'perhaps you can tell me what's really going on.' She folded back the sleeve of her chiffon blouse, checking her watch. 'And by my estimation we have approximately fifteen minutes until we're over-run, so do get a move on, please.'

Sue was glad Lucia had followed Amy out. Talking about Peter's death, suggesting there was something untoward about the Gallivans – it made Sue no better than the rest of them. The ones who picked over Anne's breakdown, vultures for a salacious story. Perhaps this was different, but still, it didn't feel right to air their concerns in front of a stranger.

She took a deep breath. 'The footsteps you saw in the hallway. It's not sand from the beach. It's silica sand. Industrial. Processed. The type used in construction.'

She headlined the facts in staccato, Diana nodding as she noted each piece of information.

Sue continued. 'The first time I visited the Gallivan house, there was an antique vase on a side table at the entrance. When I was there last Sunday, the day er—'

'When Peter died. Go on.'

'Right. That evening, by the time I got there, it was gone – smashed into pieces on the floor, from what I could tell.'

Diana sat back in her chair, hands neatly folded on the table in front of her. 'Let's hypothesise: someone gets in, he leaves the trail of sand. But Peter disturbs him. The vase gets smashed in the melee. Peter gives chase, the intruder takes off, and Peter starts to clean up the vase, but the shock of the disturbance and the strain of the physical altercation send him into cardiac arrest.' Even Diana looked unconvinced by her proposal.

Sue frowned. 'But nothing was stolen. Was it?'

'Perhaps burglary was not the objective. What if someone wanted to threaten him, or give him a scare?' Diana reached into her handbag and retrieved a small leather-bound notebook and pencil. She held the tip to her lip, frowning in concentration. 'The other outstanding issue is how on earth did someone get in without leaving signs of breaking and entry?'

Sue's shoulders sank. 'That one's quite simple, I'm afraid. Spare key under the plant pot.'

Diana was outraged. 'You can't be serious.'

'Afraid so. Under one of the planters by the front door. I noticed it had been moved – the lichen, it was in the wrong place. Moved recently, I'd guess.'

'A key under the plant pot, for a property like that?' Diana shuddered. 'Never mind. Continue.'

Sue shook her head. 'That's all I have, really. That, and the family stuff. The son was arguing with his parents, then there's the daughter that everyone forgot to mention. We overheard them discussing the business, lying low until the dust had settled.' She waved a hand, dismissing the thought. 'You'll have to ask Amy. I'm sure she remembers better than I do.'

The clatter of the front door startled them both, with Diana regaining her composure first. 'Really, Susan.' She tutted. 'You're ever so jumpy these days.'

The chime of giggles filled the hall; not Hannah's girlish twittering, but someone else.

Amy's best friend Rachel came into the kitchen, closely followed by Mike.

'Sorry,' he said. 'I didn't know anyone was home yet.'

'We're almost done,' said Sue. 'Just clearing up a few things.'

Rachel squeezed onto the bench beside Diana. 'Putting the world to rights, are we, ladies?'

Diana closed her notebook and slipped it into her bag. 'Something like that.' She sighed. 'We were just discussing the circumstances of the unfortunate and untimely demise of Peter Gallivan.'

Rachel's smile fell. 'Yes... I was sorry to hear about that. Poor Fiona.'

'Peter Gallivan?' Mike opened a packet of crisps and ate them standing, and Sue couldn't help but think about the floor she had mopped that morning. 'Couldn't have happened to a bigger bastard.'

At Sue's tut, he glanced sideways at Diana, his eyes quickly falling to his feet. 'Excuse my French...'

'Mike,' Sue chided. 'Show some respect.'

He held up one hand, flecks of crisps and salt glistening on his fingertips. 'Sorry. But the man was a... he wasn't a very nice bloke.'

Diana turned to face him. 'An acquaintance of yours, was he?'

Mike shrugged. 'I wouldn't say I *knew* him personally. He kept himself to himself, down at the club.'

'The *club*?' For some reason, Sue got the feeling that Mike was enjoying this.

'Yeah, the golf club. He played most weekends, lording about the place. Never joined in a round with the rest of us mere mortals. Hired his own caddy to carry his gear and everything.'

Recognising a captivated audience at the same time as he spotted the open biscuit tin, Mike slid onto the bench to join them at the table. 'Rumour has it that tax dodging wasn't the worst of his repertoire.'

'What?' Diana couldn't keep the urgency from her voice. 'What else did he do?'

Mike hesitated.

'Go on,' said Sue. 'You might as well tell us now.'

'They said... Well, I mean, I heard.' Mike searched for the words. 'He was... *unfaithful.* Like a serial cheater, or something. But the last one was his downfall, apparently.'

Diana frowned. 'Why?'

'He did it to his friend and business partner.' Mike cringed. 'Rumour has it that Peter Gallivan had an affair with his best mate's wife.'

36

TOM WAS DELIBERATING WHETHER IT WAS ACCEPTABLE TO TAKE the book with him.

In some parts of the world, he had no doubt, it was entirely the done thing. He pictured himself sitting in a piazza somewhere in Italy, sipping an Aperol spritz in the late afternoon sunshine, reading a John Grisham, only glancing up occasionally from the pages to people-watch.

Unfortunately, it was probably not something that folk around here considered reasonable behaviour for a bloke in a pub on a Friday night.

He could see why Sue chose this one. Don't get him wrong, Tom loved a war story as much as the next man – or woman – but this was something else. They'd studied the classics at school and none of this had ever come up. It was a trend, he knew that. Women reclaiming the narrative. *Herstory*. Injecting female perspectives into stories where, for centuries, there had been none.

He placed the book on the side table by his reading chair and left Agnes to her evening rotation of soap operas.

It was starting to get milder, the days stretching longer into the evening, shades of grapefruit and lilac staining the sky. His footsteps echoed rhythmically down the back lane, a percussion against the squat stone cottages, the perfume of salt on the breeze.

This was beginning to feel like a routine, and Tom liked that. *His routine.* There was a comfort in the repetition of faces and places, a succour that almost resembled belonging. He'd been denied it long enough that he could appreciate the beauty of monotony.

He assumed his usual perch at the bar, the seat from which he could observe the door, because some old habits were impossible to break. Gina greeted him with a dull familiarity and although he longed for more, part of him relished the greyness of their exchange. He ordered a glass of wine.

'Have you read the book?'

Confusion flashed behind Gina's eyes, just for a second, before she remembered. 'Oh right, it's next week. I can't believe it's been a month already.'

She gnawed at the inside of her lip as she set his drink down in front of him.

Tom cleared his throat. 'I'm actually rather enjoying it. Wasn't sure that I would. You know, all that rape and pillaging and sacking.' He felt his face growing red, hot. 'Not really my bag...'

Gina mumbled something that sounded like acquiescence, despite not really paying attention.

Never mind.

The man next to him was enormous, his faded Aran jumper holey and threading at the cuffs. Tom tried to make eye contact, preparing to offer a smile and possibly even pass a comment on the weather, but the man didn't take his eyes off his beer. Probably a good thing, on balance. Tom doubted they'd have much in common.

The door opened; the sudden cool draught sent a briny whisper around the crowded bar. Amy and her aunt bundled in, followed by Helen from the gift shop and another woman that Tom didn't know.

She bore an uncanny resemblance to Sue, except her hair was longer and wound up in a chignon on top of her head. Whereas Sue was on the sturdy side, this other woman – who Tom quickly chalked up to be a sister – was a wispy thing, all cheekbones and angles. He could see how skinny she was even from here and despite the flowing layers she was drowning in. A string of Tibetan prayer beads hung around her neck.

They sat at a corner table, none of them noticing Tom at the end of the bar.

He toyed with going over to say 'hello' and felt the familiar anxiety rising in his chest. He closed his eyes and did as Fran had suggested: visualising the encounter in his mind, projecting the conversation like a script in his head. Trying it on for size. Even in his mind's eye, he looked like a prat.

Gina kept glancing at the clock. *Who is she waiting for,* he wondered? He tried to imagine the kind of company she kept. What kind of man it would take to make a girl like that tick?

His question was answered when Carrie breezed in.

––––––

Gina was relieved to see Carrie, even if she was late. But one glance at her friend's face told her something was wrong.

She pulled her into the hallway, out of sight and beyond earshot of the bar. 'What happened?'

'It's Chris, he was—' Her voice cracked.

'Oh, love.' Gina folded Carrie into a hug, mindful of not letting her friend's mascara anywhere near her top. 'It's OK. You're here now.'

Carrie sniffed, desperately trying to compose herself. 'I don't know what to do. It's not his fault, you know? It's the weed. That's what makes him like this.'

Gina said nothing, afraid of what might come out if she opened her mouth.

'He fell asleep, so I just left him there. He'll be fine once he wakes up.'

Gina very much doubted that Chris would ever be 'fine', but the main thing was that Carrie was safe now. 'Come on,' she said. 'Let's get you upstairs.'

Gavin could handle the bar on his own, and she'd have him bring the Chinese up when it arrived.

They turned towards the stairs.

Suddenly, there was the thunderous clatter of the outside door, a crash that echoed through the pub and made the walls shake.

'Where is she?' Chris bellowed into the stunned silence.

At the foot of the stairs, Carrie stiffened, the colour instantly draining from her face. Gina held a finger to her lips and shook her head. Only the strains of Tina Turner on the pub sound system, previously drowned out by chatter, were audible.

Think, think. Blood pounded in Gina's ears as she weighed up her options for damage limitation. The safest bet was to send Carrie upstairs out of harm's way, then deny all knowledge of her whereabouts. Hopefully, they could persuade Chris to go home and sober up.

She pressed the key for her flat into Carrie's palm. 'Go', she mouthed, pointing at the stair door.

Carrie opened it a few inches and edged through.

'I said, *where is she?*'

Gina leaned back against the wall, still hidden in the shadows. *One elephant, two elephant...* She had to give Carrie enough time to get safely up to the flat.

Gavin's voice broke the silence. 'Howay, mate. Come on. Everyone's just out to enjoy the evening. Either take a seat and calm down, or leave.'

His bravado rang hollow.

There was the shuffle of footsteps and a gasp, and when Gavin spoke again, his voice had transformed to a thin strain. Even without looking, Gina knew that Chris had his hands on him.

'Look, I'm sorry, yeah?' Gavin mumbled. 'We don't want any bother.'

'Where is she?' Chris ground the words out through a clenched jaw.

Seven elephant. Eight elephant.

Gina could hear Carrie fumbling with the lock on the landing upstairs.

'You.' Chris's tone was icy cold.

Who's he picking on now? Gina wondered.

'I know you.'

She froze. *Nine elephant. Ten elephant.*

'I... I don't think so.' Tom stuttered.

Oh, god. Not Tom.

'Yeah.' Chris's voice was a sneer. 'And you know my girlfriend.'

Gina stopped counting.

'It's OK,' she said, emerging from the shadow of the stairwell. Hands held up in welcome, surrender. She attempted a reassuring smile at her punters. 'Apologies for the disruption, ladies and gents.' She fixed her stare on Chris. 'Why don't you head home and cool off?'

He lunged at her.

Chris pinned her against the wall before she had time to draw a breath. Strong hands on each of her shoulders immobilised her arms while fear paralysed the rest of her body.

And the humiliation, that's what really stung. In her own bloody pub.

Old Harry Whitefield got up from his seat at the bar, striding towards them. 'I wouldn't do that if I were you—'

'Yeah? Well, you're *not me*,' Chris hissed. His eyes were bloodshot, but there was something about them – a flatness.

Harry persevered. 'Leave her be, lad, or you might end up with something worth crying about.'

Chris laughed. A chuckle before those flat eyes sparked to life. He released Gina and turned his attention to Harry. 'Or what? Eh, old man? What are you going to do about it?'

'Chris!' Carrie appeared at the bottom of the stairs, her eyes wide and wild with fright, and Gina's heart sank.

'Stop it. Now.' Carrie's voice was breathy. Full of air.

Chris licked his lips, a smirk dancing on his mouth. He eyeballed Gina. 'Now that wasn't so hard, was it?'

'You can't do this.' Gina heard the tremor in her voice, as if someone else spoke her words. 'Carrie – stay right where you are. I'm calling the police.'

Carrie was at her shoulder. Their eyes met. 'No need. It's fine, honest.' Her words were flat, cold. Her expression frozen. She shook her head and gave Gina's arm a gentle squeeze. 'I'll ring you tomorrow.'

Chris was already holding the door open. 'Ladies first.' He sneered, without taking his eyes off Gina. Carrie didn't look back.

————

Amy stood and excused herself, sidling up to Gina, who was staring at the door. She placed a tentative hand on Gina's shoulder, feeling the tremble beneath her fingertips.

'Spare a ciggie?'

Amy led Gina outside to the small yard at the back of the pub. The street was already empty, Chris and Carrie's footsteps reduced to an echo on the breeze.

Gina was wide-eyed. 'I don't know what else to do, Amy. I'm at my wits' end.'

Amy exhaled a feather of blue-grey smoke. She'd get a lecture from Mike when she rocked up smelling of cigarettes, but that was a problem for later. 'You should call the police—'

'No,' Gina muttered. 'I can't do that.'

'Carrie might not want to press charges, but you never know. They might be able to help her.'

Gina shook her head. 'I'm scared. I'm scared of losing her.'

Amy understood. Carrie, it was clear, was teetering on the edge of something. The slightest nudge either way could send her plummeting into an abyss.

Even in this light, Amy could see the dark circles beneath Gina's eyes.

'I'm getting desperate.' Gina's voice was small.

'Sleep on it for tonight.' Amy extinguished her cigarette, half-finished, under the toe of her boot. 'Everything will look much better in the morning.'

She wished she could believe that.

37

HELEN LOCKED UP EARLY. SUNDAYS IN MAY WERE STILL QUIET enough, and the tail end of the afternoon especially so, as weekenders raced to get home. Helen could never understand their rush to get back to reality. What she would give for a holiday. Somewhere hot, preferably, where the sand was warm between her toes and everything smelled like coconut, and the sea was the same shade of turquoise as the travel supplements would have you believe.

But when she imagined herself exploring far-flung exotic destinations, it wasn't Roy she pictured at her side.

Yesterday, she had somehow managed to acquire a fifth mirror from Anne's collection. It was like the blooming things were breeding on her shop wall. Anne insisted that she had refined her technique, and this latest offering should be displayed centrally as the cornerstone of the artistic narrative... yaddah yaddah yawn. Helen agreed just to get her on her way.

It had been more than a week since anyone heard from Fiona, and eventually, Sue suggested that they call around to check in on their new friend. Helen hastily signed up.

They were supposed to meet at the shop at four, and Helen spent the last two hours watching the clock.

She had rummaged through her dresser that morning and found an old eyeshadow palette. There was a lipstick, too, long since dried out. Perhaps that was for the best. It wouldn't do to turn up looking like they were ready for a night on the tiles when the woman only just buried her husband.

She thought back to the years after Sue returned. Matthew was just a baby, and Helen was still adjusting to the weight of her new responsibility. She'd wanted him so badly – god knows they'd both waited long enough. And yet... she had struggled to recognise herself in the mirror. A stranger in her own skin. And as much as everyone told her to enjoy those first, precious years, Helen was burdened by a single pervasive thought: *what if this is this all there is?*

The Mortons lived on the coast road, back then, in that big house just a few doors down from where Fiona lived now. Her old friend Sue, with all her education and fancy job and stories that began, 'In Aberdeen...'. Sue, who'd managed to get so far away from here, only to be snapped right back to where she started. Helen had always wondered if she was going to leave again, but here they both were, all these years later.

On cue, Sue appeared at the corner. Helen's shoulders sank when she saw Anne by her side, and she chastised herself for thinking unkind thoughts.

'Right, ladies.' Sue assumed command, rubbing her hands together. 'Ready?'

The green sports car was parked on the road at the bottom of the Gallivans' garden. Other than that, it was impossible to tell if anyone was home. Those windows stared down at them from the imposing façade like accusing eyes.

Sue had baked a cottage pie, despite her blackberry crumble still having elicited no response. At this rate, Fiona would soon possess her entire collection of oven dishes.

Anne stopped halfway along the garden path, her nose held high in the air and her eyes closed. 'I don't like this vibe. So much negativity. Can you feel that?' She looked at Sue and Helen for validation. 'I did bring a rose quartz crystal, just in case—'

'No, Anne.' Sue didn't break her stride. 'I told you, we're not doing that today.'

She pressed down hard on the enamel doorbell, letting the determined chime ring out for a fraction longer than necessary.

The door creaked open, just wide enough for the person behind to see who was calling.

Caitlyn Gallivan looked so much like her mother. The same pixie nose and wide blue eyes. She was fresh-faced, a smattering of freckles sprinkled over her cheekbones, the trademark highlighted hair fixed up in a loose knot. She folded her arms across her chest, cocooning herself in an oversized sweatshirt. 'Can I help you?'

'We're friends of your mother. Is she home?'

'Friends… right.' Caitlyn looked the trio up and down, taking them in. 'I'm afraid she's unavailable. But I'll let her know you called.' She went to close the door.

'Wait—'

Caitlyn hesitated, glowering at Sue.

'When do you think she might be up for visitors?'

'Not for the time being, I'm afraid.' She forced a smile

that almost looked sincere. 'I'm sure she'll be in touch if she wants to see you.'

Sue squared her jaw. If Izzy or Amy ever spoke to one of her friends like this, she would have had words. 'Do you want to take a note that we called, perhaps?'

'Great idea,' sighed Caitlyn. 'Let me just grab a pen.'

She shot a glance over her shoulder, then disappeared back inside, pulling the door to an inch. Sue and Helen exchanged an eye roll.

Anne drifted back down the path, captivated by the vista. It was, Sue realised, almost identical to the sea view from her sister's old house. Seeing the dunes from this perspective must feel like bumping into a long-lost friend.

Sue turned to look back up at the house. You couldn't deny it was incredible what they'd done with the place. Apart from those hideous new windows, of course. Although, who could blame the Gallivans for wanting to keep prying eyes out? They were giant mirrors, reflecting the clouds back down at her.

Although from this angle, without the sun shining on them, they weren't entirely opaque. Almost, but not quite. In one of the rooms upstairs, Sue saw a shadow moving. She couldn't be certain – it was very difficult to see, after all. But it looked like Fiona was waving at her.

38

Out of respect for Peter Gallivan, Sue had quietly postponed last week's book club, rescheduling it for the coming weekend. Now, doing a quick count in her head, she realised they had lost three members in their first month, which was quite a feat.

'We haven't *lost* them.' Amy was clearly growing weary of her histrionics. 'Lucia can't make it because she's going away on a business trip, and Gina has to work.'

She didn't mention Fiona. Or Carrie.

Sue pursed her lips, her face creased in a frown. It was impossible to hide her disappointment. She'd had high hopes for her little club. 'What should we do about Carrie?'

As much as Sue was loath to interfere in someone's private matters, watching that heinous man attack Gina and drag his girlfriend off into the night had been enough to give her nightmares. As the days ticked by, regret started to seep in, remorse superseding her initial anger. Why didn't any of them stop him? Harry Whitefield braved a shot, bless him. But the rest of them? Herself included – they just stood by and watched it unfold, rubberneckers at a car crash.

'Carrie will be OK. And there really wasn't much we could have done – he would have jumped on anybody who got in his way,' Amy said, an edge of sadness to her voice. 'And just to put your mind at ease, I've raised a safeguarding concern through the hospital's system. The police will find some excuse to call on Chris and check up on his girlfriend.'

That did help, thought Sue, as some of the tension in her neck eased.

'Anyway, we're still getting together.' Amy's voice rang with forced cheerfulness. 'Rachel will be there, and Diana, and Tom, I expect.'

'Of course... Tom.' Sue rolled her eyes. 'How could I possibly forget about our friend Tom?' She sat back, pressing a finger to either temple, pushing away the threat of a headache. 'And Diana isn't happy with the reading list, apparently. Says she would prefer less dismantling of the patriarchy and more who-dunnit. Honestly.' She threw her hands in the air. 'I'm not even sure why I bothered.'

The doorbell interrupted her tirade, and Sue glanced out of the bay window to see the lady herself standing on Amy's doorstep. 'Speak of the devil...' she muttered.

'Ready, dears?' Diana was a vision, as ever, in a belted jacket and wool fedora adorned with pheasant feathers. Quite an outfit for the bi-monthly Lifeboat Institute committee meeting.

Sue just hoped they could complete the five-minute car journey without reigniting the debate over her taste in books.

It was a pleasant afternoon, and if Sue got a lift, she would have just enough time for a stroll along the seafront before she had to collect Lucas and Betsy. Helen's son Matthew had shown them how to count their steps on their mobile phones. Apparently, you were supposed to do ten thousand steps a day and although Sue didn't always hit the target, she had lost slightly more than a stone since they started.

Amy pulled into the harbour carpark opposite the RNLI centre. A mild breeze puffed white clouds across a cornflower sky. Sue got out of the car and closed her eyes, feeling the warmth of the sun on her eyelids.

'Eurgh,' Diana harrumphed, albeit quietly. 'Look who the cat dragged in.'

Sue followed the direction of her gaze to see Chris ambling along the coast road towards them, his thuggish gait unnaturally wide for his thin limbs.

He spotted the three of them staring and a smirk smeared across his face.

Sue locked eyes with him. *What a hideous man.* The embodiment of so much that was wrong with the world. Something inside her hardened. A little stone in the pit of her stomach. As Chris drew closer and those pale, scowling eyes bored into her, the stone grew. Emboldened her.

She took a step towards him, still holding his stare.

'Auntie Sue...' Amy sounded far away.

Her unwillingness to wilt enraged him; Sue saw the anger flash behind his eyes. He was close enough now that she could see the pockmarks on his cheeks, the silver-pink thread of a scar running through his left eyebrow. Her heart fluttered, a panicked pounding in her chest, but still, she did not bend. It was about time someone stood up to him, and it turned out, she realised, that *someone* was her.

He stopped in front of her, too close to be friendly. 'You got a problem there?'

Sue felt the heat of his breath. She could smell him: sweat and dirt and cigarette smoke. He was half a head taller than her, and she drew herself up straighter. That stone inside her stomach was molten, red-hot lava, ignited by a spark that she thought was long extinguished.

She felt truly herself in that moment. Not this fifty-three-year-old who had dreamed and loved and lost it all, but who she was before all of that. That girl with a fire in her belly, whose ideas were too big for a sleepy fishing village and who refused to force herself to fit. She wasn't scared of a stupid boy any more than she was scared of small-town mentality and this time, she wouldn't run away.

Her voice came from nowhere and everywhere. 'Actually, I do have a problem.'

Without thinking, she squared up to him, leaving little more than a fist between their faces. Her heart fluttered like a trapped bird, its wings beating against the cage of her chest.

She steeled her eyes on his and when she spoke, her words were clear and unwavering. 'I have a problem with men like you. Men who think they *own* women. Men who abuse and manipulate and control the people they claim to love.'

His hand twitched at his side, his fingers reflexively curling into a fist.

And still, she carried on. 'But make no mistake: one day, lad, you'll get what's coming to you.'

There was a second – an eternity – in which she anticipated a blow, a jab, a slap. She was ready for the pain, yet braced herself for a hit that could not and would not hurt her.

His lips moved as if to retort, but the words – any words – evaded him. Instead, he scoffed, a laugh that rang false under the weight of too much effort and landed somewhere close to incredulity.

Sue planted her feet into the ground and pressed her hands firmly to her hips, solidifying her frame.

Chris blinked first, suddenly less certain of himself. He threw a glare from Amy to Diana and back to Sue, his lip contorted in disgust for good measure, and started to walk away – glancing back twice, the sneer undiminished.

'Christ, Auntie Sue,' said Amy with a heavy exhale, a whoosh of air. 'Where did that come from?'

Sue was too numb to answer. Inside her chest, the cage bars had disappeared, and the once-trapped bird soared high on a warm sea breeze.

39

WELL, WELL, WELL, THOUGHT DIANA. SHE DID NOT SEE THAT coming.

Sue Palmer, of all people. It just went to show... well, what did it show? That people can change? Or that we never truly know them in the first place?

If decades of teaching in an all-girls school taught her anything, besides her ability to spot a liar at twenty paces, it was how to judge a character.

Over the years, she had fine-tuned her process for wheedling out the bullies, the ne'er-do-wells, and other less-than-desirable types, to the point that she could pick them out of a line-up with her eyes closed. From the first day of each new school year, Diana knew who would get the best exam marks, who would make the hockey team, and who was most likely to be caught *in flagrante* with one of the boys from the grammar school a mile away. She was rarely wrong.

The ringleaders were the easiest to spot. The popular girls, usually quick to appoint a trusty second-in-command and attract a small herd of followers. Then the rebels – even if they didn't know it yet themselves. Diana saw something in those girls that, eventually, made them tick. Bullies, if spotted early enough, could be crushed before they had a chance to cause any lasting damage. And the wallflowers, the girls who would spend adulthood looking back on *the best years of their lives* and thanking providence that they survived them.

Identifying the personalities, the groups and the extremes – this was always Diana's priority. Establishing the pecking order early on was the critical foundation of a successful term.

The first-year Sue Palmer had stood out for all the right reasons. From Diana's point of view, at least. She challenged leadership, asked intelligent questions that others dared not to, and fought for what she believed.

They did their best to hammer it out of her, of course – that was the way of teachers, back then. Mould students into disciplined, regimented beings, capable of following a structure and sticking to it. Diana remembered with glee how their attempts at stifling Sue bore little fruit. The girl eventually headed off to pursue a career in science without so much as a glance back at St Helen's, and Diana had – much to her chagrin – all but forgotten her. It wasn't until more than twenty years later, when she started to become concerned about Izzy and Amy Morton, that she remembered their aunt.

How sad, Diana thought, that Sue had been forced to forsake it all.

She tuned out the droning discussion of the Lifeboat Institute meeting. They were at the accounts now – always her least-preferred part of the committee. Yes, it was critical, life-saving work, but her energy levels were depleting, her enthusiasm waning with them. At least her age absolved her of any expectation of playing an active role, should she prefer to take a back seat. Better to let the younger ones run the show. She caught the eye of Richard Pringle, the young headmaster at North Sunderland, and smiled sweetly.

Sue Palmer, eh. There was still some fire in the old girl, after all. Had it always been burning, invisible to the naked eye? Or had someone struck a match, unaware of the gunpowder that lay beneath the surface?

She glanced at the clock, willing the meeting to finish and expending a disproportionate amount of energy on simply keeping her eyes open. Sandra had not only given her a lift to Amy's but offered to collect her afterwards and take her home, feigning some excuse to be in Seahouses on a Tuesday evening. Diana had been too weary to do anything but accept. As much as she was determined to keep driving until the DVLA ripped her license from her hand, even she had to admit that sometimes, these days, she found herself too tired to make the journey safely.

Your problem is that you're just too stubborn, Lionel had been fond of saying. Unfortunately, it was a trait that Sandra had inherited, and they frequently locked antlers over Diana's determination to preserve her independence. She liked to think that it came from a place of love, but with Sandra, she wasn't always certain.

Richard Pringle's voice brought her back to the room, and the mist of her wandering mind evaporated.

'Diana? Anything to add?' His eyes flashed with kindness, and he spoke just a little slower than was necessary, as if she was one of his primary school pupils. 'We're just checking if anyone has any other business?'

She folded her hands in her lap, doing her best to pretend that she understood exactly where they were at in the agenda. 'Nothing from me, dear.'

They wrapped up twenty minutes early – and Sandra wouldn't be here until ten past.

Following any other RNLI committee meeting, Diana would sit and chat to Clifford Groves, the helm, whose wife occasionally baked shortbread just for her. Amy once called him *a silver fox,* hiding her giggle behind a hand. Diana could see past the matinee idol good looks and was far more interested in the daring tales of sea rescue – Hollywood sagas themselves. But not tonight. Something was troubling her.

From here, the Gallivan house was only a short walk away. What harm could it do to pay a visit?

Diana tugged her collar up as high as it would reach, pulling it tightly against the southerly gust which had picked up considerably since the early afternoon.

The wind on this stretch of the coast was pernickety, seemingly changing direction and speed any time it pleased. This afternoon's breeze of warm, dry air rolling over from the Cheviots had been displaced by an icy draught which coiled down from the North Sea, whipping the surf into an agitated fervour.

She pulled the garden gate closed behind her and paused for a moment at the bottom of the path. From here, there was no sign of life at the Gallivan house.

After Lionel passed away, she'd wanted nothing more than to shut herself off from the glare of the world and hide in that sacred space where everything she saw and smelled and touched reminded her of him. She would have quite happily crawled into their bed and stayed there forever, inhaling the memory of him from the pillow. But her daughters, Sandra and

Jennifer, flung open the curtains, fed her, forced her to dress and walk outside. Forced her to see that grief is hour by hour, day by day, and week by week, until life inexplicably continues.

But that, she felt with a growing conviction, was not the case here. Those Gallivans were far from the family in mourning. What on earth were they up to?

On the threshold, Diana raised a finger to the doorbell, then hesitated. She could see now the urn that Sue had mentioned, and indeed, the lichen was clustered together, scaling the side facing south. *A spare key left outside for a home like this.* Diana tutted, shaking her head. A pot of lavender caught her eye, an overweight bee dancing among fat buds of blossom. Its scent was heady, and the fragrance almost masked the smell of something else. She inhaled deeply, and it hit the back of her throat.

Burning.

The smell of smoke made her heart flutter. From somewhere close by, she heard voices.

Not from inside the house, but round the back of the property.

Well, thought Diana, *it's only proper to check.* After a cursory glance over her shoulder, she stepped off the path and onto the lawn, following the wall of the house around to the right. She would never admit it, not even to herself, but her toes tingled with anticipation.

Diana rounded the annex and hesitated at the corner. The old garden had been re-landscaped and from here, she could make out the edge of a newly paved terrace. From above the building, a narrow column of smoke snaked skyward. The voices were sharper and clearer than before. She crept as close as she dared, taking care to move as quietly as a mouse.

Ben's voice was the first she could clearly determine. 'I can't. I can't do it and I won't. End of story.'

'Darling.' Fiona sighed, exasperated. 'It's hard, I know. We all know you don't want this right now. But it's our legacy. *Your* legacy.'

'No, it's not. It was *his*. I want nothing to do with any of it, with any of him. You should just sell, take the money and let's leave it all behind us.'

'This is your future.' Less frustrated now. Pleading. 'All the mistakes he made – now you can put them right. It's our second chance.'

Ben laughed, dry and forced. 'No, Mum. This is *your* second chance. I'm done. Understand? *Finito.*'

Diana pressed her back against the wall as the silence hung there between mother and son.

When Ben spoke again, his tone was conciliatory. 'Sell up now. The share price is high, and we won't get another deal like this. I don't understand—'

'Of course you don't understand.' Fiona snapped. 'But just think for one second about how much *I've* sacrificed. What all this has cost *me*. Money, it's—' Diana heard her frustration as she searched for the word. 'It's not everything. It's not even close.'

'Easy for you to say...' Ben mumbled.

'Forget about that now,' she said dismissively. 'That was what *he* did. That was how he kept us all right where he wanted us. But those days are over. It will be different now. You'll see.'

'And what about Lou? You think he'll just roll over and accept it if I step in and take over?'

'With all due respect to Lou, it's not his company. It's ours.'

Ben sighed, possibly mulling this over. There was the click of a latch and the sweeping sound of a door opening.

'Gorgeous evening for a bonfire. Need a hand?'

Caitlyn. Diana pictured her as she was in the church, glowering at her and Lucia. The silence went on for a moment too long to not be awkward.

'Well, don't stop on my account.'

'Can you help her understand?' Ben asked. 'Help me convince her that we're better off just walking away?'

A tut. 'I'm right here, you know,' Fiona huffed.

There was the sound of a chair scraping back, iron on stone. Caitlyn making herself comfortable. 'I don't know, Benny-boy. Can't see yourself as CEO, is that it?'

'Caitlyn,' he growled. 'This is serious.'

'Well, since you ask...' Caitlyn purred. 'In my opinion – as humble as that may be – I'd forget about it. Forget legacy, forget redemption. Did Dad ever think of those things?' She laughed. 'Can either of you tell me the last time he was thinking about any of *us*?' A pause. 'Thought as much. So, yes. If it were up to me, I'd burn the whole lot of it to the ground.'

The flower beds on this side of the garden had been replanted and were already blooming. From here, Diana could smell more than she could see. Suddenly, something tickled at her nose – pollen, or cold air – whatever caused it, it caught her off-guard. Her chest burned as her eyes began to stream, and Diana fought against it to no avail.

She sneezed – not a quiet snuffle that she could catch in her handkerchief, but a full-blown chest sneeze, deep enough to make her throat hurt.

There was a pause, then Fiona spoke. 'Did you—'

Caitlyn interrupted her with a hiss. 'Shh. Quiet.'

. . .

Diana couldn't outrun them – at her age, such things were sadly no longer an option. Better to adapt the plan than to embarrass herself by making a mad dash for it.

'Hello?' she called out, adding a quivering inflection to her voice. 'Is anybody home?' She trundled into the back garden, emerging from her hiding place with a well-rehearsed waddle that instantly added a decade.

Diana pretended not to notice the three Gallivans trade glances – the unspoken discussion that families can conduct using only their eyes. At least Fiona had the manners to appear somewhat pleased to see her.

Caitlyn, meanwhile, exuded her usual glacial chill. 'I'm sorry, but I didn't realise we were expecting company.'

Diana eased herself into the seat next to Fiona. 'Diana Wheeler. I'm a friend of your mother's. I rang the doorbell, but no one answered. I was about to leave and then I heard voices.'

Caitlyn scowled. 'I didn't hear the bell.'

Diana held up a hand, waving away her concerns. 'That's perfectly all right, dear.' She turned to Fiona, pressing a hand on hers. 'And how are you?'

'Well,' said Fiona, her voice small. 'It hasn't been easy.'

Diana nodded sagely. 'I can only imagine. It must have been a terrible shock. To lose him at such a young age!' She nodded towards Ben and Caitlyn. 'My most profound condolences to you all.'

'You were at the funeral,' Caitlyn stated, no hint of a question in her voice. 'I recognise you.'

Diana shifted in her seat. 'Yes, dear. I did call to pay my respects. As one of the most senior members of St Cuthbert's, the wellbeing of our parishioners is an obligation that I take very seriously.'

In truth, Diana only ever made it to church a couple of

times each year. She prayed none of the Gallivans would think to name-drop her to the vicar, whose name she now struggled to remember. 'The reverend often asks me to check in on families who have lost loved ones.'

Thankfully, this seemed to placate Caitlyn.

The fire had burned down to its embers and Ben prodded it with an iron, revealing the charred remnants of what looked like a stack of papers.

'Having a clear out, were you?' Diana's gaze snagged on Caitlyn's steely regard and she realised, too late, that she might have overstepped the mark.

'A small de-clutter,' said Fiona. 'Just some of the paper-work from the renovation. I'm the most terrible hoarder, and Ben can't stand mess!' She looked at him and smiled. 'He's such a good boy, always thinking of his mother.' The smile didn't reach her eyes.

Diana nodded. 'They say it can help the healing process.'

She wasn't entirely sure that they said anything of the sort, but she could feel the suspicion radiating from Caitlyn, who continued to glare at her.

'As I'm sure you can appreciate, we're getting through this very difficult time together as a family, so unless there's anything else...?'

From the corner of her eye, Diana saw Fiona shift uncomfortably in her seat. Quite rightly so, she thought. This Caitlyn was a piece of work.

'You are absolutely right, my dear. I had better make a move.' Diana stood to leave. 'However, nature calls. Ben, could you kindly escort me?'

He glanced at his mother, who gave a barely perceptible nod.

'Thanks for stopping by,' Fiona said with a weak smile.

There was something in Fiona's expression. Something like regret. Diana had the impression that if it was up to her, Fiona would have rather enjoyed an extended visit. But why wasn't it up to her? This was her house. What was going on here?

Ben showed her to the cloakroom, as he called it, and retreated to the polite distance of the kitchen. When Diana reappeared, he was sitting at the central bar, hunched over and jabbing at his mobile phone.

'Is that Lucia that you're texting?'

Ben's eyes widened at the mention of her name, and he cast his gaze down, a faint blush blooming on his cheeks. *So it was.*

'She mentioned the wonderful evening the two of you spent together.' Diana chuckled. 'I hope she'll forgive me for saying so, but I do hope you will...' What was the phrase they used these days? *Become an item?* It sounded like one of those ghastly movies that Sandra insisted on watching. '...continue to enjoy one another's company.'

They walked into the hallway and ground to an impasse, Ben inching towards the door, Diana fixed firmly and in no particular rush.

She beamed at him. 'I say, there's something different.' She held a finger to her lip, feigning profound concentration. 'The vase.' She pointed to the empty space where it had stood. 'Yes, that's it – there was a vase here, the first time I visited. A beautiful old piece.'

She blinked up at Ben. 'Did your mother move it, perhaps?'

The blush worsened, his cheeks reddening.

'Actually, it was me.' He massaged the back of his neck. 'I knocked it over the other day. Smashed it into smithereens. An accident. Obviously.' His laugh was uneasy.

'What a pity. Although it's understandable that you were so distracted, dear boy. Grief can make one quite clumsy.'

A voice made them both jump. 'Are you still here?'

Caitlyn had appeared in the hallway, leaning against the wall, arms folded across her chest.

'Cait!' Ben spat, throwing her a frown.

Unperturbed, she slinked towards them, her eyes never leaving Diana's. 'Forgive me, but are you always this *curious*?' Caitlyn rolled the word in her mouth, giving it a new meaning.

'I'd better be off,' Diana said, as if this thought had just occurred to her.

Caitlyn opened the door, hip jutted to an angle, her jaw set. Saying nothing.

On the doorstep, Diana paused, glancing back at Caitlyn and Ben. 'Do take care of each other and let me know if there's anything at all I can—'

Caitlyn closed the front door, cutting her off.

Diana walked down the garden path towards the sea, silently seething. Money might buy many things, but no price could be put on the value of good manners.

Ben's response to her question about the fate of the vase was interesting. Diana had encountered many accomplished liars in her time, and Ben Gallivan was not one of them. Who was he covering for?

And Caitlyn. Was she keeping the world from her mother, or keeping her mother from the world?

40

HE WAS SUCH AN IDIOT. EACH AND EVERY TIME HE WAS ON TO a good thing, Ben messed it up. Guaranteed.

Even with his mother practically holding his hand and walking him through it step-by-step, he still managed to screw it up. He was an abject failure. Plain and simple. Perhaps Dad was right all along.

He still couldn't get over the way he'd poured his heart out to Lucia. He'd been so full on, so needy. *So unlike him.* Every time he remembered it, he grimaced, his stomach curdling at the memory. Baring his soul, telling her stuff that he hadn't even told his therapist.

Fair enough, Mum paid for Zizi, the therapist, and for all her promises of patient confidentiality, Ben never had complete faith in her not to report back to whoever picked up the bill.

But Lucia. What was it about her? She hadn't even had to coax him. Not in the way his ex, Tammy, had nagged at him to *share his feelings,* as if they were on a reality TV show. Or Lysette, the hot Australian lawyer he dated for three months before she broke things off with him, who told him he needed to open up and *let her in*.

Ben winced.

If only he hadn't had that stupid row with Dad. That's where it all went wrong.

He'd stormed out of his parents' place and driven straight back to Jesmond, seeing red. Ignoring Zizi's warning ringing in his ears, he had WhatsApped the familiar numbers in his address book until someone gave him the answer he wanted. He hadn't had to wait long for his delivery to arrive.

There had been a moment – mere seconds, perhaps – when he questioned whether he really wanted to do this, but old habits die hard. The prospect of release was seductive, and before Ben knew it, he had snorted his way through £120 of coke, sank the best part of a bottle of scotch, and lost a day of his life. They called it a blackout. An entire twenty-four hours, forgotten to darkness.

Was the row with Dad even that bad, or had he been looking for any excuse? Sure, the old man had hurled a few spiteful comments, but when didn't he do that?

Zizi had spoken before about self-sabotage; when someone subconsciously indulges in thoughts and behaviours that drive them away from their goals. Ben thought it was rubbish, mostly, but if Zizi was ever looking for proof...

It was almost poetic, in a way, that when his father died, Ben was wasted. When the call came to tell him the old man had snuffed it, Ben was sleeping it off. He woke up in a bed that didn't belong to him with zero recollection of how he got there, his head full of questions that, even now, he still wasn't able to answer.

Because this was what Ben did: he messed up. Only this time, he had made things ten times worse for himself. He'd managed to screw up a good thing with the most perfect woman he had ever met, before it had even got off the ground.

Lucia deserved better. His mum might not see it, but Lucia was on another level, and it sat way, way above him.

Of course, Caitlyn saw it differently. *She would.* She'd spotted Lucia at the back of the church during Dad's funeral and hissed to Ben, one eyebrow raised, realising right away that it was probably *one of his lady friends.* Caitlyn never had the time of day for any of the girls Ben liked. According to her, they were only ever interested in him because of his money – which was why they left so quickly when they learned he didn't have any.

Mum wanted to change all of that. Plant the son in the same spot as the father had once stood.

If only it was that simple.

He understood where she was coming from. Of course he did. She wanted her old life back, or as close to it as she could get, and this was the easiest way. Poor Mum. After everything that went down with Lou and Esme, she had a point to prove. Ben wished she could care as little as he did.

He wished he could remember that night. It turned out they called it a blackout for a good reason.

Each morning of that week, he went for a jog along the coast road, trying to get everything straight in his head. 'Clear your mind', Zizi had taught him. 'That's how you focus – by not thinking of anything.' Ben listened to the rhythm of his feet against the ground, the beat of his heart in his chest and the whorl of the wind in his ears, but when he closed his eyes, all he saw was Lucia.

They'd been texting after that weekend, at first. Every time his phone pinged, his heart leapt. But the mortification of what he'd done started to get to him. The worst part was the blank space where his memory should be. It eroded his insides, eating at him like acid.

He had almost given up on her until that old lady had mentioned her name. Diana Wheeler. Mum met her through a book club, of all things. Apparently, the same place she met Lucia.

Ben was pretty sure it was now Officially Too Late to call her. Wasn't it? What could he possibly say to her now?

He could apologise and blame his lack of communication on his dad's death – tell Lucia that he got overwhelmed by the grief, in being there for his mother, in the administrative tasks of the multi-million-pound company he had inherited. It wasn't like that would impress her. Caitlyn was wrong. Lucia wasn't like the others.

Or he could tell her the truth – that shame and guilt were eating him alive. That it proved she was too good for him.

That his little bender and subsequent blackout could have been just the tip of a very long downward spiral had he not woken up on Monday afternoon to the news that his father was dead and the nightmare, at last, was over.

41

CARRIE SLOSHED A FINAL SQUIRT OF BLEACH INTO THE TOILET.
The Victoria Hotel in Bamburgh had been almost at full
occupancy, and there were only the three of them to clean
all the rooms. She took a second to catch her breath. A
rivulet of sweat trickled between her shoulder blades.

Margaret and Brenda were already loading up the van. It
was Thursday, which meant they had a list of houses and
flats to clean this afternoon before the influx of weekenders.
B&Bs with magnolia walls and signs that pointed 'To the
beach'. Generic IKEA bedspreads and framed prints that
said 'Live, Laugh, Love.' They'd be back on Monday to do it
all over again.

Brenda drove the van and Margaret ticked off the
addresses from the spreadsheet. As the youngest, fittest, and
the lowest in the pecking order, it was understood that
Carrie would pick up most of the slack caused by Cath
pulling a sickie that morning. That was fine. She could
simply lose herself in her thoughts.

The job required nothing more mentally demanding
than going through the motions. Dirty bedding off, bins out,

dust, polish, clean the bathroom, new towels in, new bedding on, vac. Step by step, that way you don't forget anything. Repeat, repeat, repeat. You only score points if you can do it faster. Don't overthink it.

No one grew up wanting to be a cleaner. Carrie could see now that she probably should have stuck at college, but the hairdressing course had been hard work and she'd hated their tutor, Amanda. That stupid bitch, with her nice car and fancy nails and snotty-nosed attitude.

Auntie Pat tried to convince her to stick at it, but she knew she would have failed, in the end. It wasn't really about the money, or the time, or how dry her hands got – and the irony of that struck her every time she put them into a bucket of sudsy bleach water now. It wasn't about any of the excuses she offered when she finally quit. It was that deep down, she understood that hairdressing would be just another thing she was shit at. Snob-arse Amanda knew it already. Why waste everyone's time?

Cleaning – well, you could hardly be bad at cleaning, could you? Carrie didn't mind the monotony, and there was a peculiar satisfaction in shining up a bathroom, scouring an oven dish, transforming a space. Putting everything back to the way it was meant to be.

Last summer, Gina offered her a job behind the bar. She needed the extra help, apparently.

Carrie's gaze had drifted across the rows of bottles, labels with names and words that were foreign to her. All those drinks that you'd have to remember... As if she could see what Carrie was thinking, Gina promised her that it was easier than it looked, and that she'd know it like the back of her hand within a few weeks. Carrie had hesitated.

'You're a smart lass', Gina said. 'You'll get it quickly enough.'

No one had ever told Carrie she was smart.

She mulled it over for a week, trying to picture herself pulling pints. According to Gina, you sometimes got tips, and they would be hers to keep. It was more glamourous than cleaning. Well, that wasn't hard, she supposed.

She'd even started to think about giving Brenda her notice. But when she mentioned it to Chris, something flared behind his eyes. He shook it off before it could take hold, but it was too late. She had seen it – a storm cloud blowing back out to sea as quickly as it had blown in.

They had only been going out for a few months back then, but they were already talking about moving in together. His caravan was big enough for them both, and it would save Carrie getting the bus every day.

It was blissful, in the beginning. Carrie spent a week's wages on new bedding, cushions, and picture frames that Chris hung on the walls. Their own little place, and in many ways, the home she'd never had. She even started saving up for a wedding dress. Imagining what their kids would look like.

Thankfully, they were able to stay there after Chris got the sack from the caravan park. Owen, the manager, already had Chris on a final warning when he caught him smoking weed behind the club house. And suddenly it fell on Carrie to pay the rent, and she didn't manage to save much after all.

A storm cloud. That was accurate. Chris's moods could go from golden sunshine – the kind of weather that warms your soul and makes you feel satisfyingly sleepy – to dark and thunderous in minutes.

She never took the job at the pub. It took Gina a while to stop nagging her about it and hire Gavin instead.

Carrie was the captain of a ship, sailing through waters that could turn before you even saw it coming. All she could do was close her eyes, keep her hands steady on the keel, and wait until the sun broke through the clouds once more.

Getting sacked from his job at the caravan park had been a massive blow to Chris. Carrie had read something about men losing their self-esteem. It was one of those stupid agony aunt letters, in a glossy left behind in a bedroom by someone who could afford to pay £2.99 for a bloody magazine. *Self-esteem.* How much you value yourself. They offered clues – a checklist of things to look for in someone who might be struggling.

Yes, she thought, as she ticked them off, one-by-one. *That sounds just like Chris.* She threw the magazine in the recycling.

Before he lost his job, he only ever smoked weed at night. As time went on, Carrie got used to getting home mid-afternoon and finding him stoned, even after he found another job.

It wasn't his fault. It was his low self-esteem. Paranoia.

As if by giving him labels, she might figure out a way to fix him.

She fingered the necklace he had given her, clutching the tiny gem between her fingertips. By now, she knew every curve and spike of the claw that held the small jewel in place. An apology present, for that time with the stupid book club that she hadn't even wanted to go to in the first place.

She struggled to work out why he was saying sorry for that time specifically, when there had been so many others. Perhaps they had all just rolled into one at this point.

It wasn't his fault.

Carrie knew exactly what Gina thought of Chris. Carrie might not have been the brightest bulb on the Christmas tree, but she was by no means a complete idiot. She saw the way her friend's jaw tightened when Chris came to meet her from work, the way Gina sneered at him like he was something she had stepped in.

But who was Gina to judge? A woman who owned a car and had enough money that she didn't incessantly worry about making ends meet come the end of the month. Who never had to time her showers or wear three jumpers because she couldn't afford the gas bill. Who had parents that not only gave a shit but actually had money to give her, if she ever needed it. Gina had a security blanket, a life-raft. When Carrie looked down, all she saw was the black and bottomless sea. How could Gina ever understand what it was like for lost souls like her and Chris?

Brenda counted out the wages – there was extra for today, because Cath had gone AWOL and her share was split between the three of them. That meant £270 for the week. Not bad.

Chris was better at maths than she was and could always work out how much Carrie should be getting, just in case Brenda ever tried to short-change her. But he didn't know that Cath hadn't turned up today.

Carrie tried to do the arithmetic in her head, her hairline sticky with the exertion of the calculation as much as the physical demands of the work.

'Can I see that a second?' she asked Brenda, her voice small, gesturing to the time sheet.

Brenda raised an eyebrow but said nothing, handing her the clipboard.

Carrie squinted in concentration, her brow knotting as she read the list of numbers, the crossed-out line that represented Cath's absence.

'Twenty-five quid, love.'

Carrie looked up. 'Sorry?'

'Twenty-five quid extra from today.' Brenda sighed. 'It should be fifteen, but I've taken a fiver each from mine and Margaret's, seeing as you did all the hard graft. Don't spend it all at once, mind you.'

Twenty-five quid.

There was an old biscuit tin under the sofa where she kept sewing supplies – what little she had, at least. Auntie Pat had insisted on teaching Carrie and her foster sister Michaela how to darn socks and re-attach buttons, claiming it would save the girls a fortune later in life. She'd been right, of course. Auntie Pat had been right about so many things.

Later that night, as soon as Chris was in the shower, she would slip the extra cash into the tin. She already had almost two hundred pounds in there. If Chris ever found it, she would tell him she was going to tell him she'd been saving for a holiday.

What was she actually saving for? A rainy day? A life-raft of her own?

Her heart raced, a pulse throbbing at her temple.

They dropped Margaret off first and Carrie moved across to the window, the seat warm from Margaret's back-side. She could smell herself – stale, her skin sour. With her head resting on the window, she let the vibrations of the engine rumble through her, soothing her tired muscles.

Brenda swung the van into the caravan park.

'I guess this is me.' Carrie hopped down to the gravel.

The sea was dimpled with waves, not high enough, she imagined, to satisfy the few surfers that had ventured out from Bamburgh. Two layers of cloud stretched towards the north, as fluffy as the whipped cream Auntie Pat put on her Sunday trifles. Carrie's stomach clenched. She really should go to see her.

'Chris?' she called out as she entered, stretching over the top step that sagged in the middle. The caravan reeked of weed.

Chris was asleep on the sofa, sitting upright with his head lolling back over the headrest. The curtains were drawn, casting a gloom in the cramped space.

For god's sake.

He was meant to be at work this afternoon, and she wondered if he had just sat here and smoked instead.

'Chris,' she said, more forcefully now.

He still didn't move.

She took a tentative step towards him. It couldn't be comfortable sleeping like that. His neck was skewed at an angle that made her ache just looking at it, his Adam's apple pointing awkwardly towards the ceiling.

She took another step, close enough now to see his face. His eyes were open, bulging. Staring into heaven.

There was a scream, a guttural howl, and Carrie was on her knees before she realised that the noise was coming from her.

42

IZZY HAD MISSED THEIR WEEKLY CALL AGAIN. *HONESTLY,* thought Amy. *What is the point in having a standing appointment if one of you always stands the other up?*

She opened Instagram on her phone. Izzy's name was already at the top of her feed. By the looks of things, Thursday had been a big night for her sister in Hong Kong.

Never mind. The weekend was almost here, Mike was on his way home, and the weather forecast was promising. All the prep for their dinner of beef and pea jelly with cauliflower bake – two of her own recipes – was already done. She had just enough time for a run before chaos descended, along with Mum and Auntie Sue.

At the top of the harbour, she stopped, the sound of a siren snagging on the breeze. She listened, tuning in to the noise. An ambulance, followed by a police car.

The noise stopped abruptly, signalling the crews had reached their destination. Amy thought of changing direction and heading towards them, but there wasn't a lot she could contribute to a team of paramedics.

She turned and ran on towards Bamburgh Castle. It took

several paces to find her stride again. She couldn't help it. The question was already turning in her mind: *who was it?*

Back at home, Amy stood under a blisteringly hot shower that left her skin pink and glowing. With her hair wrapped in a towel, she applied some of the face oil that the kids bought her for Mother's Day, considering her reflection in the mirror. Some days, she barely recognised the woman who looked back at her. She traced the web of fine lines that had appeared at the sides of her eyes. Evidence of a life well-lived.

Down below, the front door clattered open, and the hallway filled with the chatter and footsteps of Betsy, Lucas and Hannah, ably shepherded by Auntie Sue. Amy glanced at her watch – Mike should have been home by now. Inwardly, she rolled her eyes. It was funny how his views about how much time she should spend at home did not apply to him.

'Mummy!' Betsy burrowed her face into Amy's thigh, Lucas not far behind his little sister. Amy bent to Hannah's head. Too cool for such babyish nonsense at twelve years old. She breathed deeply, inhaling the scent of her first born as she planted a kiss at the top of her forehead.

She checked her phone. Rachel was on duty this afternoon, and Amy had sent her a message to ask if the ambulance call-out was anyone they knew. There was no reply. She wondered again: who was it, and what had happened?

43

It was strange, looking back at old photos. The black and white images captured a moment in time that, in Diana's mind, remained vivid technicolour.

Sandra had insisted that leaving personal items in a holiday rental was strictly a no-go, but for Diana, the framed memories of her and Lionel were as much a part of Puffin Cottage as the foundation stones.

Lucia had called her, asking if she could pay that month's rent in advance because she was leaving for a few days. A *work trip*, she said. Diana was still itching to know precisely what line of so-called *work* this young lady was in. Time would tell, she was sure. Secrets, she had learned, rarely remained hidden forever.

For now, she was quite distracted by another mystery entirely. What was going on with those Gallivans? That ghastly daughter and the charming – albeit feckless – son were definitely up to something. Hiding their mother away like that, a bonfire of paperwork and all that hushed talk of selling the company and finding redemption. Diana never required much excuse to visit Puffin Cottage, and the prospect of picking Lucia's brains had been more than the temptation she needed.

A photograph on the chimney breast caught her eye – her and Lionel at a correspondent's dinner in London, some award or other. He didn't win, but that didn't matter. Rarely did regional newspapers like The Chronicle ever receive the grand accolades. They were happy just to be invited.

That evening came to her as if it was yesterday. Those wide glasses of champagne, the borrowed shoes that pinched her toes, the jazz band playing until the early hours under a fug of cigarette smoke. Lionel pulling her close to him, spinning her, dancing until they were giddy and panting for breath.

For a moment, she quite forgot Lucia was there.

'I love this one.' Lucia pointed to a picture of the façade of Puffin Cottage, a young Diana and Lionel standing on either side of the newly painted door. Three years after their wedding and just a few weeks pregnant. The stone doorstep sagged in the middle, worn smooth by centuries of feet crossing the threshold. From the angle of the camera, it looked just like a smile.

'Young love.' Diana shook her head. 'Nothing but a memory for me now, dear.' She sat in the armchair, making herself at home. It was her home, after all, and Lionel used to say that people were always more willing to talk once comfortably seated. Lucia perched at the edge of the sofa, mirroring her.

'And what of your young gentleman friend? Any word?'

Lucia's shoulders sank. 'I'm afraid not. But you know, with his dad passing away...'

'Give it time, my dear. Grief... it can put anyone out of sorts.'

The younger woman nodded, absorbing this advice.

'You could call him, you know,' Diana said. 'I may be old-fashioned, but even I understand the rules of the game have changed. Just check in with him, see how he's coping.'

———

The old lady was right. Lucia knew it. As soon as she got back from Kuala Lumpur next week, she would text Ben.

She escorted Diana out of the cottage and back to her car, opening the door for her. From close by, there was the sound of sirens. The two of them paused for a second, looking in the direction of the noise. Diana's face lit up, her eyes flashing with something that Lucia could swear might pass for excitement.

'Safe travels, dear girl. I shall look forward to hearing all about your trip on your return.'

Lucia waved her off, the car zipping down the back lane towards the main road faster than Lucia might have expected Diana to drive.

She wondered if she might be imagining things, and second-guessed herself before the realisation sank in.

Diana wasn't in a hurry to get home that afternoon. She was heading directly towards the drama.

44

HE CAME TO HER THAT NIGHT. GINA HADN'T SEEN HIM IN MORE than twenty years and suddenly, there he was.

That face that she had tried so hard to erase from her mind until one day it vanished, just a blur, features indistinguishable. Now he was back, as clear as day, just as he had been the last time she saw him.

Tony.

She tossed and turned, fighting the nightmare, pulling herself up but unable to break the surface, the current pulling her back down to murky depths.

She cried his name, begging, pleading with him. *Don't do this. Please.* A deserted riverbank in a small town that was little more than a place-between-places. His grip was like a vice on her wrists.

She couldn't believe this was happening to her, not after everything. Not after she thought she'd escaped him for good. After three years of being ground down to a fine dust, of being fragmented, torn, piece by piece, she had finally broken free of his clasp.

Tony. Tony.

For those past two weeks, she had woken up in her old bed back at her mum's, that narrow single bed in which she tossed all night. Every creak and groan of the house woke her at all hours, convinced each time that he had come back for her.

But he didn't. She had done it. She had escaped.

Gina explored the boundaries of this new freedom, trying to recall the shape of herself. Either her old personality, or who she was now – she wasn't sure. What she liked, what she wanted. Pushing herself to remember the most basic things. Taking it one day at a time.

The hands around her neck had been the final straw. A ring that stained blue and purple, a necklace of shame. The shackle of bruises eventually faded and two weeks later, only she could see the imprint he had left on her.

Tony. Tony. Tony.

She began to relax. It was safe to go out in this small town where she knew everyone, Gina told herself. What menace could possibly lurk in daylight? She had to pull herself together and stop cowering. Her own shadow was making her jump. It was no way to live, Mum said. And he wasn't that bad, Gina told herself in a small voice.

She was wrong about that.

He came out of nowhere, but she realised later that he must have been watching her and waiting for the right moment. The wrong moment. The instant she let her guard down.

As he dragged her away by her hair, she almost felt relief that finally, it was over. The waiting and not knowing, the dread and trepidation. Surely that was worse?

She was wrong about that, too.

The grass was wet underneath her. A blow of Tony's fist to her head left her foggy, and she was thankful for that small mercy. She numbed herself, ignoring the burning between her legs.

Detaching her mind from her body, she floated up towards that vast grey sky, looking back down at herself on the ground, pinned beneath him. She closed her eyes again and all she could hear was the river. *Listen to the river.* Let it wash over you, wash out to sea. *This too shall pass.*

The sound of sirens. Coming to rescue her?

But no, there was no siren. There had been no rescue.

It was the phone.

She sat upright in bed, breaking the surface of her nightmare. No longer drowning.

'Hello?' she panted, catching her breath in ragged gasps.

'Gina?' Carrie choked back a pained sob.

Oh my god. Carrie.

Gina pressed a hand to her throat, willing her racing heart to slow. She tried to say something, but when she moved her mouth, no sound came.

'I didn't know who else to call.' At the other end of the line, Carrie sobbed. 'Gina, it's Chris. He's dead.'

45

GINA WASN'T THE ONLY ONE WHO SUFFERED A NIGHT OF interrupted sleep.

It took Sue a few moments after waking to remember her late-night call. The sight of the phone on the bedside table brought it back, and she wondered, just for a second, if it was a dream.

No, she was quite sure it had been real. And more was the pity.

Diana, calling at goodness knows what time of night, raving about a serial killer on the loose. The official definition of a serial killer was three murders, but Sue hadn't wanted to point that out. It felt like tempting fate, for one thing.

But was she right? Again, doubt needled at Sue, pushing her to trust her gut. As much as she disliked people who interfered in the affairs of others, this was her village. She had a right – no, a *duty* – to know what happened within its boundaries.

She flipped the pillow over, burying her face into the

cool side and closing her eyes, determined to make up for the time she lay wide awake during the small hours. From the kitchen below, she heard voices. Not just one voice – not her sister Anne indulging in her unnerving habit of casually chatting to her late husband – but a second voice, too.

Sue groaned.

Diana.

She dragged herself out of bed and tentatively inched down the stairs, trepidation churning in her stomach.

'Cup of tea?' Anne had made porridge and an inch of lukewarm gruel sat waiting in the pan on the stove.

Sue took a seat at the table. 'Yes please,' she replied, thinking that she might need something stronger than tea to get through this.

Diana nudged the sugar bowl towards her. 'Now, we have a lot to deal with, so I called an early start.'

Sue said nothing.

Diana spread her hands, planting her fingertips into the table. 'First victim. Peter Gallivan, aged sixty-one. Death initially presumed to be natural causes – a heart attack. Second victim: Chris Carter. Aged twenty-seven. Died of a suspected heart attack—'

'Let's just take a step back, for a minute,' said Sue, pinching the bridge of her nose.

'You're quite right,' said Diana. 'We need Amy, too. Let's head over there, pick her brains. After all, she was at the scene of the first—'

'Don't say it, OK? Please. Don't say *murder*.' She didn't mean to sound so belligerent.

Diana smirked over the rim of her cup. 'I was about to say *crime*, but now that you mention it...'

'I'm sorry. It's just a lot to get my head around, that's all.'

Sue thought again of the sand in the hallway, the smashed vase, and how easy it would have been for someone to gain entry thanks to that spare key. Did the same person break into Chris's caravan?

'Apparently you threatened him,' said Anne, joining them at the table.

'What? I did nothing of the sort!'

Anne exchanged a rueful glance with Diana, who shrugged.

'You did tell him that he would get what's coming to him...' Diana's words hung there like a question, and Sue didn't respond. She didn't like where this was conversation was heading.

'So,' Anne shrugged. 'If it does turn out to be murder, you might be a prime suspect.'

Sue ignored her sister. 'Diana, let's start from the beginning. Tell me about Chris. When did it happen?' She took a sip of too-hot tea. 'And also, how on earth did you find out?'

'Yesterday afternoon. Carrie found the body when she came home from work. Fortuitously, I happened to be in the area and heard the emergency vehicles approaching. I arrived promptly at the scene and was able to ascertain that the victim was deceased.'

Why was she speaking like that? Sue clenched her jaw. *Angela Lansbury, eat your blinking heart out.*

Diana continued. 'Upon further enquiry, I was able to determine that the suspected cause of death was a heart attack.'

Anne gnawed at a cuticle. 'It is quite worrying when you think about it.'

'Precisely.' Diana slapped her palm against the table. 'This could be a public safety issue.'

She leaned forward in her seat, lowering her voice to a whisper. 'Ladies, please understand that I do not say this lightly.' She licked her lips, and Sue did her utmost to ignore just how much Diana was relishing this moment. 'But there is a murderer in our midst.'

46

AMY WAS SURPRISED BY THE STRAGGLE OF MID-MORNING visitors on her doorstep, but knew better than to show it. Wordlessly, she waved them inside.

Poor Auntie Sue. Her hair was flattened on one side of her head and there were shadows under her eyes the shade of rain clouds. Diana was in fine form, as ever. Amy couldn't remember a single day when she had seen that woman looking anything other than immaculate.

'Morning, love.' Her mum greeted her with a kiss and held her at arm's length to get a good look at her. 'Your father says hello.'

Amy ushered them into the kitchen where Rachel was already sitting by the Aga.

'I'll put another pot on,' Rachel said, getting to her feet.

'Ladies,' said Diana, installing herself at the head of the table. 'First things first – may we all swear a solemn vow that nothing we discuss here leaves this room. Not until we are all satisfied and in agreement for it to do so.'

Amy glanced at Sue, holding her gaze for a fraction of a

second, long enough to show Sue that she was equally bemused.

Not allowing herself to be derailed by the lack of assent, Diana ploughed on. 'I have a working theory: that Chris Carter and Peter Gallivan were murdered by the same person or persons. What we need to do now is to establish just who that might have been.'

'This is the part I can't understand,' said Sue. 'They both died of a heart attack. No murder weapons, and no signs of violence or foul play. Amy attempted to resuscitate Peter. She'd have known if something wasn't right.'

Sue looked to Amy, who shrugged and nodded. But the news of Chris's death had reached her this morning, and it did seem odd for someone so young to suffer a cardiac arrest. Diana had roused her curiosity – just to see where this was going, if nothing else.

Diana dismissed the interjection with a wave of her hand. 'Look at the similarities, the *modus operandi*. Less than three weeks after Peter's death, and a second victim shows up with an identical cause of death.'

'That's just it, though.' Sue held her hands out, palms up. 'I know it looks suspicious, but they both suffered cardiac arrests.' She cleared her throat as if to steady the tremor in her voice. 'You can't *cause* someone to suddenly have a heart attack.'

Amy and Rachel exchanged a glance and quickly looked away. Rachel served tea, studiously avoiding eye contact with Sue.

'What?' said Sue. 'What's going on? Tell her, Amy. Tell her it's not possible to give someone a heart attack.'

Amy sighed. 'Actually, it is.'

Diana clasped her hands together. 'At last, I think we are getting somewhere.'

'How?' Sue was incredulous.

Amy hesitated, then sighed. 'It wouldn't even be that difficult if you know what you're doing. There are a few combinations of drugs that would do it.'

'Go on, dear.' Diana gave her an encouraging nudge.

'Well, if it were me – and this is just my best guess, here – I'd mix meds that enlarge the vessels around the heart with something to reduce blood pressure and add a thinner at the same time.' As she spoke, a knot of nausea tightened in her stomach. Was that what happened to Peter Gallivan? No. Surely not. She pictured his face again, his eyes wide and lips blue as she tried desperately to resuscitate him on his living room floor. *Did someone do that to him?*

'Well, I never,' said Sue. 'You learn something new every day.'

Diana considered this, her lips pursed in concentration. 'We already had our suspicions about the circumstances of Peter Gallivan's death, if not on how he died.'

Rachel took a seat next to Diana. 'Tell me what I missed.'

'There were signs of a possible break in. Oh, and I almost forgot...' Diana slapped a palm to her forehead. 'I spoke with the son. He claimed responsibility for the broken vase. But I got the distinct impression he's hiding something. We also have the sand in the hallway. Silica sand, I believe you said, Sue?'

'Yes. From a building site, most likely.'

Diana pressed a finger to her lip. 'We should check whether Peter's business interests include construction.'

'Mike would know how to find out,' said Amy. 'He's gone to Newcastle for a meeting, but he'll be back in an hour or two.'

'Good, good,' Diana mumbled.

'I suppose the most important thing to work out is if they knew each other?'

'Thank you, Rachel. I was just coming to that.' Diana seemed annoyed that someone else got there before her, but quickly regained her composure. 'As I was about to say, it is critical that we establish the connection between the victims. What, or who, is the link between these two men?'

'Peter Gallivan and Chris Carter?' Sue scoffed. 'I can't imagine that they knew each other from Adam. What on earth could those two possibly have in common?'

Diana folded her hands together, pressing her index fingers to her chin. Amy noticed the glint in the old lady's eye as a thought formed.

'I can think of at least one thing they have in common...' Diana looked Sue in the eye. 'Your book club.'

———

'Obviously, this has nothing to do with the book club,' said Sue. 'So, let's quickly move on from that suggestion, shall we?'

She could see exactly what Diana was playing at. *Her book club*, indeed. She could also see how much her friend was enjoying this. Diana was positively in her element.

'Now, we have several lines of enquiry. I suggest we attempt another interview with Fiona Gallivan. Amy, I think it's high time you and I paid a visit to our friend,' Diana said.

Amy nodded, and Diana continued to instruct her team. 'Rachel and Sue, you can do some digging. Facebook and...' This was clearly unfamiliar territory for Diana, and she hesitated, seemingly searching for the right words. '... the social media.'

'Copy that,' Rachel replied with a grin.

'Well, I can't help you, I'm afraid.' Anne folded her hands in her lap. She had been quietly observing this discussion, so quietly that Sue had quite forgotten she was there. 'But I'll be in my studio if anyone needs me.'

Something throbbed behind Sue's eyes, and she felt the familiar pressure building at her temples. Just what they needed right now – more shell mirrors. At her last count, Anne had produced nine 'pieces' so far, and Sue still had no idea how they were going to get rid of the damned things.

She wished they could give Anne a task – anything – to make her feel useful and give her something else to focus on. Then again, given the way things were going, perhaps it was safer to have her sister distracted and out of their way.

'Thank you, Anne.' Diana placed a hand on hers and gave it a reassuring squeeze. 'We'll keep you updated as our enquiry progresses.'

———

Amy set off with Diana on the short drive to the Gallivan place, a light rain misting the windscreen.

Her mind was racing – running through the drugs that should never be prescribed together because their combination would do more harm than good.

Had someone known that? Had she never stood a chance of saving Peter?

At Seafield Road she pulled onto the pavement, averting her gaze from the spot at the top of the dune path where her father fell all those years ago. She'd been powerless to help him, too, but it didn't make her feel any better.

She saw it as they walked up the garden path – the

murky shadow of a figure moving behind the upstairs window.

'Now dear, to make this work, we have to suggest that you're here on official duty. District nurse bereavement follow-up, or something.'

'Diana, I can't—' But Amy was forced to cut her protest short as Caitlyn Gallivan appeared at the door before they reached it.

Amy took her in. The resemblance to her mother was stark. Fiona's features were mirrored back at her, the same face and that thick, blonde hair. But instead of her mother's generous smile, Caitlyn's mouth was a flat, tight line.

'Good morning, dear,' Diana chirruped, disguising any hint of residual antipathy from her last encounter with Caitlyn. 'I'm not sure you've met Mrs Sanders – Amy, to her friends, of course – our local district nurse.'

Caitlyn's eyes darted between Amy and Diana, the hard line of her mouth softening slightly.

'We're here to see your mother.' Amy's heart fluttered. She knew she was a terrible liar. 'It's part of the protocol, following a bereavement.'

From her coat pocket, she retrieved her NHS ID card and offered it to Caitlyn. *Go hard or go home,* she told herself.

Caitlyn scanned the card and handed it back to Amy, one eyebrow raised. 'You'd better come in, then.'

Amy shoved the card back into her pocket with a trembling hand.

Stepping into the hallway, the memory of that night hit her. She'd been preoccupied with attending to Peter, of course, and hadn't appreciated the grand renovation the Gallivans had done to the place. Everything was white and gleaming, and felt like that boutique hotel where she and Mike spent their wedding anniversary.

'This way, please.' Caitlyn led them into the living room and Amy carefully stepped around the spot on the floor where Peter had lain. She took a seat at the edge of a wide sofa, next to Diana, who had confidently planted herself in the centre.

'She'll be right with you,' said Caitlyn, forcing a smile.

47

As soon as they were alone, Amy scanned the room. It looked different in daylight. She thought back again to that Sunday evening. It had been too gloomy to see some of her kit, the room lit only by side lamps.

She saw it now, a small side table with a heavy gold-based lamp, a shade of crystal beads. Pretty, but it had cast a low gleam. And on that night, there was something else... She closed her eyes, willing the memory to solidify in her mind's eye.

A glass. Amber liquid. A decanter with a crystal stopper.

She opened her eyes at the sound of footsteps approaching.

'Diana, Amy.' Fiona beamed. 'How wonderful to see you.'

'This is an official call, actually. Bereavement can be a very difficult process and we can offer you a number of referrals for patient services to make it easier. Counselling, therapies, even medication, if you need it.' Amy's heart was hammering, but she knew she sounded convincing, even enough for Caitlyn.

'And I'm here from St Cuthbert's. A follow-up to the funeral service. I trust that everything met your expectation?'

A gasp snagged in Amy's throat. Surely that was a step too far? Diana's audacity was astounding, and only just a little bit impressive.

Caitlyn perched on the arm of her mother's chair, a guard dog keeping watch. Amy tried to read her face but got nothing.

'We're doing well, I think,' said Fiona after a moment. 'Of course, it hasn't been easy. And Peter's company...' She rolled her eyes. 'There's so much administration after the death of a—'

'Never mind all of that, Mum.' Caitlyn cut her off, a forced lightness to her voice. 'Boring!' Her mock laugh rang hollow. 'Let's just focus on you for a moment, eh?' She squeezed Fiona's shoulder. 'I'd say you're coping remarkably well. Besides, you've got Ben and me to look after you. Right?'

Fiona laid a hand over her daughter's. 'Absolutely.'

'No trouble sleeping?' Amy ventured.

Fiona shrugged. 'A little. Tossing and turning. And now that you mention it, I'm beginning to get a headache. Darling,' Fiona turned to Caitlyn. 'Be a gem and pop upstairs to my bathroom, could you? There's paracetamol in the cupboard.'

Amy watched Caitlyn hesitate for a moment, hovering above her perch before darting from the room – presumably keen to complete her errand as quickly as possible and avoid leaving her mother un-surveilled for too long.

Fiona's shoulders relaxed the instant her daughter left. She sat back in the chair, crossing her legs, and Amy sensed that she had deliberately sent Caitlyn away to give them some privacy.

'That night. Peter had been drinking, hadn't he? There was a glass of whisky on the side table, right there.'

Fiona followed the point of Amy's finger, her gaze resting on the table as if she expected to see the empty glass. 'Yes...' she said, remembering. 'Yes, there was.'

'And you came home to find him collapsed on the floor and having difficulty breathing?'

Fiona took a deep breath. 'That's right. The house was quiet when I came home. I assumed Peter was in his study, or his media room. But then I heard something. I came into the living room. He was on the floor.' She looked down at her feet. 'I called for an ambulance right away.'

Amy's brow knotted. That more or less tallied with what she already knew. Above them, she could hear Caitlyn's footsteps on the landing.

'My dear,' said Diana, edging forward in her seat. 'Do you know a man named Chris Carter?'

Fiona considered this for a second, then shook her head. 'Who is he?'

'He lives in Seahouses,' Diana said quickly, before Amy had a chance to speak. She noticed that her friend spoke of Chris in the present tense. 'Ring any bells?'

'I'm afraid not.'

Caitlyn's footsteps moved towards them. Diana spoke with urgency. 'That night – is there any chance that someone might have been in the house while you were out? Before you got home?'

'Not at all. I mean, I certainly didn't see anyone.'

'Is there any possibility that someone else was here? That they got in without you knowing?'

Fiona shrugged. 'The door was locked. Nobody else has a key...'

Her voice trailed off and Amy saw it – the embryo of a thought flashed behind her eyes. It vanished as quickly as it surfaced, just as Caitlyn reappeared and Amy knew that the discussion was over.

———

'Curiouser and curiouser,' Caitlyn muttered as they watched the women leave. Despite the anonymity of the reflective glass, she stood half-concealed behind the thick white drape.

'They're well-meaning.' Fiona offered. And they were, but Caitlyn wouldn't have appreciated the line or tone of their questioning. It seemed wide off the mark for what one might expect from a district nurse and the local parish councillor, or whatever Diana was.

Fiona had been so relieved that Amy wasn't asking too many probing questions about Peter's heart attack that she was caught off-guard when they mentioned that other chap. Chris Carter – she committed the name to memory. Later, when Caitlyn eventually got bored of babysitting her, Fiona would do some digging of her own.

The paramedics had questioned her about the heart attack the night of Peter's death, and she'd done her best to give the answers they needed. Everyone seemed satisfied. Didn't they? There was no reason why anyone would think to dig deeper. Besides, he was buried now. It was over.

In the rational part of her brain, Fiona knew this – and still, her heart thundered in her chest.

The image came back to her of Peter lying on the floor,

curled on his side, his hands clasped so tightly to his chest that his knuckles had turned white.

She shuddered.

'Don't worry, Mum.' Caitlyn's voice jolted her back to the moment. 'I know what you're thinking, and just don't.'

Fiona attempted to steady her pulse with a slow exhale.

Caitlyn sighed, exasperated. 'It's done. He had a heart attack. You called an ambulance. End of story.'

'Yes, I know. It's just—'

'Just nothing, OK? We have a plan. Now let's stick to it.'

The plan. How could she forget the plan? The plan that she had been outnumbered into.

She had missed Caitlyn these past several months, but each day brought a fresh reminder of how controlling her daughter could be. Caitlyn wasn't happy unless Caitlyn was in charge. Peter had a point – Ben was too soft, sometimes. She wished he would stand up to his sister.

'Any news from your brother?'

Caitlyn shook her head. 'He's with the accountants now and they're working on it. Dad put stuff in place to optimise the tax bill in the event that we did sell, and it's just taking them a while to move things around, that's all.'

Fiona hated the way the children spoke to her some-times, as if she hadn't been the one doing the books for the first few years after Sparkbrook was founded. As if she and Peter hadn't written their wills together.

'I still wish Ben would take over,' she said, her voice small. 'It would be so good for him.'

Caitlyn glided towards Fiona, silhouetted against the daylight. She dropped to a crouch beside her, brushing a strand of hair away from her mother's face with a mani-cured finger. 'No, Mum. It would be good for *you*. Not Ben.

And it will be best for all of us when you sell and walk away.'

Fiona gazed out the window. The rain had stopped and, out at sea, blue sky nudged dove-grey clouds aside. At this rate, they might even get a glimpse of sunshine this afternoon.

And what was all that nonsense about someone breaking in? Where did that come from? She chewed at the inside of her lip, biting hard enough to draw blood. The tang of iron was sharp on her tongue.

Fiona thought of the spare key that they kept under the plant pot.

Peter had insisted on it after an unfortunate incident at the house in Durham when he lost his house keys on the golf course. He'd had to wait an entire forty minutes on the doorstep for her to come home. His mood was thunderous by the time she arrived, and he didn't care in the slightest that she'd had to cut short a perfectly lovely lunch with Esme to rescue him. God, he had been a difficult man.

But Diana's question replayed in her mind. *Is there any possibility someone else was here?*

Was someone else here that night?

Had someone seen what she had done?

48

BACK IN AMY'S KITCHEN, SUE AND RACHEL WEREN'T MAKING much progress. While Peter's Facebook page gave them nothing at all, Chris's offered way too much.

He had posted almost daily – often several times in the same day, and at all hours of the night. Chris had a view on everything from global warming to immigration and the topics of his musings were varied, his thoughts scattered and incoherent. He had checked in at multiple places of employment, a potted history that suggested a struggle to commit to anything for very long. None of them, however, were Sparkbrook.

Sue's heart sank lower as she waded through rant after rant, random and contradictory thoughts piling high, littered with spelling mistakes. She wondered, guiltily, just how deeply Chris's problems might have run.

Peter Gallivan was not among the almost one thousand people on Chris's friends list. Nor were Peter's wife or children.

Rachel sighed. 'I suppose that would have been too easy.'

'Maybe they don't know each other,' Sue mused. 'At least, not directly. Or not well enough to consider each other friends.' She didn't want to repeat the suggestion that they were connected, somehow, through the book club. *Her* book club.

They turned back to the screen, scrolling, looking for something. Anything. *Come on,* thought Sue. *What aren't you telling us?*

They both jumped at the sound of the front door.

'Anyone home?' Mike called out.

He stepped into the kitchen, his face falling when he saw that it was just the two of them. 'Amy not back yet?'

'She's just popped out on an errand,' said Sue. 'She'll be home soon.'

Rachel turned in her chair to face him. 'We were waiting for you, as it happens. Fancy giving us a hand?'

At the prospect of being useful, Mike's face lit up. *Men,* thought Sue. *They really are the most basic creatures.*

'We want to find out everything we can about Peter Gallivan's business. Any whiff of trouble, tax-dodging or scandal, you name it.'

Mike raised an eyebrow. 'That could be a long list.'

'OK,' said Rachel, thoughtfully. 'In that case, why don't you focus on anything that might have made someone want to kill him?'

Sue frowned at her, then shrugged. That should, in theory, narrow their enquiry.

As Mike disappeared upstairs to his study, Rachel and Sue turned back to the computer. They scrolled through page after page of photographs documenting Chris's life over the past decade. Despite his dodgy demeanour, his life was an open book. It was difficult to know where to start.

'Take a look at this,' said Mike, reappearing in the kitchen twenty minutes later.

Sue glanced at her watch. 'That was quick...'

He shook his head. 'Nothing definitive, just something to tell us where we should look.' On the smooth oak table, he spread out several pages.

'The Companies House records. Sparkbrook is the name you see on the shop, but in fact, there are several holding companies behind it. For example, Sparkbrook doesn't actually employ anyone except the executives – all their shop staff work for this company.' He jabbed a finger at the page. 'SPC Retail.'

'That's weird,' said Sue. And it sounded like an accountant's worst nightmare.

Mike shook his head. 'Not at all. It's fairly standard. It spreads the risk and liability, rather than putting all your eggs in one basket. So, when Sparkbrook got in trouble for forcing zero hours contracts on to their distribution employees, it wasn't their company that got fined – it was a contractor, even though the same people technically own both firms. This one... BSC Fulfilment. They even have their manufacturing under a different umbrella company. They make the goods and sell them to themselves.

He glanced up to check that they were still following. 'Pretty smart when you think about it.' He said with a shrug. 'I've printed off a list of the subsidiary companies, plus the directors and executives that Gallivan appointed to run them. If you're looking for someone who might have wanted him dead, from a business point of view, at least, this would be a great place to start looking.'

Sue glanced over the pages. Mike was right – this may not be an answer, but it was a good place to begin.

49

SUE HAD MISSED THEIR USUAL FRIDAY AFTERNOON COFFEE. IT wasn't a formal arrangement, anyway, more of a habit that they had fallen into. Certainly not set in stone.

Regardless, by three o'clock that afternoon, Helen found herself pacing in front of the shop window. She cast her eyes up and down Main Street, habitually checking her phone for a text. Nothing.

Something must have come up with Amy and the kids, or that dotty sister of hers. But as the afternoon went on, her niggling questions intensified.

Where had Sue got to? Had something come up, or was she just tired of Helen and their idle Friday afternoon chats?

It wasn't as if Helen had anything particularly interesting to offer. Not to someone like Sue Palmer with that brain of hers. Helen had seen some of the books Sue read – doorstoppers about the rainforest and volcanoes and the like. That was probably it. Sue had simply grown bored with her.

There were plenty more interesting people around these days. Not like the years when they were growing up, when everyone fished or farmed. Or even when Sue first came back from Scotland. Tourism had taken a firm hold since then, and the villagers had shifted gears from sustaining themselves to accommodating others. Seahouses had doubled in size just in Helen's lifetime and was now home to all sorts of people.

Perhaps Sue had gone off with that Fiona Gallivan. Helen couldn't be sure, but she bet Fiona had gone to university, too. She seemed the sort. Bright, full of things to say. Someone who had been places and seen things. Seen some of the life that existed just beyond Helen's farm gate – the life that was within touching distance, yet somehow remained forever beyond her reach.

Or Tom, perhaps. That chap from the book club. Sue didn't seem that keen on him, but maybe it was like one of those Mills and Boon stories when they start off despising one another but fall into bed by chapter ten.

Except Helen knew that Sue was not like that.

She recognised this feeling: a pang in her gut, a fist gripping its fingers around something in her chest.

Jealousy.

Helen chided herself. Jealousy over what? Because her pal made a couple of new friends lately? They weren't schoolgirls anymore. Besides, things hadn't been any easier back then.

When she still hadn't heard anything by the following afternoon, she decided to call over at Sue's after closing up. The drizzle had kept most of the would-be weekenders away and the shop had turned a meagre profit for a Saturday.

Helen was nonplussed by the poor takings. She spent the afternoon with one eye on the clock, counting down the minutes until she could leave.

Anne answered the door in a peacock-green kaftan and waved her inside. 'She's working at the computer,' she said with a theatrical eye roll.

Sue jumped to her feet as Helen entered the living room, her shoulders sinking as soon as she saw her. 'Helen – I'm so sorry.' She ran a hand through her hair. 'I got caught up in all of this and completely forgot our Friday coffee.'

That's good, thought Helen. Sue called it *our Friday coffee.* That felt official enough.

Sue gestured to a pile of paper beside the computer.

Helen leaned in to get a closer look. 'What's that you're working on?'

'Didn't you hear? Chris Carter died on Thursday. Heart attack.'

Helen chewed her lip. Chris Carter... the name rang a bell.

'That... man, Carrie's boyfriend. From the book club. The one who dragged her home from the pub the other night.'

Helen's eyes widened, her breath a whoosh of air. '*Him?*'

Sue nodded. 'I'm starting to wonder if it might have been deliberate, and whoever killed him might be responsible for Peter Gallivan's death as well.'

Deliberate... It took a moment for Sue's words to sink in.

Sue shrugged. 'Amy says there'll be an autopsy and a police investigation into Chris's death, so I'm focusing on Peter for now. These are his company records. I'm trying to work out who might have wanted him dead, and how Chris might be connected to any of it.'

Helen picked up the first page, her hand trembling slightly. *Two murders in Seahouses?* When she spoke, her voice was thin. 'How far have you got?'

'It's complicated, but Gallivan had several companies

within the same group. Not even his name on all of them. One business to pay the staff, another to manufacture the merchandise, another that oversaw the online stuff and the deliveries. I've been researching them, trying to weed out any enemies he might have made. It's a lot to go through. There are zero hours contracts, offshore holding companies, disgraced directors... you name it.'

In her notepad, Sue had constructed a diagram of Peter's business interests. Helen traced the spidery lettering and read the angry words, some of them underlined. *No tax. Zero hours.*

'Maybe Chris worked for him? That could be the connection.'

'I don't think so. That was the first thing we checked. Chris clearly struggled to hold a job down for long, but none of them were at...' Sue hesitated, her brow knotting. 'But then again... I looked through that before I had the list of Sparkbrook subsidiaries. He didn't work at Sparkbrook, but what about the others?' She raked a hand through her hair. 'Have I missed the bleeding obvious?'

She turned to Helen. 'Can you get onto Chris's Facebook profile?'

Helen took a seat beside her, her face so close to Sue's that she could feel her breath on her neck. She pulled up Chris's page and clicked on *check ins*. The list expanded.

They saw it instantly. *BSC Fulfilment, Newcastle.*

Sue turned to Helen, planting both hands on either side of her face and planting a kiss on her cheek. 'You did it! Helen, you absolute genius!'

Sue turned back to the screen, jabbing at it with her index finger. 'That's how they knew each other. Chris worked for Sparkbrook.'

Helen was glad that her friend didn't see the blush rise

in her face, or the way she touched her thumb to her cheek, tracing the spot where Sue's kiss had landed.

It didn't surprise Helen when Sue insisted on going straight to Amy with the news. The bond between Sue and her niece was stronger than many mother-daughter relationships.

Helen had always wanted a girl. But they were blessed with Matthew, and she knew better than to wish for anything more than she already had.

As they walked down Main Street, Helen noticed a spring in her step. It was a minor triumph, but she replayed it over and over in her mind, picturing Sue's face the moment she cracked the puzzle... even if it might have been slightly obvious, in hindsight.

The rain had finally stopped, but it had drained the day of colour, the dusk sky now a wash of thin grey. Lights flickered on inside the homes they passed, golden windows illuminating their way as people settled in for a Saturday night at home.

Amy's face was flustered when she answered the door, two spots of rose high on her cheeks. In a certain light, she looked just like her mother. Except Helen knew that whereas Anne was made of porcelain, Amy was as strong as steel.

The three kids were home and producing the equivalent noise of a playground full of children.

'Let's have a bit of quiet time now, shall we?' Amy's voice resounded authoritatively over the din, resulting in an immediate hush. She pulled the living room door to and turned to Sue and Helen, rolling her eyes. 'God, give me strength...' she muttered.

'Is Mike out?' Sue asked as she filled the kettle.

'Golf.' Amy's terse reply betrayed precisely how she felt about her husband's absence. 'Should be home soon.'

'I don't suppose there's any news yet on Chris Carter and the, er... investigation?'

A shadow fell across Amy's face. 'Nothing official, not yet. But the lad took industrial quantities of drugs, apparently. That's probably what caused it. They'll know more after the autopsy.'

———

Sue grimaced. Hearing Amy calling him a *lad* was a stark reminder that Chris had been a vulnerable young man. Sure, they might have fallen on the wrong side of him, but he was clearly battling with his own demons.

'Well, we – or Helen, at least,' – Sue nodded to her friend – 'worked out how they might have known each other. Chris worked for Sparkbrook's distribution company, based at a depot down in Newcastle. He started there in February 2009.'

'Interesting...' Amy pressed a thumb to her mouth. 'The distribution company was the business that got knocked hardest in the zero hours contracts scandal.'

She flicked back over the notes she had scrawled in a ring-bound pad. 'It hit the headlines sometime after that, but Chris would have been one of the affected workers.'

Sue remembered reading about it in the papers. The trade union had organised a strike. The media covered it for weeks. Eventually it snowballed into a national campaign. Was Chris out to avenge shoddy employment law by murdering the CEO? It seemed like an elaborate plot and something about it failed to add up. Chris seemed more... how would she describe him? *Animalistic.*

'Peter Gallivan certainly wasn't popular,' said Sue. 'I dug up all sorts, not just the zero hours stuff. He got into huge trouble over his taxes – or rather, the lack of them. Sparkbrook funnels their profit through some island in the Caribbean and hasn't paid a penny in the UK for almost a decade.'

Amy shook her head. 'The brass neck of the man.'

'Yup. He was even hauled before a parliamentary committee to answer for it. And then there were rumours of numerous extra-marital affairs. Poor Fiona – looks like she's put up with a lot.'

Helen's eyebrows knitted in a frown. 'So, if Chris did kill Peter – and I still don't understand how he could have done that, by the way – then who killed Chris?'

It was a good question, thought Sue.

'There has to be a third person,' said Amy. 'Someone who knew both Chris and Peter.'

Their discussion was interrupted by the sound of the front door opening, sending the children back into a high-energy spin. Mike padded down the hall in his bare feet, Betsy and Lucas tugging at his arms to come and play with them. He shooed them off with a promise of being there in a minute, and they scuttled back to the living room.

'What's this?' He took a Coke Zero from the fridge and drank straight from the can.

Sue helped him catch up. 'Chris Carter and Peter Gallivan. Peter wasn't a popular man, as you made quite clear. He could have had all sorts of people after him. And Chris had enough problems of his own. We're trying to establish the connection between them. Apparently, Chris used to work for Sparkbrook – one of its subsidiaries, at least. He was one of the workers who got short-changed by their zero hours policy.'

Mike's gaze bounced between the three of them, the hint of a smirk dancing at the corners of his mouth. 'You've been trying to work out how they knew each other?'

'Yes.' Amy's voice was taut.

'I wish you'd said so at the beginning. I could have saved you a bit of time.' Mike scoffed, and Sue got the feeling he was resisting the temptation to laugh. 'Peter played golf. Chris Carter was his caddy.'

50

Gina's hands were shaking – the slightest of trembles. A leaf quivering in a warm breeze, nothing more. But enough for Tom to notice.

The poor thing.

The village was awash with gossip, buzzing like the bees in the potted lavender bushes in their cottage garden. Agnes had received a phone call from a friend, who had walked into Clarke's bakery on Friday morning and heard from someone who was there when the ambulance arrived. Agnes hadn't left home in almost a year, and even she was in the loop.

According to a reliable source, *that man* – Tom didn't even want to think his name – died of a heart attack a couple of days ago. Tom tried to think of something poetic, some witty quip about karma being a bitch, but nothing came to mind. There was just that quiet anger sitting high in his stomach, like indigestion. Besides, it wasn't right to speak ill of the dead, no matter how horrendous they were in life.

He had got quite good at looking-without-looking. From

his usual seat, he adopted the pretence of fixation with some detail in the bar – the brass barometer of a fishing boat or antique diving gauge – only allowing his gaze to float softy towards Gina when he could be certain she wasn't watching him. Thankfully, there were plenty of objects with which he could feign mild fascination.

This new skill of discreet observation still required some work, and once or twice Gina had met his eye. She looked away as quickly as he did. In the lulls between serving customers, she pressed her hands against her jeans, ostensibly smoothing down some invisible crease but, Tom suspected, trying to stop the shiver that wouldn't go away.

———

Gina had gone straight to the hospital after Carrie rang on Thursday night. It had been overcast, the moon blotted out behind cloud. It took her no time at all to find Carrie. Alnwick Infirmary A&E was deserted, save for a lone figure sitting hunched over in a plastic seat, her knees pulled up to her chin. Her cheeks streaked with silver tears.

The police had already spoken to her, but Carrie wasn't able to relay the specific details of this to Gina, who frantically demanded answers. Was it a formal interview? Had they offered her a solicitor?

Gina's memory stumbled over itself to a time many years ago when she was a frightened girl, asked questions she didn't know how to answer.

It had taken Carrie several hours to call her. With a pang of needle-sharp sadness, Gina realised that she was possibly the closest thing that Carrie could count as family. Those that she hadn't pushed away, at least. Gina cursed herself again for not trying harder, back when she first saw the signs. She should have forced Carrie to listen. But what more could she have done? At least Chris could no longer hurt her now.

They drove back to the pub in silence. Gina tucked Carrie up in her bed and took the sofa so that she would be close if Carrie woke. It was a question of when, not if, the nightmares came. Gina knew that much. She dragged the throw over herself and didn't even bother with a spare pillow, exhaustion weighting her limbs like lead. But when she finally closed her eyes, sleep did not come.

Carrie had left the following morning – there was an aunt in Berwick, and she couldn't tell Gina when she might come back. *If she ever would.* Carrie collected her stuff from the caravan and Gina almost wept when she saw that her friend's worldly possessions amounted to two bin bags, engorged and gleaming in the morning sun. Carrie insisted on taking the bus and Gina bit back her tears as she hugged her goodbye, feeling Carrie's bird-like frame beneath her hands, bones pressed up against Gina's rolls of flesh. Crying wouldn't help anybody now.

Gina had been setting up for a busy Saturday night and was restocking the spirits when she heard the door. She silently cursed herself for forgetting to lock it again.

'We're not open yet...' Her voice trailed off when she saw the uniforms.

'Gina McGee?'

'That's me. How can I help you?' Her heart fluttered already, fingers drumming on her ribs.

'We have a couple of questions about Chris Carter.'

She turned back towards the bar so that they couldn't see her face and took a slow, steadying breath. 'Just give me a second.'

They sat down at a table as if they were mates on a night

out. A younger guy who Gina might have found hot in other circumstances, and an older woman with over-processed blonde hair. Gina pegged the female officer as the more senior of the pair, not only because of her age. She took the lead.

'We understand that you had a falling out with Mr Carter in the days before his death?'

Gina scoffed – she couldn't help it. 'I'd hardly call it a *falling out*.'

'His girlfriend seemed to think that the two of you weren't...' —she turned to her colleague— 'what were the words Ms Brannigan used, Constable Daley?'

Daley didn't take his eyes off Gina. He had cheek bones to die for, but that uniform was an instant red card. 'Carrie said you had argued and, at one point, things got physical.'

Something lurched in her chest, her pulse racing even faster now. *What was Carrie playing at?*

'Yeah, *he* got physical. With me and a member of my staff. A pub full of people saw what he did.'

They let the silence sit there, and after a moment, Gina could no longer fight her compulsion to fill it. 'Chris was abusive. He was controlling and manipulative; he trapped that poor girl and she couldn't see a way out. She would have been stuck with him until...' Gina trailed off, catching her breath and pausing to choose her words. *Stuck with him until what? Until the day he went too far? Until Carrie snapped?*

The older copper had a pinched mouth, her lips a tight line ringed by the creases of a decades-long nicotine dependence. She still said nothing.

Gina shifted in her seat. 'Anyway, he died of a heart attack, didn't he?'

'Something like that,' was all the woman said.

That's when the shaking started.

The police left, and Gina resumed Saturday night with a shadow hanging over her.

Carrie's phone was switched off and Gina's calls went straight to voicemail, her messages showing undelivered. Not that she expected Carrie to answer.

The pub was packed, that night – nothing like bad news to turn the entire village out. Gina kept smiling, saying nothing beyond her usual banter. At least the work provided a good distraction. But no matter how hard she tried to take her mind off it, the shaking in her hands would not stop.

51

'I'M SORRY, COULD YOU REPEAT YOUR NAME FOR ME?'

Diana slammed the receiver back into its cradle. It had been fun while it lasted, but the pathology technician at Alnwick Infirmary had eventually cottoned on to her ruse. The police were all over Chris Carter's death by now, and presumably it was their instruction, rather than Diana's failure to sound convincing as a journalist, that prompted the hospital to draw an iron curtain around the case.

It was Lionel who had inspired her, as he so often did. 'Show your press credentials and open any door,' he told her once. They had sneaked backstage at the London Apollo in 1968 and met the cast of Madame Butterfly before an angry theatre director ejected them, giggling, into Shaftesbury Avenue.

Four nights ago, she'd only had to mention that she was calling from The Evening Chronicle before a duty doctor was willing to confirm the suspected cause of Chris's untimely demise.

Sadly, it seemed that her journalist cover story was no longer an option.

She reached for her notes and read them again. The pathologist had confirmed a cardiac arrest, and although they'd found illegal drugs at the scene, the official report would state that other toxins had probably caused the heart attack.

What other toxins, she wondered? Somehow, she needed to get a copy of that toxicology report.

Diana cast her mind back to that day. That little caravan had been a mess – goodness knows how they managed to live like that. The air was filled with a bizarre perfume, pungent and sweet, a botanical scent that Diana had not encountered for many decades.

In the heat of the moment, she had decided to take a small souvenir for their investigation. Amidst the chaos of police and paramedics, she elbowed her way through and managed to remove a tiny Ziplock bag, secreting it in her handbag until she got home. The contents were dried leaves, pungent with that unmistakable aroma, and even though she knew this should not be in her possession, or perhaps because she did, simply holding it in the palm of her hand was exhilarating.

If any other drugs were present, she hadn't been able to see them before that too-polite young officer insisted that it was a crime scene, and she really did have to leave.

Sue had called her that morning with an update, having taken the entire weekend to establish that Chris was employed by Peter as a golf caddy. Diana had been working on various theories as to how the two men knew each other, but all her scenarios had involved Sparkbrook. Now she was picturing the unlikely pair meandering their way across the golf course.

It had taken quite some convincing to persuade her golf fanatic son-in-law that yes, this was an urgent issue and no, it could not wait until he finished work. In the end he caved and answered her questions, only, Diana imagined, to get her off the phone.

She now understood that the role of the caddy involved carrying the golf bag, helping the player select the right club for the shot, and advising on the particulars of the course. A delightful young lady at Bamburgh Golf Club named Shelley informed her that the majority of their members played without caddies, but one could be arranged if the member insisted.

She wondered whether Peter had been introduced to Chris through the club. There was no way that Chris wouldn't have known who he was. Perhaps he had even engineered the opportunity to caddy for Peter, giving him a chance to get close. What had they talked about during those long hours spent in each other's company? Had Peter known that Chris used to work for him, once upon a time?

Diana made a note of each question as it came to her.

After a working lunch for one, she dragged a stool across the living room floor to the foot of the bookcase. Gingerly climbing, she reached the top and steadied herself with a hand on the wall. From here, she could just about reach the second-highest shelf.

Fifteen years ago, she hadn't needed to stretch to get there. *Age is such a terrible pity,* Diana thought as something in her back clunked awkwardly out of place. Sandra would have a fit if she saw her mother clambering to such a height, and that thought alone steeled her determination.

Safely back on the ground, she blew a film of dust from the hardback *Encyclopaedia Britannica*, volume M–Z. Perhaps it had been longer than fifteen years, after all. She flicked through until she found the page she was looking for.

The dried leaves in that little cellophane bag didn't much resemble the line drawing on the page. *Keep an open mind*, Lionel used to chide her. But try as she might, she couldn't fathom any other possibility. *Marijuana*. She drew three lines under the word she had jotted down earlier in her notes.

The encyclopaedia entry was enlightening – a stimulant and a depressive, a narcotic hallucinogen commonly used in pain relief. No mention of causing cardiac arrest.

She had never tried it, not even back in the days when it seemed that everyone and their grandmother were getting stoned – she and Lionel just weren't into that sort of thing. But now she was curious. Had Chris's marijuana been spiked with the deadly cocktail of heart attack-inducing drugs that Amy had described? Or had it distracted him sufficiently for someone to slip him something else?

Always look for the gaps in the story, Lionel was fond of staying. The biggest gap for her right now was whether Peter knew that Chris had been one of his underpaid workers, or whether he simply knew Chris as his the man who carried his golf bag.

Her mind spun with the possibilities this now opened, and she listed them in her notes. *Blackmail. Extortion. Drugs. Revenge*. She underlined that last one twice.

The hairs on the back of her neck stood on end and she shuddered, excitement rippling through her. And despite the body that occasionally failed to cooperate and the mind that let her down with increasing frequency, Diana felt more alive than she had in years.

52

IT HAD WORKED. THE JUJU, THE *STREGHERIA* – THE OLD religion – the ancient sorcery that both of Lucia's grand-mothers swore by while knowing it by different names. Two women whose paths never crossed in life and yet whose blood mixed in her veins. Whatever it was, it had worked. The magic of vanishing, of disappearing, of distance.

Lucia had even attempted a visualisation, picturing Ben in her mind's eye and willing away whatever obstructed his energy. Willing him back to her.

And it had worked. Ben had got in touch. Whatever had been troubling him, it seemed to be no longer an issue.

Heathrow Airport shrank smaller and smaller beneath them as the plane climbed north, the last leg of the journey home. Lucia sat back in her seat and closed her eyes. She shouldn't be this happy over a boy. The sensation was foreign and frightening, yet familiar at the same time. It wasn't happiness as much as relief. What she felt for Ben was real, and he felt the same.

It was difficult, he'd told her by text. *I'll explain face-to-face.* Once the messages started, they came in a flurry, like the first snowfall of the season. His dad's death had hit him hard, and he'd been dealing with his mother and the company and the grief. Between all of that, he hadn't had the emotional energy to deal with anything else. He hadn't forgotten about her, though. In fact, according to Ben, he had thought about Lucia every day.

The apricot light of the late afternoon streamed through the cabin window as they rose above the clouds, reminding Lucia that even when you can't see it, the sun is always shining.

She would be back in her own bed tonight. *Her own bed.* She thought of climbing between the cool crisp sheets in Puffin Cottage and waking up to the sea view from her window. *Perfection.*

It had been a successful commission and even though she hadn't needed the money, falling back into the rhythm of travel had been like visiting an old friend.

That was the part she enjoyed the most. The formula. Checking in. Flight codes. Security protocols. Baggage rules, cabin crew prep, safety briefings. The language of announcements and warnings and reminders. A glimpse of a cockpit full of dials. A meal of measured portions, served at set times, a choice between only two options. Following the signs to the taxi rank, the hotel room. Doing it all again the next day. The rhythmic familiarity of it all.

The rank, the file. Order among chaos. Crossing the globe in a day. Putting your life in someone else's hands.

Going anywhere in the entire world and seeing life from a different perspective – not just seeing it, but living it, if only for one day.

If things did progress to the next level with Ben, she would tell him what she did. There was no need to hide it, after all. The only reason she wasn't upfront with everyone was that people didn't understand. How could she convince them that it was all above board when some days, even she thought it was too good to be true?

Lucia was a courier.

Not drugs – never anything illegal. Her consignments were precious cargo, the belongings and acquisitions of the rich and powerful that were too valuable to entrust to an anonymous agency.

This time it had been a watch, purchased in Switzerland and custom-modified by a London jeweller. A wedding anniversary gift for the wife of a Malaysian millionaire. Not that Lucia cared much about the recipients.

Occasionally, it was just paperwork. Companies with a contract that had to be signed by two parties on either side of the Atlantic on the same day, a real estate agent purchasing property overseas, or a popstar scoring the deal of a lifetime. Sometimes it was the most ridiculous things: prototypes of gadgets, samples of sneakers, an old family photo album... Lucia had transported items of all shapes and sizes. The precious, the rare, the urgent, or the sentimental. They went with her in her hand luggage, often locked under a code until she had to declare them at customs.

It was only supposed to be that one trip back in the beginning. She had been so desperate to escape that she barely entertained the thought that it could become a long-term thing. Then another job came up soon after the first, and another after that.

Escaping became her crutch and the music of travelling became a salve to her anxiety, the dread that crept in whenever she sat still for too long. For hours, the hum of an aircraft could drown out the voices in her head and soon she would be in another place, where nobody knew her and her problems remained far away.

She didn't belong anywhere – not Ghana, not Italy. Definitely not Manchester. But perhaps that meant that she belonged everywhere. She considered this. If she belonged everywhere, then it was her choice. For the first time since it started, all those years ago, Lucia felt the beginning of true freedom.

53

FIONA WAS RIGHT – EVENTUALLY, CAITLYN GOT BORED. IT took longer than she'd expected; she had to give her daughter that. But Seahouses was far too quaint for Caitlyn, who seemed to require artificial lighting and wine bars and Ubers to survive in the way that most people need water and oxygen.

Fiona had watched as her daughter's claustrophobia grew each day, suffocating her until one morning midweek she declared her imminent departure. She was needed back at the office in Edinburgh, some urgent client issue. And despite the pitiful excuse, Fiona let her have it.

Ben was heading up at the weekend, and although Fiona hoped the primary reason for his visit was to spend time with his mother, she expected that Lucia played a large part in his decision. Never mind. They just weren't that sort of family. She had to admit that now.

He'd been holed up with the accountants and lawyers for days before he had the decency to call her with an update. Hopefully, all was not yet lost. After all, these things usually took months, not a couple of weeks.

She could easily picture Ben as the new CEO of Spark-brook. Sharp in a new suit and the Hermès tie she bought him for Christmas last year. It was his destiny – he just needed to see that his father had been wrong. With Ben in charge, they could do things differently. She would walk back into Durham with her head held high and the past would soon be forgotten, even by Caitlyn.

It was no use trying to persuade him on the phone, not now that Caitlyn and Lou had already got to him. Her best bet was to get him alone, just the two of them. Ben had always been a mummy's boy deep down, and she was confident that she could at least get him to see her point of view. She was owed that much. Wasn't she?

She wondered if he knew about that awful business last week. That young man, not much younger than Ben, who died at the caravan site. It was a tragic loss of life, but Fiona wouldn't have given it much thought if Diana hadn't asked if she knew him.

What a strange question, she had thought. That evening, she went online and brought up his Facebook profile, seeing a face she recognised from that night at the book club. Still, the name meant nothing beside that, and she quite forgot about him in the days that followed.

It wasn't until she was in Peter's office looking for some cash that the name came to her again. Peter was terrible for squirrelling money away and would frequently forget where he had stuffed wads of notes. Fiona was searching his desk, turning out envelopes and fanning notebooks, strongly suspecting that Caitlyn had been through there before her.

A cheque. She could make a cheque out to herself and cash it. She was certain that was still allowed, and if anyone tried to tell her it wasn't, she would feign ignorance. It would be easy to fake his signature and backdate it by a month. Just a little petty cash until everything was in place. It was all hers now, anyway.

Peter's office smelled of him – like soap and leather and something bitter, tinged with the faded memory of a sneaky cigar. Being in his space was emboldening. Peter had never allowed her to venture into his sanctum, and they had an unspoken yet mutually understood rule that she should never be here unsupervised.

She had almost dared herself to, once. Peter was down in Newcastle for meetings, not long after they arrived in Seahouses, and before he stopped doing any work at all. In his absence, the house felt lighter, more open, and for the first time in weeks she was able to breathe. It would be hours until he got back. She knew that as soon as he set off, and a desperate urge rose in her chest, pulling her towards this room. Only the thought of what he might do if he found out – if he so much as sensed that she'd been snooping – restrained her.

But there was nothing stopping her now.

Peter's chequebook lay prone in the desk drawer, half used, its cover well-thumbed. Fiona opened it on the first blank cheque, then hesitated, her curiosity getting the better of her. She flicked back through some of the stubs. And that's when she saw it. C Carter.

She went back through again, checking methodically this time, her heart fluttering.

Several cheques from Peter's personal account had been paid to Chris Carter over the past eight months. Most of them were for a hundred pounds each, except for two.

'Two thousand pounds...' she mumbled to herself.

How did Peter know him, and why on earth had he given him two cheques at one thousand pounds a time?

For all his faults, Peter was a generous man. She'd

known him to bequeath large sums of money on deserving strangers as the mood took him – which tended to be erratic. Their friends had feigned embarrassment at Peter picking up the entire restaurant bill and lavishly tipping the waitress with a fifty-pound note, his eyes glistening merrily in the candlelight. Those were the moments in which Fiona had still found something to love about her husband, even if he did tend to favour younger wait-staff, particularly those with shapely legs.

Chris wasn't Peter's usual type, and Fiona couldn't imagine why he would have been on the receiving end of her husband's generosity. She thought back to that bizarre discussion with Amy and Diana. Did they know something that she didn't? Was Chris's death linked to Peter's, somehow?

No. That wasn't possible. Peter died of a heart attack. She saw it with her own eyes.

Or had she only seen what she wanted to?

54

FIVE DAYS. FOR FIVE AGONISINGLY LONG DAYS, GINA HAD heard nothing from Carrie. As the hours and minutes dragged by, the sense of unease in the pit of her stomach grew. Her phone remained a black mirror, stubbornly silent. More than once her finger twitched reflexively over the call button, but she resisted, tucking the device into the drawer by her bed each night to hide the temptation.

She wished she knew what was going on in Carrie's head. Had Carrie mentioned Gina's name to the police because she suspected her friend had something to do with Chris's death, or simply because she was terrified, alone in the world once more, with no one to turn to?

Gina had almost expected Carrie to turn up this morning with the housekeeping girls. She had stopped her inventory-taking as they arrived, willing Carrie to walk through the pub door with the rest of the group. Of course, she didn't.

If she didn't hear anything by Sunday, she would drive up to Berwick. She hadn't a clue where Carrie's aunt lived, but nothing could stop her cruising the cobbled streets of the town, her eyes scanning the faces of everyone she passed. The place wasn't that big. She would drive around all day if that's what it took.

No, she wouldn't do that. She had to wait.

It was only a matter of time, surely, until Carrie came home.

Gina thought back to the last night out they'd had – the last proper night out. Almost a whole year ago. Carrie had only just met Chris, and he was on the periphery rather than at the epicentre of her life. She could still breathe without him.

They got ready in Gina's flat, sharing half a bottle of prosecco to get them in the spirit. She painted Carrie's nails and curled her hair in rollers, all for a night of bingo at the caravan park. What a laugh they'd had.

Yes. Carrie would remember all of this and would come back.

The police must have said something to her – made some comment or raised a question that tipped Carrie from numb grief into suspicion and paranoia. Something that made her wonder if there was more to Chris's death. Why else would she have told them about the argument in the pub?

Or perhaps she just needed a break. Perhaps it was Gina who was being paranoid.

She couldn't help it. Police made her nervous.

She thought back to what happened before, all those years ago. This was like watching a movie when you had already read the book.

Gina opened her window a slice, enough to let a cool trickle of briny air fill her bedroom. From the harbour down below, the rhythmic percussion of the waves sounded a steady hypnotic beat. She slowed her breathing to the cadence and began, finally, to drift off to sleep to the tune of the tide, white noise that quietened her troubled mind.

He came to her again in the crush and sweat of the dark hours, plummeting to the depth of her dreams.

Tony.

A grassy riverbank, still glossy with morning dew. Nobody could see this spot from the little stone bridge, and they were hidden from the road by the wall. Gina's mind wasn't cloudy this time. She could see everything in electrifyingly frightening detail. A drop of sweat ran down his temple over a bulging vein, his face red and taut. *Look up,* she told herself. *Keep your eyes on heaven.*

Tony. Tony.

She floated out of her body and this time, when she looked down from above, it was Carrie who lay on the ground. She couldn't see Chris's face, but she didn't need to – it was undeniably him.

What was he doing here? How did he find them? Carrie's eyes were wide with panic. Gina tried to scream for her, but when she opened her mouth, no sound came.

There were no sirens this time, but suddenly the grass wasn't wet beneath her. No sign of Carrie, either, or Chris. Their apparitions vanished from her dream as quickly as they had appeared.

Gina's feet were planted against the solid gravel ground in front of the bridge, sharp stones digging into her bare feet. Bodies all around her, jostling for position. Craning their necks.

In her nightmare, there were people standing on the tow path, but there hadn't been anyone there that day. Had there? A crowd gathered now, on the bank of the river in that place-between-places. Police officers in fluorescent yellow jackets and spectators wrapped up against the perpetual damp in a town where it seemed to rain more often than it didn't. What had they come to see?

Gina was among the crowd, cocooned from the cold in her big coat. There was nobody in that spot where the grass had been flattened two weeks earlier. Her shoes were back on her feet.

It was a month after she broke up with Tony. No, she told the officer; she hadn't heard from him since then.

The policeman didn't ask about Carrie and, for some reason, Gina knew she shouldn't mention it.

Divers searched the river. A call from one of them sent a murmur through the crowd.

Tony. Tony. Tony.

'Good riddance,' Dad said.

Gina went to the inquest. Mum didn't understand why she wanted to, but Gina needed to hear it with her own ears, and Mum came with her in the end. They sat in a stale courtroom as a judge read out a long legalese from which Gina could only pick out parts. *Depression. End of his relationship. Suicide.*

They determined, in the end, that Tony jumped from the bridge, smashing his skull against the rocks at the bottom of the shallow river below. An image that, once conjured, Gina could never un-see.

She sat upright in bed now, breaking the surface. Panting to get her breath back. No longer drowning.

The nightmare was finally over.

Outside, the sea continued to sing its lullaby, but Gina's heart would not stop pounding.

55

A FAMILIAR FIGURE WAS WAITING ON THE GARDEN BENCH WHEN Sue got home from walking the little ones to school. She cursed silently to herself. *There goes my morning.*

Diana was dressed from head to toe in shades of lavender and violet, with the sole exception of her practical brown leather brogues.

'Good morning, Susan.' Diana offered her hand for Sue to help her up. 'We have quite a lot to catch up on.'

It almost escaped Sue's attention, but Diana was carrying what appeared to be a laptop bag. She sighed. She would no doubt get the full story soon enough.

Sue imagined what she should be doing, instead. Her monthly copy of National Geographic had arrived yesterday, featuring a spread on the avifauna of Costa Rica by a rather dishy Irish photographer. She would have made a cup of tea, grabbed a couple of biscuits and sat down in her favourite armchair to admire closeups of toucans and hummingbirds.

'Now, Sue,' Diana said, once they were seated at the small kitchen table. 'You're a woman of science, aren't you?'

Sue wasn't sure if this was a rhetorical question. With Diana, it was best to be non-committal. She struggled to see a way out of this one, though. 'Yes. Well, I was a geologist. *Am* a geologist,' she corrected herself.

'Perhaps you can officially identify this.' Diana placed a tiny Ziplock bag on the table in front of her.

Sue's eyes widened. 'You' – she lowered her voice to a hiss – 'you can't have that in here!'

'Oh, relax. It's not like I'm proposing you roll it up and smoke a joint.'

Sue leaned back in her chair, instinctively scanning the hallway and the back door, checking that they were alone. Anne had been down in her studio since early that morning and thankfully had not yet re-emerged.

'Diana, this is a class A drug. You can't carry stuff like that around with you.'

It might not have been class A. Sue wasn't an expert on such matters, and it felt like a moot point. Bottom line – she didn't appreciate it sitting on her kitchen table.

'Why ever not?' Diana purred. 'It's hardly as if they would stop and search me, is it?' Her eyes sparkled mischievously in the thin morning light. 'Besides. This is evidence.'

Sue held her head in her hands, wanting to avoid it, but also needing to ask the obvious question. 'Where did it come from?'

'It was left at the crime scene.' Diana anticipated Sue's protest and held up a hand to stop her, bony fingers elegantly pointing skyward. 'There was plenty more where that came from. I'm sure the police took everything they require.'

Misinterpreting Sue's shocked silence as a curiosity to know more, she went on. 'Anyway, as samples go, it's quite redundant. The pathologist confirmed that marijuana,' – she waved the small bag in the air – 'did not contribute to Chris's death. The toxicology report indicated that other substances led to the cardiac arrest. They found nitric oxide in his tissue, and his blood vessels were dilated. We'll have to get Amy's professional opinion, but it seems that her initial guess was impressively close to the mark.'

Sue sighed. She didn't want to know how far Diana went to find all of this. Yet despite her alarm, she felt a vague admiration for her old friend's tenacity.

Diana retired the drugs to her handbag and retrieved her second piece of evidence. 'I removed this from the property this morning.'

'You have got to be kidding me.' Sue gawped at the laptop Diana placed on the table. 'You can't just break in and take evidence from a crime scene.'

'I did not "*break in*" – the caravan wasn't locked. If you can even call that a lock – it barely merits the name.'

Sue winced.

'And for the record, it is no longer a crime scene. The police have already removed all the evidence they need for their investigation. Of course, they might need this laptop at some point in the future, if their investigations ever catch up with my thinking on this case.'

Sue shook her head. 'This seems wrong. It *is* wrong,' she corrected herself. 'We shouldn't have this.'

'Well, let's find what we need and then we can return it.' Diana shrugged as if this was a reasonable proposition, like borrowing a cup of flour from a neighbour or asking someone to water your plants when you went on holiday.

Sue shuddered. *None of this was reasonable.*

And yet... If Chris had been murdered – and that was still an entirely hypothetical scenario at this stage, as far as she was concerned – and Chris knew Peter, that would make Peter's death an extraordinary coincidence. Heart disease or not, the timing and the connection between the two men were making her second-guess... well, just about everything.

Sue pulled the laptop towards her and took a deep breath. 'OK,' she said. 'What, exactly, are we looking for?'

————

A pop-up window appeared as the computer blinked to life. Sue sighed. 'It's password protected.'

Diana was unfazed. 'Unfortunately, most people set incredibly obvious passwords. Unfortunate for them, but hopefully good news for us.'

'Any suggestions?'

Diana had considered several passwords but hadn't dared to try any of her ideas. She didn't own a computer but knew that multiple attempts at an incorrect password could shut the machine down, and she didn't know what, if anything, came after that. It felt safer to go through this with someone else at the keyboard.

'One-two-three-four-five.'

'Seriously?'

Diana nodded, and with a shrug, Sue typed.

'Incorrect.'

'Try *password*. Just the word, all lowercase.'

Sue tried it and sighed. 'It's not that either, I'm afraid.' She leaned back in her chair, her gaze drifting towards the ceiling. 'It could be anything.'

Not quite anything, but Diana didn't say this to Sue. Logic dictated that there was a finite list of possibilities. She had gone for the most commonly used passwords on the basis that Chris had seemed like the sort to make such an obvious mistake. Perhaps he was more intelligent than she gave him credit for.

'What about Carrie?' said Sue. 'His girlfriend's name?'

'No.' Instinct told Diana that wasn't correct, but why? She didn't know enough about Chris to determine whether or not he had been the romantic sort. They had all witnessed the extent of his preoccupation with his girl-friend, but in Diana's view, that sort of passion did not signify love. It was about possession and control. Chris's relationship with Carrie was more about him than it was about her.

'Carter.'

Sue turned to her. 'His name?'

'Precisely.' Behind her back, Diana crossed her fingers.

The pop-up disappeared and the women suddenly found themselves face-to-face with Chris Carter. Diana's eyes met his as his face filled the screen, so large that she could count the pockmark scars on his cheeks. Behind him, over his shoulder but occupying only a corner of the image, Carrie grinned at the camera.

'Now,' said Sue. 'Where to start?'

Diana blinked hard, shaking off the distraction and trying to avoid Chris's disconcerting gaze from the screen. There were ways of seeing which websites people had visited, and she hoped Sue knew how to find them.

'His browsing history. Let's see what captured Chris's attention in the days before he died.'

Sue performed a series of clicks. 'That's odd,' she said, her face creasing in a frown. 'There's nothing here. It says it's in incognito mode.'

'We'll come back to that. What about the documents? Anything interesting?'

Sue bit her lip. 'His Facebook suggests that Chris was a

prolific over-sharer. Maybe he saved some of the photos on his computer?'

She clicked on an icon and the screen filled with thumbnails of photographs. She selected a couple randomly, and Diana watched as images of a life cut short tumbled across the screen in front of her.

'There must be thousands of photos on here,' Sue murmured. 'These date back more than a decade.'

Diana drummed her fingers on the table. This was all well and good, but she had hoped that Sue's computer skills might extend beyond knowing how to access old photo albums. Besides, all this voyeurism was making her friend melancholy – she could see it in the sag of Sue's shoulders and the downturn of her mouth. They didn't have time to be despondent. They needed that browsing history.

Diana considered where to go for support. Sandra was out of the question, and Jennifer was so busy with the business these days. Besides, both of her girls had inherited her curious mind, and there was a risk they would demand to know more than she could tell them.

Mike was tech-savvy and would be at home this time of day, but it probably wouldn't do to involve too many people in this.

There was one other person that they might be able to call on. Someone young and bright enough to know their way around a computer, and someone who, Diana suspected, was quite adept at keeping secrets.

56

IT WAS WARM – STILL SWEATER WEATHER, BUT PLEASANT enough to sit outside. Sunlight pooled in the little yard at the back of Puffin Cottage and the scent of honeysuckle filled the air.

Lucia heard them approaching, two sets of footsteps and the unmistakable voice of her landlady. She put her book down and listened, a smile spreading over her face. *Better get the kettle on,* she thought.

She had picked wildflowers and grasses on her morning walk and arranged them in a green glass vase, the display earning her a curt nod of approval from Diana as she entered the kitchen.

Amy's aunt was with her, although Lucia had come to understand that she was more like a second mother to Amy. Sue bore little resemblance to her sister Anne. They were a study in contrasts, both in their outward appearance as much as their characters. Whereas Sue was practical and solid, Lucia could tell that Anne had a wounded soul.

She wordlessly set out the tea on the table, using the pretty set adorned with hand-painted flowers and gold leaf. A discreet glance at the clock told her that she still had a few hours until Ben arrived, unless he decided to surprise her by turning up before she expected him.

It wouldn't be the first time.

Tea served, Diana got down to business. 'I'm afraid this is not strictly a social call. We need some help.'

'IT support,' added Sue. She placed a laptop on the table and opened it. 'We've tried to access the browsing history, but the results are hidden – incognito, I believe.' In the way that she said 'incognito', Lucia guessed she had only recently learned the word.

She smirked, unsure if this was a windup. These ladies seemed to be constantly up to something.

'Seeing as you're a digital...' Diana paused, frowning in concentration. 'What was the word, my dear?'

'A digital nomad,' Lucia mumbled. She felt the warmth of a blush rising in her cheeks and willed it away.

'That's it.' Diana clicked her fingers. 'A *digital nomad*. Whereas Sue and I are quite the dinosaurs when it comes to all things technological.'

Lucia very much doubted that, but said nothing. 'It should be straightforward.' She noticed the briefest glance pass between the two women.

Pulling a notepad from her bag, Sue nudged her chair towards Lucia's place at the table.

'I'll take notes. Just in case I need to do it again.'

Lucia made a series of perfunctory taps. 'Hopefully, it'll all be saved in the cache. You go into Control Centre, open a command...' Her fingers glided across the control pad. 'There.'

A list of websites unfolded across the screen in front of them. Lucia quickly scanned it, unsure what, exactly, she should be looking for, and whether it would give her any clues as to what these two were playing at.

The most recent sites were points on Google Maps, mainly spots around the village and out toward the golf course that Lucia could identify by road name. She scrolled down, and saw Peter Gallivan's name appear, repeated like lines written for punishment. Her eyes widened.

The laptop snapped to a close, the screen disappearing from in front of her eyes and in its place, Diana smiled back at her, one hand on the computer.

'There's no need to do all of that now, ladies.' She addressed Sue directly. 'Lucia has very kindly shown you how to access the history, but let's save the rest for later.'

Sue nodded. Lucia might have imagined it, but she appeared to be squirming in her seat.

'We should get out of your hair, anyway,' Sue said, as she carefully slid the laptop back into her bag. 'I'm sure you have much more exciting plans than tea with us.'

Lucia smiled politely and went through the motions of urging them to finish their tea and call over any time.

Three hours until he got here.

That was more than enough time to clean up the impromptu tea party, refresh herself, and prepare the modest dinner she had planned.

She waved Sue and Diana off, watching them trundle back down the lane in the direction they came from. Then she set about the washing up.

What are they up to? she wondered. And why on earth were they going through Chris Carter's laptop?

57

THE SKY HAD BEEN CLEAR ALL AFTERNOON, PUNCTUATED ONLY by sporadic clouds whose edges were tinged pink in the falling dusk light, petals from a wilting bouquet. In the distance, the rocky outcrop of the Farne Islands rose from the sea. Even from here, Tom could see the swirling and swooping of the birds as they fished for their evening catch, plunging from great heights into the icy depths below.

He looked down at his own fish supper and found that he had somewhat lost his appetite. In truth, he wasn't all that hungry to start with, but it seemed like a normal thing to do. At least it gave him a reason to get out of the house.

These days, Tom found that he increasingly spent his time on tasks for the sake of tasks. *Normal things.* Purposeless, except that they were a purpose in themselves.

Fran had nagged at him to *expand his circle* – meet new people and increase the circuit of places in which he spent time. 'Don't fall into forming habits that impose new limits,' she had instructed. Eating fish and chips while watching the trawlers make their evening return to the harbour was a novelty, so there had to be some merit in that.

At least it got him out from under Agnes's feet. They had fallen into a comfortable pattern of coexistence in which neither relied upon nor indeed expected very much of the other. Crucially, Agnes didn't ask too many questions. Tom appreciated that more than anything.

He checked his watch. In twenty minutes, he could turn up at the pub.

Before all of this upset, he had taken to midnight walks. In the small hours, after the day trippers had returned home and when everyone else was in bed, Seahouses was dark and as still as air, the sky a velvety canopy of stars. On those nights when Tom's dreams stopped him from sleeping, or worse – when a nightmare shook him roughly awake – he slipped out of the house and paced away his demons, winding his way quietly through the slumbering streets with no goal in mind other than to keep moving.

Even in a place like Seahouses, you saw things differently at night. Under the fluorescent haze of streetlamps and the pale light of the moon, the narrow streets had a new eeriness, and the harbour gave way to nothing but oily blackness.

Now, in the comfort of the fading daylight, he popped one last chip into his mouth. It was cold, soggy, and left a slick of grease on his lip.

A seagull stalked him on the short walk to the litter bin, eyeing him menacingly. After cramming the remains of his meal through the slot, Tom scuttled away, the bird still glaring at him.

He was almost at the top of the hill when the green sports car flew past, driving far too fast for this stretch of road, as the types who drove such cars were wont to do.

Tom tutted under his breath. Mr Flash, back for more. Still in a hurry, too, by the looks of things. But where was he going this time? His parents – or rather, just his mother now – lived in the opposite direction.

Probably calling in on the supermodel. She lived in one of the little fisherman's cottages that overlooked the harbour. It was inevitable, Tom supposed. Money and beauty and glamour were drawn to each other. The pair of them were two of a kind, pulled together like magnets.

Confirming his suspicion, the car bypassed the pub and snaked down one of the side streets towards the water. Hopefully Flash would park up and call it a night wherever he decided to lay his head. He'd almost killed Tom that last time he took a late-night spin, careening through the dark like a madman.

Tom's midnight walks were on hold, for now. The police had been in Seahouses again today, and the village was beginning to buzz with the suspicion that Chris's death might have been a smidge more complicated than a straightforward heart attack after all.

He had self-imposed a curfew – at least one that kept him largely at home during the nights, if only to avoid having to answer any difficult questions down the line. There had been press interest in Peter Gallivan's death and they would swarm like flies if there was a whiff of murder. Tom wanted – needed – to keep his name out of this.

The last thing he needed right now was to draw attention to himself.

———

At the same time, only a stone's throw away, Helen was closing the shop for the evening.

She left the till open to warn any would-be thieves that there was no cash on the premises, although a burglar with half a brain would surely find the security box in the back. It was a mandate from their insurance company, just like the CCTV camera that bumped up the electricity bill and the Health and Safety training refresher they made her do once a year. Completely unnecessary but it allowed someone somewhere to keep ticking their precious boxes. As she locked the door, five versions of her reflection from Anne's sea glass and shell mirrors winked back, mocking her.

The weather forecast had predicted it would be dry all day, so Helen had left her car at home that morning. The weight was melting off Sue, and apparently it was all down to getting her steps in, so Helen set off for more of the same. Who needed fancy aerobics classes and Lycra leotards when you had a mile and a half walk to get home? She could swear that Sue now had the beginnings of what looked decidedly like cheekbones, and Helen focused on this as she plodded through the village and out towards the farm.

The sun cast long shadows out into the lane, and gravel crunched under her feet as she walked up the drive, the flowerbeds losing their colour in the fading day. A light was on downstairs and the curtains were open, its glow spilling into the yard outside.

Roy was already asleep – she sensed it in the stillness of the farmhouse before she heard his snores. His mud-crusted boots lay discarded by the kitchen door, the dirty plates from his tea stacked in the sink.

Poor bloke.

Matthew should have taken over by now. Except it wasn't like the old days anymore, and they could hardly expect the lad to earn a bachelor's degree in marketing only to spend the rest of his days working on a farm.

Helen put another log in the hearth and watched as the flames flickered back to life. Roy didn't stir. She sat down with her book in the armchair opposite her husband. Roy's head hung at an angle like a scarecrow, a thread of dribble leaking from one side of his mouth. She would wake him in an hour or two, just for him to drag his weary bones upstairs to their bed where he would sleep like the dead until dawn broke, at which point he would do it all again.

She tugged off her socks and flexed her toes, warming the soles of her feet in the heat that now radiated from the fire. She picked up the novel they were reading for the book club, but the words on the page swam together. Helen couldn't muster enough concentration to focus on the story and keep those other thoughts from nudging their way into her consciousness.

A memory replayed in her mind from a lifetime ago. Two girls on the cusp of womanhood. They had drifted away from the rest of the group, a shadowy gaggle of teenagers whose faces, illuminated by the bonfire, were indistinguishable. They only saw each other.

Neither of them meant for it to happen – it just did. As if they would always be there at that moment, as if it were written in their stars. Pressed so close that she could feel the warmth of her friend's breath on her lips.

She put the book down on the coffee table, open on the page that she had tried and failed to read, and allowed thoughts of Sue to occupy her mind.

Helen woke an hour later. It was dark, and she still hadn't closed the curtains. The embers glowed in the glazed brick hearth. She glanced at Roy and a knot tightened in her stomach. In her mind, a pendulum swung back and forth, back and forth.

Yes, she had done the right thing. Thirty-five years – it was nothing next to one silly teenage kiss on a beach a lifetime ago. She and Roy had been happy, whatever that meant.

She sighed to herself. Some things were just not meant to be. But tonight, as on so many nights, her head brimmed with questions. *What if?*

It was a different time back then. They were so sheltered. The swinging sixties and the hypnotic liberties of the seventies happened elsewhere – New York and London and places that might as well have been on another planet. It was decades before any of that stuff reached Seahouses.

But what if things had been different? If they had been born thirty years later, at a time where parents didn't line up suitors and anyone could marry whomever they pleased, and people aspired to more for their daughters than to settle down with a farmer who had a decent herd and a handsome farmstead?

Helen would never say these things aloud, not even to Sue. She was coming over for a coffee tomorrow, and Helen had saved half a packet of the fancy shortbread for her visit.

But she wondered – did Sue ever think of that night? Did she ever wonder what might have been?

58

ANNE WAS SULKING. FROM THE TILT OF HER HEAD AND THE curve of her shoulders, hunched as she was at the kitchen table, Sue could sense it before she even saw it on her sister's face.

This was so typical of Anne. Really, the woman could be maddening at times. Sue didn't know anyone else quite like it. Anne's constant need for attention was an insatiable appetite, never to be fulfilled. When she wasn't getting it from Amy – who was pretty good with her mother, all things considered – she demanded it from Sue.

A few weeks of Sue going off and doing her own thing had rubbed Anne up in quite the wrong direction. And even though Sue's instinct to apologise and make amends needled at her, she took some delight in this. She normally ran around after Anne, at the mercy of her sister's every whim. The shoe was on the other foot now, and Sue was surprised to discover that it was a comfortable fit.

'I suppose you're off out again today?' Anne huffed without taking her eyes off her sudoku puzzle.

'Seeing Helen for coffee, just as I do every Friday.' She

anticipated Anne's next question before it came. 'And no, none of the mirrors have sold, before you ask.'

She barely registered Anne's attempt at a nonchalant shrug as she swung out of the door, forgoing breakfast. A growling stomach was a price worth paying to wind her sister up.

There were customers in the shop, a Scandinavian couple trussed up in walking gear. Sue went through her practiced routine of play-acting a casual browser. Aideen McIntyre, the owner of the gift shop, had never explicitly said that staff couldn't invite friends over for tea and biscuits, but Helen was always cautious, nonetheless.

As soon as the hikers left, Sue dropped the pretence.

'I've got so much to update you on!' Her voice lowered to a stage whisper even though they were alone. 'Chris Carter and Peter Gallivan knew each other. Not only did Chris work for Sparkbrook, but get this – he caddied for Peter at golf.' Sue straightened with pride. She had no benchmark, but as amateur detective work went, it seemed quite impressive. 'And that's not all. Diana got hold of Chris's laptop.'

'What? How on earth...?'

Sue held up a hand. 'Honestly, the less we know, the better. But still. Can you imagine what she might find out from that?'

Helen said nothing, but Sue was unperturbed. 'We found loads of photos. And Lucia hacked his browsing history – all the websites he'd visited. Seems that Chris spent quite a lot of time researching Peter Gallivan, reading articles about him and what-not.'

Sue felt the warmth rising in her face, a rosy flush blossoming on the apples of her cheeks. She hesitated, waiting for Helen to say something.

It struck her, in that moment, that she really cared about

this – not just about the evidence they had uncovered, but about finding out what happened. About seeing justice served. There was a difference, she realised, between spreading gossip and sharing knowledge. Knowledge itself was not a bad thing. What you did with it; that's what mattered. They weren't meddling – they were doing a good deed. And this was her village, after all.

Helen sank down into the chair opposite. 'So, do we have a working theory?'

Sue took a sip of too-hot tea, swallowing it in a gulp. 'I reckon Chris had something on Peter. Maybe some scandal that never made the papers. He could have threatened to expose him. And when Peter refused to play ball...' She swiped a finger across her neck.

'But then who killed Chris? It makes no sense.'

'There must be a third person. Someone who didn't like that Chris had something over Peter, but also had something to gain from Peter being killed.'

'One of the Gallivans?'

Sue shook her head. 'Fiona was over at mine the evening Peter died. She found him like that when she got home. And Ben wasn't here that night – Amy saw him leave Seahouses that afternoon. There's the daughter, too, but she didn't appear until her dad's funeral.

Helen knotted her brow in concentration. 'There's got to be some explanation...'

They were disturbed by the tinkling of the bell.

'Ladies,' said Diana, announcing herself from the threshold. 'I believe I have found what we are looking for.'

Diana had taught enough Shakespeare to know a thing or two about dramatic tension. She refused to reveal anything until they were safely secluded in Sue's kitchen with Amy at the table, insisting everyone needed to hear this.

The desire to know had been enough to convince Helen to close up before lunch and to drag Amy away from the unenviable task of balancing the accounts of the Lifeboat Institute committee. They had decamped promptly, with Diana leading at a brisk trot.

Amy glanced at the clock. 'So, you've got us all here. What have you dug up?'

Diana opened the laptop and typed in the password using her index fingers, her varifocals reflecting the blue square of the screen in front of her.

'Receipts. Lots of them. I got into Chris's email. It looks like someone had been on a shopping spree lately. PlayStation. H Samuel. ASOS.'

Diana had never heard of ASOS until last night, when she spent an hour researching the items and outlets corresponding to the order confirmations in Chris's inbox. Why anyone would spend such a ludicrous amount of money on a pair of trainers was beyond her. But it was a trail of breadcrumbs. She had quickly understood that this young man who lived in a caravan and worked as a casual labourer had enjoyed full pockets of late.

Sue chewed pensively on her lip. 'So he had money. Any idea where it came from?'

'That, I can't tell you. Not unless I'm able to get access to his bank accounts.'

Diana's daughters had tried to get her to use online banking, but she had never been keen. Who in their right mind would open their bank accounts to possible attacks from Russian hackers? She shuddered at the thought and clicked open a window from Chris's browsing history that she had bookmarked for later reading.

'Lou Renwick. Does that name mean anything to you?'

'Peter's business partner,' said Amy. 'His right-hand man? Or something like that? Peter had an affair with his wife, according to Mike. It's an open secret, apparently,' she added with a sigh.

'That's what they want everyone to believe.' Diana regarded each member of her audience in turn. 'Lou's wife – fifty-eight-year-old Esme Renwick. Glamourous, fair, good build...'

Diana studied the picture on the screen in front of her as the others crowded around for a glimpse. 'They kept it out of the papers, for the most part. This was the article that broke the story, and it doesn't name the unfortunate soul on the receiving end of Peter's affections.'

She scrolled down, giving the others enough time to read the headline: 'Millionaire's Marriage At Breaking Point'.

Without going into too many specifics, the piece simply stated that Peter Gallivan and his wife were in crisis talks after the latest round of infidelity accusations. It was positively restrained in its condemnation of Peter, with only a nod to the fire he came under for his zero hours contracts and tax avoidance.

'How does one keep one's dirty laundry out of the press...?' Diana said, posing the question to the group.

'Money,' said Helen. 'Everything comes down to money. Always.'

'Exactly!' Diana wagged a finger in the air. 'Not only is Sparkbrook a major advertiser of The Chronicle, but Peter owns a stake in Newcastle United – another significant revenue stream for the paper. Just imagine, for one second, what would happen if The Chronicle published all the gory details? They'd risk being blacklisted. The publishers can't afford to print a story like that, no matter how many copies it would sell.'

'So he kept the sordid details out of the papers.' Amy shrugged. 'So what?'

'What we need to ask ourselves, my dear, is what exactly was he keeping out? What was so terrible that the publishers dared not venture close to the truth?'

Sue sighed. 'I don't know. An affair with your business partner's wife is rather bad PR.'

Diana nodded. 'Indeed. But what if it was actually much, much worse?' Wordlessly, she clicked open another window.

'Erin Renwick,' said Amy, scanning the profile piece from a lifestyle site. Diana looked again at the photo that accompanied the article. Erin was a younger version of her mother, and only a slightly different variation of Fiona. Or Caitlyn, come to that.

'Erin Renwick.' Diana repeated the name with a sigh of resignation that did little to mask the satisfaction in her voice. 'Peter wasn't having an affair with his business partner's wife. He was having an affair with his business partner's daughter.'

59

DIANA HADN'T WORKED IT OUT QUITE ALL ON HER OWN, OF course, although she had no doubt she would have got there, eventually. As it happened, she'd had a helping hand.

Earlier that morning, she had put in a call to Roger Mason – once a young protégé of Lionel's, now a balding news journalist with a middle-aged paunch. She had almost cried with delight when she'd first seen Roger's name under The Chronicle's articles on the Sparkbrook scandal.

After having his wings clipped by his editors for trying to run the story in its original form and with the promise of an exclusive if Diana uncovered something, Roger had been glad to divulge which parts of the story didn't make the cut. He provided Erin's name, and Diana had only had to match it up to some of the websites in Chris's browsing history to understand that he'd cottoned on to Peter, too.

But the ladies didn't need to know that. Not yet, at least. As Lionel always told her, keeping your cards close to your chest was part of the game. A good investigator never reveals their sources, and journalists that Lionel knew personally had gone to jail to protect the identities of the men and women who fed them information.

'His best friend's daughter.' Amy shuddered.

Sue sank into the chair opposite Diana. 'Let me get this straight: Peter cheats on his wife with his mate's daughter but manages to keep it out of the papers. Chris finds out and blackmails him, then someone kills them both. Why?'

Diana regarded her fingers and offered a considered shrug. 'Revenge? Financial gain? To hide a secret?'

In truth, she still was not clear on who, exactly, could have killed both Peter and Chris. There were several people who would benefit from Peter's death and a smaller number who might wish ill on Chris, and very few fit into both categories.

'So where do we go from here?' Helen asked.

'We need a plan,' said Sue, her face knotted in thought. 'We need to look again at all the evidence and piece it back together. The sand in the Gallivans' hallway the night Peter died – we still haven't found out who could have trampled it in or which building site they came from. The money in Chris's account. How he died. Who benefits from the deaths? We need timelines... and that sort of thing.'

'We could form our own detective agency!' Diana clapped her hands together. 'Northumberland Ladies Investigations.' She hoped it sounded as if the name had only just occurred to her, and scanned her friends' faces for a response. When it came, it was lukewarm. She shrugged it off.

'Perhaps we don't need a name just yet. But we certainly have our work cut out.' Diana nodded at Amy. 'You're on Fiona's detail. There's something she's not telling us, and we need you to find out what it is. Sue – I want you to go through Chris's computer. Comb through his Facebook again, and those blasted photos. Anything at all. I know he published a lot, but there has to be something we're missing.'

'What about me?' Helen said, after an uncomfortable pause.

'You're on the golf course,' Diana replied. 'That's where they spent time together. Perhaps they left a clue. Take your husband, have dinner, make conversation with the members. Ask around.'

Helen nodded, wide-eyed.

'We each have our assignments,' said Diana, without mentioning what, exactly, she would be doing. 'We rendezvous Monday morning at my house.'

She was the first to depart. Her car was parked in the public carpark behind the gift shop, and she ignored the temptation of a celebratory ice cream as she walked past Coxton's.

The air was crisp, but the sun had burst through the clouds, burning off the threat of rain that afternoon and leaving a broad blue sky speckled with pockets of cloud. There was one more thing to do before returning home.

Instead of turning right towards the road to Beadnell, she turned left at the roundabout, winding her car carefully through the lanes above the harbour. And there it was – a familiar green sports car parked snugly up to the low stone wall outside Puffin Cottage. Just as she had expected.

Had folk always been so predictable, she mused, *or was that the benefit of experience?*

The Gallivan boy had clearly not only spent the night but stuck around for lunch – and then some. She just hoped that Lucia knew what she was getting herself into.

60

'MUM, MY BUN ISN'T STRAIGHT.' HANNAH'S WHINE CAUSED Amy to clench her jaw.

She had exactly eighteen minutes before she had to get everyone out of the house. Their first stop was to drop Lucas at football practice, then Hannah at ballet, and she would take Betsy to soft play before dragging her out thirty minutes later so that they could collect the older two on time. Just another typical Saturday for the Sanders.

Except that Amy was on a mission. She laid awake in bed last night, staring at the ceiling, playing it through in her mind while Mike snored softly. She had to get to Fiona.

Short on better ideas, she had decided to bake a tart – yet another thing to add to her to-do list. There would be a window later that afternoon, once the kids had finished lunch and were playing happily, and Mike had settled on the settee with a beer and whatever sports he could find on TV. Approximately an hour before she would have to get everything ready for dinner. Just enough time to call over to Fiona's on the pretense of depositing baked goods and pray that she could muzzle her way in for a chat.

Fiona didn't seem like the kind of woman who could murder her husband. But then again, did homicidal women sport a definitive look? Was there even such a thing as your average husband-killer? Fiona certainly wasn't crazy or deranged by anger or abuse. In the brief time that Amy had spent with her, she had seemed kind and gentle. Although who could say what they would be capable of after walking a mile in her shoes?

All afternoon, Amy's mind flitted back to that evening. She allowed the image of Peter Gallivan to occupy her thoughts, lying on his living room floor as life ebbed away from him. The same picture came to her in her dreams some nights. And sometimes, instead of Peter's face, she saw her father's. Emboldened by daylight, she confronted it now.

Yes, Gallivan had done some heinous things. But surely, nobody deserved to meet such a cruel fate.

Amy wanted answers. For Peter, but also for herself.

The pie turned out quite well – she had followed a recipe from her own book, which she'd written largely by taking classics and substituting key ingredients for whatever she had to hand, making notes of anything that worked. She'd settled on a Christmas pudding pie – a pastry case filled with a mixture of seasoned raisins, currants, and candied peel. Who cared that it was May? Amy's secret ingredient was peas – once enveloped in the mix of dried fruit, it was impossible to taste them, and their green hue faded quickly. By the time the pie was topped in a dusting of icing sugar, few people thought to question the added crunch.

Ben's car was outside the Gallivan house, and for a moment, Amy hesitated. She gripped the sides of the pie dish as she walked up the path to the ornate porch. Closing her eyes on the doorstep, she pictured Peter's face. By the time she opened them, her resolve had steeled. She pressed hard on the doorbell, hearing the chime echo on the other side.

'Amy, what a lovely surprise.' Fiona seemed genuinely pleased to see her, and Amy felt the tension in her shoulders melt away. 'Care to join me for a glass of wine?'

It wasn't yet three o'clock, but this was her ticket. 'That sounds wonderful.'

The hallway seemed bigger than before – the gleaming white space had been cleaned since her last visit. A bouquet of fresh lilies sat in a glass vase where Amy knew an antique ceramic had once stood. All traces of the sandy trail were long gone.

'Come on through, come on through,' sang Fiona as Amy kicked off her shoes.

She followed Fiona into the kitchen, and took a seat at the island.

'Here,' said Fiona, handing her a glass with a generous pour of rosé. As Fiona slipped the bottle back into the fridge, Amy clocked that it was already half-empty. A telltale flush high on Fiona's cheeks was evidence of where the rest had gone.

Amy took a sip, wondering where to start. She needn't have worried.

'I've been meaning to get in touch,' Fiona said. 'To apologise for my daughter's ill manners, firstly. She's grieving.' She took a gulp of wine, her face taught. 'But last time you were over here, you mentioned that man – Chris.'

Fiona looked at Amy, her eyes wide and her expression blank, and Amy recognised it was her cue to continue.

· · ·

'Chris Carter. He died last Thursday. They thought it was a heart attack initially, but now they're looking into it in more detail.' Amy's voiced dropped to little more than a whisper. 'Suspicious circumstances.'

She fingered the stem of her wineglass. *How much should she say?*

Fiona pursed her lips. 'And Peter knew him, if I understand correctly?'

Amy sipped her wine to disguise her expression while she regained her composure. 'We— I think so. But I'm not sure how.' She longed, in that moment, for some of her sister's bravado. Izzy always knew what to say and could effortlessly handle even the trickiest of situations. Even a dose of Diana wouldn't go amiss right now. But here, alone in this gleaming white spaceship of a kitchen, Amy had almost forgotten why she wanted to come here in the first place.

'Peter was paying him.' Fiona's tone was matter-of-fact, with no room for ambiguity or interpretation. She set her glass down and met Amy's gaze. 'We're talking thousands of pounds. For what, I'm not sure.'

Amy squirmed. 'I don't know. I don't know what to tell you...'

'Oh, I don't believe that for one moment.' Fiona's eyes glistened, but beneath the sparkle, Amy could see the grit. 'I think you know more than you're letting on.'

The accusation hung in the air between them, amplified by the silence of the grand old house. Even the muffled voices from the television upstairs had grown quiet.

'Could Chris have been blackmailing Peter, perhaps?' Amy ventured. Her heart fluttered in her chest.

Fiona sighed. 'Perhaps. But despite outward appearances, Peter was not a soft target.' She took measure of

Amy's response and waved her hand dismissively. 'I know what he was up to. Believe me, I know *all* of it. We were married for forty years, for heaven's sake. Try as he might, Peter was incapable of keeping a secret from me.'

She gazed out of the kitchen window to the landscaped garden and beyond. A blackbird landed on the old stone wall of the herb garden.

Amy bit her lip, wondering what knowing *all* of it actually meant. She fought back against the urge to ask. *Did you know he was sleeping with his best friend's daughter?*

Fiona rolled up the sleeves of her cashmere sweater, the warmth of the wine and the underfloor heating causing a flush to radiate across her cheeks.

'I never wished him dead,' she said. Just like that.

Amy blinked.

'I mean, there were times when I wanted to strangle him for sport, and plenty of days when I knew my life would be better if he wasn't in it, but I married for love.' Fiona regarded Amy, waiting for her to understand. '*For better, for worse,* and all that. Well, I had to take more than my fair share of the *worse*.' Fiona sighed deeply and downed the rest of her glass. 'But none of this is answering my question – who on earth is Chris Carter, and what did he have to do with Peter?'

Without warning, the door flung open with a crash, startling Amy so much that she jumped on her stool.

'You. Again.' Caitlyn sneered.

Caitlyn? Amy's eyes grew wide. She had assumed that only Ben was home. 'I... I just called over to see how your mum was doing. I... I brought a pie.'

Amy glanced at Fiona for validation.

'Darling.' Fiona purred. 'Pour yourself a glass and join us.'

'I'd rather not,' said Caitlyn, never taking her eyes off Amy. 'And I suppose you're here on *official business* again?' Sarcasm dripped from her words.

'I—' Amy started. She took a deep breath and channelled some of her Izzy energy. 'That's right. I wanted to make sure your mum was coping, and remind her that if she needs any support, services are available through her community nursing team.'

It sounded good, but Caitlyn's gaze didn't veer from Amy's face.

'Well, it's a relief to hear that you're not prying. So, I'll simply thank you for your visit, *nurse*, and politely ask you to go.'

'Caitlyn!' Fiona was horrified. 'You'll do no such thing. Honestly...'

Caitlyn turned to her mother, softening her tone to melted butter. 'Come on, Mum. Remember what we talked about? About going back to Durham?'

Fiona visibly stiffened and said nothing, her lips pursed into a tight line.

'Now,' said Caitlyn, looking back at Amy, her eyes falsely bright and a fake smile plastered across her face. 'Weren't you just about to leave?'

———

It was only supposed to be Fiona and Ben that weekend. Just her and her boy.

Yesterday, she made the aubergine parmigiana that he loved and she'd bought two salmon steaks for their lunch today. She'd planned for them to eat in the kitchen, away from the memories of their last meal in the dining room and the phantom menace of his father, and they would talk.

Mother to son. Once she got him alone, it would be easier to get him to see sense on all this nonsense about selling the company, no matter what paperwork he had signed.

But Caitlyn showed up an hour after Ben arrived yesterday evening, while he was still unpacking in the guest room that Fiona had designed with him in mind. Her daughter had offered no explanation about her sudden arrival, which had thrown Fiona's plans into disarray, merely grunting greetings as she politely kissed her mother on both cheeks.

When did they start doing that? Fiona wondered. Once upon a time, she embraced Caitlyn with a bear-hug whenever her daughter returned home. How had she allowed this distance to creep in between them?

Now, Caitlyn was *here,* occupying all the space that Fiona needed if she was ever going to get through to her son. Fiona sighed. She had no doubt that it was a strategic ploy. While Ben possessed many of his mother's qualities – caring, nurturing, sensitive – Caitlyn had learned much from her father. Even if she would sooner die than admit it.

Scaring Amy off was the final straw, and something in Fiona snapped. 'She was only checking in on me. There was no need to be quite so insolent.'

Caitlyn picked an apple from the fruit bowl, which Fiona had replenished ahead of Ben's arrival, and took a deep bite of a Granny Smith. She wiped a speckle of apple juice from her lip with the back of her hand.

'She's not your friend, Mum. None of them are.' She considered the apple, contemplating the outline of her bite on its waxy skin. 'You do know that, right?' She didn't meet her mother's eyes.

Fiona tensed. 'We have become friendly, actually. And she's concerned about me, that's all.'

She didn't want to tell Caitlyn about Chris Carter, about the cheques, about the growing knot in her stomach whenever she thought about how he had died just three weeks after Peter. A death which, Amy had now confirmed, was being treated with suspicion.

'Listen,' said Caitlyn. 'All you want – all you ever wanted – was to get your life back. "Just to go back to the way things were", that's what you told me. Before all that awful business.'

'With Erin,' Fiona said slowly, monitoring her daughter for a reaction.

Caitlyn's mouth pulled into a tight line. 'Yes. Before any of that happened. When your life was a merry-go-round of lunches and parties and fundraisers...' She rolled her eyes.

Caitlyn was belittling her. As if Fiona's social life – her entire existence – were crumbs to sweep off the table.

'You can have all of that back. Esme should never have taken her side and said all those awful things. But she must know, deep down, that you had no idea what Dad was up to. How could you have? Once you clear the air with her, the rest of them will welcome you back with open arms, I'm sure of it.'

Caitlyn still made no mention of Erin, and Fiona realised that she couldn't bear to even speak the name of the girl who used to be her best friend. Fiona pictured the two of them together at the riding club, aged twelve, jodhpurs and velvet helmets and shiny black boots that were astronomically expensive.

They had been inseparable all through their school years and even after going away to university in different cities. Almost twenty years of friendship obliterated in one single evening, and a perfectly lovely party ruined after Erin confessed to having been Peter's latest conquest. The girls had rounded on Fiona, taking Esme's side and echoing her accusation that Fiona must have known what Peter was up to.

Fiona had wandered out into the garden, plonked herself into a deckchair, and gazed up at the stars scattered across the sky with only one question on her mind: where had it all gone so horribly wrong?

Everyone had known about Peter. The boy from the rough side of Birmingham, who couldn't quite believe his luck at how his life had turned out. Who must have woken every day and pinched himself.

Perhaps that went to the heart of it, thought Fiona. For Peter, it had all been too good to be true. As much as he enjoyed the trimmings and trappings of his success, deep down, he had been hell bent on sabotaging it. Salting the earth beneath their feet.

It had been easy enough to turn a blind eye when it was anonymous, nameless women. Hotel bills itemised with a bottle of champagne and receipts for dinner for two. Even when he had flings with women she vaguely knew, Fiona could hold her head up high and get on with life. Until one day, she couldn't.

Had Chris known about Erin? Peter kept it out of the news for Fiona's sake, and for Caitlyn's, but he hadn't cared. Not really. That hurt Fiona most of all. Lou and Esme knew. All of Fiona's so-called friends knew. The damage was done, as far as Peter was concerned. So why the cheques to Chris?

Caitlyn opened the fridge, illuminating her profile with a hazy blue light that sent her shadow stretching across the gleaming white tiles. She poured herself a glass of rosé.

'He's gone, Mum. It's over. The best thing for us now – for all of us – is to move on. Everything can go back to the way it was. Or something like it.'

Fiona wanted to believe that. She really did. She had spent months with an ache in her bones and an urgent craving for some return to normalcy.

And then she thought again of Chris, and of Peter, and how they might have been connected. Normal still felt like a galaxy away.

61

SUE SAT HUNCHED OVER CHRIS CARTER'S LAPTOP. ANNE WAS still sulking out in the workshop, although no new mirrors had appeared in days. Hopefully, that spelled the end of this particular crafty chapter.

Diana had given Sue an instruction to dig, and that's what she was doing. Most of Chris's files were photos, and her starting point had been to organise them by year. She was beginning to build up a picture of a young man who had come from inauspicious beginnings. His earliest pictures showed him as a gangly pre-teen on a camping holiday with a woman Sue assumed to be his mother. How poetic that he'd ended up living in a caravan.

A quick scan through the images showed Chris falling off the rails – or perhaps that was how all teenagers behaved these days. Dimly lit photos of anonymous youths drinking from cans and smoking goodness-knows-what. There were pictures of Chris larking about in various warehouses, white vans and factory floors, and Sue imagined him bouncing from dead-end job to dead-end job, spending his weekends getting wasted and then doing it all again. None of the photos appeared to have been taken on a building site, unfortunately.

The most recent photos were of Chris and Carrie, selfies taken on the beach, the iconic silhouette of Bamburgh Castle looming in the background. Sue felt a familiar pang of regret, tinged with fresh guilt. She had been quick to judge him without considering the forces that shaped him. They all had, but if anyone understood that people were merely products of their environment, it should have been her.

A pop-up appeared, a message from her Wi-Fi network, prompting her to save her files to the cloud. Mike had set it up for them after she complained their computer ran slowly. Only after she had clicked *yes* did she question whether she'd made a mistake. Could they trace her back to Chris's laptop through her cloud account?

She decided to come back to the photos later. After all, there was nothing in there to suggest a link to Peter Gallivan. She needed to focus.

Deep in thought, she scrolled through Chris's Facebook posts. Beyond his vitriolic musing on Brexit, politicians, and immigrants, she could see an angry and confused young man. But was he manipulative enough to seek revenge? Angry enough to kill?

Sue was concentrating so hard that she was startled by the voice behind her.

'Still working on your little detective project, then?' Anne's tone was cool.

'Yes,' said Sue, without taking her eyes off the screen. 'Just background research.'

'Only I was talking to Edward, and he offered a lead.'

Sue stiffened. She was used to her sister communicating

with her late husband, but it never got easier to be on the receiving end of a message from beyond the grave.

Anne looked pleased with herself. 'Apparently, you should look harder at Lou Renwick.' She let that hang there, studying Sue's face for any indication of interest.

'Lou Renwick?' Sue said after a moment. How did Anne even know his name? Had she really connected with Edward? A shiver rolled down her spine.

'Yes. Apparently, some of Lou's investments and business interests merit closer inspection.' Anne licked her lips, and Sue got the impression she had rehearsed this.

'Projects not related to Sparkbrook. A construction site in Gateshead – that's where you need to be looking. I wrote down the name.' Anne sighed as she slid a Post-it across the table to her sister.

Sue's chest tightened.

Lou Renwick and a construction site?

Anne shrugged. 'When you consider what he stands to gain from Peter's death, and the fact that it was his daughter between Peter's sheets, I'd say it was a reasonable lead. Although, of course, what would I know? I haven't been involved with any of this, so it's hard to put it in context.' She waved a hand towards the computer, her thin fingers stroking the air with feigned nonchalance.

Sue glared at the address on the Post-it in front of her.

She thought again about the builder's sand in the hallway and her eyes widened.

———

It was hurtful, that was the word. Anne had let Sue live with her all these years, allowed their lives to grow entwined, and now Sue was drifting away from her. The distance between them could once have been measured in inches. Now Anne felt Sue pulling with the strength of the tide, all thanks to Diana's little clique.

Anne had never liked cliques. She also didn't like it when Sue wasn't focused on her.

She really did talk to Edward. He rarely replied, but that didn't matter to Anne. Edward had always been a good listener. Often, she didn't need him to say anything at all.

There had been that awful time after his death, when he had been taken from her so suddenly that the grief was suffocating, blinding. Anne drowned in her loss, unable to see up from down, and sank like a stone to the bottom of a deep ocean. There, alone in the murky depths where only sadness could exist, she glimpsed a hint of sunlight winking at her from the surface far above. She followed it, and when she eventually resurfaced, she saw that in her desperation, she had cast aside everything that mattered to her. She had left her girls adrift at sea.

Thankfully, Sue showed up in a life raft. And more than twenty years later, she was still helping Anne to tread water. But still, Anne was entitled to feel a mild bitterness from time to time. Sue had a very high opinion of herself, and despite what she said, Anne knew that her sister had never truly forgiven her for leaving the girls while she escaped to find herself. And despite all her university degrees and books, Sue didn't know everything.

Because there was another layer to this existence. Few people felt it, even fewer were sufficiently attuned to it that they could connect with the spirits that dwelled beyond this plane. For all the heartache it caused her, Anne considered herself one of the lucky ones.

Edward hadn't exactly told her to look at Lou Renwick. Not in so many words, at least. He hadn't, in fact, said anything on the subject of the two men who recently lost their lives. But while explaining her predicament to him, only yesterday, Anne had sensed that he was pointing to that little knot of hurt in her stomach.

They had almost forgotten she was there that day in Amy's kitchen. None of them thought much of her. She knew that. Not Helen, and especially not Diana, who barely gave her the time of day. She hadn't even assigned Anne a task in their investigation.

But Anne had followed the discussion with interest. *Sand from a construction site.* In her heart, or her soul, or her sixth sense, she felt Edward nudging her back to that vital piece of information.

So, she did a little research of her own. It was easy, and she was surprised that neither Sue nor Diana had got there before her. After all, it was staring them right in the face.

Lou Renwick, Peter's business partner and friend. He would benefit from Peter's death – Anne's internet research churned up tons of speculation that he was set to buy out the family members who had inherited Peter's shares. When Anne thought of what must have gone through Lou's mind, the day he uncovered the depths of Peter's betrayal, she could imagine the hatred he might have harboured for his once-friend.

And Erin was his daughter. If Lou found out that Chris knew the whole story and was ruthless enough to blackmail Peter, who knew what lengths Lou might go to in order to silence him?

She'd only had to find a link with a building site – Diana had been quite clear that it was a crucial piece of information.

After a long pause, Sue spoke. 'And Edward told you all of this?'

'Yes,' Anne fibbed.

She watched her sister now, the cogs of Sue's mind whirring as she computed this new information. This prime suspect fit everything they were looking for, ticking all their boxes, and Anne tingled with the satisfaction of someone who had cracked a complex puzzle. What would Diana and Helen have to say about that?

Anne imagined Amy's face when they told her that she, Anne, had solved the case – with a little help from Edward. She realised in that moment that, more than anyone else, it was Amy she most wanted to impress. This was her chance to show her daughter once and for all that her mother wasn't completely useless. And that, Anne realised, was what she wanted more than anything.

62

SHE HAD BOTTLED IT. HELEN WOKE THAT MORNING WITH every intention of going on her assignment, and now she'd bottled it.

She hadn't wanted to tell Diana that she had never set foot inside Bamburgh Golf Club in all of her fifty-three years, and that she wouldn't know a birdie from an eagle if it hit her on the nose. Or that Roy worked seven days a week and would laugh her down to the coalhouse if she so much as suggested they went out for dinner. And now she was knee-deep in the proverbial.

One glance in the mirror had been enough to convince her that any of the golf club staff, let alone the members, would see right through her. While Matthew's old PE gear had cost her more than a week's wages, back in the day – she cringed anew, remembering the price tags of the designer sportswear he insisted on – the clothes were now faded, frayed, and worn thin from too many washes.

It wasn't just that her outfit wasn't up to par – which, she now knew, was a golfing expression. There was an entire social code and a language that she didn't speak. Venturing down there would be like stepping into a foreign country, and Helen hadn't been abroad since her honeymoon in Brittany thirty-five years ago.

And she knew this wouldn't be friendly territory. She could already picture the snooty club members looking down on her in Matthew's tatty old trainers. The sportswear that she'd salvaged from his wardrobe had seemed vaguely passable when laid out on the bed. Now that she was wearing it, her heart sank into her shoes.

She dressed again in her normal clothes and sat back on the bed, contemplating her next move. Down in the fallow field, Roy's silhouette made its way towards the pasture, hunched like a comma against the hedge.

Sue picked up on the third ring. At the sound of her voice, something inside Helen's chest clenched.

'Are you busy this morning?' she asked, her eyes still on Roy. The rain was stopping, the clouds parting above him. 'I need you.'

Safety in numbers, that's what Helen always said. Already, with Sue by her side in the car, she felt like a different woman. Or perhaps that was just the effect that Sue had on her.

'It's Anne,' said Sue, her eyes on the road in front of them. 'She came up with a theory – well, she says Edward told her—'

Helen scoffed. She couldn't help it. Sue's sister was a special character, and her quirks were a long-standing joke between them.

'Apparently, Edward told her to look more closely at Lou Renwick. As of now, Gallivan's death is a pay cheque for Lou – he's set to buy the company. He wouldn't want anything to scupper that – especially not something that threatens to tarnish the precious reputation of his darling daughter.'

Helen considered this. It made sense – most parents would move heaven and earth to protect their kids. And that poor girl. Peter Gallivan had preyed upon her. That's what it was. The papers were full of it, these days.

Sue drew a deep breath. 'Turns out that when he's not working for Sparkbrook, he's also the director of a construction firm. And get this – they're currently building a housing estate in Crawcrook, just outside Gateshead.'

'The sand...'

'Exactly.' Sue shifted in the passenger seat. 'I'm still trying to see how and when he could have done it, exactly, but the motive is there.'

'And it stands to reason he might have had builder's sand on his boots.'

Their discussion was stopped short as Helen swung her Volvo into the gravel carpark of Bamburgh Golf Club.

'Here goes nothing,' she said, switching off the engine.

'Wait!' Sue clasped a hand on Helen's arm.

Helen followed her friend's gaze. 'Is that Tom?'

They watched as a lone figure hauled a set of golf clubs from the back of his car and hefted the bulk onto his back.

'Let's give it five,' said Sue. 'Wait until he's gone.'

Moments later, they were standing in reception. Thankfully, Tom was nowhere to be seen. Helen had to agree with Sue – there was something off about that man, no matter what Amy said.

———

In all her years of living just a couple of miles away, Sue had never once set foot in Bamburgh Golf Club. She wasn't sure what she had expected, but it certainly wasn't this. The place was cosy, warm almost. It was more of a Scout hut than a fancy club house.

A young woman beamed at them from behind the reception desk. 'How can I help you ladies?'

'We're thinking about taking up golf,' Sue answered earnestly. 'We were hoping for a tour of the facilities.'

The girl's name badge said Shelley. She bit her lip, looking from the outdated computer monitor in front of her to something on the desk. 'I don't seem to have you booked in. I'm sure I can find someone—'

'No need. But perhaps we can look around ourselves?'

At this suggestion, Shelley frowned. 'I'm afraid I can't authorise that,' she said, trying to sound officious. 'But I can show you, quickly,' she muttered, glancing at the entrance. 'I just can't leave reception for long.'

Helen returned Shelley's smile. 'I'm sure we won't take too much of your time.'

The tour began in the ladies' locker room, taking in the trophy cabinet on their way out. Despite her age, Shelley was impressively knowledgeable about which members currently held the various titles, all of which had long and complex names. She pointed out the restaurant, detailing the dress code before explaining the menu.

Conscious that time was slipping, Sue interrupted her. 'And what if we wanted to use a caddy?'

'Funnily enough, you're the second person to ask me that this week. Short story is, we don't do caddies.' Shelley shrugged. 'I guess Bamburgh just isn't that sort of golf club. But it's an option. You can hire someone privately. There are a couple of local lads – er, I mean boys, men – who can caddy for you.'

Sue couldn't help but notice the inflection in Shelley's

voice – the poor girl was clearly holding back tears. She must have known Chris, at least to say hello to.

Shelley regained her composure. 'I expect you want to see the green?'

'Yes please,' said Helen.

'Actually, I have to use the ladies'.' Sue met Helen's eyes. 'You go on ahead without me. I'll catch up.'

As soon as they were out of sight, Sue darted back to the reception desk. It was crowded with paper – evidently, Bamburgh Golf Club had not yet gone fully digital. A ring-bound folder lay open, occupying most of the surface. On the left was a list of names under the header 'Sign in'.

'Tom Grey...' Sue read out loud, banking that information for later. She hadn't known Tom's surname, and for some reason, this felt like an important detail.

Shelley, for all her manners and professionalism, had not locked the computer. Sue wiggled the mouse and saw the cursor move on the screen. She just had to work out what she was looking for. She cocked her head, listening out for anyone coming. Only once she was satisfied that the coast was clear, she took a seat.

It took seconds to find Peter's membership record. He had joined eight months previously and had played seventy-six rounds to date.

'Someone's getting their fees' worth,' Sue muttered to herself.

The club – Shelley or another member of staff – had noted that Peter hired a private caddy. Underneath, there was a phone number and a name. *Chris Carter.*

A tab at the top of the page was labelled 'guests'. Sue clicked, and two entries popped up. Her eyes widened as she took in the name. The big man had played alone, for the most part – except for two occasions when he had registered a guest to accompany him. One was the day he died.

'Well, well, well...' Sue whispered to herself. *Ben Gallivan.* Sue drew a finger across the screen, double-checking the date.

The sound of footsteps coming back down the hallway startled her. She checked the screen again, just to make sure she wasn't missing something. Blood pounded in her ears, drowning out the chatter of Helen and Shelley as they approached. She had just enough time to close the window and make it back to the correct side of the reception desk as they turned the corner.

Shelley blinked at her through impossibly long eyelashes. 'Did you find the ladies'?' She spoke the words slowly, drenched in suspicion. Her eyes fixed on Sue's.

'Yes.' The response snagged in her throat. 'Yes, I did, and then, I just thought...'

'The green is beautiful,' said Helen, catching her. 'You'll really love it.' She turned to Shelley. 'So, I have all the information about the dues and the application forms. Thank you ever so much. You've been most helpful.'

'Extremely,' Sue added. 'Thank you.'

'My pleasure,' replied Shelley, glancing at the desk, her eyes scanning to see if anything was amiss. Satisfied, she looked up at them, the smile returning to her face. 'Hope to be seeing you both soon.'

As they left the clubhouse, Sue exhaled, a slow release. Her heart galloped in her chest.

63

HE'D PLAYED A LOUSY GAME. TOM WAS NEW TO GOLF, AND SO far, he had to disagree with everyone's suggestion that it was a therapeutic hobby.

'Just give it time,' Fran had said when he initially expressed his frustration. Tom had time in spades these days.

He dropped his clubs back at home, showered and changed, and made spaghetti Bolognese for Agnes.

'Aren't you having any?' she asked.

He swallowed. 'I'll get mine later.'

The mischievous twinkle in her eye alleviated some of the guilt he felt at leaving her alone with only the TV for company. 'Off gallivanting on the town again, are you?'

'Something like that.' Indeed, Tom wished it *was* something like that.

He walked through the village towards The Ship. It had rained again that afternoon. The reflected lights of homes and cars shone on the oil-slick shine of the road and pavement. Far out at sea, from its perch atop the Farne Islands, the lighthouse winked at him. His footsteps echoed in the street.

Once upon a time, not so long ago, a Sunday night out for Tom meant big city lights, bars in Soho or Mayfair, depending on how the mood took them.

How small his world had become.

He refused to despair. All things considered, he was lucky to be here.

The bar was invitingly warm, and he took comfort in its intimate familiarity. Even if he could feel Gina's anxiety from here.

Tom tried to distract himself with his surroundings. The curios fighting for space on every wall and ceiling captured his attention momentarily. If Gina ever decided to close the pub, they could convert this place into a local history museum.

The seat next to him, usually occupied by a trawlerman named Harry, was empty tonight. At the corner table, a foursome of young men and women laughed loudly, their faces flushed.

He glanced across at Gina, his fingers gripping the stem of his glass. Cheap wine, nothing like what he was used to, once upon a time. What he wouldn't give for a 2007 Sancerre. Gina avoided meeting his eyes, and instead, picked pensively at a cuticle with her teeth.

Her phone buzzed on the counter, too far for Tom to see who the message was from or what it said. He'd have to guess by measuring her reaction.

———

Gina quickly scanned the bar, noting that nobody needed service, and permitted herself the indulgence of checking her phone.

Her heart fluttered when the name appeared on the screen.

Carrie: *How r u?*

Gina sighed. A whole bloody week of radio silence and all she got was a casual *how r u?*

I'm fine, she typed. She deleted it. *I'm good. How are you? I miss you.* She added three kisses for good measure. The icon told her that Carrie was drafting her response.

Carrie: *I'm sorry.*

Gina heaved a sigh of relief, her eyes on the screen as Carrie continued to text.

Carrie: *The police told me not to talk to anyone.*

That was understandable, Gina supposed. But it meant that they were treating Chris's death as suspicious, and that wasn't good for any of them.

Carrie: *I didn't mean to land you in it. They were pushing me.*

Gina put the phone back on the counter and gazed up at the ceiling. This was good, she forced herself to admit. If Carrie thought she was responsible for what happened to Chris, she wouldn't be sharing any of this.

It's OK, she typed. *I just want you to be OK.*

Tears welled in her eyes, the text blurring on the screen, and she bit back against the urge to cry. She knew what it was like – to be young and daft, and to lose a boyfriend like this. If only she'd been able to tell Carrie what had happened to her back then. If only Carrie could have learned from Gina's mistakes.

But no, she couldn't tell anyone what happened. Not even Carrie.

Her phone vibrated.

Carrie: *I'll be back soon.*

That was enough for Gina. Almost.

Gina: *When? Can I come and get you?*

Three dots. Carrie was typing.

The dots stopped abruptly, Carrie was no longer on the chat. Gina's shoulders sank.

————

Tom saw her disappointment from his seat in the corner. When he first met Gina, he was struck by her confidence – the woman was a swaggering tower of hairspray and bronzer. Now, under the harsh lights of the bar, reflected in the brass dials and gauges that hung overhead, she looked different. Younger, somehow, and softer. More vulnerable.

Her expression twisted – into regret, resolve, and then something in between, and Tom experienced a pang of recognition. He saw then that Gina was hiding something deep within her.

64

DIANA WAS READY FOR THEM. SHE'D EVEN BAKED SCONES THAT morning, thinking that everyone might get peckish later. The more they had to nibble on, the longer they would be inclined to stay. After all, they had lots to cover.

It had been necessary to convene a meeting of the book club. On what other premise could Diana invite the core party to her house in the middle of the day? She had suggested to Sue that they might forget to invite Tom, just this once, and her friend had readily agreed.

But this was no ordinary gathering of a ladies' reading circle. The living room of Diana's cottage had been transformed into a makeshift incident room. Last night, she removed the paintings and photographs from the furthest wall and, in their place, tacked up a timeline that stretched across its entire width. To that, she added photographs and Post-it notes detailing key moments and the observations that constituted their evidence at this point. She had extended the dining table to its full length and repurposed it as a grand desk that bore their small collection of forensics – a laptop and a small bag of marijuana – alongside a myriad of notes, printouts and more Post-its.

Sue arrived first, her friend Helen in tow and Anne trailing behind them. Diana watched from the upstairs window as they parked in the lane outside and walked up her garden path, admiring the old climbing rose that had been Lionel's pride and joy. If only he could see her now.

She met them at the door and ushered them inside.

'Amy's on her way, as soon as she's finished—' Sue broke off, her eyes fanning across the living room and her mouth falling to a small circle. 'My, you have been busy,' she mumbled.

'We have a lot to get through. First things first – our victims.'

Diana had printed out photographs of the two men and pinned them to the timeline. These were separate to another pool of headshots, photos taken from Facebook and the Sparkbrook corporate website. *Persons of interest.* It had been quite an effort, but Diana felt that it lent the investigation board an air of professionalism.

'Our first victim—'

She was interrupted by a knock at the door and excused herself to retrieve the visitor.

Diana returned seconds later with Lucia, whose eyes widened as she took in the scene.

'I thought we were discussing the book...' she trailed off, scanning the headshots on the wall.

'There'll be plenty of time for that, dear.' Diana patted her arm. 'In the meantime, we have a real mystery on our hands.'

She registered the alarm on Sue's face. It was, Diana supposed, one thing sneaking around crime scenes and quite another to extend the circle of those who were privy to their investigation. Nor could it be denied that they – chiefly, Diana – had employed some dubious methods to acquire the evidence that they had gathered. Still, she had exercised the necessary precaution. After all, Lucia was no stranger to keeping a secret or two.

She did her best to allay Sue's evident concern. 'I thought we could use an extra brain. Especially one who can help us with the technological aspects of our investigation. I'm sure Lucia will be happy to help.'

Diana resumed her opening remarks before Lucia had a chance to object. 'Our first victim – Peter Gallivan. Passed away on the evening of Sunday twenty-ninth. The initial supposition was that he died of a heart attack. No immediate cause for suspicion, apart from a smashed vase in the hallway and a trail of sand leading from the doorway into the living room, where Peter was found. On closer inspection of the premises, we can be confident that someone was able to gain entry thanks to a spare key kept under the plant pot.'

She glanced at her audience, checking that they were following. 'Victim number two. Chris Carter. Aged twenty-seven years old. Found dead by his girlfriend upon her return from work on Thursday, the seventeenth. He was under the influence of drugs at the time and the cause of death was assumed to be cardiac arrest, possibly resulting from recreational drug use, however a post-mortem revealed it to have been induced by a cocktail of medication – not marijuana. We don't know, as yet, how these drugs were administered to him. Given the proximity of our victims and a consistent cause of death, we have presumed that Peter's heart attack may also have been chemically induced.'

Lucia's eyes widened. 'Peter's death wasn't an accident?'

'My dear, I appreciate this is a lot to take in.' Diana

gestured to the wall. 'Peter had a history of heart disease, which, conveniently, meant that no post-mortem was carried out. However, in light of Chris's untimely demise, we are reconsidering this.'

'Who is *we*? Does the family know about this? The police?'

Sue shifted uneasily in her seat. 'Suffice to say, this is an unofficial investigation at this stage. We just want to know what happened. Perhaps it's nothing...' she said, although the state of Diana's living room suggested that remark was entirely disingenuous.

Lucia exhaled, a sigh that came from the bottom of her stomach.

Diana spoke softly, the way she had done many a time to an errant adolescent girl in need of a gentle coaxing. 'My dear. If this isn't for you, then you're free to leave. All we ask is that you keep shtum. If, however, you want to be part of our efforts to uncover the truth, you are welcome to stay. It is that simple.'

Lucia bit her lip and glanced at the door, the way she had just arrived. She hesitated, a beat, before turning back to Diana.

'I'm in.'

———

Amy pulled up at Diana's house and parked behind her aunt's car.

She'd only been able to get the morning off, thanks to submitting her shift change request at such short notice. Once she'd completed the school run, done two loads of laundry and prepared the family's evening meal, there was scarcely enough time left for her to make any meaningful contribution to the proceedings – whether it really was a book club discussion or, as she suspected, Diana gathering the ladies for a meeting on their investigation. She was turning up in a show of support, knowing full well that she had little else to offer.

But what she lacked in time, she made up for in curiosity. After her run-in with Caitlyn Gallivan at the weekend, Amy was more convinced than ever that something decidedly dodgy was going on with that family.

Diana met her at the door of her cottage. 'They're all here,' she whispered under her breath, steering Amy through to the living room. 'Including your mother.'

Amy didn't have time to question any of it before she was confronted by the scene. Sue and Helen were sitting at a large table, scrolling through pages of paper and armed with highlighter pens, while Lucia was elegantly poised on the sofa, the laptop that Amy knew belonged to Chris balanced delicately on one long, slim leg. Her mother was... doing what, exactly? Anne was folded into the lotus position in the middle of the floor, her legs crossed at an impossible angle, clutching something in her hands. Her eyes opened as Amy entered the room.

'Amy.' Anne glanced up at her youngest daughter and smiled, then opened her hands to reveal a small bag of cannabis sitting neatly on her palm. 'I was trying to channel Chris's energy. This could have been one of the last things he touched.' Anne sighed sadly, shaking her head in disappointment. 'So far, he's not giving me anything.'

Diana politely ignored her. 'Now that everyone is here, let's compare notes. We all took a homework assignment this weekend, and hopefully your findings will help us fill in some of the blanks.' She moved towards the wall.

'We know that the victims knew each other – they

possibly they met while Chris was employed at Sparkbrook, and certainly spent time together on the golf course. The question is, who might have had wanted them both dead?'

'I'll go first,' said Anne. 'Here's my theory: Chris found out that Peter was hiding something – that he'd had an affair with his daughter's best friend. So Chris blackmailed him. Enter Lou Renwick. Lou's daughter was Caitlyn's best friend. Not only does Lou resent that Chris was threatening to expose his business partner and ruin his daughter's reputation, but he stands to gain enormously from Peter's death. Even as we speak, he is buying up the family's shares in the company. And,' she said, clearly relishing the attention, 'Lou's business interests outside Sparkbrook include a construction firm.'

Her mother failed to conceal the satisfied smirk that danced on her lips. 'So, there you have it – a clear motive, and a prime suspect.' She unfolded her legs and took a seat on the settee next to Lucia, placing her hands in her lap and glancing nervously at Diana, no doubt eager to get something right, just for once. Just for a change.

Diana, however, was merciless, and responded with a dramatic roll of her eyes. 'Seriously? Lou Renwick? You didn't imagine that possibility had already crossed my mind?'

Her mother squirmed and shot a pleading look at Auntie Sue, who simply shrugged in response.

———

Diana sighed, exasperated. She didn't have time to deal with amateurs.

'Lou Renwick. The business partner, the best friend, the aggrieved father. Of course, he's an obvious suspect. But motive is only one piece of the puzzle – what about opportunity? On the day that Peter died, Lou Renwick was in London for a football match between Newcastle United and Chelsea. Not only do I have it on good authority that he never misses a game, the man was on national television, cheering from the directors' box. He couldn't have made it to the murder scene even if he travelled by private jet. Which he did, by the way. The flight log from Newcastle Airport shows him arriving shortly after 10:00 p.m. that night.'

Anne glowered at her feet, suitably admonished.

Diana turned to Sue. 'What did you find on the laptop?'

'Sadly, not much. Mainly just photos. And of course, his browsing history, which shows he was very interested in Peter and Erin Renwick.'

Nothing new. Diana pressed her fingertips together, her hands forming a prayer, and closed her eyes. 'Hopefully Lucia will be able to tell us more.'

'I'm on it,' Lucia mumbled in response.

'And Helen? Please tell me your visit to the golf club was fruitful?'

Helen swallowed. 'Yes. Sue came along with me, actually.' She glanced at her friend, her eyes pleading.

Sue picked up on her cue. 'Peter Gallivan played a *lot* of golf. The register shows that twice, he reserved a place for Ben to join him. In fact, Peter had been due to play with his son on the day of his death. But I don't think they made it. I saw Ben driving off at lunchtime. There was an argument, and he left.'

Diana kept her eyes on Lucia, who followed this with a feigned passive interest, all the while saying nothing. Apart from Amy, the others didn't know that she and Ben had been romantically involved. Best to keep it that way, for now. Perhaps Lucia knew more than she realised.

In fact, Diana was counting on it.

Sue cleared her throat. 'It might not mean anything, but we saw Tom at the golf course yesterday. That man who joined our book club.' The rest of the group offered disinterested, non-committal shrugs. She persevered. 'I mean, if we're thinking about who else knew both Chris and Peter, well... Tom knows Carrie and Fiona. That makes him another potential suspect.'

Diana's shoulders sank. 'As I've said, more than once: *motive and opportunity*. Tom appears to have neither. Indeed, apart from you finding him slightly annoying, there's nothing to suggest his involvement in either crime.'

It had been a morning of disappointing results, all things considered. At least Roger Mason over at *The Chronicle* had come through.

It transpired that Roger had been fed most of his intelligence on Sparkbrook from a single employee, and that person had been incredibly generous with their information. *A whistle-blower* was how Roger referred to his nameless source.

He had an entire dossier on Peter Gallivan and his various scandals and had generously invited Diana to come by the office and look through it. She intended to take him up on his offer and make the hour-long journey to Newcastle as soon as she could think of an excuse that would convince Sandra to drive her there. Until then, she'd have to make do with picking his brains by telephone.

She had homed in on the crucial piece of information she needed. With barely any questions asked, Roger had posted the employment records to her that same day. It was a list of more than seven thousand names, detailing everyone who had worked for Sparkbrook and its subsidiary companies stretching back for more than a decade. She had tasked Sue and Helen with combing through it, searching for Chris Carter to confirm the dates when he had been a pawn in Peter Gallivan's empire, as well as any other familiar names.

Diana studied the wall once more. Of course, she had done her own research, and had also jumped to conclusions when she realised that Lou Renwick counted a construction company among his many and varied interests. It hadn't taken her long to scratch beneath the surface and discover that Renwick was merely a non-executive director. Nor had it taken her long to find out that he was at a football match three-hundred miles away on the evening Peter died. The longer she dwelled on it, the less Diana could imagine Lou doing anything sufficiently menial to get builder's sand on his shoes.

'We need to add Caitlyn's movements to this,' said Amy, joining Diana. 'It's funny how she wanted nothing to do with her parents for months and now she can't seem to leave her mother's side.'

Amy didn't need to add what she thought of Caitlyn – they had both felt the steely weight of the woman's ice-cold glare. Remembering the chilly reception she received at the Gallivan house two days ago caused Diana to shudder. She reflexively wrapped her arms around her body.

'Sorry, but I can't stay.' Amy stood. 'I'm on shift at the hospital this afternoon.'

'I need to get going, too,' said Lucia, gathering up her things.

Diana saw them out, waiting until Lucia's car disappeared around the corner at the end of the lane before retreating once more into her house. Re-entering the living room, she sighed despondently. Sue and Helen were only partway through the enormous list of past employees. She saw the evidence wall afresh and recognised what it was – a mishmash of information, speculation and hear-say, dots that did not connect. She caught the eye of Lionel, captured in time and framed in gold on the mantelpiece, and his reassuring gaze steadied her nerves.

What were they missing?

'Here's Chris.' Sue was studying the page in front of her with a frown. 'In 2009, he was employed at BSC Fulfilment for ten months, working at a depot in Newcastle. That tallies with his check-in on Facebook.'

'This is interesting.' Helen's eyebrows knotted. 'It says that Ben was based in the Newcastle depot for three months of that summer. Four hundred people worked there, but their paths could have crossed.'

It could have been a trick of the light, it could have been the jubilation that sent her heart rate soaring, but Diana was sure that, from behind the glass of his frame, Lionel winked at her.

Having reached a minor milestone, the other women decided to call it a day. Anne started muttering about needing to get back to her *art*, and Sue, as always, quickly indulged her, neatly attuned as she was to her sister's fickle sensibilities. There was no chance that Helen, who had never managed to move beyond the anxiety of Diana that she'd harboured since her school days, would stay once they left.

Despite Diana's powers of persuasion and a substantial quantity of scones, Helen, Sue, and Anne departed with a promise to return in the morning. *Honestly*, thought Diana.

Would Jane Marple have solved a single case if she stopped every time she made a breakthrough?

Resuming her position in front of the evidence wall, she moved Ben's headshot into the line of suspects. It had been a necessary precaution to omit it, until now, due to Lucia's attendance at their meeting.

He was handsome, she supposed, although she couldn't comprehend the current fashion for men to sport absurdly feminine hairstyles.

Roger had told her all about how Peter employed his son fresh out of university, installing the boy in a role of inflated responsibility while showing him the ropes, training him to be the future CEO, until he'd had an abrupt change of heart. And it was interesting that Ben worked at the Newcastle depot during the time Chris was there.

She cast a glance towards the employee list and felt certain that the name they were looking for lay somewhere on that list. Was it Ben? Or was there another name buried in there, waiting for them to find it?

It had been an exhausting morning, playing the roles of hostess and lead detective simultaneously, and weariness threatened like a grey cloud on the horizon.

Diana took a seat in front of the wall and wondered how the pieces connected. Two men from very different worlds, and yet those worlds had crashed together in a fateful, fatal collision. Someone knew Peter and knew Chris and hated both men with sufficient passion to take their lives. Someone who either stood to benefit from removing them both from the picture or stood to lose if either of them had remained. She closed her eyes, deep in thought.

Hours later she woke, surprised to find that she had fallen asleep in Lionel's old armchair. The rain that had threatened the morning was long past, washed out on the afternoon tide.

Something had shifted in the room. Diana couldn't put a finger on it, but something felt out of place. Had she left the cushion askew on the settee like that? She padded into the kitchen, pondering the question, and noticed that the cutlery drawer was open. Had she forgotten to close it when she made tea?

Or was someone in here while she was asleep?

Diana shook off her unease. There wasn't a burglar in the world inept enough to leave a kitchen drawer open and a cushion at an angle while forgetting to steal anything. Her disquiet was swiftly replaced with sadness at the realisation that it was nothing more than a cruel trick of old age.

She turned her mind back to the investigation. *Look more closely at the discrepancies,* she told herself. Where the story doesn't quite fit, that's where you'll find the truth.

Ben was supposed to golf with his father on the day he died, but he left Seahouses early that afternoon. There was a row. Fiona was upset. A lovely weekend *en famille* came clattering to the ground like a shattered antique vase.

What happened to make Ben drive off in such haste? *And what if he turned back?*

Sue had witnessed him leaving. But what Sue saw was not necessarily the full story. Diana began to devise a plan that would help Sue to understand exactly what she had seen that day and what, if anything, she might have missed.

65

SUE HADN'T MISSED A THING — OF THAT, SHE WAS CERTAIN.
Why couldn't anyone else see what was patently staring
them all in the face?

Tom.

He had appeared in Seahouses out of nowhere, it
seemed, and within a couple of months of him showing up
in the village, two men were dead.

She wasn't just looking for Chris's name in the employment records yesterday; she had been scanning for Tom's
too. She didn't find it, but that didn't deter her in the slightest. Call it female intuition or a sixth sense or a keen nose,
Sue was grappling with a growing conviction that something about the man didn't quite add up.

It wasn't that she felt threatened by his presence, and
Amy was wide of the mark with her insinuation that Sue
disliked the fact that a man had joined her book club.

She sighed. The book club. Nobody had even
mentioned their latest read – a beautifully crafted retelling
of Homer's odyssey and the Trojan Wars from the perspectives of the women who had, until now, existed in the

spaces between the narrative. Sue decided to park it for now.

Anne had been in a huff since yesterday, shuffling about the house in her slippers and muttering about how silly it all was whenever Sue was within earshot. Sue spent the afternoon in the garden tending to her vegetable patch just to put some distance between them. Her sister's moods dictated the climate of the home they shared, with her bouts of depression that often blindsided Sue, who did her best to hide those black moods from Amy.

She peered out of the window, checking on her sister. Anne had shut herself up in the shed shortly after dawn and Sue braced for another mirror to add to their collection by nightfall. There was no point, she knew, in asking if Anne wanted to come back to Diana's house this morning.

Helen was waiting for her at the gate, and they made the short drive to Beadnell in silence, the car meandering down the road that lay snug against the coastline. The forecast of fair weather had been accurate, but Sue felt little appreciation for the vast expanse of navy that stretched out toward infinity. Her mind was on Tom, and she used the journey to think of how, exactly, she could articulate her suspicion without sounding foolish.

Diana had continued the work after they left yesterday. That much was clear from the new additions to the evidence wall, and she launched into her update while Sue and Helen shrugged off their coats.

'Ben Gallivan. We know he worked in the same depot as Chris, but did they know each other? Caitlyn Gallivan also stood to gain from her father's death, although we must question how she might have known about the blackmail – if, indeed, that was what was happening. Both Gallivan children appear to have had strained relationships with their father. And I'm sure both of them would have known where the spare is kept.'

She steepled her fingers. 'My feeling is that the murderer was someone close to home. With Peter Gallivan, it was revenge. In Chris Carter's case, someone was tying up loose ends. We should focus on who wanted Peter dead, and I'd say both Gallivan offspring are high on that list.'

'What happened to *opportunity*?' Sue asked. Neither of the Gallivan children were here the night Peter died.'

They were going around in circles, coming back repeatedly to a cold trail. Why couldn't Diana consider other possibilities?

Sue sighed, exasperated. 'On the night of her father's death, Caitlyn Gallivan was at a work event in Edinburgh. There are photographs of her at the party on the company website, and there will no doubt be countless colleagues who can provide her with an alibi. And I saw Ben leaving the village that afternoon. He drove off after the row. We've been through this.'

'And yet, someone killed Peter Gallivan that night, and all evidence suggests this same person or persons murdered Chris. Ben had more motivation than anyone.' Diana locked eyes with Sue. 'It's time to retrace your steps.'

Despite her foreboding that this would be a pointless exercise, Sue reluctantly agreed to Diana's proposal. All she could hope was that Diana didn't envision a full scale reenactment, Crimewatch-style. With Helen in tow, they piled into Sue's Vauxhall and drove back to Seahouses, pulling up on the verge opposite the Gallivan house.

Diana, as usual, had dressed for the occasion. Her belted jacket and matching hat lent her an air of sophistication that wouldn't be out of place in the middle of hunting season.

The wind whipped at them as they climbed out of the car, forcing Diana to hold her hat in place with a hand. She turned to Sue. 'Describe the scene that day.'

'We were here, more or less.' Sue cast her eyes down to the grass bank that lay between the pavement and the dunes, trying to recall the exact spot where Amy's car had been parked that afternoon. 'I brought Betsy up from the beach and she was sitting in the boot, getting out of her wetsuit. I heard something.' She looked across to the Gallivan house. 'Raised voices. Shouting. The door was open, and Ben came outside with his mother following him.'

What had they argued about? It had been impossible to make out their words above the wind, and Sue was careful not to replace any blanks in her memory with her imagination.

'He was more sad than angry. In fact, he was crying – they both were. Ben came out of the gate and got into his car, and Fiona let out the most terrible wail. He drove off back towards the village at quite some speed.'

Sue shuddered as she remembered how distraught Fiona had been. She had hidden out of sight, and Sue now wondered if she ought to have done something to help the situation. Perhaps Peter Gallivan might still be alive if she had.

———

Across the road, from the comfort of the high-backed chair in her reading room, Fiona was watching the trio with the foreboding of one who knew they were being talked about. Goodness knows her ears had burned enough in her time.

But if they knew what she had done, why hadn't they gone to the police already? And what did that other man have to do with it all?

She pushed the thought away and took a deep, calming breath. They had no idea. Nobody was there that night. Her secret was buried with Peter. Whatever they were on to, it was something else entirely.

Sue was doing most of the talking, occasionally gesticulating towards the house, the other two ladies following the story with a keen interest.

She might have expected Diana Wheeler to be slightly more circumspect. In fact, just then, the older lady motioned to Sue with her hand out flat, fingers splayed, urging caution.

But it was too late.

―――――

Earlier that morning, Lucia had set out for a walk along the beach in what had quickly become a daily routine.

For someone who had flitted across the earth for almost a decade, forming a habit came surprisingly easily to her. Each day, while the tide was out, she strolled through the village and down to the beach, crossing the broad sand until she reached the little stream that spilled out into the sea, at which point she turned and came back the same way. Her route took her past the Gallivan house, but that was unavoidable. At least, that's what Lucia told herself.

She had almost reached the top of the steep path that snaked up the dunes when she saw them. Instinctively, she fell into a crouch behind the deep ledge of a high tuft of dune grass, tucked just metres below Sue's car. Diana hadn't explicitly asked her to join them again that morning, but Lucia didn't want to be forced to make excuses. Avoidance was always the simplest solution.

Her rudimentary plan was to hide there and wait until they left, all the while praying they didn't head for a walk along the beach. If any of them ventured close to the edge of the verge and looked down the dune bank, they would see her straight away. She stilled her breathing, willing herself to stay calm.

She didn't intend to eavesdrop, but their words were so clear. Lucia's heart broke again for Ben as she overheard Sue describing the scene that day when Ben fled in tears.

A shout interrupted their conversation. It pierced the air, carried on the wind towards her, and Lucia instantly recognised the voice. Cold dread seeped through her.

———

Fiona heard Caitlyn before she saw her.

'Oi!' Caitlyn yelled, her carefully cultivated honeyed tone forgotten, leaving only a harsh, crude pitch in its place.

Fiona rolled her eyes. Her daughter had always possessed a flair for the dramatic, and it was almost comical how the girl could go from plummy to fishwife in a matter of seconds when the occasion called for it. Fiona peered down to see her stomping down the garden path towards the women.

'What on earth do you think you're doing?'

The ladies were caught off-guard, and Fiona saw the alarm register on their faces.

Caitlyn didn't give them a chance to answer. 'You're rubbernecking, that's what it is! You can't mind your own bloody business and let a family grieve in peace. You're like vultures. Vultures!'

Caitlyn was almost at the gate now, and Fiona considered it a small mercy that the rest of their conversation was carried away on the breeze.

———

At the sight of Caitlyn Gallivan marching towards them, Sue's heart thundered in her chest. She knew it was a mistake to come down here, but it was too late to regret ignoring her instinct. Caitlyn's eyes blazed with fury.

'My dear,' Diana said, seemingly unfazed. 'This is public land and we have every right to be here. We have no intention of intruding on anybody.'

'Don't patronise me. I know what you're up to.' Caitlyn's voice was reduced to a snarl.

'We haven't done anything—'

Caitlyn cut her off, jabbing an accusatory finger in the air just inches from Diana's face. 'Coming around here and bothering my mother while she's vulnerable. It's harassment!'

Sue felt the blood drain from her face. 'Now hang on there,' she said, with as much bravery as she could muster. 'You can't speak to her like that...' She faltered, silenced by a withering glare from Caitlyn.

'Listen. And make sure you understand. If you or any of your little friends come anywhere near my mother again, I'll call the police and have you arrested for stalking.'

'That's your prerogative,' said Diana with an easy shrug and a sad shake of her head.

Sue thought of the stolen laptop sitting in Diana's kitchen, not to mention the bag of cannabis or the employment records she had managed to snag. Once again, she found herself admiring the woman's audacity.

'In fact,' Diana continued, 'we could call them now? If that might help us to clear up this little misunderstanding?' She took her mobile phone from her handbag and offered it to Caitlyn. 'Shall I do the honours, or would you prefer to call them yourself?'

At this, Caitlyn faltered. Her mouth narrowed to a pinch. 'If I see you here again, you're in trouble.' She looked at Helen and Sue. '*All* of you.'

Thankfully, Diana saw the sense in allowing Caitlyn to have the last word.

———

Behind the dune, Lucia was trapped. Her mind raced through worst-case scenarios. The women finding her. Caitlyn finding her. Ben coming out to see what all the fuss was about and finding her.

After what felt like an eternity of silence, she heard Sue speak again. 'I told you this was a bad idea.'

'Not quite, my dear girl.' Diana's voice was cool, calm. 'Caitlyn may have just given our investigation a nudge in the right direction.'

'Really? And how's that?'

'Didn't you see how she responded when I suggested calling the police? That woman is desperate to avoid the involvement of the authorities.'

'Maybe because she's covering up for her brother?' Helen offered.

Lucia's hand flew to her mouth.

'Something like that,' Diana replied, thoughtfully. 'Let's head back. The employment records aren't enough to support the connection – there must be something else that proves they knew each other. My hunch is that if we look more carefully at Chris's photographs, we'll find Ben in at least one of them.'

Lucia clutched a hand to her chest, pressing her palm against her ribcage to slow the fluttering of her pulse. *Shit.* Ben was now their prime suspect.

'Diana,' Sue protested. 'There are thousands of pictures on that computer.'

'But now that we know when Chris worked in Newcastle, our search has been vastly narrowed.'

'Only down to about a thousand photos.' Sue sighed. 'Perhaps we're better off visiting the golf club? Asking around, finding out how well Peter and Chris knew each other and if either of them knew Tom?'

Diana was unpersuaded. 'Tomorrow, perhaps. The photos – that would move this forward.'

Moments later, Lucia heard car doors closing. The engine spluttered to life then droned to silence as it disappeared into the distance.

She leaned back and heaved a sigh of relief. The sand was cool against her back despite her layers, and she massaged her calves to relieve the cramp that had begun to seize her legs. Slowly, she counted to thirty, then emerged.

———

Two cars behind, Tom eased himself from the uncomfortable slouch he had assumed when he first saw Sue and her friends pull up. He'd slunk down as low as possible in the driver's seat, presuming they intended to take advantage of the fine weather with a stroll along the beach. How wrong he'd been.

With his window wound down an inch, he had managed to hear the entire row.

And then, just when he thought it was finally safe to sit up again, Lucia's head popped up from behind the dunes. Tom slid back in his seat, propping himself up at eye level so that he could watch her.

Lucia hastily scanned the road in both directions before taking the last couple of steps back up to the path. She hurried along the road towards the village, her hands digging deep into her pockets and her head bowed low, and from her posture, Tom knew she had been listening, too.

The plot thickens, he thought.

66

THEY WERE QUIET ON THE DRIVE HOME, EACH WOMAN LOST IN her own thoughts.

Diana knew that Sue was sulking. She had every right, Diana supposed. After all, Diana did appreciate that she had catapulted them all into a high stakes scenario – although she would never admit as much. She also knew that Sue's sulks rarely lasted long, and her friend was incapable of bearing a grudge. It was one of the qualities that Diana most admired in the woman she had watched grow up, starting all the way back when Diana was barely much of a grown up herself.

She thought again of Caitlyn Gallivan. Diana knew the type – she knew all the types. Caitlyn was a bully and a narcissist who was too accustomed to getting her own way. The only question in Diana's mind was why Caitlyn was so preoccupied with keeping her mother from the world. Was it to protect Fiona, or protect a secret she was hiding?

Sue was silent in the seat next to her, and Diana noticed her hands gripping the wheel more firmly than necessary. But as the car wound further along the narrow coast road,

Sue's shoulders eventually relaxed to their normal position from where they had been bunched up high around her ears.

Diana sighed. That was a close call back there. From now on, they needed to be more careful.

That Caitlyn was certainly a piece of work. Part of her hoped that Caitlyn did have something to do with the murders, if only to see her brought down a peg or two. Diana could imagine how that would wipe the smile off her smug little face.

Back in Beadnell, they pulled up outside Diana's cottage. She hesitated, searching for the word, then laid a gentle hand on Sue's arm. 'Thank you.'

Sue nodded, her mouth still pinched, and said nothing.

Once inside, Diana resumed control of the operation. They needed to channel their frustration into productive activity.

'Helen, let's have you checking the employment records – see if there are any other names in there we recognise.' Diana heard herself – her old teaching voice – and resisted the temptation to smile. After all, this was getting serious. 'Sue – let's go through those pictures on the laptop. Ben Gallivan's face has got to be in there somewhere.'

Diana watched as Sue opened the laptop and issued a series of clicks.

'What? I don't... I don't understand.' Sue stuttered. 'What did I do?' She jabbed at the mousepad. 'It – they were right here.' Her brow furrowed. 'The photos – they've all disappeared.'

She looked up, seemingly hoping her friends might be able to offer an explanation.

'Are you sure you're looking in the right place, for starters?' Diana almost laughed at herself, the memory of the phrase she had uttered so many times to forgetful and careless schoolgirls. Not to mention Lionel.

'Maybe it's a virus?' Helen said optimistically.

Diana had heard of computer viruses, of course, and anti-virus software, although she couldn't fathom exactly what that entailed. She paused for thought. That meant Chris Carter was probably aware of anti-virus software, too.

'I don't understand this at all...' Sue mumbled. 'Well, not to worry. It should all be backed up on the cloud. I'll download them tonight.'

A satisfied smile spread across Diana's lips. She had no idea what a *cloud* was, but from Sue's face, she sensed her friend had it in hand, even if it did delay the investigation.

With the laptop out of order, Diana moved across to the wall. 'We need to add our latest findings. Number one.' Diana held up an index finger. 'Caitlyn is hiding something. More specifically, she is hiding her mother.' She hesitated, a beat, as she considered this. 'As well as other things, potentially. Number two – we have a loose end with that sand in the hallway. Ben must be involved with a construction project somewhere. We need to find it.'

'And what about Tom?' Sue frowned. 'I can't help but notice his mug shot hasn't made it on to the leader board, and I'm telling you, I have a bad feeling about that man.'

Diana didn't agree, but she tried to look as if she was at least considering this possibility. She needed to keep Sue on side, even if she struggled to understand what her friend had against their newcomer.

This was the problem with these two: no focus. Too easily distracted, allowing personal opinions and paranoia to cloud their judgement.

Diana sank into Lionel's armchair. It had been a tiring

morning, and now that her adrenaline had subsided, their run-in with Caitlyn had left her drained.

Sue seemed to sense this was their cue to depart. 'We'd best be on our way.' She glanced at her watch. 'We can pick up where we left off tomorrow.'

Diana lacked the energy to persuade them to stay.

The house was quiet once they left, and the silence allowed Diana to concentrate.

Instead of examining her evidence wall, she turned her attention back to the laptop. It was strange that an entire folder had disappeared without a trace. Could someone have deleted it deliberately?

She thought again of the disquiet she had felt after her snooze in the chair yesterday afternoon.

Diana shook off the idea as soon as it occurred to her. That was the stuff of Watergate, of *News of the World* phone hacking, of scandals in far-away places. Nothing like that ever happened around here.

Then she thought of Peter and Chris. Perhaps it was time to start locking her front door.

———

Back at home, the familiar fragrance of burning incense greeted Sue.

Anne had finished another mirror, which was propped up beside the others in the hallway. Sue supposed she should be thankful that it was just the one. None of them had sold yet, and this added to Anne's dark mood. It was a good sign that she was meditating, though. It never failed to soothe her. This evening, Sue didn't want her sister's mood to be a distraction.

At least she had planted the seed of suspicion with

Diana about Tom Grey. She would give the suggestion time to germinate, to grow in Diana's mind. Meanwhile, Sue planned to do some digging of her own.

As soon as Anne was settled with the Radio Times in the living room, Sue logged on to the computer and opened Facebook. She didn't have an account – never having understood the appeal – but thankfully, Anne was already logged in. A search for Tom Grey returned hundreds of results. It was, she supposed, a very common name.

She scrolled through the thumbnail photographs, scanning for his face. Nothing.

'What are you doing?' Anne set a steaming mug of herbal tea on the computer table, which Sue gratefully accepted. She felt on edge and could use something to calm her nerves.

'I'm trying to find out more about Tom, that man who joined the book club.'

Anne peered at the screen. 'Tom Grey? Is that his name?'

Sue heard something in Anne's voice, something that only a sister would hear. Anne knew something. 'Why? What else could it be?'

'Oh, nothing.' She waved a dismissive hand, then paused. 'But I thought he was Agnes's sisters' boy. That's what Brenda told me when I bumped into her in Clarke's. The sister married a man with a fancy name.' Anne lifted her gaze towards the ceiling, as if searching for it. Nothing seemed to come to her.

'Who's Agnes?'

'Agnes Bellamy. You know her. Or actually, maybe you don't. You were away at the time.'

Sue heard a note of bitterness in her sister's voice. All these years later, the old resentment rose to the surface: that Sue once imagined a life beyond Seahouses.

Anne continued. 'She must be in her eighties now, but she's still around. Her sister was Dorothy. That's Tom's mother.'

'You *know* them?'

'When Edward was alive, I knew a lot of people around here,' she said with a sad sigh.

Sue thought of Anne's husband, the charismatic local doctor. He had never been the type to keep himself to himself. Sue, on the other hand, had purposefully shied away from getting too well acquainted with others in the village.

'After Dorothy married she moved away, somewhere down south, as I recall.' Anne shrugged.

Down south didn't exactly narrow the field. Sue took a deep breath. 'If you could remember his name, that would be extremely helpful.'

Anne's eyes widened. 'You don't think he had something to do with all this, do you?'

'Well, if we knew his name, we might be able to find out.'

'Wait right there. I'll ask Edward.'

Sue wanted to bury her face in her hands, but this was not the time to get into a row about her mocking Anne's spiritual sensibilities.

With her eyes closed and her arms spread out like wings, the tips of her index fingers pinched against her thumbs, Anne began to hum. The noise came from deep in her chest, and she gently swayed to her own beat. It would have been hilarious, thought Sue, if the stakes weren't so high. She took a sip of hot tea.

After a moment, Anne's eyes burst open. 'Montfort. Told you it was fancy.'

'Tom Montfort,' Sue mumbled, turning back to the computer. That search returned a much shorter list.

Sue spotted him immediately. His profile picture was black and white, taken quite some time ago, but there was no doubt it was the same man. 'It says here that he lives in London. Works at HSBC in Canary Wharf.'

It was Tom, but there was something different about him. The pictures showed a man enjoying middle-age and living a full life – travelling, exotic beaches, skiing holidays and fancy cocktail bars. Something about it reminded Sue of Izzy, her other niece, who was forever sending her pictures of nights out, mountain hikes, and photos of her toes against a backdrop of luxury swimming pools.

What made him trade all of that for a quiet life in Seahouses?

She searched for 'Tom Montfort, HSBC.' The first result was an article about a merger he had overseen. She combed through the other results, but there was nothing recent. The latest mention of Tom Montfort was five months ago, in an article about the woman who had replaced him in his job.

'It looks like he just packed up and quit his life,' Sue muttered. 'But why change his name? And what made him come here?'

'Maybe he wanted to be closer to his family?' Anne offered.

'But his parents don't live in Northumberland. Why would you give up a high-flying city career and come to Seahouses to live with your elderly aunt? And none of that explains why he changed his name.'

'Perhaps he was running away.'

Sue's throat tightened. 'I think you're on to something.'

Her hand hovered above the mouse, and she noticed it was trembling.

67

SUE HAD BARELY SLEPT LAST NIGHT, CONSUMED BY TROUBLING thoughts of Tom Grey, or Tom Montfort, or whoever he was.

She cradled a cup of milky tea in two hands, now, unable to muster sufficient focus for even the simplest task. The tea eventually got cold, a translucent film forming on its surface.

Tom's name – his real name, that was – must be connected to Sparkbrook. Perhaps he was the banker behind some of Peter Gallivan's business dealings. He might even be the whistle-blower who tipped off the press about the company's tax affairs. Whatever he had done, he had gone to great lengths to cover it up and sneak back into the Gallivans' orbit undetected.

And what about Chris Carter? Tom must have uncovered the link between Chris and Peter – whether that was blackmail, or merely the fact that Chris had become acquainted with his former boss. Clearly, Tom had been tying up a loose end.

She cast her mind back to that night in the pub, when she had first gathered a group of women – and Tom – for a book club. Chris stormed in, and his treatment of Tom was frosty. Sue chewed her lip. *Frosty* was probably putting it mildly. Chris must have recognised him from somewhere. What appeared to be an indiscriminate threat to a stranger might in fact have been a warning blow to someone who Chris knew perfectly well.

Her mind burned with the possibilities and the ramifications.

Diana would need more than proof of an identity switch to convince her. Sue's heart sank as it dawned on her – all they had was evidence of a name change and an abandoned career. She needed to find out more.

The sun was in its ascent when she left home, dousing the windows of the houses on her quiet street in marigold light. Not a soul stirred.

Anne had told her where Agnes Bellamy lived. On the outskirts of the village, on the road towards Beadnell, a short row of cottages sat discreetly in a natural curve of the land. Each one was white, with the same blue windows and doors. Sue parked her car at the end of the street, out of sight, and waited, watching.

She had no plan other than to catch another glimpse of Tom. With every minute that passed, she became more enraged that a con artist lived among them, tricking them into believing he was someone else. Her instinct had been right from the start.

Just before 10 a.m., the door to one of the cottages opened and Tom emerged. He slipped on a pair of sunglasses, his head bowed and his eyes on his feet. He was dressed for a game of golf, in pressed cream chinos and a black weatherproof jacket.

Tom climbed into a Mini, and, because she had no better plan, Sue decided to follow him. She set off, leaving a safe distance between herself and the Mini as they wound their way through the quiet village.

She passed the gift shop and saw that it was already open, the door propped with a heavy stone. Helen was at work today, having been unable to convince Sharon, the weekends-and-Wednesdays girl, to cover for her. Sue longed for the reassuring presence of her friend. Instead, she found herself alone, and in pursuit of a potential murderer. It was just observation, she told herself, as the blood thundered in her ears.

Tom picked up speed as he passed the Gallivans' house at the top of Seafield Road, a clear stretch of pale tarmac unfurling in front of him. Sue followed, maintaining the distance between their cars. The magnificent hulk of Bamburgh Castle looming larger the closer they got.

She slowed as she approached the base of the ancient fortress. Tom's car indicated right, and Sue followed him into the narrow lane. The Wynding arced around the castle green, then curved to run parallel to the beach. She held back, knowing that the road led to only one destination. Soon, the golf course came into view.

Her tyres crunched obtrusively over the gravel of the carpark, but Tom, who was already on the steps of the club entrance, didn't turn around. Sue watched him in her rearview mirror.

She knew that she should turn around and go home, that there was nothing to gain from this folly. But something told her to press on.

Ignoring the sign that designated the carpark as strictly 'members only', she walked in the direction of the green. The wind was sharp, whipping the sea into a frenzy fifty meters below and smoothing the golden sand, erasing any evidence of the people who had walked this stretch of beach that morning.

She yanked at her collar, pulling it as high as it would go, and buried her hands in her pockets. Without a glance back towards the club house, she set off along the boundary of the green, where the neatly trimmed grass bordered the perilous drop down to the beach.

A squat building came into view on her left. A shed, of sorts. It wasn't much of a hiding place, but it was the best shelter she could hope for out here. She crouched down, hoping to remain unnoticed by the few hardy golfers who tackled the course despite the wind, and waited.

———

Three miles away, back in the warmth of the pub, Gina checked her phone.

She had been buoyed by Carrie's text on Sunday but had heard nothing since and was now sinking into a despair even more profound than before.

What had Carrie told the police? She read over their conversation again. Was Carrie apologising for the radio silence or for dobbing her in?

Gina was paranoid, she recognised that. She knew that the practical, sensible thing would be to get her ducks in order – to make sure she had a ready and watertight alibi for the day that Chris died, just in case the police did come knocking. She should prepare an explanation, she thought, about how Chris was abusive towards Carrie and she, Gina – the concerned friend – was only looking out for her pal.

A story to make the cops believe she was incapable of harming another person. But what if they saw right through her?

Gina shook her head. She was just paranoid; that's all it was. She had nothing to hide. And if she wanted anyone else to believe it, she had to first convince herself.

The bottle optics were buffed and sparkling, the drip trays stacked in a sink full of disinfectant, and the brass artefacts around the bar – which numbered well into the hundreds – were polished to gleaming. Keeping her hands busy stilled her troubled mind.

Gina caught sight of herself in the mirror behind the bar. Under her eyes, shadows had appeared beneath the pallor of a complexion that could benefit from a little sunlight. She needed a holiday. Maybe, if Carrie came back – *when Carrie came back*, she corrected herself – they could have a week in Mallorca or Tenerife. But most of all, Gina craved a good night's sleep.

The nightmares were becoming more frequent. Every night, after dark, his face appeared in her dreams, shocking her awake at all hours, leaving her panting for breath.

The floor. She had vacuumed the carpet that morning, but could still detect the stale odour of spilled ale. There was some carpet shampoo in the cleaning cupboard, and an hour to go before she opened. Gina got to work.

———

Tom was thinking of Gina at that moment. Perhaps that's what was putting him off his game. Not that he really *had* a game, per se. This morning's round was his first practice session without Billy, the optimistic instructor who had encouraged him to spend some time alone on the course, getting a feel for the terrain and the wind.

His golf club clattered against the ball and he lost sight of it momentarily as it arched uncontrollably into the air before the wind carried it miles away from the area of green he had been aiming for. Tom swore to himself. How did anyone find this remotely relaxing?

As he walked towards his ball, a gale buffeting against his back, he thought of ways to approach her. He could suggest a film at the cinema in Berwick, or dinner in Alnwick – he'd read some great restaurant reviews online. Perhaps that was too grand. She might think he was hitting on her.

He needed something more low-key. A game of pool, perhaps. He could even make a casual suggestion to get fish and chips one night.

It would never happen.

Tom swung wildly at the tee, sending tufts of grass splaying. The ball landed in the bunker. He swore again, louder this time, and glanced around. The nearest golfers were a few holes ahead, and nobody else was within earshot.

Suddenly, his frustration at the way things had turned out bubbled to the surface. That anger – at the things he had been forced to do, forced to sacrifice – burned in his chest. The rage that he had grown adept at burying was in his throat, a fireball of hate.

Turning to face the sea, he cursed again, even louder. It felt good. He balled his hands into fists and screamed as loud as he dared.

He had no idea that he was being watched.

———

From her hiding place behind the shed, Sue observed Tom as he approached. His shots were all over the place and his swing lacked control. Even at this distance, and knowing nothing about the game, she could tell he wasn't very good.

When he began screaming like a madman, she moved back a few inches, her body flush against the wall, and kept her sights trained on him. She pressed a hand to her chest, willing her racing heart to still. That frustration, she sensed, came from more than just a round of golf.

He lurched forward, marching towards the spot where his ball had landed, fists clenched at his sides as if ready to punch something. He dropped over the edge of the green into the sandy bunker, and Sue's heart pounded in her ears.

The sand. It hadn't come from a building site, after all.

She gasped, her hand flying to her mouth.

―――――

Against the quiet of the course, Tom heard something.

He whipped his head around, scanning the green around him. Had he imagined it?

No, there had been something. A distinctly human noise, coming from the storage shed in the middle of the green, some thirty metres away from where he stood.

His skin prickled with the sensation of being observed. He hesitated, then took considered, tentative steps in that direction.

―――――

Sue knew instantly that she had been too loud. Tom was looking in her direction – he might even have seen her – and she pressed herself flat against the shed, her hands splayed against the wall, her pulse galloping.

She dared not risk another glance – she had to get out of

there. But where could she go? The course was open and flat, and Sue was no athlete – whichever way she ran, he would see her.

She inched her way to the back of the building, the side furthest away from the sea. There was nowhere to hide. Her breath was coming in shallow gulps. *What to do?* She would phone for help.

She slid her mobile phone out of her pocket with a trembling hand. No signal. *Damn it!*

A ride-on lawnmower was parked at the rear of the building, flush to the wall, as sheltered from the wind as possible. She imagined hot-wiring it and riding to safety.

A soft thud reverberated through the feeble metal structure, a hand slapping angrily against the corrugated tin wall. She had no idea if he was approaching from the left or the right. The closest golfers were a jumble of colour in the distance. Would they even hear her if she screamed?

———

The shed, to which Tom had never paid much attention, was deserted. He tried the handle of the door, giving it a vigorous shake.

'Hello?' he called out.

Slowly, he started to make his way around the side. The structure was windowless, and the only door was on the side he had just come from.

He could have sworn he had heard something. *Someone.* He approached the back of the building. An old lawnmower sat forlornly, speckled with rust.

There was no one here. Perhaps it had been a bird, or the wind playing tricks on him. Or perhaps it was just *him.*

Tom shivered. Thoughts of the past, the echoes of painful old memories, messing with his head.

He stood there for a moment longer, then turned and strolled back towards the course.

———

Just inches above him, lying flat on the roof, Sue let out a slow sigh of relief.

She rolled onto her front and eased herself up into a half-crouch, tentatively raising her head. Only once she was certain that Tom had gone did she edge towards the lawn-mower, trembling as she lowered one foot slowly towards the seat, and climbed back down the way she came.

It was Diana's fault. She had been so convinced of a connection to a building site that they had been blinkered to the blindingly obvious.

Well, Sue supposed, she had played a part in that. She had told everyone, confidently, that silica sand was used in construction.

She conducted one last check that the coast was clear. Tom had moved on to the next hole, holding up a hand to shield his eyes from the pale sun.

Was this what she wanted, when she wished for more excitement? She thought of the home she shared with Anne, sipping coffee at the giftshop with Helen, of doing the school run and a thousand other mundane things, and wondered whether a simple, uneventful life is perhaps not such a terrible thing after all.

68

SUE DASHED BACK TOWARDS THE CARPARK AS FAST AS HER LEGS would carry her, fumbling with the key. Her hands were still shaking as her car wound back through Bamburgh and out on to the strait towards Seahouses.

As tempting as it was to stop at the gift shop – the prospect of a hug from her friend and a hot, sugar-laden cup of tea almost brought tears to her eyes – she kept going. She passed the turning for Amy's house, driving past the road where she lived, and headed straight to Diana's place.

The primal fear that choked her for most of the drive began to subside and, in its place, anger smouldered. What did they think they were playing at?

Diana thought this was all some stupid game and Sue saw now that it was completely out of hand. She could have been killed back there. As she marched up Diana's garden path, she imagined the many horrible ways that Tom Grey – or Tom Montfort – might have seen her off. Reaching the doorstep, she paused to compose herself before knocking.

The door opened after a heartbeat.

'My goodness, Susan. Whatever happened to you?'

Sue opened her mouth, the tirade bubbling on her tongue, when she spotted Lucia sitting in the living room. Her lips clamped shut. She would have to wait. They were already in enough danger, and she didn't want to put anyone else at risk with her knowledge.

Sensing her change of heart, Diana waved her inside.

The kitchen was filled with the scent of baking, cinnamon combined with something bitter as it met Sue's nose.

'Let's get you a cup of tea and a slice of apple pie. I baked it myself.' Diana ushered her through to the living room.

'Hi,' Lucia said, her face falling as she took in Sue's appearance. She opened her mouth, then closed it again. Whatever else she was about to say, it died on her lips.

Sue passed the mirror in the living room and caught a glimpse of her reflection. She had been growing her hair, fancying a change of style. While the longer length looked great after a blow dry, right now it was a royal mess. Strands stuck out at ugly angles and the front flopped towards her face, buffeted in all directions by the wind on the golf course. She raked it back into place with her hands. There was little she could do about the paleness of her skin, still white with shock, or the dark shadows under her eyes.

'I asked Lucia to come by and have another look at that blasted computer,' Diana explained.

Lucia nodded, biting her lip, a frown forming on her perfect face. 'There's not much I can do, I'm afraid. I've no idea what happened to all those photos.'

'Lost for good, I suppose,' Diana said with a sorry sigh.

Sue was about to remind her that she had saved a backup of the entire file on the cloud and point out that it was a waste of time to have sought Lucia's help, but Diana caught her eye. The glare silenced her.

'Well, allow me to thank you properly with pie.' Diana smiled innocently and shuffled back into the kitchen. She re-emerged momentarily with two steaming slices, the pastry golden and the apples glistening.

———

Diana watched as Lucia hugged the knee of a long, Lycra-clad leg towards her body. She sensed the young woman had something on her mind, and despite having been there for forty-five minutes, had not yet plucked up the courage to spit it out.

She had hoped the pie might make the girl more forth-coming, but Sue turning up looking traumatised had killed any chance of that happening. Lucia had now clammed up entirely.

Diana sighed. If only Sue had left them to it. Who knew when she might get another chance to hear Lucia's piece?

The three of them ate their pie in awkward silence, both Lucia and Sue sporting anxious expressions. Each burdened by something and neither wanting to talk in front of the other.

Diana was troubled. What had Lucia wanted to tell her? And what on earth had happened to Sue?

Plates cleared, Lucia made her excuses to leave. After seeing their young visitor out, Diana made two fresh cups of tea, adding a generous spoonful of sugar to Sue's. There was no mention of the evidence wall or the photos. Instead, Diana provided the silence her friend needed.

'It's Tom. Tom Grey. Only that's not his real name. He's actually *Tom Montfort*. At least, he was...'

Diana's eyes widened. The name rang a bell. 'Excuse me? You mean he's Dorothy's boy?' *Odd that he had never mentioned anything,* Diana thought, but allowed Sue to continue.

Her friend clasped the hot mug with two hands, her knuckles paling. 'He was a banker down in London. But he quit his job and changed his name, and he's been living up here with his aunt.'

Agnes, thought Diana, remembering her. Agnes had a fall, which resulted in a hospital stay, and Diana had not seen her in over a year. Possibly two.

She shared none of this with Sue. The woman was clearly building up to something big.

'After realising he isn't who he said he is, I decided to follow him. I tailed him to Bamburgh Golf Club. It wasn't building sand in the hallway, Diana. It was sand from the golf course.'

Of course, Diana thought. She kicked herself for failing to see it. Mind you, the geologist should probably have worked that one out. 'But what's his connection to Peter Gallivan? Or Chris?'

'Diana.' Sue fought to keep her voice level, clearly struggling against the urge to cry. 'We are not detectives. It's not our job to solve a crime. I could have been *killed* out there today.'

Diana resisted rolling her eyes when she saw that Sue was on the verge of tears. 'My dear girl, what on earth happened?'

'He *saw* me! I was spying on him, and I made a noise. He turned around—' Sue stopped herself, her voice catching. She pressed the back of a trembling hand to her lips, waiting for the threat of tears to pass. 'I had nowhere to hide. I had to climb up onto a roof, for goodness' sake. He was snarling like a... like a wild animal, and I swear, if he had found me...'

It sounded far-fetched, but Diana could not deny that her friend was truly afraid. Real fear was hard to disguise, and even more difficult to fake. It set her on edge.

'We should check the employment records. Maybe Tom—'

'No. Don't you understand what I'm telling you? This is where it ends. I want you to get rid of all of this.' Sue gestured around the room with a flailing hand. 'And we're going to call the police tonight.'

'But we're—'

'No.' Sue's lip trembled.

Diana nodded glumly. 'All right, dear. If you think that is for the best.'

Together, they took down the pictures and notes from the evidence wall. Weariness consumed Diana, and it was all she could do not to retire to the chair and simply watch Sue finish the clean up on her own. Her bones ached with the fatigue of every single one of her eighty-two years.

She stacked the paperwork in piles by the grate and laid a fire for later. The employment records, timeline, and suspects' headshots would be kindling in a few short hours. Their investigation reduced to ash.

All that hard work had come to nothing.

'I'll take the computer back.' Sue gnawed on a nail.

Diana shook her head. It would be risky, she knew, returning to the caravan. She wouldn't put that on her friend.

Together, they dragged the table back to its original position and placed the dining chairs around it. The room started to regain its familiarity.

Diana caught Lionel's eye from his frame on the mantelpiece. A shadow danced across the photograph, and Diana recognised the look on his face. She turned away, unable to bear the weight of his disappointment.

They had been so close. But Sue was right. It was over now.

She wiped down the laptop with Vanish, uncertain that it would be wholly effective at removing all traces of DNA and what-not, but it was the best she could think of. Her chief concern wasn't being caught, but getting the others in trouble. She had dragged them all into this – she knew that, deep down – and if anyone took the heat for it, it would be her and her alone.

They drove off together in their separate cars with an agreement that Sue would call the police at 7 p.m. That would give Diana enough time to get to the caravan and back, and get a good fire going once she was home.

It wasn't much of a plan, but they agreed that Sue would give an anonymous tip off to lead the police to Tom, citing his change of name, and the fact that he had befriended both victims' spouses through a local book club. *Some plan indeed.* Diana could see the flaw, the absence of almost any proof – not to mention that they had been unable to ascertain neither motive nor opportunity – but Sue would hear no more talk of gathering further evidence.

'They're quite capable of solving this themselves,' she said, not even attempting to hide her exasperation.

Diana, who always knew when she was skating on thin ice, conceded.

The caravan park was quiet and nobody witnessed her prising the lock at lot thirty-two. She returned the laptop and slipped out as quietly as she entered. Anyone who happened to pass by would see her stumbling into the wrong unit and would attribute it to the innocent faux pas of an elderly lady.

That's all she was now. A useless old woman.

The caravan park was perched on a crop of headland, the well-tended lawns giving way to a cliff face that dropped dramatically toward the sea.

Diana paused beside her car, closing her eyes, and feeling the agreeable warmth of the afternoon sun on her face as the wind whipped at her hair. She took in the view. A rich navy eternity, broken only by a dusting of waves, and a piercingly blue sky illuminated by buttery sunshine. Only those who knew what to look for would recognise the storm that was approaching.

She had tried.

The ache now seeped into her bones, and it took all her strength to climb back into the car and make the short journey home.

Her cottage felt emptier than ever – impossibly quiet. The thick stone walls blotted out the noise of the wind, which had picked up clouds from the sea, rolling in from the horizon, threatening heavy rain by nightfall. Dust motes danced in the silence of her living room, and she turned on the television in the vain hope of filling the void.

She lit a fire in the hearth and watched as golden flames flickered to life, casting long shadows across the room. The stack of papers sat beside her. Tentatively, one by one, she began to throw them into the grate, entranced as the flames lapped greedily.

———

A couple of miles away in Seahouses, Sue spent the evening pacing. She could sit still for a moment or two, but it was impossible to relax. Outside, the weather worsened by the minute, but Sue barely noticed the sky fade to dark. The hands of the kitchen clock ticked by impossibly slowly.

Finally, it was time. She looked up the phone number of Alnwick Police Station and made a note of it in her address book. Her hand trembled as she dialled.

'Yes? Hello? I, er...' she stuttered. 'I'm calling to report a crime of murder.'

69

A STORM WAS ROLLING IN. FIONA WATCHED THE DAYLIGHT SLIP away prematurely, blotted out by angry clouds that spread like ink across the sky. The sea whipped into a frenzy and waves pounded the shoreline, crashing against the rocks and sand that were now grey in the gloom.

From the floor below, she heard the voices of Caitlyn and Ben. She edged to the door of her reading room and prised it open, just a crack, to better hear. But they were speaking in conspiratorial whispers, and Fiona couldn't make out what they were saying.

They were taking it in shifts, she had realised, to babysit her. At first, she found it endearing that both of her offspring would rush to their mother in her hour of need. It took her a few days to realise that their attentiveness might be driven by an ulterior motive.

She padded down to the first floor and paused on the landing. At the sound of her footsteps, their chatter dimmed.

What were they up to?

Fiona made her way to the kitchen and retrieved a bottle

of Gavi di Gavi from the wine fridge. It was crisp on her tongue, and she closed her eyes as she savoured the first few mouthfuls, knowing that she would finish the bottle before bed.

She had nothing better to do.

All her suggestions of lunch at country pubs, of afternoons exploring the antique shops of nearby villages and even forays into Seahouses had been met by the same responses. At first, it was murmured non-commitments and half-hearted excuses. Neither Caitlyn nor Ben seemed to want to leave the house. The problem was that they didn't want her to leave, either.

She polished off her glass just as the rain started; fat drops smashing soundlessly against the triple-glazed windows.

Esme. She would call Esme.

There was enough water under the bridge by now – months' worth – and Esme must surely have known, deep down, that none of it was Fiona's fault. Besides, she needed a friend right now. It was a risk worth running. She took a gulp from her second glass for courage.

Bracing herself, she picked up the phone and dialled the number she knew by heart.

The handset was mute.

'Mum.'

Fiona started. Distracted, she hadn't heard Caitlyn coming downstairs.

Caitlyn hesitated in the doorway, the words she had been about to say dying on her lips as she eyeballed the handset in Fiona's hand. 'What are you doing with that?'

Rage simmered in the pit of Fiona's stomach. 'Why is the phone not working?'

'Who were you calling?'

Fiona closed her eyes, willing herself to remain calm. 'Caitlyn. I asked you a question. Why is the phone not working?'

Caitlyn was incredulous. 'Who on earth has a landline these days? I was going through the bills and sorting stuff out. I just assumed you never used it. You have your mobile and the internet, you don't need a landline as well.'

'I didn't ask you to go through the bills.' Fiona's cheeks burned. It could have been the wine, or it could have been the unique rage that only her daughter could elicit.

'So, who were you calling?' Caitlyn's tone had changed. The edge disappeared from her voice. She took the Gavi from the fridge and topped up Fiona's glass.

Fiona took a sip. 'I was going to call Esme, as it happens.'

'You can't be serious...' Caitlyn rolled her eyes.

'Why? Why not? She's my friend. *Was* my friend,' Fiona corrected herself.

Caitlyn leaned back against the kitchen island, regarding Fiona with something that could have passed for pity. For a woman that so many considered beautiful, her daughter certainly had an ugly side. 'I'm sure you'll see her soon enough once you're back in Durham—'

'When?' Fiona cried, louder than intended. '*When?* You keep talking about *going back*, but you won't let me leave the bloody house!'

Caitlyn threw her a scornful look and spoke slowly, as if speaking to someone very old, or particularly stupid. 'Once the sale goes through—'

'I don't give a hoot about the sale! It's not what I wanted, and you ran roughshod over my wishes, but it's happening, and I—'

The kitchen door creaked open and Ben padded in. He

looked older than his years, with dark circles under his eyes and the stooped shoulders of one carrying the weight of the world on his back.

'Come on, Mum, don't be like that...'

A scream swelled in Fiona's chest and she stomped out of the kitchen before it could escape, the bottle under her arm, ignoring the glance exchanged between her children. She thundered up the stairs.

The reading room was dark now, the sun having disappeared beyond the horizon, the line between sea and sky completely obscured by the wet, black night.

On the road below, three police cars approached from the direction of Bamburgh, their lights flashing blue.

They were coming for her.

The wineglass slipped through her fingers and fell to her feet, the contents pooling onto the thick carpet.

She pictured Peter lying on the floor, gasping for breath, begging for her to call an ambulance. Above, she loomed, larger than him now. For the first time in their miserable marriage, she held all the cards.

And she did nothing.

She watched the life drain out of him, struggling to feel pity or remorse or... well, anything.

Until death do us part.

But the police didn't stop.

Fiona watched as they slowed, a convoy heading into the village. Only once they were out of sight did she realise she was holding her breath.

―――――

The flashing blue lights lit up the facades of the buildings around The Ship, and Gina pressed herself flat against the wall of the back yard, almost dropping her cigarette. Her breath snagged in her throat. She could have sworn that, just for a second, her heart stopped beating.

But the cars swung around the roundabout and headed inland, in the opposite direction to the pub. She exhaled slowly, her heart continuing to pound as they disappeared from view, the lights blurring into the rain.

She frowned, wondering where they could be going at this time of night.

It was raining heavily now. The kind of rain that wouldn't let up for another full day at least.

Gina walked back into the pub, her hand trembling lightly as she gripped the cool brass of the door handle. From the pocket of her jeans came the shrill squawk of her phone. She jumped, cursing under her breath.

The police always put her on edge.

She shook it off and peered at the screen.

Carrie: *I'm ready. Coming home Sunday. See you then x.*

For the second time in as many minutes, Gina's heart galloped.

The warmth of the pub enveloped her as she snaked her way through the bar that was already full, thanks to the inclement weather. After seeing the forecast, Gina had roped in Gavin for an extra shift, knowing it would be busier than a typical Wednesday. And she was right – the trawlermen were hedging on a day off tomorrow. Harry Whitefield had been joined by a whole crew of them – youngsters jostling among the old-timers who crowded the bar, too macho to sit at a table.

Roused by beer and merry from company, a few of them started to sing, an old shanty of lyrics which meant nothing to Gina. A group of hikers looked on from their table with bemused grins.

She dried a pint glass, getting ready for the fishermen to order another round.

Where were the police going?

Carrie was coming home. That was all that mattered.

70

On the other side of the village, Tom was watching a comedy show. He'd had such little time for television, before, and saw now that he hadn't been missing much.

Agnes had gone to bed after supper, complaining that the weather made her arthritis worse.

He was laughing along to the TV and didn't notice the blue lights illuminating the quiet blackness of the night as the squad cars arranged in formation outside the house. When the knock at the door came, he sat upright in his chair.

Padding through the kitchen in his socks, he was surprised by the outline of several figures silhouetted in blue light behind the textured glass of the door. His brow knotted to a frown as he opened it to the rainy night.

'Tom Montfort?'

Reflexively, Tom drew a sharp breath. He hadn't heard that name in months.

It was over.

'We'd like to ask you a few questions. Can we come in?'

It was a young police officer who spoke. She must have

been barely out of school, or university – he was unsure of the requirements to qualify as a police officer these days. Rain dripped from her hat.

He glanced over his shoulder, listening. Laughter tinkled from the TV, and beyond that, there was only silence. He hoped Agnes was still sleeping.

As if reading his thoughts, the officer spoke again. 'We can take you down to the station if that's easier?'

Tom shuddered at the prospect of a police station. God knows, he'd spent enough time in them. He did a quick headcount of the officers on his doorstep.

'It's... My aunt is sleeping. I don't want to wake her.'

The young officer turned to her colleague, a stout man who appeared to be on the verge of retirement, who issued a curt nod in response.

She looked back to Tom. 'We'll be quiet.'

The two officers trudged into the tiny kitchen and a numbness set over Tom as he watched them remove their hats and raincoats. Wordlessly, he gestured to the kitchen table and closed the door to the living room, hoping it would afford them some degree of privacy.

'I'm Constable Tamsine Young,' said the girl, without a hint of irony. She looked even more baby-faced without the hat.

Seriously, thought Tom, *how old is she?* But his mind raced, and it was impossible to curb the elation he felt. Their presence could only mean one thing.

The nightmare was over.

'We're here to ask you about Peter Gallivan and Chris Carter.' Constable Young blinked, her Bambi-brown eyes framed by a smattering of freckles.

Tom's ears started ringing. 'But I thought...' His words hung in the air.

'Mr Montfort, where were you on the evening of April the twenty-ninth?'

Tom heard a wail from somewhere, and, after a moment, realised it was coming from him. Before he could stop himself, tears rolled down his cheeks.

'Sorry,' Tom said, composing himself. 'I'm so sorry. Where was I...?'

He glanced at the calendar on the kitchen wall, which showed that Agnes had two hospital appointments last month. The rest of the days were empty. A sob escaped before he could stop it.

'I have no idea,' he said, mopping at his eyeline with his finger.

The young officer shifted nervously, but her colleague's face remained impassive. 'Perhaps you can tell us how you knew Peter Gallivan?'

'What on earth...?'

Constable Young cleared her throat, uneasy now. 'We believe you're acquainted with his widow, Fiona Gallivan, of Seafield Road. Peter died on the twenty-ninth of April.'

'Oh. Right. Of course.' Tom straightened in his chair and took a deep breath. 'I didn't know him, as such. Never even met the man.'

'What, might I ask, is so upsetting, Mr Montfort? Or should I call you Mr Grey?'

At this, Tom howled.

The young officer's cheeks reddened.

'I'm so sorry.' Tom gulped for air, dabbing his eyes with the cuff of his sweater. 'I take it you didn't have a chance to check my file?'

Constable Young gave up. She huffed a sigh and turned

to her colleague with a look that made it clear she was done. 'Mr Montfort—'

'Please.' He sniffed. 'Tom is fine.'

'Tom.' The older officer stroked a bushy moustache. 'Can you tell us why you changed your name?'

Tom wondered where to begin. 'I used to live in London...' he began. 'Lived there most of my life, actually. My ex... well.' He felt his face reddening.

He hadn't spoken these words for a long time, not to anyone other than Fran during their monthly therapy sessions on Skype. She told him it was healthy to say it out loud.

'My ex was... *difficult*. I was advised by the police...' He took a deep breath and continued only when he was sure that the threat of tears had passed. After all, the story must be told. He started again from the beginning.

'My former partner was abusive. Your colleagues were unable to charge him, however, and, through concerns for my safety, on the advice of the police, I changed my name and moved up here.'

He left out the part about the stalking, his breakdown, the career that it had cost him, and how the court case had crumbled through a lack of evidence and the unwillingness of witnesses to testify. They would find all of that once they did their homework.

'I thought you'd come here tonight to tell me you'd finally got him,' he added quietly.

The male officer made once last push. 'Tom, we received an anonymous tip off this evening that you were acquainted with Peter Gallivan and Chris Carter, both of whom have died in recent weeks, one under suspicious circumstances. Can you tell us anything about either of those men?'

From upstairs, Tom heard Agnes stir, and realised he barely cared. 'On that, I'm afraid, I haven't the foggiest.'

'Apparently you knew them both through a local book club?'

Tom could no longer help himself. He dissolved into sobs, his head folding into his arms on the tabletop, tears streaming down his cheeks.

71

DI TWEDDLE'S STOMACH RUMBLED. IT HAD BEEN A LONG shift, and he was about to tuck into a Pot Noodle when they received the call about a murderer on the loose in Seahouses. He eyed the chippie as they drove back down Main Street. Hopefully, there'd be something left by the time they finished their final call of the night.

He hated these small villages, with their gossiping busybodies, causing upset to perfectly innocent folk.

It had always been his plan to see out his career in rural Northumberland, away from the more demanding city policing of Newcastle and its higher crime rates. He'd pictured genteel villages where the worst crimes were cakes being stolen from the church fete and missing cats. He hadn't been prepared for the relentless snooping and curtain-twitching that, almost exclusively, resulted in wasted police time.

Their investigation into Chris Carter's death had drawn a blank, which irritated his Chief Constable – a blip on her precious performance stats. She'd been delighted to receive a tip off and promptly dispatched a full team to follow up on it, never mind that most of them hadn't eaten since lunch.

It didn't take them long to trace the call. When would people learn that withholding their number was powerless against the technology that the area command office had at their fingertips? Time-wasting curtain-twitchers, the lot of them.

'I'll take this one,' he grumbled to Tamsine as they pulled up outside the semi-detached house belonging to their most recent nosey parker.

There was only one way to deal with people like this.

———

Amy was sitting with her aunt at Sue's kitchen table when the knock came. They exchanged a glance. Who could it be, so late on a night like this?

'I'll get it,' Anne called, before either of them had a chance to move. Without conferring, they both dashed to the front door.

The three of them jostled for position on the threshold, confronting a portly police officer.

The man sighed, signalling his annoyance. 'An anonymous call was placed from this address earlier this evening. Which of you would like to tell me what that was all about?'

Sue's heart thundered in her chest. 'It was me.' Her voice was small.

'Name, please?'

'Sue Palmer – er, Susan,' she stuttered.

Amy scanned the street. This would be the talk of the village before morning. 'Why don't you come inside?'

The policeman sighed as he followed them through to the kitchen.

Amy filled two glasses of water and sat next to her aunt. Her mother hovered by the kitchen door, maintaining a safe distance, the anxiety betrayed in the lines between her brow.

Amy noticed Sue's hand trembling on her glass and gave her aunt's shoulder a reassuring squeeze. 'Officer—'

'Detective Inspector Tweddle,' he corrected.

Amy took a deep breath. 'Detective. My aunt acted in good faith. Two men have died, and there were concerns about the suspicious behaviour—'

Detective Tweddle cut her off. 'Tell you what, why don't we let Susan here explain herself?'

Sue took another sip of water. 'We were there the night that Peter Gallivan died. Amy here, she's the district nurse. Fiona – that's Peter's wife – was over at our house just before it happened. And when Chris passed away so soon after, we became suspicious that the two deaths were linked. Tom – he knew them both, or knew *of* them, through the book club I started. I felt responsible. I thought you needed to know.'

Amy thought of Diana. Who knew how far she had got with destroying the evidence of their little investigation? They'd all be in huge trouble if the police found out about the laptop and employment records.

'I take it he didn't do it?' Sue asked.

Tweddle ignored her question. 'You suggested that he knew both of the deceased through your book club. It turns out that Mr Montfort only met Chris Carter once, and actually only met Fiona Gallivan on one occasion – facts I believe you know to be true. Are you aware that wasting police time is a criminal offence under section five of the Criminal Law Act 1967? And that knowingly making false reports to the police is a crime? My best guess is that you took half an egg and made an entire omelette.'

'Sorry,' was all Sue managed to say.

———

It had been a mistake to mention food. Tweddle's stomach rumbled again, and he glanced at his watch. As much as he deplored time-wasters, the chip shop would be closing soon, and his priority was to get some food in him and get home.

'Let this be a warning to you. I don't have much patience for people who fancy themselves for amateur detectives.'

Susan Palmer winced, and he saw that he'd hit the nail on the head. That bloody Netflix had a lot to answer for.

'Try anything like this again, and you'll be in trouble.'

She hung her head. 'I understand.'

He stood to leave and issued a parting shot. 'I suggest that in future, you leave the policing to the police.'

72

'I COULD MURDER DIANA WHEELER. I REALLY COULD.' AFTER her ordeal last night, Sue could barely bring herself to utter the woman's name.

Helen nodded in agreement as she set out two steaming mugs of tea. 'She's certainly got a lot to answer for.'

Sue's anger simmered. It had all been so silly, really. Who did they think they were, running around trying to solve a murder? Diana had made them all look like fools.

'And Amy's none too pleased with me, either. She's worried they'll find out at work.'

Her niece had given her quite an earful last night, once the police left, which only made Sue feel even more rotten.

'Perhaps no one did it. I mean, maybe Peter died of natural causes and Chris died because of the drugs?' Helen mused. 'If it wasn't Tom...'

At the mention of his name, Sue dropped her head into her hands. God knows how he had felt when the police showed up on his doorstep.

The rain pattered against the window, warding off any would-be visitors and ensuring the streets of Seahouses remained grey and empty. At least they had the gift shop to themselves.

'I'll have to apologise to him. The police asked him about the book club, so he'll know the call came from one of us.' She sighed. 'It's the right thing to do, I suppose.'

'Take your time. You'll feel much better about this in a couple of days. I'm sure he'll understand.'

Sue wasn't so sure. 'In the meantime, I need to pay Diana a visit.'

She drained her mug and shrugged on her coat. She was furious with Diana, but there was no point in putting off a difficult conversation.

The village looked sad. Devoid of people, the streets of Seahouses echoed with the rain, which continued to fall, casting a grey filter over everything. The windscreen wipers on Sue's Vauxhall worked overtime as it meandered along the road that hugged the coastline and through the quiet streets of Beadnell.

———

Diana was pleasantly surprised to have unexpected company, but one look at Sue's thunderous expression told her that this was no ordinary social call.

'The police came to our house last night,' Sue blurted without preamble. 'It turns out that they can trace anonymous calls.'

Which is why any sensible person would have used a public phone box, Diana thought, but said nothing. In Sue's current mood, it wouldn't do to antagonise her by pointing out such an amateur error.

'They said I was wasting police time. It's a criminal offence.' Sue folded her arms across her chest.

'So, Tom is innocent.' Diana pressed a finger to her lips. 'Or at least, he was able to concoct a story that convinced them. Any idea why he changed his name?'

'I don't care. It's none of our business. None of it is any of our business. Amy could lose her job if they find out she's involved.' She shuddered as she pictured that fat policeman and remembered his warning. 'They mentioned the book club, so Tom knows we're behind the tip off, which means I now owe him an apology.' Sue felt her face reddening and willed herself to remain calm.

'Did you get rid of everything?'

A beat. Diana nodded. 'Yes. It's all gone.'

'Good. Because I never want to hear about any of this again. You could have got us all in very hot water.'

Diana sighed. 'Now hold on a moment, Sue. Two men died – what were we meant to do? Sit back and watch someone get away with murder, right here in our village?'

'We accused an innocent man of a terrible crime!'

'We don't know for sure that he's innocent.'

'I can't do this...' Sue muttered, shaking her head.

'Come on, Sue. You were just as concerned as I was. It isn't like I forced you. I still believe we did the right thing, on balance—'

'No.' Sue straightened up and looked Diana in the eye. 'I'm not doing this. Until you see sense, I suggest you stay away from me and stay away from Amy.'

Diana flinched.

Sue opened her mouth to say more, then thought better of it. Wordlessly, she turned and left.

73

Amy was determined. Her aunt had moped around for two entire days since the police visited, and enough was enough. It was time to put it behind them and move on. Before they could do that, there was one person they needed to see.

Gina had reliably informed her that Tom came into the pub most Friday nights, and Amy decided it was the best opportunity they would get.

She had made the mistake of telling Mike the whole story. Once upon a time, he might have been sympathetic, forgiving the quirks and eccentricities of her mother and aunt with a shrug of his broad shoulders. Now, he was furious that she could have got into so much trouble.

'There was no harm done, not really,' she said, wondering if Tom would ever feel that way.

'Don't you think you have enough on your plate? You're working, you've got three children,' — she noted that he said *you,* not *we* — 'you don't need this kind of drama.'

Amy sighed. It wasn't like she had gone out looking for trouble. And as much as she despised the way gossip spread like wildfire in a small village, she realised that the benefits outweighed any downsides. In a place as close-knit as Seahouses, everyone was a neighbour, and neighbours have to look out for one another. Even if it did lead to tension, from time to time.

Besides, if she stayed at home like Mike's mother did, she'd have ended up the same way – a housewife with nothing interesting to add to their conversations. A woman who'd tell anyone that would listen how her family meant everything to her and had little else to say for herself.

And that was not the woman Mike had married.

Amy had orchestrated the whole evening. They would arrive early and get a corner table, and give Auntie Sue enough time for a glass of wine before Tom arrived. Lord knew she would need the Dutch courage.

The three of them walked down the lane to The Ship, the rain glossing the pavements to a shine.

They didn't have to wait long for the pub to fill up. The inclement weather might have kept the walkers and day trippers away, but the locals – who had spent the best part of two days cooped up indoors – were desperate for any excuse to leave the house.

Amy scanned the faces, smiling to herself as she realised that she knew every single person in this pub. She loved her sister but could never understand Izzy's desire to live in a big city where no one knew you. Who could wish for any more than this?

At seven thirty, just as Gina had predicted, Tom walked in.

By now, most of the village knew that the police had called on him, then paid a prompt visit to Sue Palmer. In a place like Seahouses, it was impossible to keep a secret for long. Several pairs of eyes tracked him as he made his way to the bar.

Then he saw them.

With a glass of Chablis inside her, Auntie Sue was ready to face her penance. *It's now or never,* thought Amy, as she gestured for Tom to join them at the table.

———

Tom caught Amy's eye first. Such a beautiful woman. Natural, too, with barely a trace of make-up and blue-green eyes that sparkled with flecks of gold. If he'd been straight, she might just be his type.

A blush rose in his cheeks as he sat down at their table. He had suspected it might have been Sue who put the police on to him, right from the moment they mentioned the book club. He had to put it down to curiosity. Perhaps he should have done a better job at telling them how he washed up in Seahouses in the first place.

'I'll go to the bar,' Anne offered as she edged out of the table. 'Tom? What can I get for you?'

'I'll have...' He trailed off, eyeing their empty glasses and the bottle of white wine they had almost finished. 'I'll have a glass of whatever you're having.'

'Tom.' Sue folded her hands on the table between them. 'I am so sorry. I did a terrible thing. I jumped to the worst conclusion.'

Tom nodded. 'I suppose I haven't been very honest with you all.' His voice was little more than a murmur.

Anne returned with an extra glass, followed closely by Gina carrying the bottle.

Tom sighed, finally ready to tell his story. He drew a deep breath. 'My ex-boyfriend was a nightmare, to be perfectly frank, and I've been through hell and back. I came up here to escape, and I changed my name so that he wouldn't find me.' He scanned their faces for a reaction and saw nothing but kindness. 'I live with my aunt, and when I'm not sitting at home with her, I like to read, or come to the pub and people-watch.'

Amy gave him an encouraging smile, and he continued.

'My name is Tom Montfort. I'm a rubbish golfer, and I haven't murdered anyone.'

Sue pressed a hand to her temple. 'Do you suppose, Tom, that we could start again?'

An hour and another bottle of Pinot Grigio later, Tom had to admit that he was enjoying his night. He laid a hand on Sue's arm. 'Honestly, that visit from the murder squad was the most excitement I'd had in months! Although it's a close tie with that time Auntie Agnes lost her false teeth in the rice pudding.'

They laughed, and he relished the sound of it. It had been too long since he felt this... *easy.*

Gina had abandoned the bar entirely and joined them, leaving the hard work to Gavin and enjoying the view from the corner table for a change.

She saw Tom differently, he could tell. As if an invisible barrier between them had broken. He realised now why he was drawn to her in the first place. It wasn't so much that she reminded him of anyone else, someone from before. No, not that. She reminded him of who *he* was before. Who he used to be. Of his life back then, when he had real friends, and the fun they used to have. That was it: Gina looked like fun.

'You know, Tom.' She leaned towards him, keeping her

voice low so the others wouldn't hear. 'They have a bingo night once a month at the caravan park. It's not London or anything, but it's a right laugh. Maybe we could go together next week?'

The smile came effortlessly now. 'I'd love to,' he said, as something inside him thawed.

Anne refilled his glass. 'I do wonder, though, what happened to those two men.' She didn't seem to notice the glare Sue threw at her. Her voice lowered to a hush. 'I mean, do you think there could still be a murderer out there?'

Tom shuddered. 'What happened, exactly? The police didn't give me the full story.'

Amy sighed. 'Peter Gallivan had a heart attack. I attended to him, and, well, you know how that worked out. And when Chris Carter died a couple of weeks later, we started to look for a connection between the two of them.'

'There were signs of a disturbance,' Sue added. 'In the house, the night that Peter died. And sand. A trail of silica sand, to be precise. We worked out that if someone was there, they had possibly been to the golf course.'

Tom considered this. 'And how did Chris die?'

'A heart attack too, but we know for sure that his was induced by drugs. A combination of prescription medication.' Amy shook her head. 'And Chris used to work at Sparkbrook. We learned that Peter liked to mix business with pleasure. He'd been having an affair with his best friend's daughter.'

Tom shuddered. 'Ghastly man. Peter Gallivan always did like the younger ones, apparently.'

Four blank faces stared at him in response.

'Did you know him?' Amy asked cautiously.

'Not at all. But I heard the rumours. We – that is, our bank – oversaw one of his acquisitions a few years ago.

There was a strict instruction to keep any young female staff members out of arm's reach, if you catch my drift.'

Sue was hit, once again, by the feeling that they had missed something. She frowned. Perhaps she had been too hard on Diana. Tom's curiosity was making her see just how fishy it all was.

He seemed to read her thoughts. 'Couldn't be the widow, could it? She stands to earn millions once the sale goes through.'

'I don't think she's particularly bothered about the money.' Sue took a sip from her glass and glanced over her shoulder, making sure she was out of anyone's earshot. 'Diana overheard Caitlyn and Ben trying to get her to sell. They couldn't persuade her, apparently. And besides, Fiona was with us,' — Sue nodded to her sister — 'when Peter had the heart attack. She got home to find him collapsed on the floor and rang 999.'

Tom hesitated. 'And the kids? Could either of them have done it?'

Sue shook her head. 'The night Peter died, the daughter was in Edinburgh and the son was at home in Newcastle.'

A beat. 'And when did this happen?'

'The evening of twenty-ninth of April. A Sunday, five weeks ago.'

When Tom spoke again, his words were careful, measured. 'I saw Ben that night. Well, I saw his car. You don't see many of those, not around here. He drove through the village.'

Amy and Sue exchanged a frown.

'At what time? Do you remember?'

Tom wouldn't have remembered at all, except for that blasted diary. Another thing that Fran insisted would help, but was, in reality, little more than a daily reminder of just how empty and pathetic his life had become. He had checked his entry for that day after the visit from the police. On the night that Peter died, Agnes went to bed early, and Tom sat alone, reading for a couple of hours before heading out for a stroll.

'Between nine and ten, perhaps? He passed me at the top of Harbour Bank, driving far too fast and swerving all over the place.'

'That's strange,' Sue said, exchanging a quizzical glance with Amy. She swallowed. 'We might have overlooked the blindingly obvious. I need to tell Diana.'

74

THAT NIGHT, IN HER FLAT ABOVE THE PUB, WITH ITS WICKER chair and palm print wallpaper, Gina slept. Outside, the sea sang a lullaby that didn't reach her ears.

She was back there again. She never left, not really.

All those years and all those miles. The river was part of her. That crystalline spring water, teeming with salmon, ran through her veins. She could never escape.

Tony's face was clearer now, and his eyes locked with hers as he smacked her over the head. In every iteration of this nightmare, he hit her, but the blow felt different each time. Tonight, it didn't fog her mind or dull her senses.

If anything, it sharpened them.

The metallic tang of blood filled her mouth. She pushed her tongue over the makeshift gag to lick at her lip, checking to see how badly injured she was.

He pinned her, his weight pressing against her pelvis and her wrists, boring down into the ground until she felt certain her bones would snap. The thought made her want to throw up.

This is how he will break me, she thought, and understood

immediately that the thought alone meant he had already won.

The wet grass was cold beneath her bare skin. In his haste, Tony had yanked her jeans down to her knees where they created a further restraint, paralysing her legs. Or perhaps that was by design. God only knew how long he had been planning this.

A scream burned inside her chest, squeezing at her heart, but she couldn't make a sound. The rag strained at her cheeks, threatening to tear her face in two. Tears leaked out of her eyes and dissolved into her hairline.

Look up at heaven. Float away. Mind over matter.

How long had he been planning this?

This isn't it.

An icy dread shuddered through her, glacial horror paralysing her and causing her heart to skip a beat.

This isn't it. There's worse to come.

One of the consequences of Tony exerting complete control over Gina was that she'd had plenty of time to learn. She knew his every tic and quirk and habit.

From above that spot on the riverbank, she looked down on herself, crushed and brutalised by a monster. She regarded him cautiously. The snarl at the edge of his lip and the vein that bulged in his temple, the red-hot hate coursing through his veins.

He had no intention of letting her walk away once he was done with her.

Her breath snagged again in her chest as the thought anchored her to the earth.

He's going to kill me.

Once more, the ground was wet against her exposed skin and the pain raged like fire between her legs. She prayed that someone would come, some passer-by would stumble upon them and fight him off. But they were too far downstream from the bridge and behind the wall, hidden from view of the road. He chose this spot for precisely that reason.

She turned her head to one side. It was a dry-stone wall. Gina didn't understand why that fact, of all things, occurred to her in that instant, but realised later it had saved her.

The pressure on her right wrist let up slightly as Tony lolled to one side, a ship tacking. It was now or never.

Breaking free from his grasp, she reached out and yanked a stone free, sending a couple of others tumbling to the ground perilously close to her head.

In one smooth arc, she swung her arm, her fingers gripping the stone with searing white strength, and smashed it against his head.

Tony barely had time to register what was happening.

He instantly went limp, collapsing onto the grass. His eyes briefly rolled back in his head and he frowned, struggling to focus.

Gina didn't waste another second.

In a heartbeat she raised the stone above her head and smashed it down, again and again, slamming it against Tony's skull with a strength she hadn't known she possessed and a hatred she barely recognised. His blood splattered on her; it streaked her face and mixed with her tears and snot and something else.

Gina sat there for a while afterwards.

Someone is coming, she thought. *Someone will come now.*

She lost track of time while she waited. A bird sang from a tree close by and she closed her eyes, listening to its refrain. The river was dark and silent, moving slowly, observing her. A fly landed on Tony's face where the blood was beginning to dry, blackening and crusted around the hollow space that used to be his right eye.

Nobody came.

It wasn't difficult to roll him into the water. At the last minute, she squeezed rocks into the pockets of his jeans, praying it would be enough to weigh him down. It seemed to work.

Methodically, she restored the stones back to their original positions in the wall. A patch of grass had been flattened, but someone would have to be looking for it to notice.

Gina washed her face and hands in the river, hardly feeling a thing as the icy water splashed against her skin. A numbness had set in, but she had the sense to go on foot rather than contaminate her car. She would come back for it later.

She took off her shoes to walk across the towpath and didn't put them back on until she was on the tarmac road and certain that she wouldn't leave footprints. The gravel was sharp underfoot.

Mum and Dad were out. She washed her clothes, throwing half a bottle of Dettol in with the detergent, unsure if that would make any difference. Finally, she showered. Gina stood under the piping hot water until her body was pink and tingling, her tears washing away down the plughole. She scrubbed her fingers with a nailbrush and rubbed the cuts on her hands until they bled again.

When she stepped out, she was bruised and red and sore and bleeding, but she was alive. The mirror had steamed up, and she wiped away the condensation with a fist, her reflection appearing from beneath the haze. She met the eyes of the woman who stared back at her and saw that she was now someone else.

75

THE FOLLOWING MORNING, DIANA ALMOST FELT LIKE HERSELF again.

Yesterday, she had finally swallowed her pride and asked Sandra for a lift to Newcastle. She'd dressed it up with an invitation to lunch in the city, but both mother and daughter knew that was not the primary objective. Sandra, in a rare episode of altruism, had been charitable enough not to ask if she had an ulterior motive.

By 10 a.m. they were on the road.

'You can overtake this lorry, dear,' Diana said, unable to help herself.

In the corner of her eye, she noticed Sandra's jaw clench.

Parents weren't supposed to have favourites. And Diana didn't, she really didn't. It was just that Jennifer was so accomplished, and so easy-going, whereas Sandra couldn't stop fussing. Always interfering. Insisting she knew and wanted what was best for Diana, as if Diana couldn't look after herself.

Sandra had been her father's favourite. Of that, Diana had no doubt.

But Lionel Wheeler had been gone for more than twenty years and Sandra was still indignant at the world for taking him from her.

Diana had no time for her daughter's melodrama today – she needed to focus. She'd given too much time to moping on Friday, raking over Sue's words like hot, angry coals. Her jab about staying away from Amy had been a low blow. Sue spoke in anger; Diana recognised that. But it didn't stop the words smarting like salt on broken skin.

At her lowest ebb she had pictured Lionel, his brow furrowed and his eyes downcast, and knew that she had disappointed him.

Sue would come round eventually. She hoped.

Diana hadn't meant for any of them to get in trouble. Two lives had been lost, for heaven's sake. All she wanted was justice.

Well, if she was being perfectly honest with herself, she had enjoyed the thrill of the chase. And who didn't appreciate a good mystery? It was human nature. Sue was only upset because she'd had her knuckles rapped.

Perhaps they had been wrong about Tom Grey – or Tom Montfort – after all. It had been too soon to alert the authorities – too many pieces of the puzzle were still missing. Diana was hopeful that, after today, she would have her answers.

Roger Mason had suggested that Saturday was a good time to visit the offices of the Evening Chronicle. With only a skeleton staff manning the paper over the weekend, they could take the time to go through his case notes on Peter Gallivan without attracting too much attention.

· · ·

The fifteen years since their last meeting had not been kind to Roger. A sedentary lifestyle of late nights and takeaways had taken its toll, and he was twice the size of the young man that Lionel took under his wing so many years ago. But when he shook her hand, Diana noticed that the mischievous sparkle in his eyes still burned brightly.

'Roger. How wonderful to see you.'

He waved her past the security guard, who barely glanced up from the football match he was watching on a miniature television. They took the lift to the basement.

'I moved my office down here,' Roger explained with a note of apology. 'I like to be out of the way.' He gestured upwards. 'Too many eyes on you, up there.'

Diana understood.

Roger's office had probably been a storage room at one point. It was windowless, its institutional walls yellowing and showing signs of water damage. Roger gestured for her to take a seat, and she gratefully accepted.

'I'm meeting Sandra in an hour for lunch.'

Roger glanced at his watch. 'That should give us enough time. Tell me everything you want to know.'

Diana did appreciate people who got straight to the point. 'Peter Gallivan. Who might have wanted him dead?'

The chair opposite creaked as Roger leaned back and sucked in a breath. 'That could be quite a long list. Sparkbrook is worth a lot of money, certainly more than they're selling it for. Lou Renwick has had his eyes on Peter's shares for years. There was something of a failed coup a couple of years back.'

Roger paused as he read over the shorthand notes in his file.

'At the general meeting in 2015, one of the shareholders

proposed a motion that Peter resign on grounds of poor mental health. Word was that Lou was behind it. I heard – unofficially – that he had Ben Gallivan teed up and ready to go. It didn't fly – it would take a lot more than that to get Peter off the horse. Lou managed to wriggle out of it, but things were never the same between them after that.'

'And Peter's affair with Erin Renwick. Motivated by revenge, perhaps?'

Roger shook his head. 'I doubt it. More likely the foible of a powerful man. Peter Gallivan's greatest weakness – possibly his only weakness – was the ladies.' He leaned closer. 'I heard he liked them young. *Too* young, if you catch my drift.'

Diana winced. *How unsavoury.*

'There were the affairs, some of which we were allowed to report. But there were also rumours, over the years. Sexual harassment, that sort of thing. And worse, to tell the truth.' He sighed. 'None of it saw the light of day, of course. Sparkbrook paid them off, and I struggled to find anyone who would talk.'

'What about the victims? Anyone I could contact?'

'There was one girl who couldn't be bought. A former employee of Sparkbrook. She went to the police, alleging that Peter raped her, but the investigation fizzled out. Lack of evidence, lack of witnesses. Same old, same old. I tracked her down, and we emailed for a while. But she was too scared to go public.' He jabbed a fat finger at his file. 'Giovanna Asare.'

'Italian?'

Roger shrugged. 'Sounds like it, although I never got as far as meeting her.'

Diana pressed a finger to her lips. 'And when was this?'

'Back in 2009.' He scanned his notes. 'She worked at a distribution centre in Newcastle.'

'So she could have known Chris, too... Any idea where she is now?'

Roger gave a weary sigh. 'Seemed like she vanished from the face of the earth.'

76

THE RAIN CONTINUED INTO SATURDAY, THE SKY BLANKETED BY a perpetual cloud that dampened Sue's mood and seemed as if it might never break.

In her mind, she replayed Tom's words. Did Ben come back to Seahouses the night his father died? Perhaps the person they were looking for had been under their noses this entire time.

As soon as it was sociably acceptable, she went to call on Diana. An apology needled at her, and she prayed that her friend would let bygones be bygones. After all, they had a murder to solve, and a new prime suspect.

But Diana didn't answer. After waiting in the rain on her doorstep for ten minutes, Sue gave up. She would try again later.

Of course, Diana might be even more inclined to forgive and forget if Sue had some fresh evidence. If what Tom said was true, and Ben was in the village the night his father died, he might have left some proof.

A bell jingled as she opened the door of the gift shop. Helen was mid sales pitch, showing a couple of children the delightful furry puffins that were among the shop's best-sellers, their parents paling at the cost of the cuddly toys. Sue waited patiently, pretending to browse the guidebooks until the tourists left with their souvenirs.

'The CCTV from the shop. Can we look at it?'

Helen glanced at the camera and offered an apologetic shrug. 'It goes onto a computer somewhere, but I've got no idea how to access it. It's all remote controlled, in the sky, or whatever they call it.'

'Remote storage? On the cloud?'

'That's the one.'

Sue pursed her lips. 'I know who might be able to help us.'

Helen locked up and turned the sign on the door to 'closed'. There were few souls hardy enough to potter about the village on a rainy afternoon, and it was highly unlikely that any of them were in the market for guidebooks or souvenirs. If Helen's boss, old Aideen McIntyre asked, she would claim to have suffered a migraine.

Huddled together under an umbrella, they walked briskly in the direction of Amy's house.

'Sorry about the mess,' Amy mumbled as they made their way into her kitchen. She moved a pile of laundry from the kitchen table, clearing a space for them to sit.

'We need Mike's help with something. An IT conundrum,' Sue said, just as the man himself entered the kitchen, drawn by the voices of their visitors.

Sue saw the way that Mike's face lit up at the prospect of being useful. It was incredible, she thought. Her niece was a remarkable woman, and yet, like so many others, she had fallen for a very weak man.

'Got it.' Mike jabbed decisively at the keyboard and

grainy footage began to stream. 'Sunday, twenty-ninth of April.'

Over his shoulders, they peered at the screen.

'Damn it,' Helen muttered under her breath. 'The camera only covers the shop entrance, not the road.'

Mike performed a series of clicks and shook his head. 'That's as wide as it goes. And the other camera isn't any better – it's pointing inside the shop.'

Sue recognised the interior, with its displays of jewellery, guidebooks, and mementos. Squinting, she could see the hand-crafted birdhouses that she'd been quite tempted to buy until she saw the price tag. In the corner of the frame, one of Anne's mirrors glinted.

'Wait a second... can you make it bigger?'

Mike enlarged the picture, the mirror's reflection almost filling the screen.

'Zoom in a bit more,' she mumbled. 'Can you move it to the left?'

'There!' Helen gasped, as the road appeared in the reflection of the mirror.

'Well, well, well,' Amy tutted as she leaned in for a closer look. 'Seems that Mum's *works of art* might not have been a waste of space after all.'

The three of them leaned in, so close that Sue could feel Helen's breath against her neck.

'We know he left his mother's house around one,' said Sue. 'Maybe that's a good place to start.'

Mike issued a series of perfunctory taps and the footage lightened to that sunny afternoon.

'There!' Amy cried, pointing at the screen. Mike slowed the video down and paused on a frame of Ben's car passing the shop.

'The question is, did he come back at some point that night?'

Mike's shoulders sagged. 'It'll take ages to go through this. I'm sorry, but I've got other stuff to be getting on with.'

Amy's face reddened as he stood to leave.

'Thank you.' Sue flashed a smile at Mike to break the tension. 'You've been very helpful.'

It was enough to make him grin like a schoolboy with a glowing report and, inwardly, Sue rolled her eyes. Besides, now that they knew how to work the thing, they would be more efficient themselves.

Helen took over. 'Make yourselves comfortable, ladies. We might be here a while.'

Sue and Amy kept their eyes glued to the screen as cars and people moved in and out of the frame, scanning the road for a bottle-green sports car. They barely noticed the hours ticking by, and the sky outside Amy's window faded from cornflower to ink as dusk fell. Sue rhythmically glanced at her watch, wondering if Diana was home yet.

The screen also began to darken, and sunlight was replaced by the neon glow of a streetlamp outside the shop. They continued to watch.

'My god,' said Amy, her hand flying to her mouth.

Helen gasped as she saw it, her hand slamming against the keyboard to pause the video.

It was grainy, and the artificial light made it impossible to clearly make out the colour, but the car was unmistakable.

'It's true. He did come back,' Sue muttered as the blood drained from her face. The three of them stared at the screen. 'Ben was here that night.'

———

'I'm going to Diana's.' Amy grabbed her coat. 'You two stay here. Load up Chris Carter's photos again and see if you can find Ben in any of them.'

They might have found a slip-up in Ben's alibi, but the fact that he was in the village on the night of his father's death was not enough to pin a double murder on him. They needed to confirm that Ben knew Chris before they could even think about calling the police again. She snatched up her car keys from the console table in the hallway.

'Are you sure you'll be all right on your own?' Sue called after her. Her aunt caught up with her at the door and reached out, stopping just short of grabbing Amy's arm.

Amy could see the unease that gnawed at Sue, throwing her off-balance. She understood. After all, there was still a murderer at large, somewhere out there.

'I just mean...' Sue seemed to search for the right words, but failed to find them. 'Just be careful, OK?'

Amy leaned forward and planted a kiss on her aunt's cheek. 'Back soon,' she whispered, and trotted down the narrow path to her car.

She floored the accelerator and sped off, her Renault nudging at the speed limit as it wound down the short stretch of coast road towards Beadnell.

The lights of Diana's cottage were on. Amy locked the car, and it beeped in response, the sound echoing in the quiet lane. The still air of the evening prickled at her skin and made her scalp tingle.

Was she being watched? She glanced around the empty street of stone cottages cast in the half-light of a dying day. A trail of smoke snaked skyward from a chimney.

She tutted to herself as she knocked on the door. Auntie

Sue had spooked her, nothing more. Her aunt's paranoia was contagious.

As soon as Diana's face appeared, Amy shook off her concerns.

Frowning in concentration, her old schoolteacher pulled Amy into the warmth of her kitchen.

'It's a girl, I know it.' Diana shook her head. 'This all comes down to a girl.'

She jabbed at the Sparkbrook employment records, which, it seemed, she hadn't had the heart to burn. 'Giovanna Asare. Peter Gallivan raped her, but the police wouldn't take her seriously. Not seriously enough to do anything about it, at least. After that, according to my source, she disappeared off the face of the earth.'

Amy winced. Peter Gallivan had been a heinous man.

'We had a breakthrough, too.'

The sapphires of Diana's eyes gleamed in the firelight, and she set aside the records.

'It was Ben.' Amy was breathless, and she willed the fluttering in her chest to quieten. 'It was him all along. He came back to Seahouses the night his father died. We saw him leave after the row in the afternoon, but he came back later that night.'

'How do you...?'

'Tom saw him.'

There wasn't time, yet, to explain just how they came to be so friendly with the man they'd accused of murder only three days ago.

'He was out walking, and Ben drove past him. Helen checked the CCTV from the gift shop. We have him on tape.'

'What time?'

Amy opened her mouth and closed it again, the wind

vanishing from her sails. They had neglected the most obvious detail.

'About an hour after it got dark...' she mumbled, trying to recall the timestamp from the CCTV footage.

'Heading in the direction of his parents' house?'

'Away from it, actually.' Amy's shoulders sank. 'But Sue's going through the photos from Chris's computer, looking for anything that links him to Chris.'

'But the girl,' Diana mumbled. 'What about this girl?'

Amy felt the weight of Diana's fatigue in her words. 'Why don't you get an early night? It's been a long day. We'll keep looking through the photos and the footage. Nothing will happen before morning, I promise.'

―――――

'Yes, dear. You're quite right.' Diana mumbled in agreement, knowing full well she would not be able to rest. 'Let's do that.'

She pictured the countless young women she had taught over the decades, their names crowding her memory, faces jostling to be remembered. Of all the girls' faces and names in her mind, one pushed her way to the front, demanding her attention. She bade Amy farewell, stifling a yawn.

She just had to make a quick phone call before bed.

77

Closing the door as Amy departed, Sue shook off her disquiet.

'Right,' she said, settling herself back at the table. 'Let's wrap this up, once and for all.'

Helen nodded. 'So far, we have Ben driving past the shop at nine-thirty, heading south towards the village. That's the opposite direction of his parents' house, and it's too late for him to be fleeing the scene of the crime – that's at least a couple of hours after the ambulance got there. I'll see if the camera got him heading towards his parents' place at some point earlier in the evening. You get back to those photos, and I'll keep checking the footage.'

Sue smirked. She hadn't seen the side of Helen that liked to take charge. Not for a long time.

On separate laptops at Amy's kitchen table, they got to work.

Sue went directly to the folder of photos from 2009, the year that Chris worked at Sparkbrook. She took a clinical approach, trying to forget, as much as it was possible, that the young man who smiled up at her from the screen was now lying in a mortuary. Methodically, she focused on the faces, scanning each one for any resemblance to Ben Gallivan. It was slow, dizzying work, and Ben was nowhere to be seen.

The faces were blurring into one another, becoming more difficult to identify with every click. Even Chris, the common denominator in every photo, was now indistinguishable from the rest of them. Sue blinked hard, clearing her vision and refocusing her attention.

A group shot swam into view, dozens of celebrants crammed into the frame. A staff Christmas party, by the looks of things. She lowered her face to the screen, scanning the line-up for anyone she recognised.

And there it was.

Her blood ran cold. Could it really be the same person?

———

Opposite her, Helen hunched over Amy's computer. They had Ben driving southbound, but where was he coming from? The road into the village would have brought him past the camera in the opposite direction unless he'd taken a significant detour. They must have missed him on the first viewing.

She trained her eyes on the cars heading north onto Seafield Road, in the direction of the Gallivan house. Her oldest friend was cast in the golden light of a reading lamp, her cheeks flushed pink thanks to her proximity to the Aga, her brow knotted in concentration.

Helen forced herself to focus on the video in front of her. She had slowed down the footage as night fell on-screen, and her eyes trailed each car that crawled across the frame. She almost missed the figure who walked by on foot.

She clicked back a few frames, wondering whether she had imagined it.

She hadn't.

The hood was pulled up, but it wasn't enough to hide the face. A face she would have known anywhere. She checked the timestamp at the top of the screen. Someone had walked past the gift shop, heading toward the Gallivans' house less than an hour before Peter died.

The image crawled through her brain, and Helen's heart thumped in her chest, the blood draining from her face as she considered what this might mean. She opened her mouth to speak – to say something, anything – but no words came.

'It wasn't him,' Sue said quietly, her voice snapping Helen from her stupor. 'It wasn't Ben...' she trailed off, and Helen saw that her friend had paled.

Their eyes met, and Helen imagined that Sue's shock was a mirror of her own.

'You... you need to see this,' Sue stuttered, pointing a shaking finger towards the laptop.

But Helen already knew what her friend had found. She had no doubt that it was the same person whose face now filled the screen in front of her.

Suddenly, Helen's fingers were cold. 'How...?' She started, staring at the computer.

Sue shook her head; defeated, deflated. 'It was her.' Her words were little more than a whisper now. 'She did it.'

78

IT WAS ALL FOR NOTHING.

The thought paralysed Fiona, and she spent the entire day in bed, unable to move. Now, as night fell, she was unable to sleep. Instead, she lay there, the pillow cool against her cheek, listening to the wind and rain outside. The reservoir of strength that had fuelled her through the darkest days, that pit of resolve and determination, was finally depleted. She was empty.

There was no going back.

Her old life was in the past, and there it would stay.

Peter's death should have meant a new beginning, a fresh start. Ben should be taking over the company, Caitlyn should be coming on board, and she should be back in Durham.

But she'd been deluding herself. *Silly old fool.*

For the first time since Peter died, she found herself missing him. She hated herself for that, despising the bitter-sweet juxtaposition of her hatred for him against... what was it? Love?

Despite the terrible things he had done, she had loved

him. In a way, at least. She loved his generosity - the way he had given that boy a couple of thousand pounds just to help him out. A sum that meant nothing to Peter, but he would have known from first-hand experience just how much it meant to someone who was struggling.

And she loved the life they had built together, the family they had created – even if he had destroyed it all.

Most of all, it was the guilt. It ate away at her, nibbling at the fringes of her soul, little by little, day by day.

She saw him in her dreams. Not Peter as he was in life, but Peter as he had been in death. Perhaps that was the reason sleep now evaded her.

She thought back to that night. The smashed vase in the hallway, one of her favourites. The flowers scattered across her gleaming white floor. All that mess. Peter lying on the floor of the living room, clutching his chest.

Instinctively, she ran to the phone, her finger hovering above the '9', but something had stopped her. Years of hurt, all the times he was unfaithful, spiteful, cruel.

The mess in the hall.

She had placed the phone back in its cradle and swept up the broken vase, collecting the fragments of something that was once so perfectly beautiful and was now shattered beyond recognition. Such a pity. Such meaningless destruction.

Fiona could picture his face again now, his flesh unnervingly pale, the whites of his eyes shattered with starbursts of red. She saw herself standing over him, remembering the way he taunted Ben, how he had humiliated Caitlyn. How her friends had turned against her for sticking by him; taking Esme's side and refusing to believe Fiona knew nothing about his affair with Erin.

How he had pushed away everyone that she cared about. Razed a beautiful life to the ground. *Their life.*

Such a pity. All that mess.

Something had eventually snapped her out of her trance, and she called for an ambulance. But only once she was certain that it was too late to save him.

She had to live with the guilt of that. But even after the darkest night, the sun rises again. Caitlyn came back to her. Fiona's life may not resemble the dream she once imagined, but at least her future was in her hands now. And so Fiona resolved to do what she had always done. Tomorrow, as sure as the sun would rise, she would pick herself up, dust herself off, and start again.

The bedroom door creaked open.

———

'I brought you some warm milk.' Caitlyn sat on the bed.

Despite outward appearances, this was progress. Her mum's behaviour since their father's death had been frankly unsettling. There are stages to grief, and as far as Caitlyn could see, Fiona wasn't even on the ladder yet. This – unable to get out of bed – was a much healthier response.

She climbed under the duvet, curling her body around her mother's, inhaling her familiar scent.

'Caitlyn.' Fiona's voice was a whisper. 'I let him die.'

'Shush, now,' Caitlyn soothed her.

When Fiona had first confided the truth in her children after Peter's death, Caitlyn's immediate response had been anger. It was visceral, a deep fury, a stormy sea in the pit of her stomach.

Not with Mum, but with *him.*

Her father had worn her mother down over decades,

like the power of the tide pounding against the rocks. He eroded her to breaking point, and on that night, she had finally cracked. Caitlyn hated him for having pushed Mum to *this*. As far as she was concerned, her father caused his own death.

She knew it would take Fiona a while to see it the same way. But this was a step in the right direction. Sometimes all you could do was burn it down and begin again.

Caitlyn hadn't known how long it might take Mum to get to this point. Her greatest fear was that Fiona would come undone, unravel like a ball of string, and who knew how that would end? It would be tangled, messy. Better to cocoon her, wait for the fire to burn itself out. Start again on unspoiled ground.

Their mother had spent a lifetime doing her best to protect them from Peter's hurt. Now it was Caitlyn's turn to protect her mother from herself. Hide her away, shelter her, until she was ready to face the world again.

She reached for her mother's hand. Icy fingers interlaced with hers, two people fused together. 'We'll be all right, Mum. You'll see.'

'You're a good girl, Caitlyn.' Fiona's words were a soft whisper, the fatigue finally swallowing her.

Caitlyn lay there, watching the rise and fall of her mother's chest. In a moment, she would get up to check on Ben, but not just yet.

He was dealing with his own issues. Guilt for leaving Mum to face it on her own. And guilt that when it finally came crashing down, he'd been too out of it to even answer his phone.

The day after their father died, her brother woke up at his new girlfriend's house with no recollection of how he got there, his memory of the previous twenty-four hours a black hole. Caitlyn had feared that this was just the beginning of one of Ben's episodes, a downward spiral that started with a bender and ended with him broken. And she couldn't cope with seeing Ben go back to rehab – not right now, not with Mum like this. But whatever Lucia said or did seemed to have the desired effect. For the first time in as long as she could remember, her brother appeared to be at peace with himself.

Lucia. She seemed to be good for Ben. Perhaps Caitlyn had got her all wrong, after all.

She brushed the thought to one side. Mum was her priority now. She was bruised and battered, a shell of herself. But they would rebuild together, stronger this time.

79

WHEN THE PHONE RANG, LUCIA WAS WAITING FOR HIM.

She spent her life waiting for Ben these days. Her hours passed by in anticipation of the next moment they could be together, longing for those brief windows of time when he felt it was safe enough to leave his mother alone with her anguish.

The old part of her hated herself for it. But the new part – the part that loved the smell of salt in the morning air and had embraced the idea of opening her heart to another person – that girl pushed her to roll with it. To stop resisting, stop fighting with the past. To listen to her feelings and ride them like the tide.

Only it wasn't him.

'Good evening, Lucia. Or should I call you Giovanna?' The voice was steady, smooth and sure.

Her heart leapt in her chest and her pulse thundered in her ears. She glanced about the room, considering the weight of her possessions and how long it would take her to pack up and run.

See, whispered that old voice in her head. *I told you. Run.*

Stay, the new voice pleaded, the voice of a weary soul that had finally found a place of peace. *We can make this right.*

'I think it's about time you and I were honest with each other,' Diana said.

Lucia didn't respond.

'I know what you did, and I believe I know why. The question is, what do we do about it?'

She said 'we'.

Run, said the voice.

Stay and fight, the other pleaded.

Lucia clasped a hand to her forehead, kneading at the pressure building inside her skull. She fought at the panic that rose in her chest like a tidal swell, swallowing hard against a wave of nausea.

'How did you...?' She stopped, knowing that she shouldn't say any more. Not while she still had a chance to escape. Her voice quivered.

'I can explain.' She took a deep breath. 'I want to explain.'

'That would be splendid, dear. I'll put the kettle on.'

———

'Where's Amy?' Helen watched as Sue paced the galley of the kitchen, a sheen glistening on her forehead. When it got to quarter past, her friend gave up.

'That's it,' Sue said, grabbing her car keys. 'I'm going over there. God knows what's taking her so long.'

'I'm coming too.' Helen stood, pushing back her chair so forcefully that it scraped against the slate tiles of Amy's kitchen floor.

'You should wait here. It might be dangerous.' She was

trying to sound brave, Helen could tell.

Their faces were close, close enough for Helen to see the lines of worry etched around Sue's eyes.

She thought of the girls they once were and the women they had become and wondered again how things might have been otherwise. How she could have done things differently, the choices she might make if she had a chance to confront them again. She knew one thing for certain: she would not lose Sue a second time.

Before Helen even knew what she was doing, she leaned forward and kissed Sue.

A bolt of electricity shimmered down Helen's spine. It fizzled in her veins. Sue's lips were as soft as she remembered from all those years ago, and Helen's heart thundered for what felt like infinity.

They drew back and stared at one another, their breath coming in ragged gulps. Helen wondered if Sue's heart was beating as hard as hers. And yet when she looked into Sue's eyes, deep pools of stormy sea, she knew.

'Helen, I don't—'

Helen touched her index finger to Sue's mouth and shook her head. 'Don't say another word.'

She knew Sue was about to say more, to tell her best friend the thing had had gone unspoken for years. She thought of that teenage kiss, a moment that changed everything for Sue while altering nothing for her.

The past, she realised, never stays where it belongs – it stays with us, within us, no matter how hard we try to bury it. It shapes our thoughts and actions and deeds. Our past makes us the person we become.

She took Sue's hand, noticing the glassy sheen that now misted her friend's eyes.

Sue spoke first. 'I'll always love you, Helen. But not like that.'

Helen nodded and offered a weak smile. It was all she had.

They were interrupted by the sound of Amy opening the front door. Reflexively, they jumped apart.

————

Amy had the distinct sense she had just interrupted something.

'Everything OK?' she asked.

Helen was pale, and Auntie Sue looked like she'd seen a ghost.

'Get over here,' said Sue, seeming to regain her composure. 'You've got to see this.' She gestured to the laptop.

Helen pressed play and the grainy image began to move. A figure came into view, and Amy gasped. 'Is that...?'

Helen paused the footage, and a face filled the screen. 'It's her, walking towards the Gallivans' house just before seven o'clock on the night that Peter died.'

Sue angled the other laptop towards her. 'See if you can spot another familiar face.'

Amy squinted at the photograph. It was a crowd of youngsters dressed for a party, with Chris Carter posing at the front. Behind him, nestled among a gaggle of girls, she saw her. She was almost unrecognisable. Chubbier, her hair darker – possibly dyed – and worn straight. And yet... There were those eyes. If Amy had any doubt, the smile on the young Lucia's face would have convinced her.

'What was she doing there?'

'Looks like she worked at Sparkbrook.' Sue wrapped her arms across her chest and shuddered. 'Funny how those pictures were wiped after she got her hands on the laptop. She deleted them so we'd never make the connection.'

Helen frowned. 'But her name wasn't on the employment list.'

'Unless that isn't really her name.' Amy shrugged, thinking about how Tom Grey had turned out to be Tom Montfort.

Sue took another look at the picture. 'What kind of name is Lucia, anyway?'

'It's Italian,' Amy explained. 'Her mum is...' She stopped, and the final piece clicked into place. 'Diana found out about a girl. An Italian name, too. Giovanna... something. She worked at Sparkbrook. Peter Gallivan...' She glanced at her aunt and Helen, wondering whether she should sugar-coat the awful truth she had learned in the last hour. 'Peter Gallivan raped her. The police didn't do anything, though, and according to Diana, Giovanna simply vanished.'

But had she turned up in Seahouses?

Sue winced. 'And how does Diana know all of this?'

'You know what she's like.' Amy sighed. 'That woman... This is like a real-life detective novel to her. It's the most fun she's had in years.'

Helen frowned. 'But she doesn't suspect it's Lucia. Does she?'

Amy thought back to the conversation she'd just had. Diana had seemed so tired, and for once, looked her age.

But she also knew that, when it came to Diana Wheeler, appearances could be deceptive.

'She knows.' Sue spoke slowly, her words carefully measured. 'I was at her place on Thursday. Lucia was there, too. Diana asked her to come over to try and retrieve the photos from the laptop, even though she knew we had them backed up on the cloud.' She pinched the bridge of her nose. 'She suspected something and was testing her.'

Amy bit her lip. 'The question is, will Diana do anything about it?'

The three of them traded a glance.

'Shit,' muttered Amy, as they raced to the door.

80

'YOU CAME.' DIANA WAVED LUCIA INSIDE. 'MAKE YOURSELF comfortable.' She gestured to the sofa.

The denouement, she thought. It was always her favourite part of the story. Solving the mystery was entertaining enough, but the real delight was to be found in the final pages. The moment when the guilty party explained everything to the detective. When the reader was finally permitted to understand the logic and reasoning of the killer.

The killer. It was bizarre to think that this divine creature in front of her had taken the lives of two men. It's always the ones you least expect.

She knew better than to be nervous about inviting Lucia into her home. Ruthless, deranged, maniacal... this girl was none of those things. Some might consider it reckless, but Diana had taken no precaution other than unlocking the back door to hasten a potential escape.

Besides, she still had questions. Curiosity was a powerful force.

Lucia clasped her hands between her knees, her eyes wide with fear.

Diana flashed her a generous smile. 'Don't worry, dear. I don't bite.'

She made a show of easing herself into Lionel's armchair, reminding the younger woman which of them had the physical advantage. Not that it would come to that.

She hoped.

She folded her hands in her lap. 'I know what he did to you, Giovanna.'

'Please,' Lucia murmured. 'It was always Anna. Before.'

'I can call you Lucia if you prefer?' She smiled. 'Such a pretty name.'

Lucia nodded. 'It was my grandmother's.' She cast her eyes down, avoiding Diana's gaze, and focused on the fire.

'I didn't come to Seahouses looking for him. I want you to know that.'

Diana nodded, willing her to continue.

'I didn't even make the connection when I met Fiona. Or Ben. Not at first.' Lucia's voice was small. 'Believe me, I've done my best to avoid thinking about *that man* for as long as I can remember. But Ben told me about his dad during our first date. About what a monster he was, the way he treated his wife and his family and the people who worked for him, and something fell into place. I realised *he* was here. Right here, in Seahouses.'

'It must have been difficult, falling for the son of the man who did that to you.'

Something flashed behind Lucia's eyes, but she recovered. 'Ben is nothing like him,' she said through gritted teeth. Her face softened. 'He's a good person.'

'You love him. Is that why you wanted his father out of the picture?'

Lucia hesitated, then shook her head. Outside, the rain continued, a rhythmic patter against the windowpane. 'It's this place. Seahouses. Finally, I found somewhere that I felt... safe. At peace.'

'And when you found out that Peter Gallivan lived half a mile away...?'

Lucia sighed. 'I slipped up there. But I can't run anymore. I'm too tired. I'm tired of constantly worrying that he'll find me.'

Diana sensed the woman's relief in acknowledging this, the fatigue that had seemingly clouded every moment of her existence. She let the silence hang there, waiting for Lucia to fill it. Silence, Lionel always said, was a great way to draw out the truth.

After a moment, Lucia spoke again. 'What he did to me, back then... it ruined my life. That man took something from me, and I've never found it since.'

Diana nodded. 'But you found him?'

'When I realised it was him, I felt like... I don't know. Fate? Like this was my opportunity to finally be free of him. I started to trail him, learning his routine. Which was difficult, seeing as he never left the house.'

'Except to play golf...?'

Lucia nodded. 'I followed him on the course. Watching him. Studying him.'

The sand in the hallway. Diana nodded.

'He played alone that Sunday afternoon. I followed him back to Seahouses, and I was going to go home, but I passed Fiona driving through the village and I figured she was out for the night. Ben had called me in tears earlier in the day. They'd had a fight, and he had gone back to Newcastle. So I knew *he* was home alone that evening, and I might not get another chance. It was like the universe was showing me the way.'

She glanced up at Diana, meeting her eyes. 'I was just a girl. There were others, too, you know. Other girls. We were powerless to stop him.' Her eyes filled, glassy with tears. 'You don't know how much suffering he caused. The world is better off without him in it.'

Diana could not bring herself to agree. It might well have been the case, but it was not for mortals to decide who lived and died. 'And so you poisoned him?'

Lucia squirmed. 'I researched it and bought the drugs online. Viagra, nitroglycerin and sumatriptan. When I let myself into the house that night, he was in the bathroom. There was a glass of whisky on the table in the living room.'

She was telling her story now. Diana felt her young friend relax into the pace and cadence of her words. A confessional.

'I didn't hang around to find out how it went. I put the drugs in his drink, then let myself out and put the key back where I found it.'

'And the vase?'

'It was dark in there. And I was scared. I tripped on the table on my way out. The vase fell, and I ran.' Lucia rubbed a hand against the back of her eyes. 'Then Ben turned up at mine a couple of hours later. At first, I thought he knew what had happened, but he was out of it. So far gone. That man – he pushed everyone to their darkest corners.'

Diana realised that Lucia could not bear to even say Peter's name. From the mantelpiece, Lionel caught her eye, encouraging her to press on.

'And Chris Carter. He knew you from Sparkbrook and found out what you had done, so you had to stop him.'

Lucia shook her head, caramel curls tumbling with the

motion. 'No. I don't think he even recognised me. I looked different back then. Before. And besides, we never really knew each other. But I could see him sucking up to Peter. His little pet,' she spat. 'He was carrying his bags around, all *sir* this and *sir* that. That man was paying him, and Chris was treating him like royalty. As if everything that happened back then, everything he did, could be erased, forgotten. All for a few quid. And his girlfriend...'

Lucia exhaled a weary sigh. 'I did it for her, and all the other women Chris would have hurt in the future. She deserves to be free. We all deserve to be free...' she trailed off, losing her train of thought. Something snapped her back to the moment.

'Don't you see? They're all the same, men like that. They think women are there to possess, like objects. They simply help themselves, taking what they want. Chris thought it was OK to knock his girlfriend around, to control who she saw and what she said and what she was thinking. Her thoughts and dreams. Everything that didn't belong to him.'

There was venom in her words.

'I could see it a mile off. Can you imagine how much worse Chris would be if he were in *his* position? If Chris had any real power?'

Diana sat back in her chair. This was not as simple as she had imagined. But then again, she had come to understand something: life was not simple. It was never black and white. It was shades and hues of grey, like the sky and the sea on a stormy morning. Sometimes, the line between good and bad became blurred.

She fixed Lucia with a smile. 'So, my dear. The question is, what do we do now?'

81

'SO, WHAT DO WE DO NOW?' SUE PANTED AS THEY REACHED the car. Her hand trembled; it was an effort to fasten her seatbelt.

Amy exhaled, a long, slow, deliberate breath, her mouth forming a little 'o'. 'We should go to Lucia's place.'

'Are you out of your—'

Amy held up a hand, cutting her short. 'Not to confront her – nothing like that. Just to see if she's home. It's closest. We need to verify her whereabouts.'

It was a risky strategy, Sue thought, but Amy's logic was sound. They could check Lucia was home, then call on Diana and make sure she was safe.

'OK,' she conceded. 'But then we're calling the police.'

Amy gave a curt nod of agreement as she swung the car out onto the road.

Puffin Cottage was only a couple of streets away. The back lane was deserted and there were any number of places where a killer might hide. Sue's eyes grew wide as she scanned their surroundings, imagining that Lucia might be lurking in the shadow of a yard wall or behind a car, ready to pounce.

'Who's going to go in?' Helen whispered.

Amy unbuckled her seatbelt. 'I'm not going *in*.' She glanced at the cottage. The curtains were open and all the lights were off. 'Perhaps none of us are,' she murmured as she climbed out of her car.

The rain echoed in the street, almost drowning out the creak of the hinge as the gate swung open. She peered inside one of the darkened windows.

Helen and Sue watched from the car, barely daring to breathe. After a moment, Amy returned.

'She left. The house is empty, all her stuff is gone. Looks like she's bolted.'

'Well, that's that, then, I suppose,' said Helen hopefully from the back seat. 'Maybe she knew her time was up.'

'Do you think she might have gone to Diana's?' There was a quiver in Sue's voice.

Amy threw her a sideways glance, catching her eye. Her niece's face was cast in the orange glare of a streetlight overhead, filtered by the rain, but even in the dim glow, Sue could see that the colour had drained from Amy's features.

Amy said nothing as she pushed the car into gear once more.

They sped down the dark coast road, taking the twists and bends at speed. Amy knew this stretch of road like the back of her hand and could, no doubt, have completed the journey with her eyes closed. That wasn't enough to stop Sue gripping the doorhandle, her knuckles turning white.

The rain pounded against the road, coating the windscreen and blotting out what little light the moon offered. Soon, the village of Beadnell loomed against the darkness, lights from its harbour and homes appearing like stars in the black sky.

Amy slowed as they turned into Diana's street.

'Shit,' she cursed. Lucia's car was outside Diana's house.

'Helen, call 999. Tell them everything and ask them to send help right away.' Amy barked the order.

'And just where do you think you're going?' Sue asked, incredulous.

'We can't just sit out here!' The panic made her voice shrill. 'I'm going in.'

'Not by yourself, you're not,' Sue muttered as she rushed after her.

Amy thumped on the door with a fist. 'Diana!' she called. 'Are you there? I need to see you. Diana?' She thumped again.

'The lights are on,' Sue murmured, peering in through the kitchen window. 'I can't see anyone, though. The living room door is shut.'

Amy tried the handle and found it unlocked.

She glanced at Sue; her voice reduced to a whisper. 'Ready?'

Sue nodded, blood pounding in her ears.

They charged through the kitchen, barely hesitating, before throwing back the door to the living room.

Diana sat alone in the plushily furnished room, contemplating the fire that burned brightly in the grate. 'My dear girls. What a wonderful surprise!' she exclaimed, as if Amy and Sue barging in on a Saturday night was the most normal thing in the world.

'Where is she?' Amy panted.

'Who, dear?'

'Lucia. Is she here?'

Diana made a show of looking around the empty room

and turned to them with an innocent smile. 'It's just me, I'm afraid. Why don't you take a seat? You look to have had the most dreadful fright.' She nodded towards the sofa.

Goosebumps rippled up the back of Sue's neck, a shiver that crawled down her spine and along her arms. Bemused, she took a seat, and Amy sat beside her.

'It was Lucia all along.' Sue struggled to catch her breath as she explained. 'She was the girl Peter assaulted. She changed her name, hid her identity. But we found a photo of her on Chris's laptop. She worked for Sparkbrook at the same time he did.' The words came tumbling out, her mouth struggling to keep pace with her mind. 'And we have her on the CCTV footage from the shop, walking towards the Gallivan place right before Peter was killed. It was her, Diana. It had to be.'

Diana nodded, but said nothing.

'This seat,' Amy said after a moment. She ran a hand against the cushion. 'It's warm. Was someone just sitting here?'

A draft of briny air tickled Sue's cheek.

Amy must have felt it too. 'Diana. Why is your back door open?'

'Is it?' Diana asked, her face creasing in feigned confusion. 'Ah yes, that's right. I was just letting some fresh air in.'

Amy and Sue traded an anxious glance.

'She's here, isn't she...?' Amy's eyes shifted about the room.

Diana sighed. 'No, my dear. She is not.'

'But she was?' Amy gasped. 'What did she do to you? Are you all right?'

'I've never been better.' Diana smiled sweetly. Within his frame on the mantlepiece, Lionel beamed with pride.

Sue's hand flew to her mouth, her eyes widening. 'You let her go, didn't you?'

Niece and aunt turned to the back door through which a sliver of dark, rainy night was visible.

Diana considered their question. 'I'm not sure anyone would be able to let Lucia go. In order to *let her go,* one must have possessed her in the first place.'

She smiled, her eyes lingering on the fire, her face cast in the warm glow of the flames. 'Far be it from me to do such a thing. That one is as free as a bird.'

EPILOGUE

Lucia sped through the night, her heart hammering. Her heart breaking.

She wiped the back of her hand against her cheek, brushing away the tears that came out of nowhere.

But she was free. Freer than she had been in years.

She wound the window down, just enough to toss out her mobile phone, and drew a deep breath. The sea air filled the car, soothing her.

The voices in her head were silent.

Seahouses just wasn't meant to be. But there would be other places. She understood that now. It was never about a place, not really. It was about him, and the vice-like grip that he'd held over her, no matter how far she ran.

But she had out-run him, now. The shackles had been broken and lay in a pile of ash at her feet.

She had jumped when the knock came at the door, but Diana was as cool as a cucumber.

'My dear girl.' She had looked Lucia in the eye, a shadow of dismay falling over her face. 'I'm afraid our time is up.'

Diana nodded towards the back door, and Lucia slipped out into the night.

She had spotted Helen in the back of the car parked behind hers. Their eyes locked, and she recognised the terror that paralysed the other woman. She had been that frightened too, more than once upon a time.

On the motorway, she allowed herself to relax a little more, even as the blue flashing lights appeared, heading in the opposite direction. It would take them ages to get to Beadnell and even longer to get the full story from Diana and her friends.

If they ever did.

By then, Lucia would be long gone.

She could catch a train. There was an express service from Newcastle to London, and from there, she could board a flight. The side pocket of her backpack contained three passports. It was time to start using her other grandmother's name.

Ben would get over it in time. She could already see that, away from the dastardly presence of his father, the man was ready to shine. He would make a fine husband for some lucky girl, one of these days.

The rain eased, the storm blowing over, the smell of salt replaced by the fragrance of the pine forest that bordered the motorway.

Lucia thought of all the places she had visited and all those she was yet to discover, deliberating on where to go next. Singapore, maybe. Or California. Or the Italian Alps.

It didn't matter.

The world opened up in her mind like an old map unfolding, the possibilities unfurling.

Finally, she was free.

AUTHOR'S NOTE

Seahouses is an actual village, although I have distorted the layout and landmarks to fit my narrative. My goal is to capture the essence and atmosphere of the village, and hopefully inspire people to visit this remarkable place.

There is no pub called The Ship, but if you do make it to Seahouses, be sure to visit The Olde Ship Inn.

ACKNOWLEDGMENTS

Thank you to you, my reader. It is an incredible privilege to have people read a story that, for so long, existed only in my head. If you enjoyed Salted Earth, please leave a rating on Amazon or Goodreads. It's the best way you can support new authors like me.

Writing is a team effort. Thanks to my editors Gabrielle Chant and Rosie Walker, whose expert eyes made this novel so much better. Thanks also to Laura Boyle for her beautiful cover design and Giorgia Rossi for my portrait photo.

Thank you to LJ Ross and Dark Skies Publishing for short-listing Salted Earth for the Lindisfarne Prize. You gave me the confidence boost I needed.

Thanks to Helen Seymour, Paul Johnson, Bernadette McGee, Jane Dineley, Lusia McCanna, Yvonne Iwaniuk, and Stew Simpson. Special thanks to Colin McGuckin for medical tips, Joanne Graham for advice on the role of a district nurse, and Andy Edwards, who enthusiastically answered all my weird questions about sand. Any factual mistakes in this work are mine and mine alone. And thanks to whoever told me about their friend who works as a courier. I honestly cannot remember who it was, but thank you for planting that seed.

This book would never have happened if it weren't for all of those who got in touch after reading my first novel, Salt Sisters. To everyone who sent me an email or posted a comment on social media: this one is for you.

Big thankyous to Living North and High Life North, and to The Coastal Custodian, who not only celebrated Salt Sisters but sent me notes of encouragement that hastened this follow-up.

One of the most enjoyable aspects of publishing my first novel was just how many people stumbled across it and got in touch. Among them I count Andy Giles, who enjoys a well-earned retirement playing golf in Seahouses.

It was my own resident golf expert who filled in a lot of the blanks. Thank you, Igor, for your love and patience, support and encouragement, and everything else in between.

As ever, I'm grateful to my sister Beth Edwards and aunt Anne Simms for constant encouragement. And, always, to Mum and Dad. Raising two women is a unique challenge, and I think you did a great job.

Need more Seahouses Mysteries? I have good news for you! Turn the page to learn more.

Thank you for reading.

Katherine Graham
October 2022

SALT GIRL

YOU CAN'T BURY A SECRET FOREVER...

What secrets did a lost girl die to keep?

When Izzy discovers the body of a teenage runaway under her conservatory, she knows that someone in this village buried a very dark secret.

Who is the girl? How was she able to vanish in a place like Seahouses? And why was her grave filled with salt?

The police are unable – or unwilling – to investigate a twenty-year-old crime, so Izzy takes matters into her own hands, teaming up with retired schoolteacher Diana to investigate.

But Diana's memory is not what it used to be. Who was the girl she knew all those years ago, and what was she running from? Diana has the answers... if only she could remember them.

Will they uncover the secrets that this postcard-perfect village is hiding, or will the truth stay buried forever?

Coming March 2023

Want a preview? Get the first chapter of Salt Girl for free now at katherinegraham-author.com.

ABOUT THE AUTHOR

Katherine Graham is the author of the Seahouses Mystery series. She is from the North East of England. When she is not writing, Katherine loves cycling, Cadbury's chocolate, bubble baths, and '90s R'n'B (not necessarily in that order).

You can find her at katherinegraham-author.com.

Also by Katherine Graham

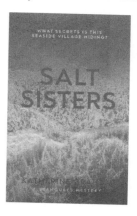

Salt Sisters

What secrets is this seaside village hiding?

Two sisters, a world apart. A family torn by trauma. And a village where no one can keep a secret except the sea.

What secrets is this seaside village hiding?

Izzy's world is shattered when her sister Amy is killed in a tragic accident. She's forced to come home from abroad, back to the small village she worked so hard to escape and a past she wanted to forget. Soon her family demands more than she is ready to give, and Izzy must reconsider her choices - sacrificing the dream life she built for herself on the other side of the world.

But was Amy's death an accident or something more sinister?

When Izzy sets out to determine what happened, she realises how little she knew her sister and how deep the mystery runs in this quaint seaside village. Can she uncover the truth while confronting the secrets that drove her away in the first place - before her life is put in danger, too?

"Katherine Graham's debut book has captured our coast perfectly and its twists and turns will have you hooked... we at Living North loved it."

Living North magazine

"Excellent... You'll become obsessed with turning the pages just to keep unravelling the mystery that unfolds."

High Life North

Printed in Great Britain
by Amazon